PATH OF JUSTICE

CADICLE: VOLUME 6

A K DUBOFF

Published by Epic Realms Press
Cover Illustration: Copyright © 2016 Tom Edwards

ISBN: 1954344031
ISBN-13: 978-1954344037
Copyright Registration Number: TXu002041935

0 9 8 7 6 5 4

Produced in the United States of America

CONTENTS

PART 1: TRANSITION

CHAPTER 1

RELICS OF WAR had no place in a peaceful future. At least that's what Wil Sights told himself as he performed his final structural checks of TSS Headquarters within Earth's moon. Deep down, however, he knew that the impending changes were actually in preparation for a new war—just one of political strategy rather than physical might.

In the three years since the end of the devastating war with their vilified Bakzen brethren, the Tararian Selective Service had been making subtle preparations for an unfolding era of Taran unification. To that end, many soldiers had retired and others had pursued more academic career paths. For Wil, those recent years spent pursuing interests outside of battle had been a time of reflection about the nature of the war and how it had divided his people. He had come to accept that he and his family were in the best position to effect change at the helm of those efforts, pairing their political influence with their positions in the TSS. The realization had left him with a new imperative to evolve the TSS to serve Tarans as a whole, and Wil wouldn't rest until the lingering threat of the Priesthood was eliminated.

With his mind set on that goal, Wil ran an ultrasonic scanner along the main support beam spanning the equator of Level 1's middle floor, similar to the others he'd already examined for the final check. Like the previous beams, this one appeared to be in good condition and should hold through the structural stress to come, as long as they were careful. *It was crazy for me to suggest transitioning the entire Headquarters facility out of the subspace bubble into normal space, but that's what we need to move forward.*

Such a radical transformation of the massive facility might appear like disarmament to some, but it would ultimately strengthen the TSS' greatest advantage over the Priesthood: the telekinetic strength of Agents.

The subspace containment shell that surrounded the facility inside the moon—keeping Headquarters suspended within a permanent subspace bubble—had offered protection from a Bakzen telekinetic attack during the war, but it also stifled Agents' abilities. Consequently, Agents-in-training never reached their full potential.

To bring down the Priesthood, the TSS would need to be stronger than ever. Looking ahead, their training grounds would need to maximize telekinetic abilities—without the dampening properties of subspace holding them back. Only then could they truly prepare for the fight to come. Gone were the days of old, fighting battles against the Bakzen with warships in the Rift; the next conflict would be resolved through finesse and persuasion, led by Agents of the future who would harness a new power for the dawning era.

Wil completed the last stretch of structural inspection and checked off the segment on his handheld. The other Agents had already reported in and given the 'all clear'. Nothing stood in the way of their plan aside from his order to proceed. *No one has ever attempted something like this before. I hope we're up for it.*

He placed his handheld in his pocket and headed to the administrative wing to retrieve Saera from her Lead Agent office, where she was reviewing the day's Rift repair activities while the rest of Headquarters prepared for the transition.

The glass wall at the front of her office was set to full transparency to indicate she was available to speak with drop-in guests. A single touch-surface desk occupied the center of the room, with a broad viewscreen along the side wall, two guest chairs on the near side of the desk, and two additional chairs against the wall under the viewscreen.

"Hey!" his wife greeted as soon as the door opened. She minimized the status report projected on the holodisplay above her desk. "Any last-minute issues?"

"No changes from our previous inspections," Wil replied. "Everything should hold up through the transition."

Saera's jade eyes lit up. "Bringing the entire structure through the dimensional veil… This'll really be something!"

"If we can pull it off."

"No way to know for sure until we try." Saera rose from her desk.

"True," Wil said. "Besides, it will be a good workaround for needing to disassemble H2 in the Rift. Not sure where we'll move it, exactly, but there will be more options."

His wife came up to him and placed her arms around his waist. "You're always thinking two steps ahead."

"Only two? I'm slipping."

Saera smiled up at him and pulled away. "We're still on for 15:00, then?"

"Yes, that's the plan."

"Speaking of plans, when are we going to tell them?" Saera asked.

"As soon as we finish the transition." He examined his wife. "Are you sure you're up for participating today?"

"I'm pregnant, not injured."

"I know, but—"

She placed a reassuring hand on his forearm. "Don't worry, I won't strain myself."

Wil let out a slow breath. "Okay." He checked the time on Saera's desktop, seeing that it was already 14:50. "Let's go meet everyone."

They took the elevator down from the command wing on Level 1 to Level 5, which had been selected as the staging ground for the transition activities. All non-essential Militia personnel had already been temporarily relocated to TSS transport ships docked at the spaceport, and four hundred of the top Agents had gathered in the Militia mess hall on Level 5 to perform the unprecedented telekinetic feat.

At the center of the room, Cris was doling out commands for where everyone should stand and directing some last-minute practices for the coordinated telekinetic engagement. He glanced over at Wil as he entered with Saera. "We'll get started soon," he said to Scott and walked over toward Wil.

"Is everyone ready?" Wil asked.

His father nodded. "I think so. We were just awaiting your final approval on the structural checks."

"We didn't find any issues. It's all on us now," replied Wil. He looked around the room at the Agents. *So much telekinetic energy in one place. It's been so long since I've felt that.*

Trying to clear his mind in preparation for the task at hand, Wil headed toward the center of the room with his father and Saera to meet with Wil's former Primus Elite Captains, Scott Wincowski, and a handful of other TSS senior Agents managing the day's activities.

"I thought you were joking about this," Scott commented when Wil reached the throng of Agents.

"Most ideas start out on a whim," Michael said, glancing up from his tablet. "Everyone is in position. We'll proceed on your command."

"Okay," Wil acknowledged as he surveyed the room.

Few actions were as nerve-wracking as the transition they were about to attempt. Inspecting the interior of the main Headquarters ring structure was one thing, but there was no way to access the containment shell that confined the subspace field— Wil's visual inspection through remote observation only told so much. They had no option but to trust that it would hold together.

"All right. Let's begin." Wil closed his eyes and extended his consciousness. The Agents around him joined in, syncing their intent to manipulate the structure.

Wil wove their combined energies into tendrils and extended the branches around them. Energy washed over the walls like a glistening silver wave in his mind's eye. The tendrils burrowed through the walls to begin enveloping the Level.

A hum of energy filled the air and the floor began to vibrate.

Groans of warping metal sounded around the room.

"Not so fast," Wil cautioned in everyone's minds. *"Let the field spread to the full structure before we pull."*

They slowed the expanse of the telekinetic bubble, allowing their focused energy to trace the intricacies of Headquarters' frame. He extended his consciousness to evaluate the full effect of their efforts, waiting until the energy completely enveloped the ten rings suspended in the center of the subspace bubble.

"Almost there," he told them. *"Now for the shell."*

Bringing the entire sphere surrounding Headquarters was the best option, since the elevator shaft and containment lock were the only means into the physical structure, irrespective of its position in subspace. Transitioning the containment sphere into normal space would ensure that the anchor points for Headquarters' rings at the surface and down to Level 11 remained intact.

Keeping himself in a state of remote observation, Wil sensed the Agents' combined energies swell in their attempt to envelop the entire containment shell. The scale would have been breathtaking to any other observer, but after Wil's own telekinetic feats on a planetary scale, he'd lost the perspective to be in awe of what they were about to do.

The output of energy swelled as they made the final push to encompass the sphere. *Just a little more...*

A loud groan echoed through the chamber, followed by grinding and a thud. The floor shifted underneath them.

Shite! Wil extended his consciousness in an attempt to locate what had gone wrong. One of the structural anchors must have given way to result in that kind of jolt.

He searched throughout the Level, but nothing seemed out of place. To go further without letting go of his physical hold on the structure, he'd need to draw more energy into himself than he had since the war. He hesitated.

The floor heaved again.

Desperate, Wil released himself—extending his consciousness to take in the entire view of Headquarters while he tried to maintain his hold on the structure hovering at the dimensional veil. The ten rings of Headquarters suspended within the subspace bubble appeared to be intact. *So, what's wrong?*

Then, he spotted the issue. The coupling between the inner containment lock and the rest of Headquarters was giving way. The shaft to the surface was slowly disconnecting. There was no way out. If it broke free while the subspace bubble was still intact…

"*We need to complete the transition. Now!*" he ordered in everyone's minds.

They renewed their efforts with urgency. The telekinetic bubble continued to expand until it brushed the inner confines of the shell. They needed to get all of it. Wil urged them onward, even as the Agents around him began to strain. He sensed Saera holding back while the others continued to push toward their limits. It still wasn't enough.

We have to do this! He let go from his physical self and became one with the shell. It was within his grasp.

The telekinetic bubble finally enveloped the full shell. "*Follow my lead,*" he instructed.

Slowly, they latched on to the shell and began pulling it back with them, in the same way they'd pull themselves from subspace back to their physical selves. The hum throughout the room intensified, but, slowly, Wil sensed the subspace shell breaking through into normal space.

With one final tug, the transition was complete. They'd done it.

However, they weren't out of danger.

Wil immediately refocused his attention on the broken coupling. He channeled all of the energy he'd drawn into the connection point with the main elevator shaft. With as much precision as he could manage from the remote vantage, he drew the Headquarters structure up into position.

The floor heaved as it came back into place. Gasps sounded around the room.

I need a temporary repair… He had no idea how long he'd be able to maintain the hold with his mind. Knowing he had to act, Wil focused on the metal surrounding the coupling. He pictured it heating up to a red-hot glow. As he fed energy into it, the pieces began to fuse together. Two minutes of intense concentration passed. When he backed away from his remote view to inspect the work, the makeshift weld seemed to be holding.

Wil released a shaky breath, quivering from the energy still coursing through him.

"What happened?" Saera asked.

"A coupling broke," he replied as he took a deep breath in an attempt to calm his racing heart. "We need to get a repair crew to the inner containment lock. They can access it now that the facility is out of subspace."

Michael smiled. "We did it."

Wil nodded. "But that was a lot closer a call than I would have liked." He reached out to Saera telepathically, *"Are you okay?"*

"I'm fine. Just didn't want to strain, like I promised."

"I'll organize the repairs right away," Cris said. He pulled out his handheld and stepped away.

"I guess celebrations are in order!" Scott grinned.

"You still have some of that whiskey stashed away from your last trip down to Earth, right?" Ian asked.

"I do," Wil confirmed.

"All right! First round's on me," Ian exclaimed.

Michael frowned. "That... doesn't even make any sense."

Ian clapped him on the shoulder. "It will after enough drinks. This way, ladies and gentleman." He headed for the door.

The others started to follow but Saera held back.

"Are you going to join us?" Michael asked her.

"Someone should supervise the repairs," she replied. "Lead Agent duties and all."

"I can stay with you," Wil offered.

"Go ahead. Have fun." She gave him a quick kiss. *"There's a lot to celebrate."*

CHAPTER 2

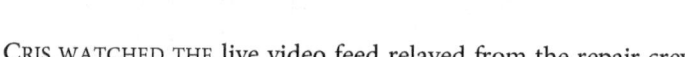

CRIS WATCHED THE live video feed relayed from the repair crew. Nothing about the shell's design made sense.

He glanced over at Saera. "How was this built?"

She shrugged. "I was hoping you knew. I always figured it was something constructed as refuge from the Bakzen."

"That was my understanding. Now I'm not so sure," Cris murmured.

The repair crew glided around in pressure suits, secured by ropes. Their movements were exaggerated in the naturally low gravity of the moon beyond the reach of Headquarters' artificial gravity generators.

Alric, the crew lead, looked into the panoramic camera mounted to a pole extending from his helmet. "Sir, I've never seen anything like this. The measuring equipment is giving off all sorts of weird readings."

"Like what?" Cris questioned.

"The dating, for one, can't be right," Alric said. "I know subspace radiation can mess with the meters, but it looks like this shell is well over a thousand years old."

"One sec." Cris muted the comm. "If that's accurate," he said to Saera, "it was built before the Taran Revolution."

"And before the Aesir split from the Priesthood," Saera added. "That would explain how they'd have the knowledge to override the command codes for the containment locks."

Cris leaned against his desk. "I never stopped to think about the origin of the structure. The idea of a subspace containment shell was… unique. Let alone the logistics of how that theory could be put into practice—"

"We couldn't have done it," Saera cut in. "I mean, constructing H2 was one thing—you can bring materials into the Rift. But the shell… That's a level of spatial manipulation that goes beyond anything I know about."

"Well, we just pulled it into normal space. In theory, the reverse is possible."

"Okay, yes. But think about how many of us it took. Moreover, the precision needed to achieve a stable position in subspace and calibrate the anchors—that'd require some really advanced tech we don't have now."

"Shite." Cris ran his fingers through his chestnut hair, touched with the first hints of gray. "How much do you think was lost in the Revolution?"

"Whatever the Priesthood found convenient for us to forget."

"But if the Aesir separated, they might still have all of that lost knowledge."

Saera nodded. "From what little Wil has said, their ships are tuned for those with abilities—like a way more advanced version of the Conquest. If abilities are central to their culture, which it seems they are, there's no telling what else they have."

"Things that have no place in the Priesthood's reality where Gifted are the exception."

"Not necessarily," Saera countered. "Such abilities are very important to them—they just want to keep that power to themselves."

Cris sighed. "Good point."

"Either way, this discovery indicates that either the TSS' history stretches back way before we imagined, or all of this was repurposed from something else."

"I could reach out to Taelis and see if he knows anything," Cris suggested.

"No, I'm still not convinced we can trust him," Saera

countered. "I'd rather keep any discoveries in our inner circle."

"Uh, sir?" Alric said over the comm.

Cris unmuted the channel. "Sorry! We went off on a little tangent there."

"Understood, sir. So, for the repairs…"

"Is it salvageable?" Cris questioned.

Alric nodded. "Yes, sir, but there's a bigger issue. I'm afraid that now that the shell is in normal space, it's going to begin degrading. This fracture may only be the first."

"In other words, we need to re-build all of Headquarters." *So much for TSS funding not being an issue.*

"That's my assessment, sir," Alric confirmed.

"Great."

Saera gave him a weak smile. "I guess some renovations are in order."

—   —   —

Wil excused himself early from the festivities. At the rate things were going, the rest of the party attendees seemed to be dead-set on having debilitating hangovers in the morning, and that was not an eventuality in which he cared to participate.

Furthermore, his friends had been quick to question Saera's absence. Though he and his wife could only dodge questions about her pregnancy for so long, select individuals should probably be the first to know before the information became public. Leaving the party was the easiest way to avoid the information getting released out of turn.

He found Saera sprawled on the couch in their living room.

"How was it?" she asked as soon as the hallway door was closed.

"Getting quickly out of hand, as I suspected," he replied with a smile.

"Figures."

"With most people distracted and in a celebratory mood, I was thinking it'd be a fitting time to share our news with my parents."

She lit up. "Good, because I just about told your dad earlier today. It's dicey talking about plans a few months down the road when we know that's coming."

"Agreed." Wil reached out telepathically to his father, *"Do you have a few minutes?"*

"Sure, come on over," Cris replied.

"How are we going to tell them?" Saera asked as she rose from the couch.

"Straight out with it, I suppose."

She shrugged. "Works for me."

Wil and Saera made the short trek across the hall to his parents' quarters. His mother answered the door and they were welcomed inside.

"Is this about the shell?" Cris asked.

Wil eyed his father. "What do you mean?"

"Oh, right!" Saera shook her head. "We made a discovery while the maintenance crew was doing the repairs on the coupling. Apparently, the shell around Headquarters is old—like, at least a thousand years old."

"Very interesting."

"Yeah. So, that's a new mystery to figure out," Cris said.

"It makes sense, though," Wil realized. "Constructing it…"

"That was our thought, as well," Saera responded. "We were wondering if maybe the Aesir had something to do with it. Back before they separated from Tararia."

Wil nodded. "It's possible. They wouldn't tell me definitively either way." *Their current technology is well beyond ours, but perhaps they simply have what was lost to us.*

"I get the impression that's not why you came here," Kate interjected.

Wil smiled. "No, it wasn't." He looked to his wife.

"Working on the repairs wasn't the real reason I skipped out on the party tonight," Saera began. "I'm expecting."

"Stars!" Kate immediately embraced her.

"I wondered…" Cris shook his head and smiled. "How far along?"

"About forty days," Saera replied. "We wanted to make sure there weren't any early complications before we said anything."

Cris smiled. "Well, he'll be very lucky to have you as parents."

"Actually," Wil cut in, "after much consideration, we opted for twins—a boy and a girl."

His parents' eyes widened.

"There hasn't been a Sietinen girl for hundreds of years!" Cris exclaimed.

"It was beyond time to mix things up." Wil put an arm around his wife. "Besides, Banks said something in his final note to me. I'm still not sure what he meant by it, but I think having a girl is the right thing. Twins just all around made sense."

Kate nodded. "I won't complain."

Wil and Saera glanced at each other. "So, that's the news," Wil said. "However, there's still the bigger issue of where to raise them."

Cris crossed his arms. "That is a complicated choice. Tararia and Headquarters do each have their own sets of pros and cons."

"Or even some third to-be-determined option," Wil countered. "It's a lot to consider, but we have several months to work it out."

His mother stepped forward and gave him a hug. "We're here to support you with anything you need."

"Thanks." Wil took Saera's hand. "For now, we'd like to keep it quiet. We'll tell our close friends next, but I'm sure word will get out soon regardless."

"Of course," Cris acknowledged. "We'll follow your lead."

Kate clasped her hands. "This is so exciting!"

Wil beamed at Saera. "It'll be a good change. We're ready to start this next phase of our lives."

They parted ways from his parents with hugs and returned to their quarters. With the news broached, they had a lot of decisions to make.

Wil stood in front of the coffee table while Saera eased onto the plush couch at the center of the living room. The quarters they shared would soon be far too crowded with two infants.

"Where *are* we going to live?" his wife asked.

"I wish I had an answer for you. There's not one obvious best option," he replied.

"I know. I just never figured everything would be this up in the air."

Wil ran his fingers through his hair. "Me either. I guess it comes down to what kind of life we want for them."

"After what you've told me about your experience growing up here at Headquarters, I can't say this is my first choice."

Even if we try to give them the best, there are no guarantees. "No, I wouldn't choose this, given an alternative." Wil paced across the room in front of her. "I'm thankful for all of the friendships I forged here, but it was tough not being around other kids. While they'd have each other, that's hardly a substitute for a proper peer group."

"Agreed." Saera rapped her fingers on the armrest of the couch. "There's always Tararia."

"Growing up groomed as heirs to the Sietinen Dynasty. That would certainly be the best path to further our political objectives."

Saera raised an eyebrow. "What a nice way of looking at it."

Wil shrugged. "That's the truth, though. If we raise them there, there's no way around the inevitable preparations for that lifestyle. We can pull them into the TSS when they're ready, but they'll be set on a deliberate path from birth onward."

"Your father escaped it."

"Oh, I'm sure we could get them to see through the layers of political shite. All the same, I don't see a childhood there being a very fun experience."

"What do we do?' Saera asked. "It sounds like there's a downside either way."

"We're not limited to those two options."

"That's true," Saera conceded. "What are our alternatives?"

"There are any number of colony worlds," Wil offered.

"Yes, but how far away from Taran government will that really get them?"

Wil considered the position. "You're right. We'd be recognized anywhere we went."

"Getting back to the heart of the issue, what kind of life do we want for our children?"

After a moment of contemplation, Wil said, "I'd like them to be able to choose their own paths, to the extent possible."

Saera nodded. "I was thinking the same thing."

"Well, there is another option, but I don't think anyone is going to like it…"

CHAPTER 3

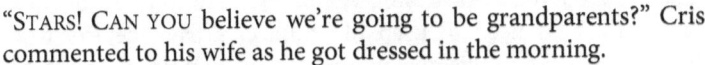

"STARS! CAN YOU believe we're going to be grandparents?" Cris commented to his wife as he got dressed in the morning.

"No."

Cris laughed. "Not the least bit excited?"

"Oh, I am." Kate got a wistful look in her glowing hazel eyes while she secured her dark brown hair in a braid. "It's just that it only seems like a few short years ago that Wil was a baby himself."

"I've felt every year. So much has happened…"

"I have, too. But you know what I mean."

Cris walked over and hugged her. "I do."

"I guess this is a chance for us to do things right," Kate said, looking up at him. "Let kids be kids. Wil had to grow up way too fast."

"I hope our grandchildren don't have to experience that. At least the war is over."

"We'll need to keep them away from the Priesthood."

Cris nodded. "Without a doubt. We'll figure out a safe place."

— — —

"Are you sure about this?" Wil asked in the morning to make sure Saera hadn't had a change of heart overnight.

She squared her shoulders. "I'm still not crazy about the idea, but I agree it's for the best."

"All right. Then we'll tell everyone and begin the preparations."

When they'd made the decision to have a family, Wil had known that they'd need to make some significant changes in their lifestyle. What he hadn't considered would be the need to start over somewhere entirely new. But as he'd discussed the possibilities with Saera, one option eventually stood out above the rest: to move down to Earth.

With Saera's roots on the planet, the proximity to Headquarters, and the operations outside of the Taran Empire, it just made the most sense. Still, Wil had reservations. To blend in on Earth, he'd need to keep his children's true identity from them. It wasn't unlike the manipulation he'd experienced his whole life, but he saw no way around it. If they were to gain a perspective of what it was like to live without the privileges of being highborn, they needed to immerse completely.

At the same time, he didn't want Saera to need to walk away from her position as Lead Agent just because she was going to be a mother. Travel would need to be cut back, surely, but the rest of her responsibilities were not mutually exclusive with parenthood.

However, they couldn't very well take a shuttle back and forth from Earth all the time. As the countries of Earth continued their own advancements in space travel, the TSS' concerns were no longer as straightforward as temporarily cloaking Headquarters whenever astronauts had a mission that circled the moon. Even though teams with top-level security clearance were able to edit out TSS Headquarters and ships from most official government and military photos and videos, masking ship transit from stargazing civilians and space tourists was another matter. Fortunately, Wil was pretty sure he had a solution to the commute issue.

The ring transport technology he'd refined to connect the Prisaris shipyard with H2—bridging two different relative positions in normal space—could likely be scaled down for transporting a person. He'd been working on a design sporadically for the last couple of years and was close to having the details worked out. Such a transport device would allow him and Saera to walk through one arch on Earth and step out of another right within Headquarters. All things considered, it'd make for a pretty easy morning commute.

Being mere steps away didn't make it easier for Wil to leave the place where he'd grown up and spent almost his entire adult life. The two rooms in their quarters were home.

The decision was made, though. It was time to tell their family and friends.

Wil decided to wait until after breakfast to break the news to his parents. He waved to them cordially across the mess hall as they ate, but it wasn't until an hour later that he tracked his father down in the High Commander's office. He requested that his mother meet them there.

When both his parents were seated around the desk, Wil took a deep breath. "About what we told you last night..."

"We'll keep it to ourselves, of course," Cris said.

"We're so happy for you, Wil," his mother added with a heartfelt smile.

They say that now, but once they know what we have planned... Wil gave her a weak nod. "It's going to mean a lot of changes for us."

"Oh, stars!" Her mother shook her head. "I remember when you were a newborn and decided that 03:00 was the perfect time for a feeding."

"You're brave going for twins," his father said.

Or just crazy. "Yeah, we'll need to ease up on our duties for a while."

"Of course, take all the time you need," his father replied. "And we can work on renovations for your quarters to add a bedroom—"

"That won't be necessary," Wil cut in. "That's what I wanted to talk about."

Kate frowned. "What do you mean?"

"I don't regret growing up here, but it's not something I want for them," Wil told his parents. "And, given present relations with the Priesthood, Tararia wouldn't be much better. After a lot of discussion, we've decided that raising them on Earth would be best. After they're born, we'll keep them away from all of this."

"I understand your reasoning. We'll come visit," Cris replied after a moment.

Wil swallowed. "No, I mean we want to *really* keep them away from all of this. As little outside contact as possible."

His mother picked up on his meaning. "But we're their grandparents!"

Cris caught on. "Why would you cut us out of their lives?"

"Not entirely." Wil sighed. "Think about how you present. You were both raised High Dynasty and have been in command positions for three decades. By human standards, you look way too young to be my parents. That's a lot to explain, and I don't think we'd ever come up with a convincing argument."

"So what?" Cris retorted. "Making them believe their grandparents don't care enough to come visit isn't any better."

"That's only part of it," Wil went on. "We need them to have an outside perspective. They need to grow up as normal people without bias toward a particular way of thinking."

"You believe we can't keep our opinions to ourselves?" his mother questioned.

"No, I…" Wil searched for the words. "I just want them to have the kind of normal life I never could. I'll have a hard enough time trying to blend in as it is. We need to give them their best chance to become the kind of people we need."

"Don't deny us this chance to be in their lives," his mother pleaded.

"If it's about how we look—" his father started to interject.

"It's everything. You aren't of Earth and could never pass as such," Wil insisted. "We don't need people asking questions. You can write emails and maybe video chat. We'll see. But as of right now, I don't think in-person visits will be in their best interest."

Cris' eyes narrowed. "I disagree."

Wil rose from the visitor chair. "We can discuss it later. But I don't anticipate my opinion changing anytime soon." He left before his parents could protest further. *We need to have a completely separate life without Taran influences. Even the smallest subtleties in their interactions could reveal how much is going on beyond Earth's view.*

As soon as he was out of the High Commander's office, Wil stopped by the adjacent Lead Agent's office to see Saera.

She looked up expectantly from a report displayed on her desk when he entered.

"I broke the news," Wil told her. "They're going to put up a fight."

"I don't blame them."

"Maintaining separation seems best…" *I hope this is the right choice.*

"I agree." Saera reached over to take his hand across the desk. "Time to start telling the others?" she asked.

"Yeah. Let's start with Michael and Elise. Hopefully, they take it better."

Their friends had remained close in the years following the war. Questions about any plans to formalize their relationship through marriage or otherwise were met with a smile and variant of 'maybe someday'. Considering that Elise had moved into Michael's quarters a year prior, Wil was certain they were in it for the long haul together. However, the path of commitment took different forms for every couple.

Being midday, the best chance to catch the two Agents was in the administrative wing of Level 1. Both Michael and Elise had stepped up as management support for the numerous transition activities associated with the dissolution of the Jotun Division and the monumental task of completing the Rift repairs.

As Wil and Saera strolled down the row of offices on Level 1 in the direction of the lobby, they first passed by Elise's office. Though the glass wall was set at half-opacity to indicate she was working, the door was open. They peeked inside and found Elise staring intently at a holographic rendering of a complex molecular model projected above her desktop.

"You do realize that these desktops aren't equipped with a telepathic interface?" Saera quipped.

Elise startled to attention. "Yeah." She laughed. "I wasn't trying to manipulate it. I'm just dumbfounded that one of my students could get something so utterly wrong."

Saera smiled. "I've been there."

Their friend studied them. "This isn't just a random social call."

"No," Wil acknowledged. "Is Michael in his office?"

Elise glanced at the staff list on her desktop. "Yes. Why?"

"Just wanted to talk about some things with both of you," Saera said.

Elise gasped and her eyes lit up. "You're pregnant, aren't you?"

Saera hesitated. "Well—"

"Stars, I knew it!" Elise practically leaped over her desk to give Saera a hug.

"How did you…?" Saera began.

Elise cocked her head and smiled. "Aside from knowing you for well over a decade, I am a biologist, remember. I know these things."

Saera smiled back. "Fair enough."

"This is so exciting!" Elise cheered and ran down the hall to Michael's office.

Wil shook his head and chuckled as he took Saera's hand.

"At this rate, the entire TSS will know within the hour," she said.

"Just wait until Ian finds out…"

Saera sighed. "I guess the whole multiverse may as well be in on the secret."

By the time they arrived at Michael's office, only seconds behind Elise, it appeared she'd already filled him in.

"Congratulations!" Michael said when they stepped into the office.

Wil closed the door. "Thanks. We're somewhere between excited and nervous."

"I'm not exactly looking forward to temporarily turning into a land whale," Saera said with a frown.

"Oh, it won't be *that* bad," Elise told her.

Saera gave a slight shake of her head. "We didn't get to the part about twins."

Michael's and Elise's eyes widened.

"Stars!" Elise breathed.

"So, yeah. That'll be fun," Saera mumbled.

"There are too many political unknowns," Wil added. "And, Saera wanted a girl."

Michael nodded. "At least with twins they'll always have someone their own age to play with around here."

"About that…" Wil glanced at Saera and she nodded. "We've decided it would be best to raise them on Earth."

It took their friends a few seconds to react.

"So, you're moving down there?" Michael asked.

"No, you can't!" Elise exclaimed.

"I'm not giving up Lead Agent," Saera explained. "We've worked out a way to commute."

"Transport arch, adapted from the rift gate design," Wil clarified.

Wil detected a telepathic exchange pass between Michael and Elise.

"Are you set on going alone?" Michael asked.

"You promised you'd never leave me behind again," Elise said to Saera.

"Well, our intent is to keep a low profile," she replied. "Limit having others with abilities around."

"We've actually talked about moving down there ourselves," Michael revealed. "You're right, this is no place to have a family. And nowhere else is especially accessible to Headquarters."

"You don't need to avoid the Priesthood like we do," Wil said.

"No, but it makes sense for us to be there, too," Michael said. "For different reasons."

"Why?" Wil asked.

Michael took a moment to respond. "Since my dad defected to Earth, I'm not eligible for Taran citizenship."

"We can't be legally married," Elise said. "Not that it matters."

"I'm sure I could—" Wil began.

"I don't doubt your political pull, but it doesn't matter," Michael stated. "You might not recall, but I'm actually 12th Generation."

"Oh…" Wil's heart ached for them. *To know that their child won't have the abilities that have been such a central part of their lives. No wonder Earth is appealing.*

"Given that," Michael went on, "a move to Earth would be a good chance to reconnect with my dad."

"And my parents haven't talked to me since I joined the TSS, so it's not like we have somewhere else to be," Elise added.

Maybe having some backup would be good—and at least Michael is actually from Earth, so that's a much better option than my parents. He inclined his head. "We'd be lucky to have you with us."

Saera took his hand. "Full circle at last."

Wil and Saera continued making the rounds to their closest friends, sharing the news in pairs and small groups. Most of the reactions were a mixture of excitement, surprise, and skepticism about Earth, but it was clear they'd have as much support as they'd need within the TSS when the twins came of age.

After hours of explanation, they were finally able to return to their quarters.

"Should our children really know nothing about their true heritage?" Saera pondered as they reclined on the couch.

"If they did, that would defeat the purpose," Wil replied.

"What if there was a way for them to be familiar with it but not know their place?"

Wil eyed her. "What do you have in mind?"

"Well, what if they thought it was fiction?" she offered.

He thought about it for a moment. "Like, a novel that documented all the people and events, but in a way that anyone would think was just a made-up book?"

"Exactly."

"You know, that could actually work."

Saera placed her hand on her stomach. "They'll never believe us when we tell them it's real."

Wil smiled. "I think they will when we show them all this."

PART 2: BIRTHRIGHT

CHAPTER 4

"Jason! Raena! School. Now," Wil called up the stairs for the third time. *It's official—I can never let Saera go on a TSS trip and leave me here alone ever again.*

He ran his fingers through his hair and leaned against the wall next to the front door. Since moving to Earth, the challenges he faced on a daily basis were refreshingly mundane—no worlds that needed saving, no diabolical enemy to destroy. But dealing with two teenagers… Some days he felt like he'd met his match.

"Coming!" Jason finally yelled down the stairs, followed by hurried footsteps. He leaped down the last four steps and landed nimbly, scooping his backpack off the ground and slipping his tablet into the internal pocket in one fluid motion. "You packed lunch, right?"

"Yes, but it's high time you did it yourself."

His son grinned back, his teal eyes sparkling beneath his styled chestnut hair. "But having you or Mom do it is so much easier."

"And with that kind of attitude you really expect us to get you a car?" Wil asked with a raised eyebrow.

"We've been sixteen for four months now. All our friends have had their own car for years and—"

"Most of your friends are also two years older than you."

"It's a time-honored rite of passage!" Jason exclaimed. "I mean, come on! The car drives itself."

Wil sighed. "We'll talk about it again when your mom gets back."

"That's what you said last time."

"We did talk about it. The answer was just 'no'."

Jason adjusted his backpack slung over his shoulder. "You're stifling our independence."

"No, I'm making sure you have some sense of discipline before you graduate high school."

"My grades are perfect. This isn't fair."

Of course their grades are perfect—they've never had a remotely challenging class in their lives. The twins had skipped two grades, but even that wasn't enough to pose an academic challenge. Any more advancement, though, would have undermined the social benefits of moving to Earth. Wil let out a slow breath. "It's not a matter of punishment or reward for academic performance. It's concern about your safety."

"Yeah, yeah." Jason headed for the door.

"Where's your sister?"

His son shrugged. "I dunno. I didn't even hear her and Katie in her bedroom."

Wil resisted the urge to facepalm. "Raena! Are you coming?"

"Just a second!" his daughter finally replied.

"Go ahead to the bus," Wil told his son. "And don't hold it for her. She said a midweek sleepover wouldn't change anything, so she can walk if she misses it."

Jason laughed. "Tough love, geez. But you know, if we had a car—"

Wil opened the door and shooed Jason out. "Have a good day. I'll see you tonight."

"Later." Jason jogged down the porch steps.

"You're going to miss the bus!" Wil shouted up the stairs. *At this point, I really don't care. They'll never learn good time management or responsibility like this. Stars! I was almost an Agent by the time I was their age.*

"Yeah, we're coming!"

Three days. Just three more days until Saera is back. Wil took a calming breath, reminding himself that running late for school wasn't the end of the world. Life on Earth in their year 2044 was easy—a place where he could forget about the complications in the rest of the galaxy and just be a father with some vague job as a contractor with the military.

As he settled on the couch in the living room to read the morning news, Wil ignored the sound of running footsteps above and smiled to himself. Their existence wasn't perfect, but all in all things were pretty good. He could only hope things would stay that way.

—   —   —

"You *cannot* tell my dad I forgot to set my alarm!" Raena hissed to her friend. She slipped on a shirt and dashed over to her vanity to locate a hairbrush.

"Relax. Nothing happens in First Period, anyway," Katie replied, calmly scanning over the books on Raena's bookshelf.

"I have a chemistry test!"

"Psh, you'll pass without trying." Katie flicked her wrist and grabbed one of the books off the shelf. "What's this? I don't remember seeing it before."

Raena glanced over at the book while brushing her chestnut hair back into a ponytail. "Oh, some new sci-fi thing my parents just gave me. It's sort of written like a handbook for citizens of the galaxy, from the perspective of an advanced alien race."

Katie read over the blurb on the back. "The 'Taran Empire', huh? Is the book any good?"

"It's really far-fetched as far as sci-fi goes and almost reads more like a textbook. But I guess that was what the author was going for." Raena finished securing her ponytail with an elastic band. "It's an okay read. You can borrow it, if you want."

Her friend eyed the book. "Brent says I need to 'expand my horizons' and start reading more diverse literature, or whatever."

Raena dashed over to her desk to grab her tablet with the notes for the team assignment that had been the excuse for Katie sleeping over mid-week. They hadn't exactly been productive, but Raena could knock out the paper herself in an hour after she got home that night. "I wouldn't call that book 'literature'. Then again, I wouldn't call Brent well-read, either."

"But he's smokin' hot, so there's that," Katie smirked. She threw the book in her backpack.

Raena double-checked that she had everything she'd need for the day and hurried to the door. "Come on. We're late for the bus!"

The two girls stampeded down the stairs. Raena grabbed her backpack and shoved her tablet inside.

"No more mid-week sleepovers if this is how it's going to be," her father said from the living room.

"Sorry, Mr. Sights," Katie said from behind Raena on the stairs. "It won't happen again."

"We can still make the bus. See you tonight!" Raena barreled out the door with her friend close behind. "We have to run!"

Katie groaned loudly but broke into a sprint next to her. In times like this, Raena was happy for the years of conditioning from martial arts and track. She barely felt winded after four blocks, but her friend was wheezing next to her. A block ahead, Raena spotted the bus approaching the stop, where Jason was waiting with three of the other neighbor kids.

"Almost there!" Raena encouraged.

Katie grimaced and accelerated to keep pace with her.

They finished their dash through the suburban neighborhood that had been Raena's home for her whole life. The homes were mostly newer, but some blocks still had renovated houses from the 1910s or even older. All her history classes in school had driven home the heritage in Virginia, and she considered herself lucky to live in a place that offered some glimpse of another time. All the same, she more often found herself looking upward toward the stars and wondering if there was any other life out there.

With Katie panting behind her, Raena slowed as she neared the bus stop. The yellow bus had on its flashers and the door opened.

Their family friend, Corine, was first to climb up the stairs.

Jason watched them approach as he boarded with a smirk of

casual amusement. The two neighbor boys, both freshmen, smiled at Raena and Katie with thinly veiled panic in their eyes.

They should have learned to talk to a pretty high school girl after two months of school. She flashed them a polite smile and then turned her attention to boarding the bus. "Good morning," she greeted the middle-aged woman who'd been on the route since her own freshman year. Though the bus was self-driving, like all other modern vehicles, having an adult around to keep order was a requirement.

Raena proceeded to her usual seat in the center left of the vehicle.

"Cut it a little close, didn't you?" Jason ribbed from across the aisle.

She glared at her brother. "You're normally the one running late."

He grinned at her. "But not today!"

She sighed and sank into her seat behind Corine. "Good morning," Raena greeted.

"Hey," Corine replied.

They'd known each other for practically their whole lives, since Corine's parents, Michael and Elise, were best friends with Raena's own parents. Though Corine was only a year younger than Raena and Jason, they'd never particularly bonded as friends. In some ways, Raena regarded Corine in much the same way as her cousins on her mother's side—someone with whom to be cordial at family gatherings, but she wouldn't go out of her way to hang out.

Katie collapsed next to Raena. "Next time, I'm setting my own alarm."

"Oh, so that's what happened?" Jason asked. He crossed his arms and leaned back, bracing one of his knees on the back of the seat in front of him. "I should have known something was up when I didn't hear you taking forever in the bathroom."

"Yeah, thanks for checking, by the way," she shot back.

"Your schedule isn't my problem. But you better watch it—I think I'm finally making progress with the whole car thing. Don't screw this up for both of us."

"I was running late *one morning*, geez!" Raena smoothed

back a loose strand of hair that had escaped from behind her ear. "Gosh, it'd really be nice to have a car to take to college. I'd hate being stuck on campus."

"Every campus has a car-share program these days," Katie pointed out.

"True," Raena conceded. "But still."

"Have you tried talking to them about out-of-state applications again?" Katie asked.

"That's going about as well as getting a car," Raena huffed. "We certainly lucked out with the most sheltering parents ever."

"I'm applying to at least three schools in California whether they like it or not," Jason declared. "I'm sick of these snowy winters."

Katie laughed. "Three? You can just apply to your top pick and call it good. Both of you are guaranteed to get in anywhere you apply with perfect SAT scores and your straight-As."

Jason shrugged. "I want to keep my options open. I haven't decided what to study yet."

"Me either," Raena admitted. "Nothing has really clicked."

Katie rolled her eyes. "I'd give my spleen to have it as easy as you two. Never having to study and still rocking it all the time."

"I study!" Raena retorted.

Her friend eyed her from above her glasses. "Yeah, college textbooks you check out from the library for fun. That doesn't count."

"Sorry, I just like physics," Raena muttered.

"I think you want to be an astronaut and won't admit it to yourself."

"Air force wouldn't be bad, actually," Jason said after a moment. "Guaranteed flight training for officers."

Raena chuckled. "There is no way Mom would agree to you joining the military."

"Grandpa worked for the FBI. It's not all that different."

"Good luck with that." Raena dug into her backpack for her phone. "Hey, is Britney's birthday party still on for Friday night? I saw a post on her Feed that she was sick."

"Last I heard it was. She just had a cold or something," Katie replied. "Are you going, too, Jason?"

He groaned. "I hate attending co-ed parties with my sister—no offense, Raena. Watching guys fawn over you is just... creepy."

"You think it's any better for me with you?"

On cue, Katie slid over to Jason's seat across the aisle and leaned up against his shoulder, playfully trailing her finger over his chest. "Like Molly Suthers at James' party last weekend—"

"Gah, stop!" he threw up his hands and tried to escape, but there were only a few inches between his present position and the window. "You may as well be my sister, too. God, Raena and I have known you since we were what—five?"

She kept up the mocking voice, "But maybe seeing Molly with you has awakened an unrequited love—"

"And what does Brent have to say about all this?" Raena cut in.

"Frankly, I think he'd be fine with sharing."

Raena laughed.

Jason let out an exaggerated sigh and gently shoved Katie away. "Go back to your seat and talk about your girl things."

"But Jason, what about our future?" Katie cried, the melodrama dripping from every syllable.

"Right now, my future is acing this chemistry midterm," he replied, but there was a mischievous glint in his eyes. "But don't worry, Katie, darling. Nothing will keep us apart."

Katie placed the back of her hand on her forehead. "But Brent?"

"I shall challenge him in a duel, and win." Jason turned on his tablet. "After this chemistry test." He withdrew into reading his notes.

Raena laughed to herself and turned her attention to her own notes. Despite the snafu with the alarm, she could already feel it was going to be a good day.

CHAPTER 5

WITH SERENITY ONCE again restored to the house after the twins were off to school, Wil took a few minutes to finish reading through the morning newspaper. Such print media had become hard to come by, but after an entire life surrounded by instantaneous electronic communications, he'd come to enjoy the quaint, tactile experience and scent that accompanied the ritual. It felt like a window into a distinct element of Earth culture and he wanted to make the most of the experience before technology took over completely, as it always seemed to on worlds with Taran origins.

Most of the news would have been depressing had Wil not had a broader perspective on the conflicts. Wars between cultures were inevitable and economic disparity could be found everywhere. There was fighting on Earth for the time being, but one day the people of the planet would realize that they weren't alone and in that moment they'd be united.

After sixteen years of living on Earth, Wil had often pondered when would be the right time to make the Taran civilization common knowledge. Taran officials had discussed the matter with the governments of Earth over the years, but human society didn't seem quite ready—not until at least some of the cultural conflicts had been resolved. To be out among other Tarans, the people of Earth would need to gain a new level of tolerance and understanding that had thus far eluded many of the planet's citizens. Although, based on the people he'd met, Wil was confident that that time would come—and soon.

Humans were curious by nature, and the government could only hide the TSS' presence on the moon for so long. Conspiracy theorists were already quite close to arriving at the real truth. As far as Wil was concerned, if anyone asked him directly, he saw no reason to deny anything. But even then, he suspected that they'd laugh it off, like Saera's family had when she'd returned from a many years' absence.

Wil finished his review of the financial section in the newspaper, then folded it and placed it on the coffee table atop the others from the week. It would appear the economy would hold out at least one more day.

Time to get to it, I guess. He dragged himself from the couch and headed toward the basement.

When he had begun looking for houses with Saera after they'd decided to move, there were several important features: the house had to back up to greenspace; it needed to reflect a typical upper-middle class lifestyle; and it needed to allow for the excavation of a basement. It'd taken some time to find the right home and the right contractor, but they had ultimately accomplished their goal to create an entire sub-level.

Wil jogged down the carpeted stairs and headed across the game room toward the false wall that led to the Secret Lair, as Saera had dubbed it. The wall was only moveable via a telekinetic tug, so there was no worry of the twins accidentally finding their way inside. He grabbed the wall with his mind and pulled until the wood panel swung inward.

Beyond the opening, lights automatically illuminated along a stairway leading downward, parallel to the back wall of the basement.

Wil descended the stairway with its smooth, stained wood walls and entered into a replica of the master closet and bathroom from the upper floor of the house. Except, rather than everyday street clothes, this closet contained TSS uniforms for Saera and him.

He stepped over to the sink to wash the newsprint from his

hands, and then carefully reached into each eye to remove the tinted contact lenses concealing the natural bioluminescent glow to his eyes. Such contacts were critical to their attempts to blend in with the native Earth population. Despite fine-tuning the design over the years, they still bothered him after days of continual wear. He blinked and gave his eyes a couple seconds to adjust to the lack of lenses.

Once his vision normalized, he retrieved a clean Agent's uniform from the closet and got dressed. The uniform, complete with tinted glasses, always felt more comfortable than even loungewear—it was a part of him after practically spending his whole life in the TSS.

Looking the part of an Agent, Wil stepped up to a sliding door on the far side of the dressing area, identical to those found in TSS Headquarters leading from quarters into a hallway. The door was outfitted with a typical TSS entryway bioscanner, just as a precaution in case someone did manage to enter the sub-basement without an invitation. Wil placed his hand on the scanner and the door slid open with a slight hiss.

Inside, the square, four by four meter room was dominated by a metal archway in the center of the space. In its dormant state, the arch appeared almost sculptural—energy conduits on the surface forming complex patterns of interwoven lines. The inner plane of the arch was smooth besides a narrow groove that ran around the entire interior and across the threshold below the arch.

Wil immediately felt calm in the arch's presence—his connection to his real home in Headquarters. Of all his inventions, the arch remained his favorite, allowing instantaneous travel through subspace between two fixed points without a craft. The attempts to name the process had resulted in some awful suggestions, but they had eventually settled on Telekinetic Spatial Dislocation, or a TSD arch for short. That singular device had allowed Saera to retain her position as Lead Agent and for Wil to retain his sanity while still calling Earth their official home. If only their neighbors had the slightest clue what his daily commute was like.

Of their relationships on Earth, only Michael and Elise knew the truth. They had a TSD arch in their own home and followed much the same commute schedule. After so many years, the routine was a natural part of all their lives.

Controls for the arch were set in a pedestal situated off to the side midway between the door and the arch. Wil connected with the telepathic neural interface and activated the arch.

A hum of energy filled the air as the arch charged, drawing power from the micro geothermal generator installed beneath the floor. White light emanated from the energy relays along the surface of the arch, glowing in the room's dim light. With a crescendoing hum, an event horizon formed within the archway like a rippling wave, warping the view of the wall behind it.

Wil reached out to the portal telekinetically to test the connection, extending his consciousness through to the other side. It was sound.

Without further delay, he strode confidently through the arch and was enveloped by the shifting blue-green light of subspace.

The transfer only lasted a moment. Wil stepped out of the arch in the common room of the Agents' quarters he'd shared with Saera for the first six years of their marriage. He reached out telepathically to the arch controls and deactivated the portal.

Though the arch took up more room in the living space than he or Saera liked, they couldn't argue with the convenience factor of the destination, just as Michael and Elise had opted for their own arch.

The brief trip through subspace left Wil feeling energized and he took a moment to let the telekinetic charge dissipate from his body. Ever since the end of the war, he was always cautious to not draw too much. The appeal was always there, though, beckoning at the back of his consciousness. Part of him thirsted for that same power that had destroyed the Bakzen homeworld, but he couldn't allow himself to go down that path.

Once he felt centered, Wil exited the quarters and made his way up to Level 1 for the scheduled meeting with the other senior officers. Due to the difference between Earth's twenty-four-hour clock and the twenty-five-hour clock observed by Tararia and the TSS, it was impossible to keep a synced schedule between both locations. In this case, however, the standard TSS meeting happened to correspond to a reasonable hour relative to the Eastern time zone on Earth.

Per custom, the meeting was held in the conference room adjacent to the High Commander's office. Michael, Ian, Ethan, and Curtis represented the Primus Elites, and Scott as well as a dozen other Agents rounded out the group. Normally, Cris and Saera would moderate the meeting as the High Commander and Lead Agent, but SiNavTech term negotiations had taken them to Tararia for a week-long visit. In such rare instances where both of them were gone, Wil stepped in as the most senior Agent to be acting commander.

All the other Agents were already gathered in the room, leaving only three empty seats. Wil bypassed his usual spot and sat down at the head of the oval wooden table.

Ian glanced at the other Primus Elites and smiled at Wil. "This is almost like old times."

Except I still have no interest in having that kind of leadership responsibility again. "This is way better. We get to talk about budgets and all kinds of fun administrative details."

Marsie Katz folded her hands on the tabletop. "Speaking of which, do you have an update on the new flight simulators?"

"There was a complication in production," Ethan replied. "Something about a titanium shortage."

Wil frowned. "That's new."

"Rather," Ethan clarified, "the main processing facilities have some sort of worker's strike going on that's messing up the whole supply chain."

"Great." Marsie leaned back in her chair.

"Is there any workaround?" Scott asked.

Ethan shook his head. "Not unless you have access to a private mine."

Wil thought for a moment, running through the SiNavTech partner contacts. "We might. I'll look into it."

"On that note, there's also the matter of budget," Michael chimed in.

And this is why I didn't want to be High Commander. "What about it?"

"Many of the raw materials for the final phase of renovations have been coming in significantly higher than the original bid," Michael explained. "Apparently, the ores market is going crazy right now."

Wil rubbed the bridge of his nose with his thumb and forefinger. "How over-budget are we?"

"Around thirty million credits," Michael replied, sounding apologetic.

That's way more than we could make up with any short-term contract. Wil drummed his fingers on the tabletop for a couple seconds. "All right. I'll wire it from my personal account. We need to get the new training facilities up and running for this next term."

The room fell into an awed silence.

"I always forget you can just do that," Ethan murmured. "Just make tens of millions appear."

Wil bowed his head sheepishly. "It's not appearing. Really, it's worthless until it gets spent. This is a good cause."

"Thanks, it'll help a lot." Michael flipped through the other notes on his tablet. "Otherwise, the classroom renovations are almost complete and the new Trainee dorms are done."

"Enrollment is up again this year, just like we hoped," Scott added. "Almost all those new rooms will be filled."

The next generation of Agents—and hopefully one of the last that will graduate while the Priesthood is still in control. "Good, I'm glad everything is coming along," Wil replied.

"There are some matters of promotions and reassignments," Michael interjected in the ensuing pause.

Wil inched back in his chair. "Can't that wait until my father returns?"

"Some of them, but we need to figure out staffing for the training year. We only have two weeks left to get everything in order," Michael reminded him.

At least for the time being, it appeared there'd be no way around the administrative responsibilities. "All right, let's go over everything."

—   —   —

Cris glowered at the SiNavTech Executive Division Manager on the other side of the conference table. "Now you're just being unreasonable."

As usual, the negotiations had hit a wall one hour into the discussion. Cris and Saera were trying to stick to their talking points as they laid out the new transit plan with Fredrik, the SiNavTech representative. He was head of the Commercial Division of the corporation, which Cris found bothersome since the TSS was closer to a government entity than a private company. Negotiations about the TSS' ability to use the beacon network shouldn't be treated in the same way as a Baellas clothing shipment.

Fredrik flashed a prim smile and folded his hands on the tabletop. "The TSS contracts are up for negotiation, and these are the new terms. It's not unreasonable to revise contracts that haven't been updated for a century."

"On the contrary, that's a good precedent to maintain a positive relationship with one another," Cris countered.

"I'm afraid SiNavTech's business priorities have shifted in the twenty years since the terms were last agreed upon."

Cris let out a coarse laugh. "I see. Allowing the TSS to move freely so it can offer military protection, moderate conflicts, and operate in general is no longer a priority?"

"It's not meant to hamper the TSS' operations," Fredrik countered. "We simply recognize that TSS funding has been an issue recently and we wish to protect our interests going forward. We simply can no longer allow free use of the SiNavTech network."

"You got the independent jump drive for free and now you want to impose a per-jump rate on all TSS transit. That's insulting."

"My understanding is that the independent jump drive arrangement was with Wil himself and not brokered through the TSS."

"A meaningless technicality."

Fredrik shook his head. "Regardless, past dealings have no

bearing on these new terms. Now that the TSS is transitioning to more academic pursuits, the original transit terms no longer apply."

"And now we'll have to pay per jump."

"Or you can enroll in an annual unrestricted use contract," Fredrik offered.

"I can't believe anyone pays that. You want us to spend one billion credits a year just to maintain our same level of access to the beacon network? That's unacceptable."

"Well, TSS transit comes at a premium because of the longer-duration nature of the jumps. The extended locks put more wear on the infrastructure."

"That has no foking basis in reality and you know it."

Saera stirred next to Cris and flashed him a warning look. *"Shouting at each other won't resolve this."*

Cris exhaled slowly. "The mechanical stress of beacon locks is isolated to the ship. Jump duration doesn't make a bit of difference when it comes to the beacons."

Fredrik consulted his notes on the tablet in front of him. "The latest reports from the Infrastructure Division say otherwise. My instructions for the term negotiations were clear."

This is the first time we've brokered a deal with SiNavTech since I became High Commander. It can't be a coincidence. "Did those directions come from Reinen himself?"

"It was a board decision."

"So, yes. Well, you'll just have to tell him that—"

Saera cut in, "There's a middle ground here where both organizations can achieve a mutually beneficial outcome."

"That requires the other party to also be dealing in reality," Cris stated, not caring that his tone was terser than he'd otherwise allow in a professional setting. Just when he thought he'd made headway with his father accepting his chosen career in the TSS, something like this always seemed to come up.

"I'll be frank," Fredrik said, "I'm not pre-authorized to go below nine-hundred million credits on an annual contract. I can tell that is still well above your acceptable threshold, so I recommend we adjourn and reconvene after you've had the opportunity to reevaluate your finances."

Or I can talk with my father directly. Dealing with intermediaries isn't going to get us the kind of outcome we need. He nodded. "I appreciate your candor. I agree that we won't be able to reach an agreement within that budget."

Fredrik inclined his head. "Very well. I'll relay your feedback to the board and we'll take it from there."

"Thank you for your time," Saera said, but Cris could tell the words were hollow.

They exited the conference room and Cris led Saera to a small room down the hall reserved for private calls.

"Wow!" Saera exclaimed as soon as the door was closed. "Are they completely insane?"

"I can only view it as a deliberate attempt to bankrupt us," Cris said with a heavy sigh. "Which makes me think this is more personal than a matter involving the TSS."

"What do you mean?"

"I have a sneaking suspicion that my father is doing this to get my attention. I've heard rumors that he's preparing to retire, and this has always been a family business."

Saera rolled her eyes. "And as soon as you agree to come take over the company, the TSS will suddenly have very favorable terms again."

"You've got it."

"Aren't those kind of backchannel dealings illegal?"

"On paper, yes. In reality, that's how the entire civilization operates."

Saera crossed her arms. "That figures."

"Question is, what do we do?"

"Well, are you willing to give up your position in the TSS?" Saera asked.

The question caught Cris off-guard. "I certainly don't want to."

"But would you consider it?"

I always knew I'd one day come back to Tararia to take over SiNavTech. I just figured it would be on my own terms. He swallowed. "I do acknowledge my responsibility and won't turn away from where I'm needed. But we have a lot going on in the TSS right now. This isn't a good time for a change in leadership."

"Can't argue that. Maybe you could just agree to a transition timeframe with your father and he'd loosen the contract terms on good faith?"

"I don't see that working, but we could try."

Saera scowled. "We really don't have a lot of options unless we want to continue privately funding the TSS. The renovations are way over budget, based on the last report I saw from Michael. I know we'll get a revenue stream going once everything is in place, but we're still at least two years out from positive cash flow."

"If not more."

She nodded. "While money isn't exactly an issue for you right now, we need to make sure we have adequate funds in place for our other plans."

"I know..." Cris sighed. "Under any other circumstances, I wouldn't have blinked at a two billion credit outlay. But there are too many unknowns to just write off that much without some serious consideration."

"What do we do, then?"

"I guess a father-son heart-to-heart is in order."

"They do support our goals, at least unofficially," Saera said. "Maybe if you put it in those terms they'll understand."

"Not without them getting what they've been asking for over the past sixteen years."

"Bringing the twins into the Taran fold."

Cris nodded. "Are you still targeting next year to bring them into the TSS?"

"Yes. We want them to be able to complete high school with their friends. Since their abilities haven't emerged yet, there's no rush."

"I'm actually shocked they haven't expressed any ability yet. Wil was only eleven."

"True," Saera replied, "but he also grew up in Headquarters constantly surrounded by Agents, whereas we limit our use of abilities around the twins. Besides, I was around their age before any of mine showed."

"I guess we should be thankful for that. Still, I hate knowing that they're so close and yet not being able to have much of a relationship with them."

Saera looked down. "Sometimes I wonder if we made the right choice."

"They got the kind of childhood that none of us did but always wished we could have, so there's that."

"Yes, true."

Before he could continue, Cris' handheld buzzed in his pocket. He pulled out the device and a message illuminated in white text on the matte black surface. It was from Kate: >>How did it go?<<

Cris slid open the handheld and texted back a response: >>They're trying to bankrupt us.<<

>>Wonderful,<< Kate replied.

He slipped the handheld back in his pocket. "Don't worry, Saera, we'll figure something out. For now, let's just focus on making Headquarters the kind of place you'll want to bring the twins when they're ready."

She smiled faintly. "Hey, we have our whole family there. What else do we really need?"

CHAPTER 6

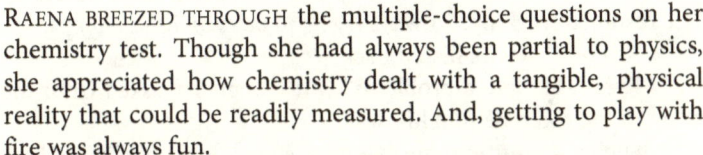

RAENA BREEZED THROUGH the multiple-choice questions on her chemistry test. Though she had always been partial to physics, she appreciated how chemistry dealt with a tangible, physical reality that could be readily measured. And, getting to play with fire was always fun.

The written part of the exam was six questions that most of the class would undoubtedly find challenging, but it only took Raena a matter of seconds to settle on her answer for each. She'd learned early on in school that it was better to work slowly, however, and not always be the first person to finish. She and Jason knew that things came to them easier than most, and it was only around each other that they really pushed themselves.

Glancing over her right shoulder, Raena saw that Jason, seated in the row behind her one aisle over, had also moved on to the written portion of the test. In front of her, Shelby Tomlin was furiously scrawling the answer to the first narrative question. Shelby had taken it upon herself to be Raena's academic rival, always trying to beat Raena's presentation scores and test percentages. Raena found the entire thing ridiculous, but by intentionally missing the occasional question, she was able to let Shelby take some of the attention from her in the interest of maintaining some normalcy in her friendships.

With Shelby forging ahead at a brisk pace, Raena resumed

her work with the intention of completing the test second. Raena read over the first question again and started to write, but a dull ache unexpectedly formed in her temples. *Great time for a headache.*

She tried to ignore the discomfort and focus on completing the question. By the time she started composing her response to the second question, however, the initial dull ache had intensified into a throbbing behind her eyes. She paused her writing to massage her brow. Normally, that kind of headache wouldn't come on unless she'd been reading small print for too long.

"I'll beat her," Shelby said suddenly. *"Almost there."*

Raena stared at the back of Shelby's curly red-haired head in front of her, taken aback that she'd speak out in the middle of the test. "Shh!"

Shelby turned around and glared at Raena. "Shh, yourself." She resumed working. *"Always trying to be such a show-off."*

"Am not!" Raena hissed back.

"Raena, is there a problem?" Mr. Dougherty asked from the front of the room behind his desk.

"Shelby's taunting me," Raena stated, only realizing how petty the phrasing sounded after she'd already spoken.

"I didn't say anything!" Shelby protested. "She started it."

"You both know better, ladies," said Mr. Dougherty. "Please let the class finish the exam."

"Sorry," muttered Raena.

"God, she can be such a prissy bitch sometimes," Shelby said in front of her.

"You're seriously going to let her talk like that?" Raena exclaimed.

"Shelby didn't say anything," Nick said from next to Shelby.

Raena stared at him with confusion, the pulsing behind her eyes creating dark spots in her vision. "She just called me a—"

"Raena, are you okay?" Jason asked from behind.

"I'm—" A burning spike bored in behind Raena's eyes. She gripped her temples in an attempt to relieve the excruciating pressure.

Whispers swirled in her mind as all attention turned to her. *"What's wrong with her?" "Did she finally lose it?" "Maybe we'll get to retake the test…"*

"Stop it, please!" Raena pleaded as a cacophony of voices overtook her. Dozens then hundreds of voices all speaking at once, each carrying with it an emotional echo of the speaker's experience. It all blurred together, too much for her to take in.

She placed her hands over her ears in a futile attempt to silence the voices. "Stop!" She collapsed to the cool tile floor, wishing she could burrow underground and escape the deafening roar.

Darkness closed in around her.

— — —

"Do you have any more anticipated cost overages?" Wil asked Michael, doing his best to hold in his frustration about the entire budget situation.

"The market is extremely volatile right now. None of these expenses were anticipated, so…" His friend trailed off.

Taran society had to choose this moment to start falling apart, Wil bemoaned with an inner sigh. The renovations and reinvention of the TSS was supposed to be an exciting occasion for Gifted people like himself, but instead it was turning into an endless string of headaches. "All right, just keep me updated. I'll let you know when I hear back from my contacts on Tararia."

"Then there's just the final order of business," Curtis began.

Wil's handheld vibrated on the tabletop. The screen illuminated with a picture of his son and the text 'Jason (Cell)'.

"Sorry, I have to take this," Wil said, holding up his finger for Curtis to hold his thought. He answered the phone in English as he rose from the table, "Hi, Jason. What's up?"

"Raena's sick," his son responded, a quaver in his voice. "She passed out in class."

Wil froze. "What happened?"

"I don't know. She started fighting with Shelby about talking during the test, and then she started screaming and passed out."

Why did this have to happen while Saera's gone? Wil ran toward the door and gestured for Michael, Curtis, and Ethan to follow. "Is she conscious now?"

"Sort of. She keeps mumbling for everyone to stop talking."

"So, she's hearing voices?" Wil asked.

Michael appeared to catch on to what was happening, and he ran ahead with Ethan and Curtis.

"I don't know," Jason said. "They want to call an ambulance."

"No. Tell them it's a migraine and she has medication at home."

"She's never had a migraine in her life, Dad. That's not what this is."

"I know. Just tell them that," Wil insisted.

"You want me to lie?"

"Doctors at the hospital won't be able to do anything for her. I'll be there soon and will explain everything."

Jason was silent for a few seconds. "How long?"

"Within twenty minutes."

"Okay." Jason still sounded unsure.

"What about you, Jason?" Wil asked. "Do you feel off in any way?"

"Not really. I have a slight headache that started around the same time Raena freaked out, but it hasn't gotten any worse."

"Okay, good." *At least we only have one major reaction to deal with for now.* "Stay calm and don't talk to anyone. I'm on my way to get you from school."

"We're in the nurse's office," Jason said. "Check in at the front desk."

"I'll see you soon. Take care of your sister—don't let them give her anything."

"Okay." Jason paused. "Please hurry."

"I will." Wil hung up and sprinted down the hall toward the central elevator lobby. Michael, Ethan, and Curtis had an elevator held for him.

"Awakening?" Michael questioned.

Wil nodded and ran into the elevator. Ethan immediately set the destination for Level 2.

"Just Raena for now," Wil replied. "But Jason might trigger at any moment. They're at school."

"Shite. No way to explain away that one," Ethan said.

Wil shook his head. "I'll do what I can."

The elevator arrived at Level 2 and the Agents ran for Wil's quarters. Wil palmed open the door and telepathically reached out to activate the TSD arch.

Energy coursed along the conduits of the arch, casting a cool glow to the corner of the room. The event horizon appeared at the center of the arch.

"Hold your breath when you enter," Michael said to Ethan and Curtis. "It's a bit disorienting."

"Yeah, I remember from when we were testing it out," Curtis replied.

Wil strode through the arch without hesitation, driven to get to his children as quickly as possible. He passed through subspace and stepped out into his subbasement on the other side.

Michael emerged from the arch after him, followed by Ethan and Curtis.

"Yep, that's still distinctly unnerving," Ethan commented as soon as he was out from the arch.

"You get used to it." Wil rushed over to a storage shelf on the side wall opposite the control podium and grabbed a tablet. He brought up a copy of the control interface for the TSD arch. "You'll need to make some modifications to the frequencies for the arch if we're going to bring the kids through in their present state. The energy in subspace might be too much for them without a shield."

"So, you want us to figure out a containment bubble on the fly?" Curtis asked.

"It's not the first miraculous feat you've pulled off. I'll be back within the hour," Wil said and headed for the stairs.

"We're on it," Michael assured him. "Let me know if you need any backup."

Wil nodded and turned to go.

"Wait, you're going like that?" Michael asked.

"No time to change," Wil replied and ran up the stairs.

The garage was accessible from the front foyer of the home, and Wil's standard SUV for everyday driving was parked in the garage next to Saera's of a similar model. However, another hidden feature within the home, unbeknownst to their children, was a parking space concealed beneath the storage area under piles of camping gear and household tools in the third parking space within the garage. Wil cleared away the items with a wave of his hand and stripped back the industrial carpet covering the space, revealing a seam in the concrete slab.

He telekinetically activated the lift mechanism to raise up a rectangular housing from under the floor, surfacing a sleek black sedan with seemingly invisible doors. The bottom of the platform was now flush with the main concrete slab and the original floor was above it, supported by four metal posts at the corners of the mechanism.

Wil jogged over to the car and placed his hand where a handle would normally be on the driver's side. The seams of a door etched into the surface with a trail of subtle blue light and the door swung forward and up at an angle. He climbed into the driver's seat and the door closed behind him, creating a perfect seal from the outside world.

The vehicle was the one piece of technology from offworld he'd insisted on bringing to Earth, aside from the items in the subbasement. Such ground vehicles were less preferable than aerial options, but he'd designed it specifically to suit his reasons for having it standing by. Not only would it serve to substantiate claims about a technologically advanced race, but he'd figured an occasion would eventually arise where he'd need to get across town quickly—and that day had come.

He opened the garage door and started up the vehicle, its near-silent engine channeling a low rumble through the interior seats. The car would no doubt draw attention, but worrying about what the neighbors thought was pretty low on Wil's current list of concerns.

Traveling at well above the legal speed limit regulated by the automated transit grid, Wil followed the familiar winding streets of suburbia to the main road and raced toward his children's school. Fortunately, the morning commuter traffic had died down so he didn't need to make too many aggressive maneuvers to maintain a clear path. The car handled effortlessly on the dry roads, and Wil smiled slightly to himself when he noticed pedestrians staring at the car with awe as he sped by.

The twins' school was a modern structure with a brick and cast concrete exterior and far too few windows to look like anything designed for daily occupation by people. As a high school, the parking lot was completely full with student vehicles. Wil circled through it once, and having seen no open spaces, headed straight for the main entrance.

Screw it. He parked the car in the front fire lane and got out.

A security guard roaming the grounds walked over to Wil as he was climbing out of the car. "You can't park there."

"I'm picking up my kids. They're going home sick. I'll only be a few minutes."

"Yeah, well, you can't park here," the guard reiterated.

"I already did." Wil ignored his continued protests and jogged down the concrete walkway to the main entrance.

Beyond the double set of doors leading into the school, the reception area was contained in a glass enclosure to the right of the entry foyer. Wil entered and the receptionist looked him over with a quizzical look, lingering on the tinted glasses.

"I'm here to pick up my kids. Raena and Jason Sights," he said.

The receptionist, whose name was Martha based on her nameplate, nodded solemnly. "I wish you'd completed a medical authorization form so we could have sent your daughter to the hospital right away. She needs immediate attention."

"Yes, I'm taking her to our family physician," Wil replied. "Where are they?"

"This way." Martha stepped out from behind the desk and waddled down an interior corridor farther into the office without any sense of urgency.

Wil followed her as she moseyed down the hall past a handful of administrative offices. On the left, he spotted a sign reading 'School Nurse'.

"In there," Martha stated. "The nurse stepped out for a few moments but she'll be back soon."

We need to get out of here before she returns. "Thank you," Wil said and opened the door to the medical room.

Jason was seated adjacent to the door, and he stood up as

soon as Wil entered. Raena was laying down on the exam bed with her eyes closed.

"Dad?" Jason questioned, looking Wil over. "Why are you dressed like that?"

"It's a long story." He crouched down next to his daughter and brushed his hand over her forehead while performing a high-level telepathic assessment. There was no doubt her abilities had emerged. She needed to get into isolation as soon as possible to limit the electromagnetic bombardment from the surrounding world. With no other options in the field, he formed a temporary telekinetic shield around her and Jason that should mitigate their exposure and lessen the symptoms.

"Raena, how are you feeling?" he asked in a soft voice.

Her eyes fluttered open. "Dad?"

"Yes, it's me," he assured her. He pulled up his tinted glasses so she could look him in the eye.

She recoiled when she saw his glowing eyes. "What—?"

"Your eyes!" Jason breathed.

Wil restored his tinted glasses. "I'll explain in the car," he said. "We need to get you home. Can you walk?"

Raena tried to raise herself up from the table. "I'm not sure."

"I'll carry you," Wil said and scooped her up in his arms before she could protest. "Jason, can you get the door?" *No need to freak them out further with telekinesis right out of the gate.*

With Jason leading the way and Wil carrying Raena down the hall, they made it back to the front reception desk.

"You'll need to sign them out," Martha stated.

"My hands are kind of full at the moment," Wil replied.

Martha shoved a tablet displaying the logbook toward him. "Policy."

With an exasperated groan, Wil shifted his hold on Raena to one arm and she held him around the neck. He scribed the necessary information on the tablet. "They won't be back at school this year."

Martha's eyes widened with surprise.

"What?" Jason exclaimed.

"What do you mean?" Raena murmured, still weak.

They can't possibly go back to school now that their abilities are emerging. I'd hoped they could complete their senior year, but... "I'll fill out the official withdrawals later. In the meantime, please alert their teachers that they won't be returning."

Martha worked her mouth. "I think they'll need more explanation than that."

"Later," Wil stated and headed for the door.

Jason ran ahead and opened the front door for him. "What do you mean we're not coming back? Don't we get a say in that?"

"This is outside all of our control. I'm sorry, I didn't want things to go down this way."

"I..." Jason was at a loss for words. "Wait, where's the car?"

"There," Wil said, gesturing toward his sedan with his head.

"Yeah, right. Did you stop by a dealership on your way over?"

"There's a lot you haven't seen." The vehicle automatically unlocked as Wil approached. "I'll explain everything, I promise."

"I don't understand what's going on," Jason stammered.

Raena began to rouse in Wil's arms, her mind finally settling within the protective shield. "What's happening to me?"

Wil leaned against the back passenger door and he stepped backward as it opened automatically.

Jason stared at the car, dumbstruck.

Wil set Raena gently in the back seat. "We're heading home, don't worry."

She sat up straighter and secured her seatbelt as he closed the door.

"What's going on?" Jason asked again as he climbed into the other back seat.

Can't delay any longer. Wil took a slow breath to clear his head as he jogged around to the driver's seat. Wil looked at his children in the rearview mirror. "I've run through this speech a thousand times in my head, but I still don't know what to say." He started up the car.

"For starters, what's this car?" Jason asked.

"I custom-fitted it for my purposes here." Wil drove toward the exit of the school parking lot toward their home. When he had merged onto the main street, he activated the autopilot and swiveled his seat around to face Raena and Jason in the back.

The two teenagers gasped.

"There's a lot we haven't told you." Wil took in their bewildered expressions. *All of this is going to sound crazy no matter how I put it.* He reached up and removed his tinted glasses, revealing his glowing cerulean eyes again. "I wasn't born on Earth and neither were you."

Raena and Jason exchanged glances.

"Dad, what are you talking about?" Raena asked in a weak voice.

Jason crossed his arms. "Is this some sort of midlife crisis?"

"Hear me out," Wil said. "There is an ancient galactic empire that exists among the worlds beyond Earth. Humans here on Earth are a divergent branch of that culture, essentially a lost colony of those seeking to break away from their fellow Tarans. One of the main differentiators of humans and Tarans is the prevalence of telekinetic and telepathic abilities. Though some humans do possess these abilities, it is far more common among Tarans. What you're experiencing right now is the Awakening of those abilities."

Jason shook his head. "Wait, Tarans? Like in *The Citizen's Handbook?*"

"Yes, exactly. We wrote that book so you'd be familiar with the terminology when the time came. Taran is the blanket term for people of our general appearance."

"This is crazy!" Jason exclaimed.

"I know it seems that way now, but it's the truth. Most divergent branches—like humans—are differentiated by the planet where the bulk of the microevolution occurred," Wil explained. "None of that matters right now, though. All that you need to understand now is that you aren't just human teenagers living on the only occupied planet in the galaxy. Quite the opposite. You're about to become a key part of that empire spanning the stars."

Raena slumped back in her seat. "This would sound insane if I hadn't started hearing my classmates' thoughts this morning."

"Awakening is disorienting under the best of circumstances. I wish we'd been able to debrief you and start integrating you into life beyond Earth sooner, but we wanted to give you the longest childhood we could. Once we leave Earth—as we now must—you won't have the same degree of freedom anymore."

Jason bolted upright. "Leave Earth?"

Wil nodded. "Now that your abilities are emerging, you need to begin training in order to gain control. Quickly. We have reason to believe you'll be much stronger than most, given your mother and me."

Raena and Jason did double-takes. "Mom isn't from Earth either?"

None of this is coming out right. "Let me back up. I wasn't born on Earth and I'm full-blood Taran. Your mother was born on Earth, but her mother was Taran and her father was half-Taran—the rest of her lineage is human. She grew up here on Earth and left to begin her training at the age of fifteen. That's when we met."

"Yep, you've officially lost it," Jason muttered, slouching in his seat.

Raena took a slow breath. "Okay, so you and Mom met at this training facility. Where is that?"

"The only sanctioned telekinesis training program is with the Tararian Selective Service, or TSS. TSS Headquarters is located in Earth's moon."

Jason chuckled. "Right."

Raena glared at her brother. "A car with no seams on its doors is presently driving itself without using the transportation grid, Dad has glowing eyes, and I can hear thoughts. Let's give him the benefit of the doubt."

Jason's smirk faded. "Sorry, Dad. Go on."

"Now, as you may recall from the book, the seat of power for the Taran Empire is the planet Tararia. The main functions of the infrastructure are controlled by corporations led by six powerful families known as High Dynasties. The Priesthood is a supposedly impartial organization monitoring everything. So, here's where things get crazier. I'm heir to the most influential of those High Dynasties—Sietinen."

"What does that mean, exactly?" Raena asked.

"Think of the Head of a dynasty being like the CEO of a company and a king rolled into one all-powerful position.

SiNavTech essentially manages the transportation network for all of Taran civilization. The Sietinen Dynasty is incomprehensibly wealthy and being born into the family gives a person every possible advantage in life."

"All right, if everything you just said is true, then… why are we here?" Jason asked.

"Because we wanted—needed—you to understand what it's like to live without those luxuries, as a regular citizen. I grew up in the TSS, so I had a decent perspective on life outside the family estate, but I also had no friends my own age until I was nearly sixteen. I didn't want to do that to you. Furthermore, everyone would still know who you were. Coming from an influential family changes how others interact with you, as much as we'd like to think it doesn't. There was no way you could possibly have a normal childhood in any established Taran community. But here on Earth, not far from your mother's family, we had a shot at giving you a life away from all of that. It wasn't without its sacrifices on all fronts, but I hope you enjoyed your childhood."

"You say that like it's ending," Raena said, her face drawn.

"Now that your abilities are emerging, we need to get you proper training. That can't be done here around the civilian population. It's time for you to understand your birthright."

"All of this still sounds crazy to me," Jason muttered.

"I know. You'll just have to trust me for now. I assure you, within a few hours you'll see that everything I've said is very real." Wil took a slow breath. "I won't lie to you—it's going to be a difficult transition. Life beyond Earth is very different in many ways, but there are also many common elements between the cultures. It's one of the reasons this was a good fit. Your mother often described it like stepping into the future."

Raena's face lit up. "Cool."

"You believe him? Seriously?" Jason asked his sister.

"We'll know soon enough," she replied. "If it is real, you have to admit that'd be pretty awesome."

Wil smiled. "Oh, it is. Jump drives for faster-than-light travel, artificial gravity, subspace communications—we have all of the things that are still only aspirational future achievements here. You'll get to step into a world where anything you can imagine is possible."

"You gave all of that up to live here with us?" his daughter asked.

"I would have given up a lot more than that."

The car slowed as it approached their neighborhood street. Wil swiveled back around in the chair to make the final approach. "Many things will make a lot more sense once I show you."

Jason sighed in the back seat. "So, the TSS... where we're supposed to get training. Is that where you work?"

Wil parked the car back in the garage where it would be out of sight from the prying eyes of neighbors. "Yes, more or less."

Raena's breath caught. "Wait, was this car in here all along?"

"Yeah, just in case." Wil closed the outer garage door.

Jason's face reddened the slightest measure as he saw the first evidence of the story he'd just been told having some validity.

Wil gave him a knowing smile in the rearview mirror. "We always told you we were military contractors, which is true—just not for any government here on Earth. I'm semi-retired, but your mother is actually Lead Agent. My father is High Commander, which is like the director of the organization. That'll change once he eventually takes over SiNavTech."

"Why did you retire?" Jason asked, less skepticism in his tone.

"That's for another time." Wil opened his car door and stepped out. *Hopefully, the arch is prepped.* "Some of our TSS friends are meeting us here to help with your transition," he explained.

Raena and Jason exited from the back seat of the vehicle.

"Other Agents?" Raena ventured.

"Yes, and my most trusted friends." Wil led the way into the house. As soon as he'd passed through the door into the foyer, movement caught his eye down the hall. He sent out a telepathic probe to confirm that it was Michael.

His friend strode down the hall from the kitchen toward them.

Raena and Jason froze when they saw Michael in the black Agent uniform.

"You too?" Raena exclaimed.

"It's a long story," Michael replied. "How are you feeling?"

"Way more confused but physically better," Raena told him.

"I grew up on Earth, too. I know how disorienting it is to find out about a whole empire just out of sight and that your parent—or parents, in this case—are Agents with telekinetic abilities." Michael examined the twins. "Don't worry, though. All of us will help you through this."

CHAPTER 7

RAENA SAT DOWN on the couch in the living room next to Jason, completely bewildered. "Is all of this really happening?"

"I'm not sure," her brother replied. "Did someone drug our water bottles on the bus?"

"Doubtful." Raena shook her head. "Say it is real… Leaving home, leaving Earth! I always dreamed about it, but the idea of going now without any warning."

"Well, we're heading off to the TSS or we're getting a one-way ticket to a mental institution along with our parents the moment we say anything about hearing voices and galactic empires. Either way, it's looking like we won't finish school."

"Or even have a chance to say goodbye to our friends," Raena realized. "I need to text Katie—"

"It's not like you'll get cut off from everyone," their father said from the entryway as he turned away from a private conversation with Michael. "But yes, it will be a while before you can come visit anyone here. And you can't tell them where you're really going."

"So, what, we just send a vague text message saying we're going away on a mystery trip somewhere?" Raena asked. "They'll think we've been abducted."

"Or institutionalized," Jason interjected.

"For now, that's all you can do." Her father combed his

fingers through his hair. "I need to go look at the transport arch to get it ready for you. Stay here and try to keep your minds quiet."

"What does that even mean?" Raena replied.

Wil frowned and then turned to Michael, who was still standing by the doorway. "Grab Curtis and have him stay up here with them."

Michael nodded and withdrew toward the basement.

"You're in a sensitive telepathic state right now," her father explained. "Being around Agents like us with strong abilities would be overwhelming were we not keeping a barrier, of sorts, around you. Think of it like a telepathic bubble that's muting the ambient noise around you."

Jason crossed his arms. "Okay... So, what are we supposed to do?"

"Nothing," Wil said. "Just try to relax."

A moment later, a man Raena had never seen before emerged from the hallway near her father. Dressed in a black uniform like the others, he had dark features and was of a lean build. His gaze passed over Raena and her brother. She could feel him silently evaluating her.

"They look just like you," he murmured in English, but with a distinct accent Raena couldn't place.

"Thanks, genetics!" Wil cracked a smile. "I'll let you know when the arch is ready."

The man inclined his head to Wil and then turned his attention to the two teenagers. "Hello," he greeted. "I'm Curtis."

"Hi," Raena and Jason replied almost in unison.

"It's hard to believe you're all grown up," the man continued.

"Have we met before?" Jason asked.

"Not exactly. You were only infants the last time most of us saw you."

Raena exchanged glances with her brother. "Where that?"

"In TSS Headquarters," Curtis replied. "Where you were born."

"How long have you known our parents?" Raena asked him.

"For a very long time." Curtis smiled. "I think I was about

your age when I first met your father. He'd been an Agent for a few years by then, but it was my first day in the TSS. I pledged to follow him then and I've never regretted the decision."

Raena tried to read between the lines. "Was he some sort of commander?"

The question seemed to catch Curtis off-guard. "What has he told you about himself?"

"Not a whole lot since the revelations about our origins came to light," Raena responded. "He mentioned something about our grandfather being High Commander and Mom is actually... 'Lead Agent', was it?" She looked to Jason for confirmation and he nodded.

Curtis sat down on the edge of a chair across from them. "Yes, that's all true. Your father used to play a more active role in the TSS than he does now. He should probably be the one to tell you about all of that, though."

"Can't you tell us anything more?" Raena pressed. "I'm still trying to wrap my head around any of this."

The Agent considered her position for a moment. "Well, I can tell you that he was my trainer in the TSS, and then my commander. There was a group of twenty of us—the Primus Elites. He trained us all as officers. Michael and I were two of his four Captains. We've all remained very close over the years. Any of us would die for him."

Die for Dad? Were they ever in real mortal danger together? She decided to keep those questions to herself for the time being. "What about our mom? Dad said they met in the TSS."

"They did, but that was before I joined," Curtis confirmed. "They had just become engaged at the time the Primus Elite group first came together. A couple of years after we began training, their relationship became public and she started training with us, too."

"It was a secret?" Jason asked, leaning forward.

"For years, as I understand it," Curtis said. "Your father had graduated to Agent by the time most are just starting training within the TSS. Your parents started seeing each other when your mom was still a first year Trainee, so it was a delicate situation for them to be involved—sometimes those things are easier to keep quiet than to address directly. On top of that, there was your father's position as a dynastic heir. The combination of the two was a lot to explain."

"But eventually, everyone did find out?" Raena pressed.

"Yes. They felt it was best to be honest about their positions for the sake of soldier morale in the war."

Raena's breath caught in her throat. "What war?"

Curtis tensed. "Um… Sounds like the arch is ready. Let's head to the basement."

"What aren't you saying?" Jason asked.

"I'll let your parents handle that one. We need to get you up to Headquarters," Curtis deflected.

What's really going on? She decided to let the topic go for the time being, seeing Curtis' discomfort. If he was an old friend of her parents', it wasn't polite to place him in an awkward position. "Don't we need to pack?"

"We'll provide clothing and anything else you may need," Curtis said. "I'm sure you can come back with your parents later to collect any personal items you want to have with you."

"About time," Jason said, standing up. "I'd like some confirmation that everything we've heard this morning is actually for real."

"With you there," Raena agreed. She rose from the couch and headed toward the hallway with Curtis and her brother. "Are we really about to leave Earth?"

Curtis smiled. "Yes, but not that far away."

The Agent led them to the basement door.

"I thought we were going to the moon?" Raena asked. "Don't we need a spaceship or something?"

"It's the 'or something' option," Curtis replied. "Your father figured out a rather ingenious portal system for short-range transport. How else do you think they had been commuting to work at the TSS?"

Raena didn't have a good reply to that.

Jason shook his head with continued skepticism but followed them into the basement.

The group jogged down the carpeted stairs. Raena's breath caught when she glimpsed the back wall of their rec room. Rather than the smooth wood paneling she had known for her whole life, there was now a doorway in the back left of the room. "No way!"

Jason inhaled sharply behind her as he saw the same thing. "Seriously, this has been here the whole time?"

"As I understand it," Curtis replied. "They finished construction before you moved down here. I believe you were five or six months old then."

None of this feels real. Raena took a deep breath and released it slowly, struggling to stay grounded as the layers of certainties within her life crumbled around her. She could no longer take anything for granted or trust in the assumptions that had been the foundation for her existence. *I have telekinetic abilities and my family isn't from this planet. Can this day get any weirder?*

Inexplicably, Jason still seemed to be in denial about the whole situation. He was eyeing the door like he expected it to either disappear or for a jester to pop out and explain that it had all been an elaborate ruse.

"Let's show you your new home," Curtis said after Raena and her brother had paused in silent contemplation on the stairs.

"There's no turning back now," Raena said to Jason.

He nodded and came down the remaining steps.

Curtis gestured for them to pass through the hidden doorway and he brought up the rear, closing the door behind him.

Raena peered into the strange space, finding it more dimly lit than the main room. The material finishes in the space were somehow foreign to her—a wood grain she'd never seen in other construction around town or in their family travels. *Was this brought from offworld?*

Still apprehensive but also curious, she headed down the stairs. The stairwell opened into a room that was eerily similar to her parents' master bedroom upstairs, but the details enhanced the otherworldly vibe. The two closets looked normal enough at first glance, but when she inspected the contents from afar, she realized that all but one of the outfits hanging in the closet were identical to the Agents' uniforms.

Further, there were what appeared to be touch-surface

interfaces integrated into the walls. While the technology itself was common in her everyday life, it was clear that these devices were in a whole other league of advancement beyond anything she'd seen demoed at even industry-leading conventions. It was alien tech—the real stuff, not like over-the-top ridiculous contraptions she'd seen in movies, but genuine, functional devices that worked seamlessly with the user to augment life in the most incredible ways. Or so she imagined as she watched Curtis interface with something resembling a palm reader next to a doorway on the far wall.

With a low hiss, the door slid to the side, revealing another hidden room. Inside, her father was staring at a small electronic device in his hand while facing a metal archway that had narrow, glowing white conduits running along its surface in intricate patterns.

"What is that?" Jason asked.

Wil looked up from the device in his hand. "That's the TSD arch. It's sort of like a teleporter, except not."

Raena gazed at the device with new wonder. "How does it work?"

"Uh…" her father searched for the right words. "Suffice to say it's like a controlled corridor through subspace."

"Cool," Raena said with a grin.

He returned her smile. "Oh, yeah."

It was then that Raena noticed another man dressed as an Agent working at a podium to her left midway between the arch and entry doorway. He looked over Raena and Jason and then said something to Wil in a language that Raena didn't recognize but it was still familiar, somehow, in its overall sound—almost like Latin.

Wil sighed in response to whatever the man had said and returned his attention momentarily to the device in his hand. He made an entry and then concentrated on the arch. A wave passed within the archway, leaving behind a barely visible shimmer within the opening, as though staring into a mirage.

"We're going through *that*?" Jason asked with a raised eyebrow.

"I've recalibrated it so it should be safe for you," Wil said in a tone that was certainly meant to assure them.

"How might it *not* be safe?" Raena asked, reading between his words.

Wil hesitated.

"It was designed for someone with full control of their abilities to go through," Michael said on his friend's behalf. "We can keep up the necessary shields, though. You'll only be in subspace for a second."

"I suppose it's too late to call for a spaceship?" Jason said with a touch of apprehension in his tone.

"I'd never put you in danger," their father replied. He turned to the friend who had yet to be introduced. "Ready, Ethan?"

The man nodded.

"I'll go through as a test," Curtis offered.

Wil nodded his consent. "See you on the other side."

The Agent strode into the archway and disappeared as he made contact with the event horizon within the metal frame.

"Whoa," Jason breathed.

Wil stood in silence for a few moments. In unison, he and the other Agents relaxed.

"He's through," Wil said, turning to his children. "Michael and I will go through with you." He extended his hand to Raena.

She stepped forward and took it with her left. "What do we do?"

"Just step through. Hold your breath as you enter. It'll be over before you know it," her father said, wrapping his hand firmly around hers.

Behind her, Michael had taken Jason's right hand and he had his left reaching out to her. She grabbed it.

"We have you from both sides, don't worry," Wil said. He stepped into the arch.

Raena was pulled through after him in an instant.

An electric tingle rippled over her as she passed through the threshold. Shifting blue-green light swirled around her—the most beautiful display she'd ever seen. As the light danced across the infinite sea, she was overcome with a sense of peace. She wanted to let go and give herself to the light, to experience everything it had to offer and be one with its eternal energy.

Except, she was being held back by a vague sense of others around her. The grip on her sense of self slipped away as she sought to become one with the light.

Then, the light blinked out of existence. A cold wave washed over Raena's skin as she stepped forward into an unfamiliar room, followed by Jason and Michael, then Ethan.

She took a gasping breath. "What was that?"

"Subspace," her father replied. "You almost let go."

"It was so beautiful," she murmured.

"How do you ever leave?" Jason asked.

"We can't survive in subspace," Wil said matter-of-factly, his tone indicating that further explanation wasn't warranted at the time.

With the topic closed, Raena took the opportunity to examine the room—her first glimpse of civilization beyond her home planet. Had she not known better, she would have thought it a nice hotel room in a sophisticated city. A padded leather couch occupied the center of the room, facing a broad screen on the wall that looked like a completely flat TV, almost indistinguishable from the painted surface were it not for the semi-glossy finish. In front of the couch, a coffee table with slightly scuffed corners and a tablet tossed on its surface made it apparent that the room was properly lived-in. She also noticed a door into a darkened bedroom and a work desk in the corner opposite the TSD arch. On various end tables and mounted to walls, she spotted pictures of herself and brother with their parents on Earth—mostly candid shots from family trips over the years. *This is where they live when they aren't on Earth.*

Wil nodded when he noticed her taking in the details. "Yes, this is our home."

"And we're inside the moon right now?" Raena asked.

"Yes."

Jason crossed his arms. "We could be anywhere right now."

Their father smiled. "Fine, then come see for yourself."

CHAPTER 8

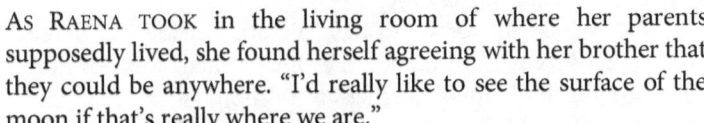

As RAENA TOOK in the living room of where her parents supposedly lived, she found herself agreeing with her brother that they could be anywhere. "I'd really like to see the surface of the moon if that's really where we are."

"In time," Wil replied. "This is the Primus residential wing within Level 2 of TSS Headquarters. There are eleven Levels total, all of which are deep underground in the moon. I'll take you on a tour as soon as you get cleared by Medical."

"Do you want us to go with you?" Michael asked.

"I'd appreciate it if you stay with us for now, Michael, as another familiar face. Curtis and Ethan, you can go. Thank you for your help."

"Think nothing of it," Curtis said with a smile.

Ethan grinned and said something else in the same foreign language, to which Wil rolled his eyes.

"What'd he say?" Jason asked.

"Right!" Wil said, shaking his head. "Second order of business is you learning New Taran—it's the galactic common language. Curtis took it upon himself to learn English when we decided to move, but very few others are fluent."

"We won't be able to talk to anyone for quite a while..." Raena realized.

"No, we have a way to speed up your acquisition of the

language, but we need to get the telepathic flashes in check before you can safely use the machine," her father explained. "We've already delayed enough, come on." He gestured them toward the front door.

"Take care. We'll see you soon," Curtis said and inclined his head to Raena and Jason.

Ethan flashed them a warm smile as he passed by to open the door.

The front door slid to the side. Beyond, a carpeted hallway nearly four meters wide was lined with sconces and small plants in illuminated, clear cylinders between other doorways. Stepping out into the hall, Raena saw that the same decor extended in both directions. Recesses with padded benches broke up the hall every five doorways. Mounted on the walls above the benches, pictures of nebulae caught Raena's eye.

She walked up to the nearest picture outside her parents' residence. From a distance, the image had looked like a photograph, but upon further inspection, it had a three-dimensional quality and appeared to be moving slightly. "Whoa."

"That's really cool," Jason commented, coming up next to her.

"We call them holopaintings," their father explained. "The art gallery tour will have to wait, though." He headed down the hall to the right.

Raena tore her gaze away from the fascinating picture and followed him. As they went further down the hall, she began to hear voices and other sounds of activity. With proximity to the other people, Raena suddenly felt pressure in her head, similar to what she'd felt in school right before blacking out. She raised her hands to massage her temples.

Next to her, Jason did the same thing. "Argh, what is that?"

Their father frowned. "You're hyper-sensitive to others with abilities right now."

"We're holding back around you, but they don't know to do that," Michael added.

"Hang on just a few more minutes," Wil said, placing a reassuring hand on Raena's back.

They made their way down the final stretch of hall, which

opened into a round lobby area with a marble-like floor and wood paneled walls. People of various ages dressed in black, dark blue, sky blue, and light gray were talking amongst themselves and passing to and from openings to other corridors at intervals around the rounded space. Some were waiting in front of what looked to be elevator doors.

Wil noticed Raena taking in the sights. "This is the central column that connects the individual Levels," he said. "The elevator shaft is the only way to access the separate rings. We're about to head up to Level 1." He activated a touchpanel next to the nearest elevator door.

A woman dressed in black was already waiting for the elevator. She bowed her head to Wil but snuck a glance at Raena and Jason, her eyes widening with surprise behind her tinted glasses. She murmured something to Wil in New Taran that was inflected like a question, and he gave a short reply. She nodded with apparent understanding as a light illuminated and the doors slid open with a slight hiss.

The five of them boarded in silence. The doors closed automatically and a white light pulsed next to the door. Seconds later, the doors opened into another lobby that was nearly identical to the previous one, but had some additional detail to the carved wood workings on the walls.

"This is Level 1," Wil continued his explanation as they left the elevator and made their way toward the opposite corridor. "It's the administrative center for Headquarters and also hosts the main medical facility."

The destination corridor immediately terminated in a reception area. Everything in the space was sterile white in harsh contrast to the soft grays and natural tones elsewhere in the building.

Wil walked up to the desk and spoke with the attendant.

A moment later, an older woman with graying red hair wearing a white jacket and tinted glasses hurried around the corner. She paused as soon as she saw them. "Stars! I can't believe you're really here," she said in English.

Their father smiled at her. "Believe me, the timing caught me by surprise, too."

"I'm Irina," she greeted as she came forward. "Let's see if we can't make you feel any better."

Raena gave her a meek smile.

"You can trust her," Wil said. "She delivered you. And me. And saved my life. Listen to her—she knows what she's talking about."

"Not that my patients listen to me half the time, present company especially," Irina said with a little huff. "This way, please." She strode back toward the heart of the medical office.

Raena and Jason followed her, with their father and Michael bringing up the rear.

Unlike the rest of Headquarters, which bore some resemblance to the architecture Raena knew on Earth, the medical facility was a whole other world that appeared to be hundreds of years in the future from her vantage. Private exam rooms lined the left wall, with transparent glass on the empty rooms and others tinted to opaque light gray. Beds in the empty rooms were just a thin frame that more resembled a poolside lounge chair than a hospital bed, though the surface was elevated on a waist-height pedestal. All vital monitoring equipment in the rooms was consolidated into a single interface above the head of the bed.

Irina stopped outside the first of two empty rooms next to each other. "Who's first?"

"Raena," Wil replied on their behalf. "She's highly symptomatic."

"It's getting worse for me," Jason revealed.

"All right," Irina said. "Martin!" she called to a middle-aged man in a white jacket seated at a station along the right wall, then said something in New Taran.

The man immediately set aside his work and hurried toward them. He said something to Wil in New Taran, and Wil replied. The man nodded.

"Jason, this is Martin," Wil said. "He's one of the doctors here and he's going to give you something to temporarily suppress your abilities while you acclimate."

"Aren't we supposed to, you know, be able to communicate with our doctors?" Jason asked.

"You'll be able to soon enough," Wil replied. "Michael can translate, if needed. But I need to step out for a few minutes. Your mom has been messaging me nonstop since I told her what was going on. I need to check in."

"Is she coming back here?" Raena questioned.

"She's on her way," Wil confirmed. "And she never would have traveled now, had we known you'd be going through this. Just let the doctors take care of you. You can trust them, I assure you."

"There's nothing to worry about," Irina stated with a tone of calm authority. "I'll come see you as soon as I'm done with Raena," she promised, looking to Jason.

He nodded his agreement, and Irina beckoned Raena into the nearest exam room.

"Come back soon," Raena said to her father.

"I will."

Raena took a deep breath as she sat down on the exam bed.

Irina slid the door closed behind her and glided her finger downward along the front glass wall, causing the glass to tint to light gray. She smiled at Raena. "Your symptoms began this morning?"

"Yes," Raena replied and gave a quick summary of the events.

"Sounds like quite an eventful day." Irina made a note on her handheld. "And how are you feeling now?"

"Uh, confused?"

The doctor gave her a sympathetic nod. "That's understandable. How about physically?"

"Well, my headache is back. I can deal with it, but I'm having trouble thinking straight."

"You're undergoing a major shift in brain chemistry at the moment. Even with the medications and therapies we have at our disposal, the transition is never easy. Plus, the stress of leaving home so suddenly will only make it worse."

Raena looked down at the white tile floor. "Dad said we can't talk to our friends about it."

"It's a difficult situation," Irina said.

"But lie to everyone?"

Irina folded her hands in front of her. "I know this is a lot to process. But think of what you've seen here. If you tried to explain this to someone who hadn't seen it for themselves, would they really believe you?"

"No," Raena realized.

"It's difficult, yes, but you're among your people now. Friendships can come and go, but our little community here in the TSS will yield the best relationships you can ever hope to find. We're one big family here."

Raena shook her head slowly. "Everyone seems to know our dad."

Irina nodded. "He's famous in almost any circle you ask. But don't concern yourself with that right now. Today is about you and finding your own identity."

"I feel lost."

"Well, you just had a veritable universe you didn't know existed open up in front of you. It's completely normal to take time to adjust."

Raena shifted on the table. "Yeah."

"And your mom will be back soon to help you navigate all this. She has a better perspective than most."

"I guess she would."

Irina gave her an understanding smile. "Now, let's have a look at you. Lie down, please."

Raena complied. Though thin in appearance, the platform was surprisingly supportive and conformed to the curvature of her back.

"I'm going to run a quick scan to make sure your systems aren't in distress," Irina explained. She tapped on the panel above the head of the bed and a beam of light projected downward just beyond Raena's feet. The beam swept upward past her head and then back downward before disappearing.

Irina studied the results on the monitor.

Raena craned her neck backward to see, but the readouts were meaningless to her untrained eye. "What's the verdict?"

"You're in perfect health, aside from the side effects of the Awakening. All within expected ranges," the doctor responded. "It looks like your contraceptive implant and nanotech immune support are in order, as well."

Raena did a double-take. "Uh… what? I have a contraceptive implant and nanobots in me? When did I get those?"

Irina's face flushed slightly. "I'm sorry. I discussed it with your parents several years back but I suppose they wouldn't have explained that to you," she said with a frown. "It's not as invasive as it sounds. All very standard. Like the ID chip in your wrist, the nanotech has been with you since you were newborns—"

"Wait, ID chip?"

"To identify you as a dynastic heir, in your left wrist," the doctor replied far too casually for Raena's liking. "As for the nanotech, I bet you never got sick like the rest of your friends, right?"

Raena nodded, still feeling unsettled about the concept.

"And I believe they arranged for one of the nurses from here to give you an exam when you were around twelve, and that's when you would have received the other implant. It's compulsory for all Taran citizens around that age—boys and girls—and especially important for someone of your birthright. With the importance of genetic legacy, an unintended pregnancy must be avoided."

Uh, yeah, that seems pretty invasive… "I guess."

"The contraceptive implants only serve that one purpose and can be easily deactivated when needed. It's quite innocuous, really."

All the same, Raena found herself unnerved by the idea that she'd been effectively sterilized without her knowledge. "I guess I'm in no position to question it if it's standard practice…"

"Well, when you have a population of several trillion people, putting some controls in place becomes necessary."

Trillions? Raena couldn't begin to think about that scale of civilization. "You need permission to have a kid?"

"Well, there's a process," Irina stated. "Anyone of note also has their genetic material on file in the Genetic Archive."

"For… cloning?" Raena speculated.

"No. Cloning is strictly forbidden—at least whole bodies."

"Why?"

"Too much conflict." Irina cleared her throat. "Now, I'm

going to give you a little something to help mute your abilities while your body adjusts to the new electromagnetic sensitivity," the doctor continued. "We'd normally keep you in an isolation room for a few days to let your body adjust naturally, but given the unconventional nature of your arrival here in the TSS, you need to go through some additional debriefing that shouldn't be delayed. This will allow you to move about freely and start getting acclimated in other ways."

"Okay…"

Irina selected a metal tube with a cone protruding at a right angle. She loaded a canister into the base of the tube and clipped a head over the cone from a sealed package. "This will sting for a moment," she said as she pressed the cone against Raena's neck.

A sharp jab caught her by surprise, but it quickly numbed. Almost immediately, her mind began to clear and the headache receded. "Wow, that's way better."

Irina smiled. "Good. It will take a few minutes for the drug to take full effect. Why don't you wait here while I check on your brother?"

Raena nodded. "May I get up?"

"Of course. I'll be back shortly."

Irina departed and re-sealed the door behind her.

Cautiously, Raena rose from the bed. Her senses were indeed much clearer than before and she was feeling more like her usual self.

As her feet touched down on the tile floor, the door slid open again.

Her father walked in. "Hey. How are you feeling?"

"She gave me something for the headache and it's way better."

"Good."

Raena looked over her father. "But uh, contraceptive implant and nanotech? Seriously?"

Wil looked down. "That was probably not the best way for you to find out."

"You think?" Raena sighed.

"I wish I could have explained all of this better. I'm sorry it's all coming at you at once."

"Yeah, well…"

Her father looked genuinely apologetic.

This is probably hard on him, too. She softened. "It's okay. There's clearly a lot I don't understand about how things work around here." She paused. "What did Mom say?"

"That she feels awful that she isn't here. She's coming as quickly as she can."

"How long will it take for her to arrive? Is she far?"

"She was on Tararia," Wil said, "which is farther away than you can possibly imagine. However, it's only a four-hour trip with our latest jump drive advances."

Raena's eyes widened. "Across the galaxy in four hours? That's crazy."

"Well, Tararia isn't exactly on the other side of the galaxy and that kind of rapid transit isn't particularly commonplace. We have some special tech in the TSS. But the point is, she'll be here very soon—she left as soon as Jason called me from school."

"I guess we can get a tour in the meantime?"

Wil smiled. "A short one, anyway. But first, let's make it so you can actually understand what others are saying. I learned American English back when I was a teenager because your mom was from there. However, as I was saying earlier, the galactic standard is New Taran. Many of the ancient Earth languages broke off from different Taran dialects, such as the origins of Latin. Since there are so many different dialects across the worlds, we have a sort of learning machine to imprint the vocabulary and syntax for New Taran so you can pick it up quickly. It will also give you a basic understanding of Old Taran, by extension."

Raena stared at him with disbelief. "You have a learning machine?"

"Technically it's an optical encoder… but yeah," Wil replied.

"So, all those years you made us go to school—"

"No, this is just for language acquisition and some other things of that nature. Apparently, your mother had the same reaction when she got here," he said with a chuckle. "What they told her then remains true today—some things you just have to learn the old-fashioned way."

"Well, I'm intrigued," Raena said with an emphatic nod.

"Good. Now, I think Jason is almost done."

Wil stepped back into the hall where Michael was waiting for them, and Raena followed. The door to Jason's room was still closed, but Raena noticed a group of people had gathered down the hall in the direction of the reception area. All dressed in white, they were whispering to each other and kept glancing at Raena and her father.

"Why are they watching us?" Raena asked in a hushed voice.

"I've always been well-known around here because of my position," Wil explained, "but you and your brother are the new, fascinating pair—High Dynasty heirs raised on Earth. That's a first."

Raena crossed her arms. "I don't really like the idea of being on display."

"The novelty will fade," Michael said.

The door to Jason's exam room opened and he stepped out into the hall.

"Let me know if you have any more issues," Irina said behind him, making a note on her handheld.

"Thanks, Irina. I'll bring them in for a checkup soon." Wil led them toward the lobby of the medical facility.

Raena turned to her brother. "Apparently, there's a machine for us to learn New Taran."

His eyes lit up. "Really?"

Wil smiled. "It's like magic!"

They approached the group of medical technicians who'd gathered to watch them. As they passed by, the staff members hurriedly pretended to go about their work, but Raena caught them stealing glances.

I'm used to getting some attention, but not like this. In retrospect, she realized that it was foolish to ever think they'd go unnoticed. They were among others with abilities and her parents had called Headquarters their home for decades, but she and Jason had been raised on Earth to escape the spotlight. Seeing the reaction of the medical technicians, she began to understand why her parents had felt the need to get away. If even those in the TSS were fascinated, she could only imagine what it would be like outside of the facility, where Agents were a novelty—especially a High Dynasty Agent.

"Ignore them," Michael whispered when he noticed Raena watching the technicians' reactions. "Act like you belong here and you will."

At the lobby, her father headed down a hallway to the right. Doors to rooms along the corridor were solid, more like those in the residential wing. He stopped at the second door on the left and it automatically slid open.

"I'll wait out here," Michael said.

Wil nodded and stepped into the room.

Inside, a single chair was in the center of the room with a contraption hanging from the ceiling. Raena examined it with dismay. "What is that?"

"This is the ·neural imprinting device to aid language acquisition," her father explained. "It looks scarier than it is."

"And that's how we'll learn New Taran?" Jason asked.

"Yep. Have a seat." Wil gestured toward the chair.

Cautiously, Jason positioned himself in the seat. The device in the ceiling descended and came forward so it aligned with his face.

Wil manipulated some controls on a console and the machine sprang to life, sending dazzling light from a viewport in front of Jason's eyes.

He tensed with surprise. "Whoa! What's it doing?"

"The transfer happens via your optic nerves. It will take a few minutes to calibrate and then complete the encoding. Try to relax."

Raena watched with fascination as the light shifted through the spectrum and pulsed with different patterns. After three minutes, the light ceased and the machine rose upward toward the ceiling.

Jason blinked rapidly. "That was… weird."

Wil said something to him in New Taran.

Jason thought for a moment, and then replied in the foreign language. He caught himself. "Wait, did I just…?"

"It takes effect quickly," Wil said with a smile. "Though, it does help that we spoke New Taran to you as babies so the basic language pathways were already there for hearing the proper phonemes like a native speaker. Your turn, Raena."

Jason got out of the chair and Raena took his place. "Does it hurt?" she asked him.

"No. It's just really, really bright."

Gripping the armrests of the seat, she let the machine work its magic. When it was complete, her head felt like it had been inside a pinball machine for the last three minutes.

"Are you okay?" her father asked.

"Yeah, I'll be fine," she replied. She caught herself; something about the words seemed strange on her tongue. "Am I speaking New Taran?" she asked.

Her father grinned. "Sure are."

"That's incredible."

Jason tilted his head. "Do these machines work for other things?"

"Not in the way you're thinking. You still have to go to class." Wil headed for the door.

"Something tells me we're going to do nothing but watch educational videos and read for the next ten years while we try to learn a whole new culture," Jason muttered while they began walking down the hallway with Michael.

"You do have a lot to absorb," Wil said, "but it won't take nearly as long as you think to learn the most critical items. I think your mom felt fairly integrated after a year. And don't worry— you won't be on your own. We've been planning for this."

Jason frowned. "It wasn't right to keep us in the dark about who we are."

"Compared to the alternatives, I stand by the decision," their father replied. "We wrestled with the choice. I know my parents were far from happy with the arrangement, but it was the only way you could come in with the fresh perspective we needed."

"What do you mean?" Raena asked.

Wil was silent for a few moments and glanced at Michael. "There's been some... political tension over the years. Our family happens to be in a unique position of power, poised to make a meaningful long-term impact. But to truly accomplish our goals, we need to make sure we're really acting in the best interests of a layperson. All of us grew up in positions of power and influence, so we wanted you to come from a more humble position. You have the name and birthright of authority but were raised in the ways of those without such advantages. We could think of no better way to position you as compassionate and understanding leaders. And from that position, we can restructure the Taran government."

"That was a big gamble. What if we rebel?" Jason asked.

"It wouldn't be the first time someone in the family has gone against the norm," their father said with a slight smile. "I just hope you'll give us a chance and maybe elect to rebel in our general direction. Take my word for now that you don't want to align yourself with the other side. If they had their way, there'd be no one with abilities and everyone would blindly follow the Priesthood's decrees."

"I guess we'll just have to see what's going on and take it from there," Raena said.

Wil nodded. "That's right. Now, come on. We have a lot to see."

CHAPTER 9

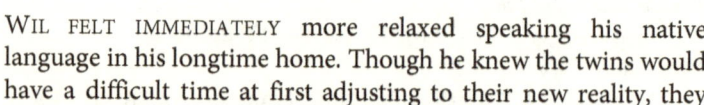

WIL FELT IMMEDIATELY more relaxed speaking his native language in his longtime home. Though he knew the twins would have a difficult time at first adjusting to their new reality, they were already taking it better than expected.

I've had my entire world turned upside down before. At least they aren't facing an all-out war. Putting it in those terms, Wil realized that his actions really had made a difference in others' lives—a positive change on a scale few could comprehend. Trying to explain that to his children was still too much for him to think about, though. He rather liked them thinking about him as a relatively normal person that hadn't grown up with the responsibilities he'd had in his real life. The persona they knew of him on Earth was his alternate reality self he had fantasized about during the worst times in his life when he wished he could escape. With that image of himself alive in his children's minds, Wil could pretend that it was true—that he hadn't done all the terrible things he was forced to do in his past. But once they knew the truth, he wouldn't be able to pretend anymore. He'd have to be himself again and remember the past he'd tried so hard to forget.

There was still time, though, for Wil to create a new vision of himself in their eyes. He was a respected Agent and leader, but his part in the war could remain a secret. The past hadn't caught up with him quite yet.

Shoving the concerns to the back of his mind, Wil returned his attention to his two children. Seeing their wonder at every little thing was a grounding reminder of the good things he'd had in his life and the even better things yet to come. "Am I going to have to explain the operation of every environmental feature to you?" he asked his daughter jokingly.

She rolled her eyes. "I just wanted to know how the plants live without water and soil. *You* were the one to go off on a tangent about the air filtration systems."

"I have been known to go off on a technical tangent or two in my day. You've been warned," he replied with a coy smile.

Michael grinned. "Take that warning seriously."

Raena let out an exaggerated sigh and resumed her intense study of the plants contained within cylinders along the corridor.

"That's great and all," Jason interjected, "but I thought we were going on an actual tour of the facility."

"Yes, we are. I guess we may as well start with the administrative wing since it's close by." Wil led the way to the nearest stairwell to head up one floor to the central command wing of Level 1.

"So, there *are* stairs," Raena commented as soon as Wil swung open the door to the stairwell.

"Oh, yeah, we'd never get rid of all the stairwells," Wil replied. "Where else would we have trainees run in circles if they get too ornery in regular practice?"

"You've made people run laps on stairs?" Jason asked warily.

"Not often, but it's happened. They did it to themselves, though—at least as far as I'm concerned. Michael might have a slightly different take on the issue." Wil held open the door for the twins to go through.

Michael only shook his head in response.

Raena paused on the stair landing. "So, you trained Michael and the others? But aren't you about the same age?"

"Yes," Wil said as he headed up the stairs. "We're all close to the same age, but I graduated when I was sixteen. I'd been an Agent for three years by the time they were enrolling as first-year Trainees."

"Being so young, were you at a low-level rank at first?" questioned Jason.

"No, Agent rank is determined by a final exam score. The biggest factor is raw telekinetic ability, so age is irrelevant."

Raena jogged up the stairs behind him. "What did you score?"

They can easily look up my CR as soon as they have access to the Mainframe. I'll have to come clean eventually. "My official score was a 13.7."

Jason glanced at his sister and she shrugged. "That's out of a twenty-point scale, I'm guessing?"

Wil was thankful he was in front of his children so they couldn't see him grimace. "It's not a set scale, but I'm the only person to ever score above a 10."

"How are you that much higher?" Raena asked.

"That's a really long story." Wil reached the summit of the stairs leading to the top floor of Level 1 and palmed open the door. He swung it inward and beckoned his children through.

Raena eyed him. "I'd wager this is a long tour."

Wil was still trying to think of a suitable response when he caught Michael's gaze. *"Time for a change of subject."*

Michael nodded. "So, what do you think of the TSS so far?"

Raena beamed. "It's incredible!" she said. "It's hard to believe all of this has been here our whole lives."

"Yes, it's a big secret to keep," Michael agreed. "We have to scrub all the surveillance footage from Earth before anything gets released to the public. The government leaders may stop obeying our agreements at any time."

Jason thought for a moment. "Wait... Are TSS Agents the mysterious Men in Black from all those conspiracy theories?"

Wil smiled. "Rumors often have some basis in reality." *Thinking about that should distract them for a while.* He gave an appreciative nod to his friend.

"What about Corine. Does she know about any of this?" Raena asked Michael.

He shook his head. "No. She grew up very similar to you."

"What about her abilities?" Jason questioned. "If you're an Agent—"

"She won't ever have abilities," Michael interrupted.

Raena frowned. "Why not?"

"It's complicated." Wil sighed. "There's a Generation Cycle, and she's at the reset point. The genetic potential is there, but abilities won't be expressed again for another seven Generations."

Jason stared at him blankly. "Huh?"

"How about we check out the High Commander's office while your dad is gone?" Michael suggested in a deflection of his own.

"Great idea." Wil led the way down the hall. "This is the administrative wing for Headquarters. The senior Agents have offices here." They passed by Saera's office. "This is your mom's office as Lead Agent. Unlike me, she actually uses hers."

Raena looked at him questioningly. "Why don't you use yours?"

"People always come to bug me about something or other. I like to work in study rooms or in our quarters where I won't have frequent interruptions."

Michael cracked a smile. "We know all his favorite places to hide out, though."

"I had to go to a whole other planet to get away," Wil joked back. "But anyway, here's the High Commander's office. As a trainee, you're either about to get high praise or you're in serious trouble if you're ever called in here."

The twins glanced at each other.

Wil opened the door to the office and stepped in. A handful of senior Agents had access to the office while Cris was away on Tararia, but usually there was no occasion to enter. The lights automatically came on as he stepped inside. "Now, you might actually spend more time in here than most, considering that your grandfather is High Commander."

"Is that weird for you, having your dad as your boss?" Jason asked.

Not as awkward as when it was the other way around. "We get along really well," Wil replied. "I'm close with both my parents. They can't wait to properly meet you."

Raena smiled. "I'm looking forward to meeting them. The vid calls just aren't the same. I guess they're not really living in a remote mountain village, like you'd told us…"

Wil nodded. "You'll meet them soon. We'll give you a couple days to let your abilities settle and then head over to Tararia."

"What's the planet like?" Raena asked.

"Well, since you brought it up…" Wil stepped over to the High Commander's desk and activated the holoprojector on the ceiling.

In an instant, a perfect rendering of Tararia appeared in midair, suspended in the center of the room. The continents depicted all the natural features in stunning realism, and even cities showed the patterns of buildings integrated into the surrounding landscape. To add to the illusion, the side of the planet that was presently in night—the First and Third regions and eastern side of the Sixth—was shrouded in shadow and the cities showed up as points of light through the darkness.

"No way!" Raena breathed.

Wil grinned back. "Like I said, it's sort of like the future—at least from your perspective. For me, going to live on Earth was like stepping back into the Dark Ages."

Michael sighed. "It's not *that* bad."

"Right, like needing to monitor file sizes to make sure everything transmits is a perfectly acceptable way of living," Wil said with a scoff.

"I'll admit, there are some downsides," Michael muttered.

"I guess I should be thankful for the recent advances, at least. I don't think we would have had a chance of blending in without some of the basic analogs to the technology I grew up with," her father continued.

"What else do you have?" Raena asked, her eyes bright with eagerness.

"Well, I guess I could show you one of the simulator practice rooms," Wil suggested.

"Like, flight simulators?" Jason ventured.

Wil smiled at his son. "Space fighters, specifically." *That should help regain a little favor.*

Jason's eyes widened. "Yes. That is the next stop of the tour."

"All right. Let's head down to Level 10," Wil said and stepped back toward the door.

"And we have to use the central elevator to travel between the rings—or Levels—right?" asked Raena.

"Ah, you were paying attention," Michael commented as he relocked the High Commander's office after everyone was in the hall.

Raena flashed a coy smile. "I try."

The four of them strode down the hallway toward the central lobby. As they neared the main intersection, two young male Primus Initiates were walking up the hall in the opposite direction. Their pace slowed and conversation died down as Wil and Michael neared with the twins. At first their focus was on the Agents and they gave a slow bow of their heads in respect, but then they caught sight of Raena.

"Hey, newbie," one said to the other.

They both looked Raena over again as they passed by.

Wil swiveled around and glared at the two Initiates. *"Don't even think about it."*

The two young men backed away.

"Dad!" Raena hissed under her breath.

"I didn't do anything—" Wil insisted.

"Sir!" A familiar voice called from down the hall. Wil turned to see a Militia officer named Dylaen, who'd been a longtime administrative support staff person for his father, running down the corridor toward them. "You need to take a look at this."

Wil sighed. "Not now. We're in the middle of something."

"This can't wait," Dylaen insisted. He thrust a tablet into Wil's hands.

"What's—" Wil froze when he saw the readings on the screen: a proximity alert for an unknown ship. *The Aesir!* "When was the alarm triggered?"

"Only moments ago. I came to find you right away when you didn't respond to my call," Dylaen replied.

Wil handed the tablet to Michael. *"They could only be here for one thing."*

Michael glanced at the screen. His face drained. *"They're not ready."*

"Not even close." Wil swallowed. "Prepare to institute an Alpha-One lockdown."

"Dad, what's going on?" Jason asked.

"Tour's over," Wil stated.

Michael glanced between the twins and Wil. *"Level 11?"*

"No, elevator car stopped between Levels 10 and 11. That will be the most difficult to access," Wil replied.

"I'll go with you to the surface," Michael stated aloud.

Wil shook his head. "You have your own family to worry about. You've already spent enough time protecting mine. Go down to Earth with Elise and Corine."

"But you need a Second!" Michael protested.

"Ethan and Ian can come with me. Three Agents or thirty won't matter—the Aesir can overpower us if they want to. I could beat them, but the facility wouldn't survive." Wil sent out a rally to the other Primus Elites with orders for where everyone should stage.

Reluctantly, Michael nodded. "Be careful." Then added telepathically, *"I'll let Cris know what's going on. Good luck."* He ran down the hall.

"Dad?" Panic was audible in Jason's voice this time.

Wil took a deep breath and addressed his children. "Some very powerful people have come here for you. You'll have to face them eventually, but this is way too soon. I'm going to try to get them to back off, but in the meantime you need to hide."

"What? Who are they?" Raena asked with wide eyes.

"A divergent branch of Tarans with exceptional abilities. They are very wise, but they don't know everything," Wil replied, dancing around the truth. "I have a history with them, and I hope that will be enough for them to see reason."

"I don't—" Jason started to protest, but Wil had too much on his mind to hear what his son said.

"CACI," Wil intoned, "an Alpha-One lockdown is now in effect. T-minus five minutes to bulkhead seal."

"Acknowledged," CACI replied from the nearest comm. The lights in the hall shifted to red. "Attention," CACI continued over the full comm system, "an Alpha-One lockdown is now in effect, T-minus five minutes to seal. This is not a drill. All personnel report to Alpha Scenario positions immediately."

Jason and Raena instinctively moved closer together.

"Come on, there's no time to explain," Wil told them and broke into a jog down the hall toward the lobby. He sped up his pace after checking that they had followed.

When they reached the lobby, three sets of elevator doors were opening and select members of the Primus Elites arrived in accordance with his telepathic instructions.

Wil approached Curtis and Tom. "You remember Curtis," he said to his children. "And this is my friend, Tom. They're going to take you to a safe place. You can trust them with your lives."

"Absolutely," Curtis said aloud. *"Midway between Levels 10 and 11, correct?"* he confirmed telepathically.

"Yes, just beyond the old containment lock. Keep them safe."

His friend nodded. *"I will."*

"Dad, can't we stay with you?" Raena asked.

"Not this time." Wil gave her a brief hug, and then Jason—his heart heavy with worry he might not see them again. "I love you both so much. I'll see you soon."

"We'll take care of them," Tom said and ushered the twins away.

The twins kept their gaze fixed on him until the doors closed, their young faces pale with fear and worry.

I'll find a way out of this. They'll be okay. They have to be. Wil took a deep breath and turned his attention to the other officers awaiting further instruction. "Ethan and Ian, you're with me on the surface. With any luck, we can prevent them from ever entering the facility."

"That'll require some luck, if I correctly recall the last time they were here," Ian quipped.

Wil boarded the elevator and set the surface port as the destination. "You were starting to go soft. It's past time I gave you some unbeatable odds to overcome to keep you in shape."

Ian smiled. "Just like old times."

"The good ol' days." *Let's just hope this isn't our last.*

— — —

Raena stared at the two Agents in the eerie red glow of the emergency lights within the elevator. "Where are you taking us?"

"The most difficult place to access in the whole facility," Curtis replied.

"But what's the danger?" asked Jason. "What makes these people so bad?"

"They aren't bad, exactly," Tom said slowly. His dark eyes darted between Raena and her brother. "They just... have their own way of doing things."

Raena frowned. "In what way?"

"Well, Taran society went to shite awhile back, but they saw it coming and got the fok out while they could," Tom continued, intermittently glancing toward the elevator doors. "Since then, they were doing their own thing until your dad came along."

"And had that really high score?" Raena prompted.

"Oh, good, he at least told you that much," Curtis breathed, sounding relieved.

"What else hasn't he said?" Jason asked.

Instead of replying, Tom made three rapid taps on the control panel next to the door. The sense of motion ceased immediately, followed by two low thuds outside that reverberated down the metal walls.

Raena's heart leaped. "What was that?"

"This car is now locked midway between Levels 10 and 11," Tom responded. "Level 11 is suspended two kilometers below the rest of the structure, outside of a containment shell that used to enclose a subspace bubble around Headquarters."

"That probably makes no sense," Curtis chimed in. "The important thing to note is any intruder would need to make their way through a double set of containment locks and then climb a kilometer down an open shaft in order to make it in here. We can wait it out."

Jason didn't look the least bit convinced. "What about food?"

"And bathroom, for that matter," Raena murmured, realizing that it had been hours since she stopped by the restroom at school in the morning.

"We have some basic necessities to hold us over," Curtis assured them. He approached the bench seat along the back wall and lifted up the cushion, revealing a stash of rations, water, and some sort of folded tent contraption, the purpose of which Raena could begin to guess based on the context.

"Great," she muttered under her breath. *I think we've officially reached the low point for the day.*

Jason surveyed the provisions with surprise. "Do all the cars have this?"

"About a quarter of them," Tom replied. "They activate in lockdown scenarios."

"Hopefully, we won't be here for long enough to need anything," Curtis hastily added. "I'm sure your dad will smooth things over with the Aesir in no time."

Tom replaced the seat cushion and sat down.

Raena took a seat on the opposite side of the bench, suddenly feeling dizzy with the thought of being suspended a kilometer from any other structure. *Come on, Dad. There has to be a way out of this.*

—   —   —

Wil, Ethan, and Ian stepped out of the elevator in the spaceport on the surface of the moon. Wil's stomach was twisted with anxious anticipation. *Why would they come for them so quickly? They have to know they could never survive the test so soon after their abilities emerging.*

"Is Saera going to meet us here?" Ethan asked.

"She's in transit, still about an hour out," Wil replied. "I'm not sure if she'll make it in time. It depends on how long the Aesir delay before boarding."

"Why *would* they delay?" Ian asked.

"There's a possibility this is a diplomatic meeting and they aren't trying to force our hands. If that's the case, they might wait for us to come to them."

Ethan raised an eyebrow. "So… why are we on our way up there?"

"We're not," Wil replied. "We're going to wait right here until either Saera arrives or the Aesir make a move."

"That seems like a feeble plan, not going to lie," Ian stated.

"Well, it's all I have for the moment."

"Why wait for Saera, though?" Ethan asked. "You said three Agents or thirty wouldn't matter."

"For stopping the Aesir, no," responded Wil. "But this is about potentially needing to hand over our children into a far from safe situation. I'd rather not make any decisions without consulting with their mother." While Wil had already reached out telepathically to her to warn of the Aesir's appearance, no remote discussion over the distance could replace a face-to-face conversation. She needed to be present so whatever happened wasn't entirely on him. He couldn't bear to hold more lives in his hands like that—especially ones so precious to him.

Ian leaned against the railing along the corridor. "All right. I guess we wait, then."

Wil gripped the railing next to his friend, his mind too clouded with possible scenarios to pay close attention to the passage of time. He occasionally checked his handheld to track the approach of Saera's transport ship. While they waited, the Aesir ship remained hidden from view somewhere far too close for comfort. But they held back, and so Wil delayed making any further move. Perhaps a fight wasn't imminent.

At last, Wil's handheld chirped with a notice that Saera's ship had locked onto the exit beacon.

"Come on, she's almost here," he told his friends.

"I can't believe the Aesir waited," Ethan said under his breath.

"Maybe they're not here for the twins, after all," Wil speculated, but deep down he knew that was the only explanation.

Ian walked alongside Wil in silence for several seconds as they headed toward a shuttle to take them up to the spaceport. "So, what's the game plan here? Are we still going the diplomatic route?"

Wil shook his head. "Honestly, I have no idea what we're walking into. I'm going to play it by ear."

Ian flashed a wry grin. "This really is turning into a proper adventure."

They boarded the shuttle and rode in silence up to the spaceport. Wil stared out the panoramic viewports, hoping to catch sight of the ethereal Aesir ship, but it had yet to come near enough for detection with the naked eye. He reached out telepathically, searching for the Aesir's presence. In the distance, he sensed a soft pulse of energy.

"We're here," a chorus of voices stated in his mind.

"Why have you come?" Wil asked, though he already knew the answer.

"We felt the Awakening. The balance of power has shifted."

"Nothing has changed yet. They are no different than any other."

"But they will be," the Aesir replied.

"We must discuss this face-to-face," Wil told them.

"We are coming."

Wil took a slow breath and released it. "The Aesir are on their way."

"Yay…" Ian said in the driest sarcastic tone Wil had ever heard him use.

"They seem amenable to conversation. Let's see what they have to say." Wil rose from his seat as the shuttle docked with the spaceport. The door opened, sending a blast of cool air into the cabin.

The three Agents stepped out into the spaceport and headed toward the concourse where Saera's transport ship was set to dock. Midway down the concourse, Wil spotted her jogging toward them.

"I picked a hell of a time to go on a trip," she said when she was within earshot.

Wil shrugged. "This would probably be a bad time to tell you I haven't done dishes for two days, huh?"

Saera rolled her eyes behind her tinted glasses.

"Kidding! The kitchen is clean. Mostly. See? Things could be worse."

His wife let out a heavy sigh. "How are the kids?"

"They're fine. And they'll stay that way if we can convince the Aesir to leave them alone."

"How do we do that?" Saera asked.

Ethan and Ian shook their heads and shrugged.

"I'll figure it out," Wil tried to assure everyone.

Before he had time to offer a more substantial plan, he felt a shift in energy in the air around him. *They're almost here.*

A moment later, he caught sight of the visitors. The five Aesir Oracles appeared to glide down the concourse, their dark robes billowing around them.

Wil stood his ground in the center of the concourse, struck by their power. It was even more pronounced than he remembered. *I'm not sure I could stand up to even five of them without destroying this port in the process. And they can always send more.*

"Bring them to us," the Oracle at the center demanded telepathically. Wil recognized the man as Dahl from when they had come for him so many years before. He hadn't aged.

"I can't do that," Wil replied aloud. "They have only just Awoken. They aren't ready for your test."

Dahl and the other Oracles stopped several paces from Wil and his friends. "This is about more than just the test this time."

"Then what?" questioned Wil.

"Tararia's future is on the cusp of change. We need to be sure it will be set on the correct path."

"How is that for you to decide?" Wil asked. "You abandoned Tararia centuries ago."

"We left, yes, but we did not abandon our world," Dahl replied. "We have been watching from a distance, awaiting the proper time for action."

Wil's eyes narrowed. "Which action is that?"

Dahl looked him over in silence. "The Taran people were once changed against their will as a result of the Priesthood's blind ambition. The Priesthood still seeks to correct their mistakes, but eliminating the Bakzen was only the first step. We know that you have learned the truth about the genetic manipulation that led to the loss of abilities throughout the general population, and that your line holds the key to repairing what was once lost. The Priesthood will once again rush the process, if left unchecked. Yet, elements of that work must progress. We must ensure the key is found."

"We already have plans to deal with the Priesthood," Wil replied. *What key are they talking about?*

"The Priesthood are more entrenched than you can ever imagine. We must walk a fine line with them. You can't simply remove the head of the beast."

"What do my children have to do with the Aesir?" Wil asked, getting back to the most urgent matter.

"Your decision to raise them away from Tararia was noble but not without its risks. It's imperative they make the right connections."

"What sort of connection?"

"Another plan that was set in motion years ago. But that must unfold naturally. We only seek to test your children now to see if they are compatible."

Wil shook his head. "Regardless of your reasons or assurances that they'll be fine, I can't hand them over to you in their current state. Even limited exposure to those with your level of ability might overwhelm them to the point of harm. You'll have to wait."

Dahl evaluated him. "If we wait, then you will forge your own path."

"I've been doing that my whole life."

"And yet that path has led you here. Our fates are forever entwined. We share your goals regarding the end of the Priesthood's reign, but we cannot allow you to disregard what we have all tried to achieve."

"I need to look out for my family," Wil replied. "You're not going anywhere near my children until I'm confident they are ready to face your tests." He summoned an aura of energy around himself, ready to lash out at the Oracles if they came any closer.

From a distance, he felt the Aesir assessing the power, weighing what it would take to strike him down. For a moment, the energy swelled around them, as well.

Behind him, Wil felt Saera, Ian, and Ethan raising their own offensive. The air hummed as the Oracles and TSS Agents prepared for an attack.

"It doesn't have to come to this," Wil said to Dahl in one last attempt to defuse the situation.

Dahl gripped Wil in a telekinetic vise. *"You cannot overpower us."* The words were spoken not only by Dahl, but all of the Aesir Oracles in unison.

Wil gasped with surprise, summoning up more energy to counter the assault. Before he had time to move, the vise suddenly released.

"To achieve the future we envision, we must cooperate," Dahl stated. "You may have five years to train your children, but then we must show them their place, as we once did for you."

Five years... That's as long as I had with the Primus Elites. It can be done. "Thank you." He started to release the potential energy he'd gathered in preparation for the fight. However, it had been so long since he'd drawn that much into himself that it wasn't so easy to dismiss—the intoxicating feeling of power and seemingly endless possibilities.

"They'll be ready," Saera said from behind him, pulling Wil back to the present. "We would value having you as allies."

Dahl inclined his head. "We hope you'll know the path when you see it. When we meet again, the time for action will be upon us."

"And we will act," Wil stated. "You've been preparing for a long time."

"We have," Dahl acknowledged.

"TSS Headquarters—you built it, didn't you?"

"This was never intended to be a military base."

"What, then?"

"It was a temple. A place of isolation to connect with oneself," the Oracle stated.

"We will try to honor that tradition."

Dahl nodded. "You already do."

Without another word, the Oracles glided back down the concourse toward their ship.

Wil let out a shaky breath. "I didn't think they'd leave without the kids."

"Maybe it was as much a test for you as it was for them," Saera offered.

"You never explained just how powerful they are," Ethan

murmured as he took a step forward. "I can't believe they pinned you."

"That caught me by surprise, too. I knew they were strong, but it's even more advanced than I realized," Wil admitted. "I guess I really don't know much about the Aesir or what they can do."

"Sounds like they're on our side. That's all I really care about right now," said Saera.

Ethan nodded. "I'll second that."

Wil flexed his hand and subtle electric sparks crackled on his fingertips. "I need to vent some of this excess energy. I haven't drawn that much for a long time. Why don't you go see the kids and make sure they get settled in," Wil told his wife.

"*Will you be okay?*" she asked privately.

"*I'm fine. Just need a few minutes,*" he assured her.

"We'll see you on Level 2," Saera acknowledged aloud while they all headed back toward Headquarters.

After traversing the surface port, Wil entered the elevator car that would take him down to Level 11 where he could unwind. The solitude would give him some much-needed time to think. *What are the Aesir planning?*

CHAPTER 10

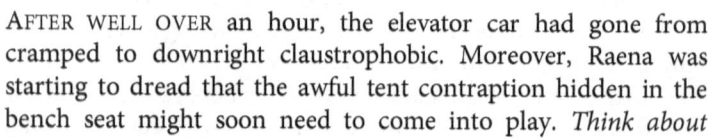

A<small>FTER WELL OVER</small> an hour, the elevator car had gone from cramped to downright claustrophobic. Moreover, Raena was starting to dread that the awful tent contraption hidden in the bench seat might soon need to come into play. *Think about deserts, and sand dunes...*

"So, I hear you were on the swim team for your school?" Tom commented, breaking the silence.

Water. Bad. Raena forced a smile. "I switched over to track two years ago. I was thinking about doing the triathlon, and then I decided that those athletes are borderline insane."

"Well, you won't find anything like that around here. We have a track down on Level 10 and a gym, but that's about it," Tom continued. "I know your dad likes water, too. That likely came out of his internship when he was around your age. He went to a world that's mostly ocean."

More water talk. Great! "I guess that would force someone to get comfortable around water."

"Are you okay?" Curtis asked, examining her.

"Yeah, I'm fine." She paused. "Any idea how much longer we're going to be in here?"

"It could be awhile—" Curtis began, but was cut off by a chime from the main speaker in the elevator car.

"The Alpha-One lockdown is now lifted," Saera announced.

"You may return to normal operations."

Raena relaxed as soon as she heard her mother's voice. "I guess that means they were successful?"

Curtis and Tom both exhaled and nodded.

"It would seem that way," Tom said. "Let's get back and get a report."

Not a moment too soon. Raena tried to keep her fidgeting to a minimum as the elevator began its ascent toward the main Headquarters structure.

"This has been such a weird day," Jason commented.

"The worst should be over," Curtis said. "Though, I suppose I shouldn't say anything until we talk with your parents."

"You don't think they'd hand us over, do you?" her brother asked with sudden alarm.

Tom laughed. "No way. I've seen how protective your dad is of people he cares about, and there aren't any circumstances under which he'd put you in danger."

"Yeah, he always has kept a close eye on us," Jason agreed.

"You're a special pair, after all," Tom continued. "High Dynasty heirs that aren't indoctrinated with the status quo of the current political system. That's a big investment."

Were we really raised on Earth to be political tools? Is that it?

"I think there might be more to it than that."

Tom caught himself. "Sorry, I didn't mean to imply that was your parents' aim. Taran politics weren't the motivating factor behind them raising you on Earth. Just… Sietinen is sort of like the royalty of royalty. Your family is known to everyone, and the continuity of SiNavTech is paramount to our entire civilization's day-to-day functions. All of us would readily lay down our lives for you because we have an inkling of understanding about what it means for you to be a part of that. It'll be up to you, though, to make that role a part of yourselves."

Raena sank back in her seat. *I do not have the mental space to process that right now.* She gave Tom a polite smile and proceeded to stare at the gray carpet on the floor.

To her relief, the elevator decelerated and the doors opened. Waiting for them in the lobby of Level 2 was her mother.

"Mom!" Raena ran to her and gave her a hug.

Saera held her close. "I'm so sorry I wasn't there for you earlier."

"It all happened so fast." Raena pulled out from the hug and gave her mother a proper evaluation in her Agent attire. "It's going to take a while to get used to seeing you dressed like that." She glanced at the other Agents waiting nearby. "This is a lot..."

Her mother placed a reassuring hand on her shoulder. "I know. We'll be here with you every step of the way."

Raena nodded. "Yeah, so... bathroom," she said quietly.

Saera smiled. "Our quarters aren't far. Come on, Jason, this way."

Raena walked with her mother and brother through the lobby and down a corridor on the opposite side. There were more people moving about than she had seen previously—mostly Agents, but also a handful of individuals dressed in dark gray. No one seemed to pay much attention to them, unlike how it had been with her father. *There really is something big he's not telling us.*

After two minutes, they reached the door to her parents' quarters. Her mother placed her palm on the panel next to the door and it slid open following a beep.

"Door to the restroom is there in the back right," Saera said.

Raena smiled with thanks and rushed across the room. She paused a couple steps from the door. "Wait, is there any special trick to how the toilets work?"

Her mother chuckled. "Very self-explanatory."

Raena was pleased to find that the bathroom was, indeed, similar to the amenities she knew from Earth. Though futuristic and foreign in their own ways, the toilet, shower, and sink were readily recognizable, and she was able to determine their basic operations within seconds. It was like the rest of the technology she'd encountered in her short time in Headquarters—optimized for user experience without adding needless frills to complicate operation. Everything just felt natural. *Maybe the learning curve won't be so bad, after all.*

When she emerged from the restroom, Raena found her mother and brother examining a series of pictures on the wall. She walked over to get a better look.

"So, this was from our honeymoon," Saera said, a far-off look of remembrance in her glowing jade eyes. The picture had the same appearance of three-dimensional depth as the holopaintings of nebulae in the corridors, but this image was of Wil and Saera in their early-twenties. "I didn't think we were even going to get a honeymoon. Your grandparents surprised us after the wedding and said we'd have two weeks to ourselves."

"I'd say you look so much younger, but you almost look the same, really," Jason commented.

"I certainly *feel* older whenever I look at you two." Saera admired the picture again. "So much has changed since then."

"Where did you go?" Raena asked. "That looks like it could be Fiji, maybe."

"Similar, but no. It was a private resort planet with exclusive islands for the super-wealthy. Naturally, your great-grandparents have an estate there."

Raena and Jason glanced at each other, jaws slack.

"I think I can get used to being in this family," Jason said after a moment.

"It does have its perks," Saera agreed. "But there's a price for everything. You'll find some... rigidity in the thinking of your great-grandparents."

Jason tilted his head. "In what way?"

"For starters, they didn't approve of me when I was just a lowly Earth-born girl. I don't want to plant any seeds of doubt, but I have to admit I'm concerned about how they're going to treat you, given your upbringing."

Raena's eyes widened with surprise. "They'd really shun their own great-grandchildren?"

"I don't think 'shun' is the right word," her mother clarified. "But they'll have certain expectations they'll want you to live up to. Leaving your past behind and becoming suitable heirs will be their priority for you."

Jason crossed his arms. "They can't expect us to give up our ties to our childhood home."

Saera shook her head. "They wouldn't think about it that way. They'd consider it you trading in a meaningless existence on a backwaters planet for a proper life befitting your birthright."

"Going to Tararia sounds like it's going to be awesome…" Raena said with a sigh.

"On the plus side, your grandparents are great—at least your paternal grandparents. My mother… Well, I'm not sure how she's going to be. I would describe my relationship with her as cordial."

Raena took a seat on the leather couch in the center of the room facing the front viewscreen. "I'm beginning to understand why you took us to Earth. These family dynamics sound exhausting."

Her mother sat down next to her. "Don't even get me started on the extended family. But hey, the community we have here in the TSS is what matters most. Your father and I have a lot of very close friends here that will be the best aunts and uncles you could hope to have. This is an escape from all the craziness in the outside worlds."

"Except today," Raena pointed out. "The Aesir were here—whoever they are."

Saera took several seconds to reply. "That's part of something much bigger than our families or even the TSS."

"What happened, Mom?" Raena pressed. "Dad initiates a lockdown and traps us in an elevator for over an hour, and then we just go on like nothing happened? Danger like that doesn't just go away."

"They won't be back anytime soon," Saera said, seeming to choose her words carefully.

Jason frowned. "But they *will* be back."

Their mother looked down at her hands. "They're giving you five years to train. Then they'll return for you," she revealed, finally meeting Raena's expectant gaze.

"But *why*?" Raena questioned.

"It's a test, of sorts—a variant of astral projection, in some ways. It will evaluate your abilities. Your father is the only outsider to be tested and pass, as far as we know."

Jason's frown deepened. "How do you pass?"

"You don't go insane or die," Saera replied a little too bluntly. "To attempt it now would have been far too much for you. We convinced the Aesir to give you enough time that you'd have a fighting chance. They recognize your importance, too."

"Outsiders with influence—a chance to effect real change," Raena murmured.

"All right, so your father did mention our little plan."

Jason laughed. "Yeah, revolutionizing the entire political system. Just a 'little' plan."

"We have a bad habit of starting trouble," Saera said with a somewhat mischievous smile.

"Speaking of Dad, where is he?" Raena asked.

"He'll be here soon. When we were meeting with the Aesir, he had to draw on a lot more telekinetic energy than he has for a long time. He needed to let it discharge before getting too close to you, considering you're still in a pretty sensitive state."

"All right, because we have a tour to finish," Raena said.

"We were about to check out the simulators," Jason chimed in, some of his enthusiasm from before the ordeal with the Aesir beginning to return.

"Definitely a highlight of the tour," Saera replied. "We can make that happen."

"But first," Raena said, "I think we need to take a detour to the cafeteria."

"I'll second that," Jason agreed. "Please tell me you have real food here and not some weird goo in packets or something."

"We have feeding tubes," Saera said with a completely straight face.

Raena just about choked. "What?"

Their mother laughed. "Your faces! That was priceless. No, we have a mess hall with three squares prepared fresh every day. And dessert, I'd like to note."

Raena sighed with relief. "You had me going for a second there."

"I guess I really shouldn't tease you after the day you've had already." Saera patted Raena's leg then rose from the couch. "Now, let's get you fed."

— — —

Wil allowed the energy to stream out of him in the practice chamber. Bolts of lightning, seen only in his mind's eye, shot from his fingertips and danced across the spherical walls of the room lined in ateron. The coating absorbed the energy and dissipated it around the interior surface like ripples on the surface of a pond.

Discharging energy in that manner was a far cry from actually focusing the power toward a target, but it felt good to have the energy coursing through him once again. *There's so much of myself that's laid dormant in the name of our new life on Earth. I'm scared to see what I might become if I tap into that power again.*

The years since the war had forced him to view his abilities in a different way—more as a remnant of his old self. However, being around the Aesir and their radiant strength reminded him of what he'd been, and what he could be again if he let loose and embraced his full self.

No, I can't. That person is who destroyed a planet and a whole people. There's no place for him in this new life. He hurriedly discharged the energy that he'd allowed to linger in his body. The emptiness that remained seemed so unnatural after the sweet power he'd felt only moments before, but he had other things to fulfill him now.

Wil left the practice chamber and proceeded up the central elevator to the mess hall, where Saera had telepathically said they would wait for him.

When he entered the spacious common area, Wil found his family seated in one of the booths along the back wall. Raena and Jason appeared to be taking in the other occupants with fascination, and Saera was in the final bites of completing her meal.

His wife looked up from her plate as Wil approached them. "Hi," she greeted. "Feeling better?"

"Yes," Wil replied, not wanting to admit that tasting the power was actually his preferred state of being. "Looks like you've all been fed?"

Jason nodded. "You know, this was actually really good."

"Told you," Saera said through her final mouthful. She

swallowed. "Ugh, I was ravenous. I got the call to come home right before lunch and completely forgot to eat on the transport ship."

"I've been there," Wil replied. *I should probably have something, myself, but I'm too wired to sit still right now.* "So, I believe we were about to check out the simulators?"

The twins straightened in their seats.

"Yes!" Raena exclaimed.

"Can we go in one?" Jason asked simultaneously.

Wil smiled. "No test flights today, but I will show you the holographic projector that trainers use to watch pilots' interactions."

Jason smiled. "All right, sounds good."

"But first," Wil continued as he slipped into the booth seat next to Saera, "we do have an official matter to discuss."

Raena's smile faded. "Why so serious all of a sudden?"

"This might be fun right now to experience new technology and have new worlds opened up to you, but there's more to this life than just playing around in simulators. The responsibilities you'll need to fulfill for Tararia run deep and are of paramount importance. Unfortunately, with a family like ours, you were born into those obligations whether you like it or not."

Jason slumped back in his chair. "That doesn't mean we can't still have *some* fun. This is hard enough as it is."

"I know," Wil replied. "But before we get caught up in other details, I want to make sure you have a clear vision of the path ahead. There are two options, really. The first is you focus on Tararia and learn everything you can about the political system and SiNavTech right away. With that path, your abilities would largely go undeveloped, and it's a big unknown how the Aesir would react in that scenario. The second option is to commit yourselves to the TSS and train as Agents. When it comes time to engage in Tararian politics, you might be underprepared, but the TSS will grant you a solid foundation for anything you may face in the future. Either way, you need to decide in short order whether you want a TSS career track or will just attend for the first year."

Raena was silent for several seconds. "I didn't realize we'd have a choice not to join."

In my mind, there's no choice at all. "I had a future thrust on me, and I vowed not to do the same to you. Some aspects are set—like needing to step up as heirs to Sietinen—but how you go about that path is your decision."

"What would you do?" Jason asked.

"Understanding and growing my abilities was how I found my true self," responded Wil. "I would choose the TSS every time, if I had to do it all again."

"Assuming this hasn't all been an elaborate hoax, it's definitely the TSS for me," Jason said without hesitation. "Politics don't interest me in the slightest."

Raena searched Wil's face. "It isn't a choice at all, is it— really?"

Wil exhaled slowly. "Some people can ignore their abilities, if they choose. For others, it's so engrained in our identity that we'd sooner die than leave behind that part of ourselves."

"I'm too curious," Raena admitted. "I was sold the moment you mentioned telekinesis in the car ride from school."

"So, you're in?"

"Heck yeah!"

Wil smiled at Saera, then looked back at his children. "Then let me be the first to officially welcome you into the TSS."

"As Lead Agent, it is my honor to offer you provisional placement in a cohort of Primus Elite trainees," Saera stated. "I think you'll find yourselves in very good company."

"Is that as fancy as it sounds?" Raena asked.

Saera nodded. "Oh, yeah."

"Cool." Raena smiled at her brother. "So much for going to college in California."

Saera frowned. "You were going to apply out of state?"

Jason inched back from her glare. "I was considering it. But it's irrelevant now—this is way better."

"You'll like it here. I have no doubt," Wil said.

Raena clasped her hands. "Awesome. Now when can we go play with the simulators?"

— — —

Cris stormed into his father's office. "You seriously want to impose beacon usage fees on the TSS?"

Reinen looked up from his desktop with surprise. "Did Marina let you in?"

"I let myself in."

"This is really a matter for you to discuss with Fredrik—"

"No," Cris interrupted. "What's *really* going on here? This is just a ploy to get me to come back to Tararia, isn't it?

Reinen minimized his open work projected on the holographic display. "Cris, I've been asking you to come home for a long time and you've never listened."

"You know how important my work with the TSS is!"

"Yes, and I've respected that. I've given you all the leeway you needed for the last two decades."

Cris sat down in the guest chair across from him. *That's true. We did have a good run after Wil's wedding.*

"Now…" Reinen's voice was uncharacteristically faint. "I'm old, Cris. I won't be Head of this Dynasty forever."

"Taxing the TSS isn't a great way to get me to take over for you."

"Then how else?" Reinen asked. "You always have an excuse whenever I ask you directly."

"There are important things—"

"You have a duty to fulfill, Cris. Soon you won't be able to avoid it any longer."

Cris hung his head and took a deep breath.

"I need to know—will you be here for our family?" Reinen asked.

"I will. You don't have to question it."

His father nodded. "That sets my mind at ease."

Cris cleared his throat. "So, about Wil and the twins…"

"Yes, I heard about their impending arrival." Reinen folded his hands on the table. "We must now focus on the next generation."

— — —

Taking in the sights within the TSS made for a thrilling afternoon, but by the time Raena had eaten dinner she was ready for some quiet alone time. Jason also seemed to be relieved when their parents showed them to temporary quarters where they could stay until TSS classes officially began in two weeks.

"Don't get used to the spacious accommodations," Wil said as he palmed open the door. "Junior Agent quarters are pretty luxurious compared to Trainee or Initiate rooms."

"Sounds like the budget for that renovation you were telling us about wasn't used so wisely," Jason quipped.

"Yeah, well, wait until you see the new spatial awareness chambers," their mother replied with a smile. She stepped into the common room. "You'll have the place to yourselves until we leave for Tararia."

Raena's heart skipped a beat. "When will that be?"

"Two or three days, depending on when Irina gives you the go-ahead to travel," Wil said. "Not surprisingly, there's some demand for you to go as quickly as possible."

"So we can be inspected for our fitness to bear the family name?" Raena asked.

Wil frowned. "I see you chatted about this with your mother earlier."

"A little advanced warning seemed prudent after my experience with your grandparents," Saera replied.

"They've gotten a lot better since then, but I won't pretend that they're the most welcoming of outsiders," Wil admitted. "I can assure you, though, that we'll be on the first transport back here if they so much as look at you funny."

That's reassuring… I think. Raena gave him a weak smile and then eyed the doors in the side walls that presumably led into bedrooms. Nothing but sleep sounded appealing at the moment.

Her mother stepped forward and gave her a hug. "Yes, go to bed. It's not surprising you're exhausted."

"Thanks." Raena held in a yawn as she pulled out from the embrace. "How do we find you in the morning?"

"There are handhelds on the charging pads next to the beds

in the two rooms at the back," Wil said. "Pick up the device and it will walk you through the setup. You'll find all the contact info you need in there. But they're blocked from communication with Earth for the time being."

Jason's eyes narrowed. "So, that's it? You take us on a partial tour like everything's fine and now you're just leaving us here alone without any connection to the outside world?"

"Yeah, what about contacting our friends?" Raena asked. "Katie will be worried."

"It's all taken care of for the short term," her mother soothed.

"We posted a notice to your Feeds that you're traveling," Wil elaborated. "We'll let you send a message in a few days once you have a better perspective on everything that's going on."

"We can't just walk away from our lives like that," Jason protested.

"I know it seems that way now," Saera responded, "but give it a couple days. It's not a matter of saying goodbye, but rather figuring out how to say 'see you later'."

"I guess anyone that doesn't understand probably wasn't a very good friend, anyway," Raena realized.

"Exactly. You'll always be able to pick up where you left off with the right people," Wil stated.

Jason shook his head, clearly not convinced.

Raena glanced at her brother. "All right, we'll give it some time."

Their parents smiled. "Good," Wil told them, looking between Raena and her brother. "Clothes are in the wardrobes and toiletries are in the bathroom. Message us if there's anything else you need."

"Fine. See you in the morning," Jason muttered.

"Good night," Saera said. "Call us anytime. We're just the next corridor over."

"Sleep well," Wil said and stepped into the hall with Saera.

"Good night." Raena closed the door. She giggled.

"What's so funny?" Jason asked.

"We're inside the frickin' *moon* right now!"

"Supposedly." He crossed his arms. "Really, how do we know

where we are? They never took us outside. All I know for sure is that I saw a lot of really fancy tech today."

Raena raised an eyebrow. "And telekinesis. Seriously, after that and those flight simulators and the engineering labs you're still in doubt?"

"I don't know." Jason frowned. "This whole day has been a completely unreal level of crazy."

"I know, right?" Raena let out a heavy sigh. *Life will never be the same.*

Jason eyed the door. "I'm way too wound up to sleep."

"Well *I'm* exhausted." Raena took a step toward the couch.

"Fine, but I'm going out. I need to see the rest of it for myself."

"Rest of what?"

"Outside Headquarters," her brother replied.

"Jason…"

"You're just going to take their word for it?" he asked. "For all we know, this is a government-run lab in Nevada and we're about to be experimented on."

Raena scowled. "I'm pretty sure Mom and Dad wouldn't do that to us."

"They did give us implants and nanobots without our knowledge," Jason pointed out.

"True, but—"

"You don't have to come." Jason walked over to the door.

After spending their whole lives together, Raena knew there was no way to talk her brother out of an idea once he'd made up his mind. She also knew it was a bad idea to let him go roaming on his own. "All right. What's your plan?"

"Head for the elevator. It goes to the surface, right?"

"That's what they said."

"They took us all around the facility but not up there. So, let's go see if we're really in space." Jason opened the door and poked his head outside, then glanced back at Raena. "It's clear. Come on."

Reluctantly, she followed him into the hall. Without an escort, the uniformity of the corridor was disorienting.

"This way," Jason said assuredly, heading to the right.

"I'm sure they'd take us up to the surface if we insisted..." Raena ventured.

"But what's the fun in that?"

Trying to set aside her misgivings, Raena followed her brother down the corridor toward the central lobby. As they approached the open space, she spotted several Agents waiting for the elevator. The Agents turned to look at them and Raena immediately recognized one of them as Tom.

She hastily turned away, but Tom called out to them, "Hey! What are you doing out on your own?"

Busted. Raena faced him and put on her best smile. "Just out for a walk."

"And your parents are okay with that?" the Agent asked.

Jason shrugged. "They didn't say we couldn't."

A smile touched the corners of Tom's lips. "Where were you headed?"

"The surface," Jason replied without hesitation.

Tom chuckled. "And you didn't think we'd have the access restricted?"

"Come on, Jason, this was a bad idea," Raena urged.

Jason stood his ground. "Are you hiding something?" he asked Tom.

The Agent took a slow breath. "Students like you are why we need security measures in the first place. Hold on—an escort will be here soon."

I never should have gone along with this. Raena edged back toward the corridor leading to their quarters.

"Really? Sneaking out to the surface?" their father said from behind them before she had a chance to retreat.

How did Dad even know where we were going? Raena wondered, then realized that Tom must have filled him in telepathically.

Jason groaned, turning to face him. "Come on, Dad! How do we know we're really in the moon right now?"

"Seeing outside will convince you?" Wil asked.

Her brother shrugged. "It'd go a long way."

Their father sighed. "All right, then we'll go to the surface." He called the elevator.

"It's not that we don't believe you—" Raena tried to explain.

"Speak for yourself," Jason interrupted. "Yeah, some weird things went on today and you've shown us some cool stuff, but traveling to a secret moon base…?"

"I guess I'd still be skeptical, too," Wil replied. "If a field trip is what you need to make this real, then we'll go."

The elevator arrived and their father stepped inside. "Coming?"

Jason hurried inside and Raena followed.

"I'm sorry we tried to sneak out," she said as soon as the door closed.

Wil selected the surface on the control panel next to the door. He was silent for a moment. "It wasn't fair of us to dump all of this on you so suddenly. This isn't how we typically handle the transition for people raised on Earth."

"What would you normally do?" Raena asked.

"Begin with a written introduction, posing as a university," Wil explained. "Make some sort of scholarship offer and arrange an in-person meeting in a neutral public location. An Agent would attend under cover to verify the candidate's ability potential, and then they'd arrange for a private follow-up interview where there'd be some presentation of telekinetic abilities. If it's the right kind of candidate we'd want here in the TSS, they'd be sold right there."

Jason softened slightly. "But Raena's abilities came on so suddenly you had to rush things."

Wil nodded. "That's right. I'm sorry, we should have been more prepared."

"It seems like a lot was working against you today," Raena replied.

"Isn't that the truth?" Wil smiled.

A thud sounded outside and the elevator shuddered slightly. Raena was about to question the sound but her father's calm demeanor indicated everything was normal.

Jason also seemed to notice the sound and dismissed it. "But Mom and Michael went through that standard intro?" he questioned.

"More or less," Wil replied. "But Michael's father was a

former Agent so things were a little different."

"How—" Jason began.

"It's complicated," their father replied with a sigh. "Suffice to say that all of us ended up where we were supposed to be."

Raena stood in silent contemplation for another two minutes while the elevator continued its ascension. Then, the pulsing white light ceased and the doors parted.

Any doubts about their location evaporated immediately.

"Whoa!" Raena breathed, taking in the moonscape outside the glass dome. Beyond the gray, dusty surface in shadow, stars gleamed in the velvety blackness of space stretching as far as she could see.

"This is incredible," Jason said, awe audible in his voice as he stepped out of the elevator.

Wil smiled. "Believe me now?"

"Yeah, yeah," Jason grinned back.

Raena pulled her gaze from space and walked forward to get a better view of the port. She spotted some small spacecraft docked down each of three corridors fanning out from the elevator lobby. "Is that what we'll take to Tararia?" she asked, skeptical.

Her father laughed. "Stars, no! All the transport ships are up there." He pointed upward behind her.

Raena turned around and looked up toward what had been to her back since she exited the elevator. Her jaw dropped when she saw a massive structure suspended above them, concourses branching from a central hub with massive spaceships docked in many of the open berths. "No way!"

Jason swiveled to see what she was looking at. "What the…?"

"How has no one on Earth seen that up there?" Raena asked. "When you said the TSS doctored footage from probes on Earth, I was thinking maybe there was a little port deep in a crater, or something. But that!"

"Well, it can't be seen from the planet since it's anchored here on the side that faces away at all times. But yeah, there are some longstanding agreements with the governments of Earth that we get to modify all surveillance footage."

"That seems impossible," Jason murmured.

"We won't be able to for much longer," Wil agreed. "All right, satisfied?"

Jason's gaze was still fixed on the massive spacedock. "Can we go up there?"

"Not now. But soon." Wil pressed the elevator call button, and the doors to the same car reopened.

Jason sighed but nodded his understanding. "Okay, I guess we really are in space."

"Very well." Wil stepped back into the elevator. "Now, we've all had very long days. Let's get some rest. This'll all be less weird in the morning."

As farfetched as that seemed to Raena at the moment, she had a feeling he was right. *I guess we'll have to get used to our new home.*

They rode the elevator back to Headquarters in relative silence. Wil escorted them back to their quarters and left them with a gentle ribbing about not trying to sneak out again.

Once inside with the hallway door closed, Raena collapsed on the couch. "We're really going to do this, aren't we? Live out some fantasy from a book we read."

"Yeah, I guess we really are," Jason replied.

Raena grinned. "You know, I think this is going to be great."

CHAPTER 11

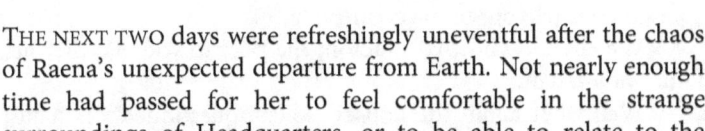

THE NEXT TWO days were refreshingly uneventful after the chaos of Raena's unexpected departure from Earth. Not nearly enough time had passed for her to feel comfortable in the strange surroundings of Headquarters, or to be able to relate to the experiences of the other members in the TSS, but it hadn't taken long for her to glimpse the feeling of community her parents had talked about.

Living in such an enclosed environment forced people to focus on commonalities rather than calling out differences, and Raena was pleased to see what a difference that made in day-to-day interactions. While becoming acquainted with new individuals, they asked about her interests, not what she'd done in the past. Values of individuality and how unique strengths could benefit the whole dominated the culture. It left her anxious for classes to start when the new term began, but there was still a lot to do before then.

On the morning of the third day after arriving from Earth, Raena was in the process of dressing in some Taran civilian clothes her parents had provided—a simple outfit with form-fitting black pants and a long-sleeve teal V-neck—when there was a chime at the front door. The viewscreen in her room illuminated and she saw that her father was in the hallway.

She quickly finished dressing and went out into the common

room to find that Jason had already answered the door.

"Good morning," Wil greeted her. "How are you feeling today?"

"Great," she replied. "The headache is finally gone."

Her father nodded. "Let's have Irina give you one final exam and then you should be ready to travel to Tararia."

"How long will we be gone?" Raena asked.

"I'm not sure. A week, maybe?"

Jason crossed his arms. "You need to let us talk to our friends back home before we go."

"Yeah, I know Katie will be freaking out," Raena said. "You promised to let us get in touch after a few days."

Wil hesitated. "What would you tell your friends?"

Raena glanced at her brother. "That you took us on a spontaneous trip out of the country?"

"We already said that much in the post to your Feeds," her father pointed out.

"Well what about the house?" Raena questioned. "Is it just sitting vacant? You'd also said we could go back for our things."

"Yes, we can go down sometime after we're back from Tararia," Wil replied. "And Michael's looking after the house for us. He and Elise are still commuting because of Corine."

"Okay, but... It's been three days since we suddenly left school. They'll be worried," Raena insisted. "Posting a generic message to our Feed isn't enough."

"All right," Wil yielded. "I'll unblock your handhelds, but please be respectful of the TSS' communication policies. You're enrolled as Trainees now even though classes haven't started, so I need to hold you to the same standards as anyone else."

"I promise," Raena said, and Jason murmured his agreement.

"As soon as you're done," Wil continued, "report to Medical. Irina is expecting you. Assuming you're cleared, we'll leave in an hour. I'll be back here to get you then."

Raena nodded. "See you."

As soon as her father had gone, Raena returned to her bedroom and grabbed her handheld from its charging pad. She tugged on the sides of the device to open it. When the main screen illuminated, she pulled up the contact list for all the numbers back on Earth that had previously been blocked. This time, when she scanned through the list, there was no longer a red dot next to those names.

She tapped on Katie's name and selected the text message option from the pop-up menu.

>>Hey! Sorry I haven't been in touch,<< she started to type before realizing that she was writing in New Taran. She erased the text and changed the entry interface to English before starting over. Nervous, she sent the message and waited for a reply.

Several seconds later, the handheld buzzed. >>OMG, where are you?! You totally ditched me on that team assignment.<<

That's right… I completely forgot about the paper. >>I'm so sorry! We had to leave suddenly on an extended family trip,<< Raena replied. >>We've been in transit.<< Her stomach knotted as she lied to her friend.

>>That doesn't make any sense. Why didn't they warn you?<<

Raena struggled to come up with an excuse. With a frustrated sigh, she jogged into the common room. "Jason, what are you telling them?"

Her brother emerged from his bedroom. "I was just going to ask you the same thing. Everything that comes to mind just sounds dumb or would bring up more questions."

"What about… 'our grandfather is sick'?" she suggested. "I went home sick with a migraine, and that night Dad got a message that his dad was ill and we went as a family to go see him, since we hadn't had the opportunity to make the trip before. He might die, and couldn't let him go without seeing his grandchildren in person."

"I guess that might work…" Jason said. "But why hadn't we been able to make the trip before? It's weird not ever seeing grandparents."

"Old family drama!" The story started to come together in Raena's mind. "Dad left home long ago and we've barely talked with our grandparents. With grandpa really sick, this was the only chance to fix the relationship before he dies."

Jason smiled. "I like it. I mean, as a story. That doesn't

explain the 'we're not coming back to school' part, though."

"Good point." Raena groaned. "I'm a terrible liar."

"No, this situation is just messed up," Jason replied. "We shouldn't have to invent a story to tell our friends."

"We can't tell the truth, though. They'll think we've lost our minds!" Raena laughed. "Well, we could tell the truth and then they'd figure that the reason we aren't coming back is because we were locked up."

"Ha! I don't think I want to be remembered as the two over-achievers that went crazy."

"Yeah, me either."

"What about... Grandpa is sick with some drawn-out illness?" Jason invented. "He has about eight months to live, which will bring us through the rest of the school year. Mom needs to be there to support Dad, so we're just going to be home schooled from..."

"Slovenia!" Raena jumped in. "Our grandparents live in a remote village no one has heard of."

Jason shrugged. "Why not? Sure."

"Okay," Raena agreed. She returned her attention to her handheld. >>Our grandfather is really sick,<< Raena texted to Katie. >>After I got home from school with that migraine, our dad got the message from his mom. We immediately got a flight to Slovenia. It took forever to get up to their village, and the cell reception is terrible. Apparently there *are* still places in the world with crappy connectivity.<<

>>That's awful!<< Katie replied. >>How long does he have?<<

>>Less than a year,<< Raena told her. >>I think we're going to miss the rest of the school year.<<

>>But Winter Formal! And prom!<<

Can't say I was terribly excited about going. >>I know. But... This is the only chance to patch things up before he dies.<<

>>Yeah, I guess that's more important,<< her friend said. Then, >>Damn, this sucks. You didn't even say goodbye.<<

>>I know, I'm sorry. Can you tell everyone I'm okay and not to worry?<<

>>You should tell them yourself! Upload some scenic

pictures of the town to your Feed.<<

Raena's heart sank. >>I don't really want to explain my family's private business in a public forum, you know?<<

>>Yeah, I get it.<<

>>I'll miss you, Katie,<< Raena said. >>I'll write you again when I can. But crappy connection.<<

>>Good luck in the wilderness.<<

>>Thanks.<< Raena tossed her handheld down on the couch. "This feels so wrong."

Jason groaned and put his own handheld in his pocket. "We're supposed to live up to the TSS' ethical code, and somehow lying to our longtime friends is the best way to do that? No."

"Katie seemed to understand—at least, that's how her messages sounded. She probably thinks we've been kidnapped."

"Well, we sort of were. Just by our parents." Jason ran his fingers through his hair. "And now we're going to leave the solar system…"

"Speaking of which," Raena grabbed her handheld from the couch, "we're supposed to get cleared by Medical."

"Yeah, let's go," her brother agreed. "We've been cooped up here for days. If we can't be at home, I guess we may as well see what space travel is all about."

"When you put it in those terms, I think I'll find a way to stay distracted from my guilt."

"Same."

They made their way up to Level 1 via the central elevator, still drawing attention from passersby in the hall for being dressed in civilian clothes while coming out from the Junior Agents' wing.

The receptionist at the front counter in Medical smiled when they approached. "Hello, again. Here for another checkup?"

"Hopefully, the last for now," Raena replied. "Our father said Irina would be expecting us."

"Yes, go on back to the exam rooms," the receptionist replied.

Raena and Jason nodded their thanks and headed to the left. They were only midway down the hall when Irina came out of another exam room in front of them.

"Hi, you two. I hear your dad wants to depart for Tararia this morning?"

"That's the plan," Jason replied. "If you clear us."

"Let's see," Irina said and led them down three doors to an empty room. She closed the door behind them, then removed her tinted glasses and concentrated on Jason.

"Should I lay down, or—" he started to ask.

"No," Irina stated. "You're fine. The dampening agent has already dissolved. Any more headaches or flashes?"

Jason shook his head.

Irina turned to Raena and likewise focused on her. Raena's skin felt electrified under the doctor's gaze.

"You'll be very gifted," a voice said in Raena's mind.

Her pulse spiked with surprise. She stared into Irina's eyes and sensed that she was the speaker.

"Anyone can receive a message. Try to reply," Irina said.

"Like this?" Raena asked, forming the words in her head.

"Precisely. You're a natural."

"What about Jason?"

Irina smiled faintly. *"He'll be stronger than I ever would have thought possible before I met your grandfather, but you take after your father. You're very special, Raena."*

"Should I be worried?"

"No. You've passed the most difficult hurdle in the Awakening. Your abilities will emerge gradually now. Believe you are in control and you will be. I anticipate you advancing very quickly."

Raena swallowed.

"Others won't be able to detect your abilities for another month or so. At this early stage, there are only spikes when you actively use the abilities. It takes time for the telekinetic aura to stabilize around you."

"And then?" Raena asked.

"Everyone will know just how special you really are."

Raena realized that almost no time had passed during the telepathic exchange. *"Why doesn't everyone communicate this way all the time?"*

"*We're trained not to intrude in other's minds. The intimacy is uncomfortable to some. And talking out loud helps us connect with the rest of the population. You'll learn the right times for these private exchanges.*" The doctor smiled at her. "All clear," she said aloud. "I'll make a note on your records that you've been cleared for travel and active duty. If you start to feel off, though, please tell your parents right away."

"Thanks," Raena replied.

"Have a nice trip," the doctor said with a warm smile. "I'll see you when you come back."

Raena and Jason returned to their quarters and began packing for Tararia. As Raena gathered several sets of clothes and began placing the articles in a travel bag, she couldn't shake the strange feeling of telepathically communicating with the doctor. *Am I really stronger than Jason? It didn't even occur to me that our abilities might be different.*

Adding to her discomfort was the bizarre situation of packing a suitcase full of items that weren't really hers. The clothes were all custom-made to her size, but they didn't feel like they belonged to her.

She was struck by a sudden pang of homesickness. *We can't talk to our friends. We have none of our old things. All that we have now is each other.*

The knot in her chest persisted while she finished packing. When the bag was sealed, Raena slung it over her shoulder and went out into the living room. She saw Jason still rummaging around in his room through the open doorway, so she sat down on the couch to wait. "Dad will be here soon."

"I know," Jason replied. "I'm ready." He came out from the bedroom with his own bag. "This was weird, right? Packing for a trip to another planet—and having none of the things be ours?"

"Yeah, this may as well be a stranger's suitcase."

A chime sounded at the door.

"Time to venture into the great unknown," Jason said as he stepped over to answer the door.

Raena rose from the couch and grabbed her bag.

Their parents were waiting in the hall.

"Ready for your first interstellar voyage?" Wil asked.

"Can't wait," Raena and Jason said almost in unison.

"Let's go." Wil led the way with Saera, each carrying their own travel bag. Raena and Jason fell into step behind them.

They took the main Junior Agent corridor to the central lobby and boarded the elevator toward the surface port.

Raena and Jason took seats on the bench at the back, watching the pulsing white light next to the door indicating movement. After a couple minutes, a loud thud sounded outside, reverberating through the car. Their parents seemed completely unphased.

"What was that?" Raena asked. "I remember it from before."

"The old containment lock from the subspace shell," Wil explained. "Back when Headquarters was still suspended in the subspace bubble, the two containment locks provided a pass-through transition from normal space into subspace. Since the transition—slightly before you were born—the locks now serve as a gateway into the sphere around the facility. Having a sealed environment around the ring structure gives an extra level of security. After all, the shell was originally constructed to withstand the structural stress of subspace flow."

"Which is a lot, I'm guessing?" Jason said.

"Yes, but highly variable and complex to represent," Saera replied. "You'll learn all about it in your navigation classes."

Raena looked at her parents questioningly. "Don't you have computers to navigate for you?"

Wil nodded. "Of course, but some things take hands-on involvement from a sentient mind. And, moreover, navigation and piloting are closely tied. If you want to fly, you need to take a few classes first."

"At least you won't have to worry about having me as an instructor," Saera said. "I used to teach Advanced Navigation, but since becoming Lead Agent I don't teach classes anymore."

That would be awkward having a parent as a formal teacher. "What about you, Dad?" Raena asked. "I can't seem to figure out what you do around here."

"I answer questions," her father replied simply.

Raena frowned. "That doesn't—"

The pulsing white light ceased as the elevator reached its

destination. The doors slid open, revealing a transparent dome rotunda and three broad corridors angled out ahead. Outside the dome, the gray, dusty surface of the moon shone white under light cast from the sun peeking over the horizon, and a magnificent starscape spanned overhead.

Raena's breath caught as she took in the sight for the second time. "It'll take a while to get used to this view."

"No kidding," Jason breathed next to her.

"It still gets me, even after all this time," Saera said with a smile.

Wil seemed amused by their fascination, shaking his head slightly as he headed down the corridor on the right.

Raena followed him, but her gaze focused upward toward the stars. The view was nothing like from anywhere down on Earth, even from up in the mountains. The stars were so much brighter and there were so many more than she thought possible. The idea of getting to see some of those distant worlds thrilled her down to her core.

One hundred meters down the right corridor, Wil stopped outside a small oval-shaped craft with a gray base and a transparent roof reinforced with metal strips around the main structural points. A protrusion from the spaceport's corridor conformed to the same arch as the craft, creating a perfect seal around the entry door. He boarded and looked expectantly at his family to follow.

Once they were on board, Wil tapped on the control console at the apparent front of the vessel. The door slid downward over the opening, and a secondary hatch simultaneously sealed off the corridor to the spaceport.

A subtle vibration resonated through the floor of the vessel and it began pulling away from the spaceport. Though there was barely any sensation of movement, Raena found herself feeling unsteady on her feet, so she quickly sat down on the cushioned seat that wrapped entirely around the circumference of the interior, aside from a break for the door on one side.

We're actually in space right now. Even seeing it with her own eyes, it hardly seemed real.

The craft gently ascended toward the space station above,

which seemed to get even bigger as they approached. Raena stared at the glowing underside of the station, noting a mammoth cable that appeared to tether it to the moon's surface. Their craft took them upward parallel to the length of the cable, and then outward to a concourse lined with small vessels identical to theirs. It slid into the berth and came to rest with a gentle bump and hiss. The door shot upward with a cool blast of air.

"All right, now for a real spaceship," Wil said, gesturing for his family to exit.

Raena collected her travel bag and stepped out onto the metal deck plates of the space station. The air pulsed with a low mechanical hum. "There's no rotation. Is this artificial gravity?"

"Yes, same as down in Headquarters," Saera replied. "Well, down in Headquarters it's more 'augmented' gravity. This is full-on artificial."

"It feels… strange," Raena commented.

"You do get used to it, but it's not the healthiest environment," Wil said. "Muscles are prone to atrophy in artificial gravity."

"So, what do you do?" asked Jason.

"Regular exercise and high-protein diet." Their father smiled. "Running laps on stairs does have some benefit."

Jason scowled. "I was afraid you were going to say that."

They walked down the concourse toward the central hub of the space station. The ceiling was almost entirely transparent, with clear panels curving upward to meet at a thin metal band overhead. Support beams arched the width of the corridor every five meters, but the flared based smooth lines tapering to meet the central support band made the structural feature come across more like a sculptural work of art. By far, the most impressive feature in the corridor was the seamless integration of information displays, with holographic projections and readouts embedded in the transparent walls.

The colorful displays transfixed Raena as she passed by, and she found herself studying star maps projected next to concourses leading out to empty berths. *So many worlds to explore!*

As they continued down the concourse, they passed by a group of four Agents walking in the opposite direction. The Agents inclined their heads to Wil and Saera.

"Where are you headed?" a woman with red hair pulled back into a ponytail asked, her eyes concealed by tinted glasses.

"Tararia," Saera replied.

"Of course," the woman said with a prim nod.

Raena couldn't be sure, but she thought she detected some hostility between the two women.

The other Agent evaluated Raena and then Jason. "A lovely family," she said.

"There's still time for you, Leila," Saera replied.

One of the male Agents in Leila's group snickered. Leila shot him a seething glare. "Safe travels," she muttered to Saera and picked up her pace.

Saera shook her head as soon as the group had passed.

Raena jogged two steps to walk beside her mother. "What was that about?"

"Oh," Saera chuckled, "Leila Gardis is one of my former roommates. We have a classic frenemy relationship."

"Did you have a falling out?"

"We were never proper friends to begin with. She came from a privileged life on Tararia and I was an Earth girl. She hated that I out-performed her in class, and as soon as things were public with your dad and she realized that I'd landed a High Dynasty heir, things really went downhill. Fortunately, most of her assignments keep her out in the field the majority of the time."

"She's a fine Navigator, but she always wanted Command track," Wil added. "She's a perfect case study for why personality is an important consideration with any assignment, not just skills on paper."

"Competitive and self-centered," Saera agreed. "I don't think she has any genuine friends left in my cohort. That Command Center crew she's with now is the first assignment that's stuck in years. Most request her to be transferred out after one or two deployments."

"Yikes. That's sad," Raena said.

"It is," Saera said, "but she brought it on herself. I tried."

"Even Elise couldn't find common ground with her, and she gets along with everyone," Wil added.

Raena smiled. "Now *that* puts things in perspective."

They reached a three-way fork in the corridor and followed the passage around to the right, circumventing the central hub. They continued to bear right at the next branch, taking them down another corridor jutting out from the hub. This one hosted much larger craft than Raena had seen elsewhere, and they got larger the farther out they went from the center—going from fifty meters to several hundred.

Raena admired the sleek forms of the ships. Their hulls gleamed under the lights of the spaceport, showing off an iridescent quality like mother of pearl. Compared to everything else she'd seen over the past several days, these ships were definitely the most alien in appearance.

"There are so many ships here," Jason commented.

"Oh, this is nothing," Wil replied. "This is a quarter of the complement we had stationed here while I was growing up."

"What changed?" Raena asked.

"The threat was eliminated and we disarmed," her father said curtly.

More dodging of the same questions. What aren't they saying? Raena looked to her mother, but Saera gave a subtle shake of her head, indicating to let it go.

Releasing a slow breath to vent her frustration about the non-answers, Raena turned her attention out the viewports toward the impressive ships. The body styles seemed to fall into one of several basic designs, but the common feature across all of them was a forked protrusion toward the back of the vessel.

She pointed to the fork at the back of the nearest ship. "Is that the engine?"

"One of them," Wil said. "It's the external component for the jump drive, which generates the spatial distortion to allow travel through subspace."

"Are some ships faster than others?"

"Travel speed is a function of the navigation system and the ability to lock onto more distant targets. That has nothing to do with the jump drive. But yes—some ships have more advanced navigation systems than others."

"Why not upgrade everything?"

"Money and politics," her father replied. "Ah, here's our ride." He gestured to a ship up ahead.

The ship was similar to many they had already passed. Boxier in appearance, there were viewports along the sides and only the slightest taper at the front. The design seemed impractical, but Raena had to remind herself that these craft were built in space and never designed for atmospheric entry and exit.

A gangway just wide enough for two people to walk abreast extended up from the main concourse to a portal in the center of the ship. Wil and Saera went first.

"I call window seat," Jason said to Raena.

She rolled her eyes. "I think we can *both* have window seats."

"Just throwing it out there in case." He grinned at her.

"Whatever." She let out an exasperated sigh and headed up the gangway.

At the top, a man dressed in a dark gray uniform was waiting to receive them. "Hello, my lady," he greeted Raena. "Please make yourself comfortable and let me know if there's anything I can do to assist."

My lady? Raena forced a smile and bobbed her head. "Thank you."

"Greetings, my lord," the man said when Jason entered.

Raena noticed her parents were heading down the hall toward the front of the ship and she followed, hanging back slightly so Jason could catch up. "What's that 'lord' and 'lady' stuff all about?" she whispered.

"I think the High Dynasties are kind of like royalty, so…"

"This is going to be so weird."

Raena followed her parents into an open room at the end of the short hall. It contained a dozen plush armchairs and expansive viewports that wrapped around the nose of the vessel.

"I don't think we'll need to fight over the window seat," she said to her brother.

"Yeah… I take it back." Jason scoped out the room and headed toward a pair of chairs adjacent to where their parents were getting situated in the middle of the room.

Raena followed him and took the other chair angled toward the viewport. "Also, I'm not sure how much a view matters when it's just one never-ending starscape."

"Oh, this'll change as soon as we get underway," Saera said from her chair as she pulled out a tablet from her travel bag.

Wil just gave them a knowing smile as he retrieved his own tablet from his bag and took a seat.

"Disengaging from dock. Prepare for subspace jump," a female voice said over the intercom.

Their mother craned her neck to look at them. "The subspace transition can be a bit unsettling at first."

"The ship won't fall apart, I promise," Wil added without looking up from his tablet.

What's that supposed to mean? Raena wondered as the transport ship pulled away from the spacedock.

Then, a low rumble began underfoot, slowly escalating until the air was filled with a buzz of energy. The ship shuddered under the intense force, seeming like it was going to rip in a thousand directions at once.

Raena gripped the armrests on her seat with white knuckles as her brother flashed her a look of alarm.

Out of the corner of her eye, Raena saw a blue-green haze forming outside the viewport. The mist swirled around the ship as the shaking came to its climax. Then, the vessel was enveloped in light.

Blue-green strands wove around the ship, dancing ribbons extending from an infinite, glowing expanse. The ship glided through the sea, magnificent forms of billowing light passing them by. The shaking ceased, replaced by a slight vibration emanating through the floor.

Raena was completely transfixed by the view out the viewport. "This is incredible."

"I've never seen anything like it," Jason murmured.

"And you won't anywhere else," Wil said. "The depth of light is a phenomenon completely unique to subspace. Even nebulas have much more definition."

"I can already tell I'll be staring out the window the whole trip," Raena commented.

"A nice sentiment," said her father, "but you have some studying to do before we arrive."

Jason frowned. "Of what?"

"Taran formal customs. I wanted to wait until we were on our way. Firstly, because it would be fresh in your minds, and secondly, because now you're a captive audience and can't steal away on a ship back to Earth."

Raena's stomach dropped. "Seriously?"

Wil nodded. "Sorry. Check your handhelds for the walkthrough. It's only half as bad as it seems at first glance."

Raena pulled out the device from her pocket and saw a message that eight new videos had been added to a shared folder. She looked over at Jason and he shook his head and sighed.

She opened the first video, titled 'Making an Appropriate First Impression', and took one final gaze out the viewport. *This is going to be some trip.*

— — —

Cris paced across the pavement at the edge of the port. Situated at the south boundary of the Sietinen estate, the port was surrounded by lush foliage that blocked the view of the main mansion. *It figures they would order this arrival be out of sight from prying eyes*, he thought sullenly.

It was no wonder that his parents had exhibited such a lukewarm reaction to news of their great-grandchildren's entry to the fold of their Taran birthright. While Cris had been reluctant to go along with Wil and Saera's plan to raise their children outside of Taran influence, he at least understood the purpose it would serve and supported the reasoning behind the decision. His parents, however, had outright resisted the plan. Were it not for some careful intervention on the part of the TSS, the twins likely would have been taken by force back to Tararia as infants. That, of course, would have undone any goodwill Cris had rebuilt with his parents over the years, but he wouldn't have put it past them to go to such extremes.

As it stood, the twins were now outsiders in much the way Saera had been at first. They had all of the pedigree and none of the conditioning to make them suitable leaders in the eyes of those that presently controlled Tararia. *Except that's what makes them so perfect.*

The sound of thrusters in the distance cut through the serene bird calls filling the gardens. As the shuttle came into view, the birds silenced.

Cris watched the shuttle land, anticipation tightening his chest. He had watched his grandchildren grow up through pictures and short videos—it would be quite a different experience to finally meet them in person.

The whir of engines began to wind down as soon as the shuttle came to a rest on the pavement. Several seconds later, the side door slid upward and the exit ramp extended at a gentle angle to the ground.

Wil was the first to emerge from the cabin. He spotted Cris and waved. "Hey!" he called out.

"Hi," Cris replied, waving back. He walked closer to the shuttle. "How was the flight over?"

"Not bad. It was actually kind of fun experiencing such a commonplace activity through fresh eyes."

Cris smiled. "I'm sure." He eyed the doorway, anxious for the twins to emerge. *I wonder who they take after more?*

Then, Raena came into view. She paused at the top of the ramp, admiring the garden. A gust of wind sent a wave of her chestnut hair into her face, and she brushed it back with one hand. She spotted Cris and grinned. Without hesitation, she hopped off the side of the ramp and jogged over.

"Hi, Grandpa Cris," she said.

Cris took her in, realizing that she was somehow a perfect hybrid of her parents. "I'll have to get used to that title. It's so wonderful to finally meet you in person."

She looked him over from head to foot. "Dad really wasn't joking about the family resemblance. It wasn't that clear on the video chats."

"Heavy filters to fit with the narrative." Movement at the

periphery of his vision caught Cris' attention and he looked over to see Saera approaching with a teenage boy that could have been Cris' twin were it not for his teal eyes. "Hello, Jason."

His grandson evaluated him. "Hey, I guess we meet at last."

"Technically, I did meet you as babies," Cris pointed out. "But I realize that doesn't count."

"And there were the vid calls, but…" Raena murmured.

"That was hardly a substitute for being there with you in person. We wanted to—" Cris tried to explain.

"It was on us," Saera cut in. "But you're very lucky now because you'll get ultra-concentrated grandparent spoiling. And they're two of the most awesome people I've ever met."

Cris perked up. "She's right. We have a lot of time to make up for."

Raena seemed to catch herself. She leaned toward her mother. "Wait, were we supposed to do the things in the videos now?"

"Stars! Please don't," Cris said.

Saera held in a laugh. "That's just for your great-grandparents."

"It shouldn't even matter," Cris continued. "We're family and should be able to just talk to each other like people."

"You're also TSS High Commander, so I'm not sure how that factors in with us being Trainees," Raena ventured.

"Do you regard your mother any differently now?" Cris asked.

Raena shook her head.

"Well, she's Lead Agent, so things shouldn't be any different with me, either." He smiled at his grandchildren. "Now, let's get you settled in. Kate's waiting for us inside."

Cris let Saera walk ahead with the twins, beckoning for Wil to hang back. *"They're absolutely stunning, Wil."*

"I'm beginning to understand the fathers in fairytales that sequestered their daughters in towers. I've already had to start scaring off TSS trainees from Raena," Wil replied.

"She's hardly a child anymore. You'll need to let her grow up."

Wil sighed. *"I know."*

"All the same," Cris continued, *"their appearance is going to make the next few days even more difficult. It was one thing when it was just their name, but seeing them now—"*

"*What are you talking about?*" Wil asked.

"*My parents are planning something and you're not going to like it.*"

CHAPTER 12

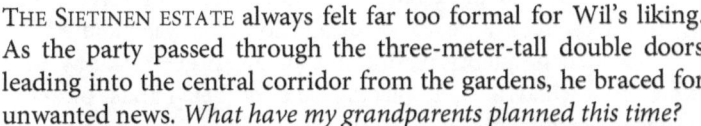

THE SIETINEN ESTATE always felt far too formal for Wil's liking. As the party passed through the three-meter-tall double doors leading into the central corridor from the gardens, he braced for unwanted news. *What have my grandparents planned this time?*

When they decided to bring the twins to Tararia, he'd had no doubt that they would be thoroughly assessed as suitable heirs. Though Saera had been officially accepted as his partner, just being the daughter of someone from a Lower Dynasty would never carry the same weight as someone truly high-born. Since Wil himself wasn't deeply connected to Taran politics, the entire family descended from Reinen, by extension, carried far less political firepower than previous generations. For the Sietinen name to be secure going forward, one or both of Wil's children would need to be paired with the right family offering continued strategic alliances. However, Wil had promised himself that he'd never let his children be used as bartering pawns for political gain. He desired for them to be able to marry for love, as he'd done. How political necessity could be balanced with a self-directed future remained to be seen.

As Wil's eyes adjusted to the interior light, he noticed his mother approaching from the western wing. She wore a flowing aqua dress with silver accents that was quite suited to the temperate weather. Accompanying her was Marina in one of her trademark green gowns.

"Welcome!" Kate greeted, fixing her gaze on the twins. She admired them for a moment in silence. "I can't believe you're all grown up."

Raena's expression warmed. "It's nice to finally meet you."

"You too!" Kate stepped forward and embraced her. She pulled out of the hug and held her granddaughter at arms' length. "You're lovely, dear." She looked to Jason. "And you..." Kate released Raena and gave Jason a hug in turn. "There is no doubt you are your father's son."

Jason glanced at Wil and Cris as Kate released him from the hug. "Yeah, I wasn't going to question it."

"And this is your maternal grandmother, Marina," Saera introduced her mother.

Marina smiled and inclined her head. "I know I haven't been in your lives, but I hope we will be able to become acquainted."

"There'll be plenty of time for us all to get to know each other now," Saera said, placing one of her hands on each teenager's shoulder.

"Have you told them yet?" Kate asked Cris.

"Told us what?" Wil replied.

Kate flashed a heartfelt smile at the twins and Saera. "Give us just a moment." She gestured toward the door and led Wil, Cris, and Marina outside.

Once in private, Kate took a slow breath. "Reinen and Alana have been somewhat... difficult regarding the twin's arrival."

"Not that that was any surprise," Cris interjected.

"What have they requested?" Wil asked, jumping straight to the point.

"They're expecting a formal presentation of the candidate heirs this afternoon," Marina began. "But they've also scheduled a reception ball—for tonight."

"No. There's no foking way I'm agreeing to this!" Wil exclaimed.

"I know, I don't like it either," his father replied in a smooth tone of feigned calm. "However, we don't have much of a choice."

"We can turn around and leave right now," Wil shot back,

taking a step for the door to retrieve his family.

Cris raised an eyebrow. "And what good would that do us when they denounce Raena and Jason as heirs?"

Wil hesitated. "They can't do that."

"It'd be an extreme measure, but it's not impossible," Marina stated.

"They were born in TSS Headquarters, which is regarded as a Taran outpost, but the argument could be made that it's technically Earth territory," Kate pointed out. "Bloodline or not, they'd need to go through a citizenship confirmation hearing."

Wil crossed his arms. "I was born in TSS Headquarters, too."

"Exactly," Cris stated.

"I've been formally named as an heir, though."

His father nodded. "Yes, but *I* named you as *my* heir. As long as my father is Head of the Sietinen Dynasty, he can meddle in the ascension lines as much as he likes."

Wil glowered. "So, we're stuck playing along or all of our plans might unravel."

"I'm afraid so," Cris said. "But the good news is that I genuinely believe my parents are on our side when it comes to matters involving the Priesthood. Really, trying to arrange some marriages is them just keeping up appearances—they have to know we'd never let anything get too serious unless it was something Raena or Jason actually wanted."

Wil shook his head. "That won't keep them from holding out hope."

"Well, let's be reasonable. We couldn't expect them to change everything about themselves. Old ways die hard," Kate said.

Wil sighed. "Fair enough."

"But hey, if nothing else, this will give us a chance to get an updated count on votes," Cris pointed out.

"I guess it will," Wil yielded. He took a deep breath and released it in a huff. "Fine, let's just get this over with."

— — —

Everything about the Sietinen estate looked like it was out of a fairytale, as far as Raena was concerned. From the perfectly manicured grounds to the expansive structures in gleaming white stone, every detail was too precise to be real.

"It's almost becoming a tradition to have Sietinen children grow up elsewhere and return when they're of age," her grandfather was saying to her father up ahead in the corridor.

"Not that everyone supports that practice," Marina stated with a prim smile.

"For what it's worth, it's not really a tradition I'm eager to carry forward," Wil replied with the shake of his head.

"When did you first come back, Dad?" Raena asked.

"I've visited here several times," he said. "The most time I spent here was when I was fourteen."

"Any particular reason?" questioned Jason.

Wil hesitated. "I was… recovering from an injury."

"This has always been a safe place for our family," Cris added.

"Yes, but even so, it hasn't been 'home' for any of us for two generations," Wil countered. "TSS Headquarters will always have that affinity for me."

Will Earth always feel like home? Raena glanced at her brother. "After where we grew up, this seems so…"

"Overdone?" Cris completed for her.

"I felt the same way when I first got here," Saera said, brushing a gentle hand over Raena's shoulder. "Even decades later, I've never felt like I fit in here."

"My parents didn't exactly make you feel welcome at first," Cris muttered.

"We're all welcome here," Kate quickly cut in.

"Of course you are!" Marina added.

So, that family drama really does go way back. Raena looked to her mother for guidance. "I'm not sure how to relate with someone who takes living in this sort of place for granted."

Up ahead, Wil turned around and smiled back at her. "That confirms that we made the right decision to raise you away from all this."

"Just nod and smile like we showed you," Saera said.

"Superficial appearance will go a long way."

The party strode down the ornate passageway, passing by windows looking out over the gardens and terraces adorned with comfortable seating and fountains. The entire estate reminded Raena of a resort out of a 'luxury living' article for the elite. Nothing about it came across as a home where anyone would raise a family.

"We have some formal clothes set aside for them," Marina said to Wil.

"No, they come as they are. The whole notion of formal acceptance is ridiculous enough already. They're not dolls to be dressed up."

Raena smiled to herself. *At least someone is going to have our backs—whatever we're walking into.*

Eventually, the corridors led to a set of double doors carved with vines and flowers, accented by metallic silver highlights.

"Everyone ready?" Kate asked.

"Let's get it over with," Wil said and stepped forward, telekinetically swinging open the doors to either side.

Raena gulped as she took in the reception room.

The two-story room had all the ornateness from the previous corridors replicated and multiplied into one ostentatious presentation of superiority. The white marble floor gleamed with an almost mirror finish, reflecting the details of the carved columns up the walls and the crown molding that transitioned into an abstract mural of a lake with forested hills beyond. Windows spanned three walls, and at the back of the room was a dais topped by a carved, white wood table and two chairs facing toward the entryway.

Seated in the chairs behind the table, two figures robed in dark-blue surveyed the party. They rose, their keen eyes fixed on Raena and Jason.

The man on the left and woman to his right projected an aura of age and wisdom, though there were few signs aside from their gray hair to denote their advanced years.

"Welcome," the man said in a commanding voice as he continued to examine them with his cobalt eyes. "I am Reinen Sietinen, Head of the Sietinen Dynasty and SiNavTech."

Raena gave a little curtsy while Jason bowed next to her. "We are honored to finally meet you," she said like the videos had indicated, keeping her gaze cast down slightly.

"And I am Alana, your great-grandmother," the regal woman next to Reinen stated. She glided around the table in her sky-blue dress. "Let's have a look at you."

Raena walked forward toward the dais, trying to feign confidence. "Yes, my lady."

Reluctantly, Jason stepped forward with her. They stopped three meters in front of the dais as Reinen and Alana came to meet them.

Raena ventured a slight smile, but her advance was ignored as the two elders circled around the twins. To her right, Jason was tense and trying to fight a scowl.

This is so weird. I figured they'd want to talk to us, not perform an actual visual inspection, Raena thought to herself when Alana brushed Raena's ponytail aside to inspect the back of her neck. Her great-grandmother then completed the circle around her side and looked her squarely in the eye.

Reinen performed a similar inspection of Jason. "There's too much green," he stated.

"Pardon?" her brother questioned.

"Hers, as well," Alana said.

Do they mean our eyes? Raena glanced over her shoulder at her parents for help.

"I don't think eye color is really a deal-breaker," Cris said, stepping forward.

"It's a defining feature of our line," Reinen replied. "Wil was deviation enough, but this—"

"These are your great-grandchildren," Cris continued. "Times change. One minor feature isn't worth getting hung up on."

"It's not just one feature. They weren't even raised on a recognized Taran world," Reinen retorted.

"Here we go…" Wil said under his breath.

"Let's look at this another way," Kate said as she came to stand between Cris and his parents. "There is now some diversity, both in terms of genetics and upbringing. All of us in the High Dynasties could use a little outside perspective."

"Still, others have expectations," Reinen insisted.

"So, what, you want us to alter their eye color?" Cris asked with a raised eyebrow.

"Well—" Reinen began.

As the situation continued to escalate, Raena couldn't keep quiet any longer. "Sorry if I'm speaking out of turn," she cut in, "but I'd like to say that I'm very happy with my eye color just the way it is. And yes, Jason and I were raised on Earth, but writing us off just because we weren't born here suggests a complete unwillingness to get to know us as people, and that's not good business. You don't hire someone on résumé alone, but rather go through an interview process. If you don't like us, fine. But at least go through the motions."

Everyone stood in shocked silence for several seconds staring at her.

Finally, Reinen cracked a smile. "All right, you got my attention. If you can bring that kind of spirit to the negotiation table, we might be able to make a proper executive out of you yet."

Cris' shoulders rounded and he let out a slow breath. "We really do need an outside perspective."

"Does this mean we get to keep our eyes?" Jason asked tentatively.

Reinen bowed his head. "Forgive me. Sometimes I forget that the old ways aren't also the ways of the future. I know you'll be far more valuable intact."

"Yeah, let's watch the commodities language," Wil pointed out. "And remember, we're all on the same side here."

"Our intent was only to make the most compelling argument possible for your other endeavors," Alana said. "To sway others you need the foundation of the familiar."

"It'll be familiar enough," Wil replied. "And what better way to make a point than by leading with evidence of that evolution."

What are they talking about? Raena's brow knitted and she looked to her mother for an explanation.

"There'll be time to discuss those details later," Saera said.

"Yes," Reinen agreed. "You'll have all the right delegates to evaluate at the ball tonight."

Wil groaned a little too loudly. "Does it have to be tonight?"

"The arrangements are made," Alana said. "You'd best prepare yourselves. Guests will arrive at 17:00."

"And you," Reinen held out his hands in a gesture encompassing Raena and Jason, "will be properly introduced as the Sietinen heirs. But who will have primary inheritance?" he asked Wil.

"I haven't decided yet," their father replied.

Wait, one of us is named heir over the other? Raena and her brother exchanged confused glances.

"Quarters have been prepared for you in the guest wing," Reinen continued before Raena could seek clarification. "You'll find appropriate attire for this evening waiting for you."

"Thank you," Raena said, though she wasn't sure the statement was specifically addressed to her. "I hope we'll get to speak more this evening."

"Yes, I'm sure," Alana said with a slight bow of her head and warm smile.

"See you then," Cris said and led the way out of the reception room.

When they were down the hall and the doors had thudded closed in the distance, he sighed loudly. "Seriously? Eye color? What the fok—"

"Dad," Wil interrupted. "Language."

"It's okay. We went to public school, remember?" Jason pointed out. "You probably don't want to know how people talked in the hallways."

"Anyway," Cris continued, "that was ridiculous. Just when I think we've finally made some progress they'll randomly revert like that."

"They came around and that's the important thing," Kate said.

"Yes," Saera agreed. "All things considered, I expected it to go much worse."

"Worse than suggesting surgical operations?" Raena asked, incredulous.

"Eye color modification is easy. Worst case would have been

demanding removal of your Dynastic Marks," Wil said. "If you'd been disavowed as heirs entirely that would have been a whole other mess."

"Yeah, what was that about picking one of us as a primary heir?" Jason asked.

"Right, that..." Wil looked down. "Another tradition that doesn't account for alternative ways of thinking."

Raena examined her father. "What do you mean?"

"It's a product of business merging with politics," Cris said. "Since the Head of a dynasty is also the heir to the family's corporate interests, an official successor needs to be named as the deciding vote on the board. While that sounds reasonable in theory, the tradition originated through somewhat questionable practices as a means to circumvent a firstborn child if they didn't live up to expectations."

"Or, if that firstborn would be more useful through a marriage alliance," Wil said.

Cris shook his head. "Yeah, that's the core of it."

"You mean marrying off a daughter and having her brother take over the company instead?" Raena asked.

"It's happened," Cris admitted.

What a delightful future. "Is that what you're planning to do with me?"

"No," Wil hastily replied. "Never."

"But if you were named the primary heir," Cris said, "you'd be the first female heir to Sietinen in two dozen generations. This family has a very long history of only having one child and having that child be male. Some families, like Vaenetri, are known for their daughters."

"Though I have a brother, too," Kate interjected.

"Practices encouraged by the Priesthood, no doubt," Wil mumbled.

"Regardless," Cris continued, "there are a lot of political implications with the decision, no matter which way it goes. We'd like to give you as much choice in the matter as possible, but the fact is that we have some serious politicking ahead of us and the more effectively we can position our alliances, the better."

"That's what tonight is?" Jason asked. "Figuring out where you stand with everyone and how we fit in?"

"It's just a getting-to-know-you affair," Wil assured him. "We won't decide your fates in one night."

Raena wasn't sure she believed him, but she nodded.

"Enough of that now," Kate declared. "Let's get you settled in and rested. It's going to be a long night." She set off down the hall.

Raena stared out the windows as she walked, trying to quiet the churning thoughts in the back of her mind about the sort of life she may be forced into. Joining the TSS had seemed like a certainty with a clear progression, but now knowing the extent of the political angle that would need to balance with telekinesis training, she no longer had a clear vision for her path.

Her mother must have sensed her distress because she fell into step with her and placed a comforting arm around her shoulders. "Don't worry. Nothing will be as bad as it sounds right now."

"I think having my fate decided is something worth worrying about," Raena replied.

"We're not deciding anything. And you should know that this family has a long history of defying the status quo."

"All right," Raena yielded. "I'll put on my best charm for the night."

Her mother smiled. "Who knows? Someone might surprise you."

After winding down several corridors, they eventually arrived in a more intimate hallway with potted plants between the doors and glass-walled alcoves that looked like small conference rooms.

"They have you in here," Cris said, gesturing to three doors in a row. Wil and Saera in the first, then Jason, and Raena. The lock is programmed to recognize your ID chip."

Raena headed for the farthest door and ran her wrist over the panel next to the door. The lock clicked open and the door swung inward.

Inside, a couch was perpendicular to the door, facing a large viewscreen on the wall. The back wall was all glass with double doors leading out onto a spacious terrace overlooking the lake. The doors were open and a temperate breeze drifted through the room.

She immediately headed for the terrace to admire the view. Sunlight glistened on the lake, and standing out in the open air made her feel like she could be anywhere in the galaxy at that moment.

Snapping herself out of the reverie, she went back inside to scope out the bedroom. The entry was on the left, adjacent to her brother's quarters, and the bathroom was accessible from both the living room and bedroom. She found a dark blue evening gown hanging in the bedroom that somehow sparkled even more than the lake. *I guess this is what I'm wearing tonight.*

CHAPTER 13

WIL EXAMINED HIS son. "Maybe we should have fitted you for a TSS uniform instead."

The charcoal gray suit Jason wore fit with the tailored finesse he'd expect from anything supplied by his grandparents for a formal occasion, but it didn't look right to see someone who so closely resembled himself in anything other than TSS attire. *It's not fair to impose that on him. That doesn't make me any better than my grandparents trying to woo them in the ways of Taran politics.*

Jason looked himself over in the floor-length mirror. "I'm not really in the TSS yet."

"You *are* enrolled... classes just haven't started," Wil pointed out.

His son sighed. "I wish we didn't have to dress up at all."

"Well, that much is unavoidable."

Jason stepped away from the mirror. "What are we supposed to do? Is this like a dance, or what?"

"No, it's not some sort of old-timey ball," Wil replied with a soft smile. "It's more like a business cocktail hour—except the business being conducted is politics and strategic alliances."

"Great." Jason's face drained.

"Don't worry, you won't have to talk about any of that. But I won't lie—you'll probably be swarmed by a number of potential suitors."

"You *have* to be kidding."

Wil gave him a sympathetic look. "I wish I was. I got roped into one of these when I was a few years older than you. Fortunately, I had your mom with me. That was the night I proposed, actually."

"So, that story you told us about Vienna…" Jason started.

"That wasn't how it happened," Wil confirmed. "We had to recreate many aspects of our lives when we decided to raise you on Earth."

"This," Jason made an all-encompassing gesture of their surroundings, "the TSS, Tararia… It's a lot to pretend didn't exist."

"It was hard. Really hard, sometimes, to keep up the front," Wil admitted. "Anytime you had a bad day at school or talked about something you wished you could do, I wanted to tell you that so much more was possible than what you could see. Especially the last couple of years when you were talking about college—we really considered telling you then. I know what it's like to have plans for the future thrown out the window with no notice. I'd always strived to avoid doing that with you, but maybe it was inevitable. Either you could grow up surrounded by this and have the pressure of responsibility gradually added over the years or live in blissful ignorance and have it all thrust upon you at once. I had both, but I thought the latter would at least grant you a few good years."

Jason released a slow breath. "Looking back on it, we did have a good childhood."

I hope he's not just saying that to make me feel better. "There's a lot for you to look forward to now," Wil continued. "While these last few days have been completely crazy, once you get settled into the TSS I'll be able to teach you some pretty incredible things. The only reason I resisted you learning to drive a manual car is because I'd have rather been giving you flight lessons."

His son's eyes widened with excitement. "You fly outside of the simulators?"

"Oh, yeah, of course. I learned to fly way before driving.

Actually, I didn't drive until I went to Earth with your mom for the first time. I started flight lessons in space when I was twelve."

"That sounds awesome."

Wil smiled. "I'll take you out as soon as we get back. I don't go out much anymore, but I love it."

"I can't wait!"

"All right, consider it done."

Jason's nerves seemed to settle. "I guess the party tonight will be the worst of it."

"That's my hope," Wil agreed. "I'll stay nearby and try to deflect all the political types from you."

"That'd be great. I have no idea what to say."

"Stars! I don't most of the time, either. Most of the people around here don't know how to interact with me since they know I'm TSS through and through, so they tend to leave me alone."

Jason frowned. "See, I'd think that'd make you fascinating and I'd want to learn more."

"Well, there's some more history behind it than that. For a long time, those with abilities were relegated to the outskirts of society. Even though the official stance of the Priesthood has changed over the last two generations, there's a lot of lingering hostility—especially in the High Dynasties. No one wants to get too close to Agents."

"Are they scared?"

"Not scared... Maybe intimidated."

His son cocked his head. "Why?"

"Abilities like ours are rare these days. We are trained and committed to using those powers to defend and protect the Taran worlds, but there's really nothing stopping us from abusing that power, and they know it. For that reason, there's always been a bit of a tenuous truce between Agents in the TSS and the rest of society."

"You mean, we could start reading their minds and manipulating them?" Jason questioned.

"Not just that, but physically overpower them. Weaponized telekinesis is very difficult to counter."

"Is that what you teach in the TSS?"

Wil dismissed the question with a wave of his hand. "We

teach students how to defend themselves, but our aim is never to hurt others." *At least not since the war ended. I'd hoped to never use my abilities like that again, but there's no telling what we may need to do to bring down the Priesthood once and for all.*

Jason examined him. "Did you have to hurt people during the war?"

"Yes." *I hope they never find out just how many.*

His son nodded slowly. "I guess that's why you don't like talking about it."

Wil searched for the right words. "There's a lot about the war that wouldn't make sense without the proper context. I just want to make sure we cover everything in the right order."

"Fair enough."

"Now," Wil said, "we should probably put that topic on hold and go retrieve your mom and sister. Being late to the party won't make for a great first impression."

Jason glanced at himself one more time in the mirror. "All right. Lead the way."

They headed out into the residential corridor and walked several meters down the hall to Raena's quarters adjacent to Jason's.

Wil hit the electronic chime next to Raena's door. He glanced over at Jason. "Sorry again about all this formality."

Jason tugged awkwardly at the bottom hem of his suit jacket. "It's fine."

"I appreciate you saying so."

His son shrugged in response.

Wil smiled reassuringly. "Look, just remember you have the upper hand. Everyone will be vying for your attention, but you don't owe them anything."

"Is that an invitation to mess with them?" Jason asked.

"Oh, please do."

The door to Raena's quarters cracked open.

"Are you ready?" Wil questioned when she didn't emerge.

"Yes, she's ready," Saera said in reply.

As the door swung open the rest of the way, Raena stood framed in the entryway.

Wil's breath caught when he saw her looking so much like

her mother when they'd first met. The sapphire blue dress interwoven with iridescent threads shimmered even in the low lighting with every movement. While the V-neck cut of the dress and wide straps were relatively modest, the form-fitting bodice underscored Wil's realization that Raena was very far from his little girl anymore. "You look beautiful," he told her.

"Damn," Jason said from next to him.

Raena blushed. "I just about died when I saw this waiting for me. It's so…" She trailed off as she ran a hand over the fabric on the side of her thigh.

"It fits you perfectly," Wil told her. "Come along, we shouldn't keep the guests waiting."

"Would it be wrong to create a literal telekinetic bubble around her?" Wil asked Saera.

"She'll grow up whether we consent to it or not, so it's probably best she learn how to fend off the animals sooner than later," his wife replied. *"All the same, I wouldn't stop you."* She flashed him a coy smile.

Raena took a hesitant step into the hall, finding her balance in the unfamiliar heels.

Saera confidently followed her out into the hall and closed the door to the room. "Four generations of Sietinens together for the first time in decades. This party will be the talk of Tararia."

The flush on Raena's face deepened. "Great."

"Yay…" Jason murmured with thick sarcasm as the four of them made their way down the hall toward the main ballroom.

"The way I look at it," Wil said, "by the end of the night, you'll either love us a lot more or hate us once you see what you were missing all these years."

"Really have my fingers crossed for the former," Saera added.

Raena glanced at Wil. "I doubt we'd hate you."

"We kept an entire galactic society hidden from you for sixteen years," Wil replied. "I expect a good deal of resentment."

"You had some valid reasons," his daughter said.

"But at the same time, we could have grown up with all this," Jason countered, making an all-encompassing gesture.

"I can't even imagine," Raena murmured. She stopped walking. "Sorry, I need to fix the strap on this shoe." She leaned her left hand on the wall and brought her right foot off the ground so she could adjust the placement of the straps on the opened-toed heeled sandal with her free hand.

Just as she finished arranging the main straps in the center into a more comfortable configuration, a segment of the wall she was leaning against pulled inward. Conditioning from years of martial arts classes helped her quickly regain her balance.

A young man in his late-teens with dark-brown hair and gray eyes appeared in the previously hidden doorway to the servant passage. He froze when he saw them out in the hall. "My lord, I'm sorry, I—" He cut off when he locked eyes with Raena in front of him.

An electric spark of telekinetic energy passed between them, invisible to most but unmistakable to Wil. The young man tore his gaze away from Raena.

Stars! Was that a resonance reaction? Wil glanced at Saera and she seemed equally confused. "Quite all right," Wil said to set the young man at ease. *Who is he?*

Saera must have been thinking the same thing. *"I'll take the kids. Get his name,"* she told Wil telepathically. "All set, Raena? Let's go." She urged the twins to continue down the hall.

Raena glanced one more time at the apparent servant before complying.

"I'll catch up with you," Wil told them. He then turned his attention to the young man who was still standing awkwardly in the recessed doorway. "Hello."

The teenager gulped. "My lord—"

"You opened a door while doing your job and we happened to be standing here," Wil stated. "It's fine."

"We're not supposed to be seen…"

Wil smiled. "My grandparents can be elitist pricks sometimes."

The servant's gray eyes widened with shock.

That got his attention. "What's your name?" Wil continued.

"Ryan, my lord. Ryan Pernelli."

"And what is your position here?"

"I'm a maintenance tech, my lord," Ryan replied, keeping his gaze downcast. "Communications systems, mostly."

It was obvious to Wil's trained senses that Ryan had latent telekinetic abilities, which was only confirmed by the charge that passed between him and Raena. However, it made no sense how someone with that magnitude of potential could be a lowly maintenance tech. "Are your parents also in the Sietinen Dynasty's employ?"

Ryan shook his head. "No, my lord. I've been a Ward since I was six years old."

Did his parents know he would develop abilities and that's why they gave him up? The TSS is the only home for people like him. Wil was tempted to offer him a training position in the next cohort on the spot, but he decided to wait. *Was the connection with Raena like what I have with Saera, or was she just the first non-bonded person with abilities he'd been exposed to?*

"Do you need my services, my lord?" Ryan asked when Wil remained silent.

"No," Wil replied. "Sorry to have held you up."

Ryan bobbed his head and stepped into the hallway, closing the door to the servant passageway so it was once again indistinguishable from the wall. He hurried down the hall and ducked into a small conference room reserved for overnight guests to make private video calls.

Wil hung back for another minute, still processing the interaction. *Someone with strong ability potential working for the Dynasty. Knowing us, that can't be a coincidence.* He set off at a light jog to catch up with his family, devising a test to help him decide his next steps. Depending on the outcome, the next few days might prove very enlightening.

—   —   —

Sounds of music and conversation filled the hall as Raena approached the reception room with her family. The indistinct hum of voices gave the impression of a large crowd. *How big is this party?*

The corridor terminated in a set of carved double doors, which were presently closed and flanked by two attendants.

"Uh oh," Wil said when he saw the closed doors. "I remember this. They probably want to formally present you."

"What does that mean?" Jason questioned with audible alarm.

"Pretty much display you on the stairs for all to see before they throw you to the wolves," Wil replied.

Raena's jaw dropped.

Her father smiled. "I'm mostly kidding. Well, not really. But we're here for backup. It'll be fine." He stepped toward the door and the attendants came to attention. "Sooner we go in, the sooner it'll be over."

Reluctantly, Raena positioned herself in front of the door.

Jason came to stand next to her. "This is stupid," he muttered.

"I totally agree but you'll be fine," Wil said and nodded to the attendants.

The attendant on the right whispered something into his jacket lapel and then stepped forward to grab one of the door handles simultaneously with his comrade. In one motion, the two men pulled the doors open.

Lively sounds of the party filled the hall at full volume as the doors opened. Raena gasped when she saw the magnificent room with crystal chandeliers and towering windows overlooking the gardens still bathed in twilight. Conversation ceased as the guests saw them standing at the top of the stairway leading down to the main ballroom. The twenty-piece orchestra playing on the right side of the room suspended their music as Reinen stepped forward from the crowd and climbed the stairs.

"Esteemed guests," Reinen began with a grand sweep of his hand over the hushed audience. "Thank you for joining us on this momentous occasion. The last time my family was gathered here, I was introducing you to Williame when he was just a young man. Now, I have the honor of formally introducing a new generation of Sietinens as heirs to our Dynasty. First, is Jason Sietinen-Alexri, a son born in the Sietinen tradition."

Jason stumbled forward next to Raena, as though he'd been pushed. Reluctantly, he descended the stairs under the scrutinizing eyes of the audience.

"But we were granted a great fortune this generation," Reinen continued. "We were also given a great-granddaughter, Raena—a twin to Jason."

Raena felt a hum of energy around her and a gentle prodding at her back. *All right, I'll take the hint.* She stepped forward and smiled politely at the audience. Several young men around the room concentrated on her and began navigating the audience to get to the front row. *Oh no...* She managed to hold her poise as she descended the stairs in her heels and long gown, stopping four steps from the bottom with her brother.

"Jason and Raena are now sixteen years of age," Reinen stated, "and I am thrilled to welcome them as formal members of this family. I'm glad we can all celebrate here this evening. Please, enjoy the party."

The audience clapped while Reinen bowed his head and descended the stairs.

"Was that just a polite way of saying 'come and get 'em while they're still single'?" Raena whispered to her brother.

"We're doomed," he replied in a hushed voice as three young women in overly revealing gowns stepped forward from the crowd.

"Good luck." Raena started to plan a path toward the buffet line on the left side of the room that would take her around the guests she saw eyeing her from afar, but before she could move a young male voice called out to her from the left.

"May I get you a drink?"

Raena turned to see that the owner of the voice had refined features and fair hair with brilliant green eyes. He looked to be in his late-teens, though it was hard to tell. Had he approached her in a hallway at school, she probably would have dropped everything to talk to him, but after her run-in with the servant only a few minutes, before she wasn't really in the mood for flirting. "I don't really drink," she replied.

"Anything?" the young man questioned with a charming upturn of his lips. "They have more than wine, you know. Some sparkling juice, maybe?"

At least holding a glass will keep me from fidgeting with my hands. "All right," Raena yielded.

Jason flashed her a wide-eyed plea for help as she passed by while the three young women descended on him.

She gave him a helpless shrug and followed the blond man toward the bar.

"I'm Elon," he turned to say to her. "I'm heir to the Gaelani Dynasty in the Fourth Region."

"Nice to meet you," Raena said, trying to remember Tararian geography from the instructional videos over the past several days at Headquarters. "It looks like a lovely archipelago."

"Yes, quite nice this time of year. Our estate is on one of the islands toward the Alarian Sea."

I have no idea where that is. "Great."

"Two aerated camillas," Elon ordered when they reached the bar.

The bartender poured two glasses of a light purple sparkling liquid and placed the glasses on the bar top.

Elon grabbed the two flutes and handed one to Raena. "Cheers."

"Cheers," she said and took a sip. The effervescent liquid had a dry grape flavor and tickled her nose.

"So," Elon said, leading her toward an unoccupied area by the wall, "we hadn't heard anything about you until this invite three days ago."

"Yeah…" Raena stared at her glass, "we grew up on Earth."

"That's strange," Elon replied. "Why would you live there?"

"Well, TSS Headquarters is right there so it made sense."

"Oh, right, the TSS…"

Raena detected a touch of disdain in his tone. "What do you have against the TSS?"

"Oh, it's just so on the fringe compared to the rest of the Taran people. I never understood how your family became so involved."

"I'm not entirely sure how it got started, either," Raena admitted. "This is still all new to me."

"Well, I'd be happy to help acquaint you," Elon said, inching closer to her.

Raena took a large gulp from her glass. "I think I'm good." She looked for an escape. Ten meters away, Jason was backing away from a group of seven young women who didn't look like they would give up without a fight.

As she scanned the room, Raena also noticed that three other young men aside from Elon were watching her movements, seemingly waiting for the right opportunity to pounce. *As soon as I step away, I'll be surrounded.*

Desperate, she looked around for her parents. However, she couldn't see them through the hundreds of guests. She was on her own.

Raena took a calming breath and put on her most charming smile. "Thank you for the drink, Elon. I should probably go mingle, being one of the guests of honor and all."

He was almost successful in hiding his disappointment with a slight bow of his head. "Of course. I hope we have the chance to speak again soon."

While she pivoted, Raena calculated the trajectory of the other suitor's paths and set a course that should necessitate only one deflection while on her way to her brother's position. Across the room, she caught Jason's eye and they silently synchronized their plans.

The suitor closest to Raena spotted his opening and approached. Simultaneously, Raena set out in the opposite direction like she hadn't seen him. The path took her on a course dangerously close to the second suitor. However, that also meant she was in direct line of sight for the third suitor, as well. While the second and third sized each other up from a distance, she darted behind a group of aristocrats around her grandparents' age.

A moment later, Jason dashed around the group to join her. "This is complete madness."

"Too much attention for a change?" Raena asked with a raised eyebrow.

"Oh, yeah, you seemed like you were having a great time with 'Slick' over there."

"His name is 'Elon'," Raena corrected, "but yeah... I think I now know how a sheep feels at auction."

"Don't devalue yourself. You're at least on the same level as a golden egg-laying goose," her brother jested.

"Very funny." Raena sighed and analyzed the room. "I'm not sure how we're supposed to get to know anyone in a meaningful way in this setting."

"This isn't for us to get to know anyone. I'm pretty sure this whole party is just to show off the newest inventory—us. Anyone interested after the show and tell can begin submitting their bids in the form of political alliances or business partnerships as soon as this event is over."

She frowned. "That sounds incredibly archaic to negotiate business deals with marriage. I thought this culture was advanced."

"Maybe archaic on the surface, but you've heard the talk over the last few days—everything in Taran culture is driven by genetics. Blending two families makes a deal official on the genetic level," Jason pointed out.

Raena scowled. "That is profoundly disturbing when you put it in those terms."

"And given those terms," a woman said from behind them, "it's not surprising your grandfather left."

Raena spun around to face the speaker, a woman with gray hair and hazel eyes. "Hi," Raena greeted. "And you are?"

"Krista," the woman replied. "Your great-aunt. Kate's older sister."

"Oh, she hadn't mentioned you," Raena continued. "Or any extended relatives, for that matter. I guess it hadn't come up yet."

Krista nodded. "That doesn't surprise me. I normally sit these kinds of affairs out, but curiosity finally got the better of me when I heard you were coming."

"I wish the invite had been optional for me," Jason muttered.

"Oh, what I'd give to have all the possibilities of youth ahead of me again," Krista said, admiring them. "But fate has a way of turning on you sometimes."

"Yeah, I never would have guessed we'd be here," Raena agreed as she looked out over the crowd.

Krista smiled. "And none of us expected there'd ever be anyone like you."

"Yeah, our uniqueness has been pretty well established," Jason said. "Personally, I'd like to see a return to normalcy for a few minutes to catch my breath."

"Oh, you still have no idea what's coming," Krista murmured. "My little sister has always been a dreamer. It wasn't until she met Cris that things began to fall into place. But the two of them with you—well, you just might be able to accomplish the impossible."

"You mean… the thing," Raena said, connecting the dots about the revolution her parents had mentioned. "Yeah, I'm still not clear on the details."

Krista nodded slowly. "In time. In the interim, know you will always have Vaenetri's support."

"Thanks?" Raena said, still not entirely sure what her great-aunt meant underneath her carefully chosen words.

With a slight bow of her head, Krista disappeared back into the throng of guests as quietly as she'd approached.

"That was weird, right?" Jason asked as soon as she'd gone.

"Oh, yeah." Raena looked down at her empty glass. "Go to the bar with me?"

"That requires leaving our hiding place."

"It's not that hidden if Krista found us," Raena pointed out, "which means someone else is running interference for us."

"Yeah, you're right. This was way too easy." Jason scanned the room looking for an explanation.

Raena did likewise. After ten seconds, she spotted their security fence. Their parents and grandparents had set up a semi-circle on the other side of the older guests Raena and Jason had hidden behind. Whenever an apparent suitor tried to approach, one of the Agents would stare at them—unmoving and without speaking—until the person backed away. Apparently, glowing eyes were enough of a deterrent. *That's actually pretty badass.*

Jason caught on to the setup at the same time. "All right. The bar should be safe for a few minutes."

They carefully circumnavigated the group of party guests and headed toward the bar. In her peripheral vision, Raena saw her parents adjust their positions to keep the buffer wall intact.

She stepped up to the bar. "Two effervescent cam…"

"Camillas, my lady," the bartender completed for her.

"Yes! That's the one," she acknowledged with a smile.

The bartender turned to prepare the drinks.

"What is it?" Jason asked.

"Sort of like a non-alcoholic champagne, I think."

The bartender placed two flutes on the countertop and Raena grabbed them, handing one to her brother. "Thank you," she called to the bartender as she searched the room for a possible hiding place that wouldn't seem too much like overt avoidance of the guests. "Maybe if we—"

Before she could complete her thought, a middle-aged woman pulled away from a nearby group of older guests and thwarted Raena and Jason's escape.

"Looks like you two finally broke free," she commented. "They're persistent, aren't they?"

I wonder who she is? "Yes, I'm trying my best to stay out of sight."

The woman looked them over from head to foot. "It would be difficult for either of you to be lost in a crowd. It looks like your family is keeping the worst at bay."

"Yes, thankfully. This is all so new." Raena eyed the woman, curious about her casual regard for them.

"Ah, of course," the woman nodded. "Your early years spent on Earth. So very quaint."

"It's more advanced now than you may realize," Jason said in their home's defense.

"Perhaps." She patted her graying blonde hair. "I suppose your absence here can be forgiven, considering your parents' ties to the TSS."

"Living on Earth did make for a reasonable commute," Raena said and took a sip from her glass.

"I can't imagine what that must have been like—growing up with a war hero," the woman commented.

"He never talked about any of that," Raena said slowly.

"Yeah, it wasn't until a couple of days ago that we even knew our parents were in the military," Jason added.

The woman's eyes widened. "He's incredibly famous. Not just for the war, but the independent jump drive, too."

"The what?" Jason asked.

Raena thought for a moment. "Does that have something to

do with navigation?"

"Yes," the woman said. "I'm surprised you haven't heard more about it. Your father cracked the code for the greatest scientific advancement in generations."

"He's been pretty reluctant to talk about himself," muttered Jason.

"Well, I suspect you'll be hearing a lot more from other people," the woman continued. "He's probably the most famous person alive. At sixteen he solved the equation to finally enable precise subspace travel without beacons, and he went on to command the TSS to victory in a war that most of us didn't even know was going on until it was almost over."

Jason glanced over at Raena. "Wait, he was in command of the TSS?"

The woman nodded. "That was my understanding, anyway."

Then why is he just an Agent now? Everyone at Headquarters did seem to treat him like he was someone of even greater authority. "I guess we have some more to talk about."

"No joke," her brother agreed.

"There you are!" Raena heard her mother say from behind.

Saera slipped through the crowd to stand between Raena and Jason. "Hello, Marilyn. Nice to see you."

Marilyn inclined her head. "Saera, you look well."

"It's been since the wedding, hasn't it?" Saera took Raena gently by the arm and guided her backward. "Well, we'll have to catch up sometime. I'm afraid I need to steal these two for a while."

Raena and Jason were pulled back past several guests into an open space near the center of the room that her parents and grandparents seemed to be patrolling. "What was that about?" Raena asked.

"Marilyn Monsari is no friend of ours," Saera replied. "Her brother is Head of the Dynasty and has expressed on numerous occasions how much he detests 'our kind'."

"That phrasing tells me everything I need to know," Raena said with a scoff.

"Exactly." Saera looked around the room. "I hope you don't mind us running interference for you."

"Are you kidding?" Jason exclaimed. "I think they'd eat us alive if that would be profitable. In the first three minutes, they were already trying to figure out my net worth under various investment scenarios."

Raena shrugged. "Elon didn't seem so bad. At least not at first. It was kind of weird when he offered to show me around."

Her mother nodded. "That was good instinct to get out when you did. The idea is to get you alone with them where there are no witnesses for what you discuss. Then they can say anything and if you deny it you'll lose face."

"And you didn't warn us about that?" Raena questioned vehemently.

"We never would have let it go that far—we were watching all the exits. I wanted to give them the benefit of the doubt, but the fact of the matter is that you're both far too big of a prize for anyone to play it safe. Sietinen is the ultimate alliance to lock down through an official joining of dynasties."

Raena shook her head. "What happened to getting to know someone and seeing if you even like each other?"

"What do you think this party was supposed to be for?" Saera raised an eyebrow.

"This is one night. And we're sixteen!" Jason hissed.

"The idea is to find someone you like, the parents vet the pairing, and if it's mutually beneficial then a formal betrothal can ensue," Saera explained. "Anything like dating would come later on, and a marriage wouldn't be for years. This is all a long game."

Raena crossed her right arm across herself as she held the glass in her left hand. "I don't like this."

"That's why we're keeping them away from you," her mother assured her. "If there's anyone you want to talk to, feel free. But I don't buy into this system and I won't let anyone force you to be a part of it."

"Won't our great-grandparents be upset?" Jason asked.

"We don't owe them anything. There are heirs for two generations—you, as the third, can take your time finding any partner that makes you happy." Their mother beamed at them. "Besides, I'm not quite ready for you to be grown up yet."

Raena smiled back. "We're not going anywhere." She swirled

the remaining contents of her glass. "What are we supposed to do for the rest of the night, then?"

Saera got a glint in her glowing eyes. "Would you like to meet our secret co-conspirators in that revolution we're planning?"

Jason perked up. "That actually sounds kinda fun."

Raena nodded. "I'm game."

"All right." Saera glanced over her shoulder and nodded to Kate. "I'm going to hand you over to your grandmother. She's kind of the master behind this whole thing—schmoozing ability off the charts."

Kate left her place in the semicircle and came to meet Raena and Jason. "You want a meet and greet, I hear?"

"How did you…?" Jason began.

Their grandmother smiled. "Telepathy, remember? Soon you'll be in the fold in more ways than one." She placed one hand on Raena's shoulder and led her and Jason into the crowd. "Let's see. Where to start…"

— — —

Wil watched his children disappear into the crowd with his mother. *Their heads are going to be spinning by the time she's done showing them around.*

He detected Saera approaching behind him. "Are they doing okay?" he asked her as she came to stand next to him.

"I think so. They're strong-willed, so I'm pretty sure they'll take anything we can throw at them in stride."

"All the same, I'd rather not put that to the test just yet."

His wife nodded. "Agreed." She glanced around them but there was no one standing nearby. *"So, who is he?"*

"His name is Ryan. He's been a Ward since he was six years old," Wil replied telepathically.

"Orphaned?"

Wil shook his head. *"I'm not sure. The program is something like permanent foster care so it could go either way. I'll need to do some digging."*

Saera thought for a moment. *"But he has abilities?"*

"Definitely. And strong ones, if the cursory assessment is accurate."

"What passed between them..."

"A resonance reaction, yes."

His wife released a slow breath. *"I guess we were that age."*

"Younger, actually," Wil pointed out.

"We should get to know him."

Wil nodded. *"I already have something in mind."*

Before he could share his plan, Wil spotted his father walking over. "What are you two scheming about?"

"There's been a... development," Wil replied.

Cris raised a quizzical eyebrow.

"On our way over here, we had a chance encounter with a maintenance tech," Wil explained. *"He has abilities—strong ones. Nearly as much as with Jason and Raena. And, there appeared to be a resonance connection with Raena."*

"That's..." Cris started.

"Yeah, it doesn't make any sense," Wil agreed. *"I can't decide if I think it's the Priesthood's doing or if there's just a genuine connection."*

Cris shrugged. *"I'll believe anything these days."*

"In any case, there are two immediate courses of action," Wil continued aloud. "First, I'd like to test if their connection is real. I was thinking we could arrange a seemingly chance encounter again to see if they really are drawn to each other."

"Isn't that a bit strange, considering this is your daughter we're talking about?" Cris asked.

Wil chuckled. "Believe me, I'm trying not to think about it. I'm taking a purely scientific vantage and attempting to return to the mindset of a teenager and how I'd want the situation handled were the roles reversed."

"I guess I did nudge you toward Saera," Cris realized.

"Aww, you did?" she asked with a grin.

"Anyway," Wil cut in, "regardless of how that works out, I move that we pull him into the TSS."

"The timing is good," Cris agreed, "with a new cohort about to start."

"Precisely." Then Wil added telepathically, *"And if he is part of a Priesthood plan, I'd rather have him close so we can keep an eye on him."*

"Unless that's what they want…" Saera countered.

Wil shrugged. "If that's what they were after, they'd make it happen one way or another."

"True," Cris conceded. "How do we proceed?"

"Leave that to me." He looked around the room. "Now, we should probably get back to the festivities before everyone becomes too suspicious of what we're talking about."

"They should be suspicious." Cris took a sip of his drink.

"Covertly planning the future of others. We've become one of 'them'!" Saera exclaimed in a whisper.

Wil wrapped his arm around her and headed toward the crowd. "On that note, let's try to get some more votes."

CHAPTER 14

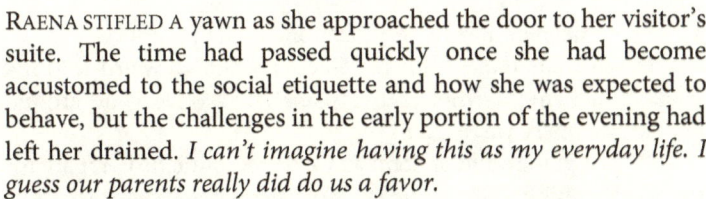

RAENA STIFLED A yawn as she approached the door to her visitor's suite. The time had passed quickly once she had become accustomed to the social etiquette and how she was expected to behave, but the challenges in the early portion of the evening had left her drained. *I can't imagine having this as my everyday life. I guess our parents really did do us a favor.*

She ran her wrist over the electronic lock panel next to the door and it clicked open. Surprisingly, the light was on inside.

As she swung the door in the rest of the way, a clang of metal on stone sounded from the lounge room. Raena froze in the doorway. *An intruder?* She took a step backward and surveyed the room from afar, looking for the source of the sound.

The head of a young man popped up from behind the couch. After a moment, Raena recognized him as the same dark-haired servant she'd almost collided with in the hall on her way to the ball.

Her heart leaped as their eyes met, reigniting the inexplicable connection she'd felt with him at their first meeting. "What are you doing in here?" she demanded, heart racing.

"My lady!" he exclaimed. "I wasn't expecting you back yet."

"That doesn't explain why you're here." *Why do I feel so drawn to him?*

"Sorry." He stood up behind the couch. "I got a notice that

your viewscreen needed servicing. Didn't you put in the request?"

She looked him over properly, deciding that his appearance rivaled the best bred suitors at the party. "No... It was working fine when I left earlier."

The servant turned to the side to glare at the viewscreen mounted on the wall. A control panel was open beneath the monitor. "Well, *someone* put in the work order. And it's definitely broken."

Who would do that? Now that she knew why he was in her quarters, Raena stepped inside. "What's wrong with it?"

He shook his head. "I'm not sure. When the screen is activated, it freezes on the VComm startup screen. After a minute, it restarts and does the same thing."

"Ah, an endless reboot loop. I've encountered that with computers back home."

"You mean on Earth?" he questioned.

"Yeah." She looked down. "Geez, it's still so weird to think about that being a whole other planet. Does everyone around here know where we're from?"

"Word got around as soon as we were notified to prepare for the event tonight," he replied. "Most people are eager to know the business of anyone with the last name Sietinen, my lady."

She smiled and let out a little laugh. "I guess they are. And you can call me Raena."

"I'm Ryan," he replied. He glanced back at the viewscreen. "I'm really not supposed to work on this while you're around."

"Why not?"

"Something about maintaining the illusion of flawless operations."

"Well, I have no such illusions," she said, catching his gaze. "In fact, I'd love to learn some more about the system. VComm is my maternal grandmother's family company, after all."

Ryan swallowed and looked down, his face flushing slightly. "I shouldn't even be talking to you."

"Well that's a dumb rule." Raena closed the door leading out into the hallway. *Who is he? I've never felt like this around someone before.* "Let me get out of this absurd dress and then you can give me an overview of the system. Maybe I can help you troubleshoot."

Ryan's gray eyes widened. "I should go—"

"No, I'll just be a minute. Hang on." She headed over to the bedroom and closed the door before she could lose her nerve, leaving bewildered-looking Ryan alone in the lounge room.

As soon as she was in the relative privacy of the bedroom, Raena let out a long breath. *What am I doing? This is insane!*

Maybe it was, but she needed to take the chance. There was something about him that made her want to know more, to see if there really was a genuine connection between them. In just a few short moments in the hall earlier, she'd glimpsed an initial spark that she could see growing into much more. Though not one for quick judgments under normal circumstances, she felt compelled to follow through in this matter. Crazy or not, the person out in the lounge room wasn't just a random stranger—instinct told her he had the potential to be someone of significance in her life. She owed it to herself to find out, despite the apparent unlikelihood.

Raena carefully slipped out of her evening gown and changed into pajama pants and a tank top layered with a zip-up jacket. She was about to take down her hair but decided to leave it up.

Taking a calming breath, she opened the door to the lounge room.

Ryan was still over by the viewscreen, shifting awkwardly on his feet. He stopped fidgeting when he saw her. "I shouldn't be here."

"I know this is all strange and unexpected," Raena began, "but there's something—"

"You're a Sietinen heir."

"So, I can change the rules."

"But I'm just—"

Raena walked over toward him. "Tell me this isn't all in my head."

He searched her face for what seemed like an eternity as they stood in silence. "I feel it, too."

The words simultaneously reassured her and made her more nervous. "Do we know each other from somewhere?"

"I've never been to Earth."

"Then why does it seem like I've known you for years?"

Ryan took a slow breath. "I can't explain it."

Raena bit her lower lip. "Okay. Well, let's just chat like normal people and maybe we can figure this whole thing out."

"All right," Ryan conceded. He looked her over. "Were you serious about wanting to learn how the viewscreen works?"

She shrugged. "Seems like as good a place as any to start."

"Diving into the inner workings of electronic devices. Yeah, that's totally chatting like normal people…"

"I can think of way less normal things to talk about."

He raised an eyebrow. "Such as?"

"Oh, I don't know," Raena said, curling up on the couch facing the viewscreen. "Anything I'd reference would be lost on you anyway. Stupid Earth stuff."

"I guess that's a pretty decent example, actually—chatting about growing up on a planet where the entire Taran civilization may as well not exist. That's way less normal than viewscreen operations."

Raena narrowed her eyes playfully. "I've already built up an immunity to the ribbing about growing up on such a backwater planet. I know I have a lot of catching up to do."

"Excuses, excuses," Ryan jested back.

"That's not very productive. Now come on! There's a viewscreen mystery to be solved."

Ryan eyed her for another moment and then turned his attention to the uncooperative device. "All right. The screen you see is actually just a thin film on the wall. The control mechanism is a central receiver for all the telecommunications in the room. That makes it easy to sync your handheld with the viewscreen and use voice commands on any of the systems, but it also makes it more difficult to diagnose the root cause of a malfunction—not that things go wrong too often."

"So, the issue now… it's possible that it's not actually a viewscreen malfunction but is just being expressed that way?"

"Yes, that's what I'm leaning toward at this point." Ryan sighed and glared at the exposed panel. "The loading screen wouldn't show up if there was an issue with the display panel itself. Voice commands are working for the lights and thermostat, so the problem must be isolated with the display. That's strange, though, since it all routes through that one control module."

"Sounds more like software than hardware."

"Yes, it does, but…" Ryan trailed off.

"But what?"

"The only thing I can think of that would cause such specific interference would require modifying the code at the most basic level—essentially deleting or corrupting the boot sequence. Otherwise, the other systems would be acting up, too."

Raena frowned. *Would someone have actually done that?* "In that case, maybe it's time to expand the investigation. Is there a way to check if anyone has come into the room since I left?"

"Of course, that's easy," Ryan replied. "You think someone may have tampered with it?"

If this was tampering, I bet I know why and I'm going to feel silly trying to explain it. Raena's face felt warm. "How do these repair assignments work? Why did you reply to this particular service request?"

"There's a central dispatcher. Most assignments are based on who's available at the time, but there are some specialists for certain issues."

"And what's your specialization?"

"Control interface coding."

Raena groaned inwardly. "Why is that not surprising? We should definitely have a look at the door entry log."

Ryan suddenly appeared concerned as he stepped over toward the door, removing a handheld from his pocket that was similar to the one Raena had received upon arrival to the TSS. "This will just take a couple seconds." He placed the top of the handheld near the electronic lock and the device chirped. "Well, your father has been by, but there's nothing else out of place."

This is ridiculous. "There you go."

"Pardon?"

Raena shrank back into the couch. "My dad is behind this."

Ryan's brow wrinkled. "Why in the stars would he do that?"

She let out an exasperated sigh. "So we'd talk to each other, I guess. Maybe he wants me to convince you to join the TSS." *Or he saw what passed between us.*

"That seems like an awful lot of trouble to go to for one person."

"Compared to the displays I witnessed this evening, it's nothing."

Ryan stared at the blank viewscreen. "Well, regardless of the motivations, this explains the viewscreen malfunction. Knowing the code was corrupted intentionally, I guess I should just run a fresh install of the operating system and resync everything. I wanted to rule out a hardware issue or a virus before I did that, and I guess this does."

"Will it take long?" Raena asked.

"No, this is the easy part."

"Then do you have any other assignments?"

"I'm not even officially on duty right now. So, no."

"All right. Finish up and then we can talk properly," Raena suggested. "We should see if there's really something here."

Ryan gawked at her. "That's a bit… forward."

"Well, unless you do join the TSS, I don't see another opportunity for us to get to know each other. What happened earlier…"

"…was nothing I should be thinking about," Ryan completed. "The long and short of it is that people like you and people like me don't ever sit down for a friendly chat."

"Maybe more should."

"I don't disagree with your sentiment, but it isn't realistic."

"We're doing it right now," Raena pointed out.

Ryan sat down on the edge of the couch, keeping his distance from her. "You know this can't go anywhere, right?"

I've never felt this instantly drawn to someone. I can't just ignore it. "I'm not ruling anything out yet."

"But this is mad! We ran into each other in a hallway."

Raena looked him in the eye. "You admitted you felt it, too."

He looked down and swallowed. "I won't deny it. But of course, anyone would be attracted to someone like you. What you see in me, on the other hand—"

"A smart, good-looking guy who's been able to conquer his fear of talking to me."

"I wouldn't say that fear has been conquered," he muttered.

"See? Some humor, too. But whatever's here isn't something that can be readily put into words. I just... know, as weird or crazy as it sounds."

"Yes, it is crazy."

"Didn't you *just* say—"

"Yes, okay!" Ryan finally exclaimed. "I feel drawn to you, too—suddenly and inexplicably. But I have a life here, and this little development doesn't exactly fit in with everything else that's going on."

"I didn't see this coming, either."

"Of course not." Ryan tousled his hair. "Look, I can't deal with this right now. There are other... complications that I don't want to get into. So, yeah, I'm going to go." He bolted from the couch. "Another tech can come do the system reinstall."

I can't be left wondering. Raena lunged from the couch and caught his hand before he could walk away. Standing before him with her hand still on his, she gazed up into his eyes. The connection she'd felt between them since their first encounter was overwhelming at that distance. A tangible electric charge filled the air, time almost seeming to stand still. Ever so slightly, she leaned up toward him.

Finally, he gave into her advance. Their lips met, sending an energizing tingle all the way to her toes. Though still strangers, there was something familiar about his touch—like old lovers finally being reunited.

They eased backward onto the couch, immediately comfortable in each other's presence. In that gentle embrace, there was no pressure for it to be anything more than a chaste affirmation of something that was impossible to verbalize. Somehow, entwined in a virtual stranger's arms, Raena felt completely at peace.

She had no idea how much time had passed by the time they finally settled on the couch with her head on his chest. They lay together in silence for a long while, but she knew one of them would have to say something eventually, and it should probably be her.

"We'll find a way," she murmured.

He squeezed her. "I suspect a plan is already in progress."

"You're probably right about that." *I bet none of the party guests would guess where I ended up tonight.* She nestled closer to him on the couch.

"I should get going." He tried to get up.

She stayed put. "Just a while longer."

Ryan relaxed again. "A few more minutes won't hurt."

— — —

Ryan's eyes shot open. Sun streamed through the open window—already well past dawn.

It took him a moment to get his bearings in the unfamiliar room. He glanced over and saw Raena still asleep on the couch next to him. *Shite!*

He scrambled off the couch, only pausing to look at the time on his handheld: 06:47. There was no way he'd be able to explain being gone all night. And if anyone caught him leaving the quarters of the newest Sietinen heir...

Raena stirred on the couch and then stretched as her eyes fluttered open. "Hey," she greeted. "Wait, it's morning?"

"I'm sorry, I didn't mean to stay. I must have fallen asleep—" Ryan tried to explain.

"It's fine, don't worry about it," Raena replied.

That's easy for her to say. She won't get shipped offworld for this. "Please don't tell anyone I stayed here."

"I invited you. What's the big deal?"

"I'm a servant here, Raena. Remember, I shouldn't even be talking to you."

She laughed. "And like I said last night, that's a stupid rule."

"You might not have such social distinctions where you're from, but the conventions are *very* clear here. I need to go."

She rose from the couch. "When can I see you again?"

He hesitated. "I still don't know how this would work."

Raena frowned. "You're ready to let some arbitrary social standing get in the way?"

Ryan crossed his arms. "I'm in a tough spot here."

"Come to the TSS with me," Raena said. "Neither of our backgrounds matters there."

"Me in the TSS?" Ryan ran a hand through his dark hair. "That'll be the day."

Raena took a step toward him. "Why not? Militia is a good career path."

"I don't know…"

"Well, I'd like a chance to spend some more time together, to see what we have between us," Raena stated, looking him in the eye.

"You may be new to the dynastic lifestyle, but you already know how to speak your mind."

Raena smiled. "Since you're not saying what you're really thinking, I figured I should speak on our behalf."

"I am speaking my mind. I can't help being rational."

"I still think you're holding back."

He sighed. "All right. The truth is that I would like a lot more nights like last night."

"Me too."

But first, I need to avoid getting killed today. "Really, though, I have to go."

Raena gave him a slow kiss. "I'll see you soon."

Ryan tore himself away from her and rushed out into the hall. *I never should have stayed overnight. This is bad—*

He rounded a bend in the hallway on his way to the servant passage entrance and almost ran straight into Wil.

"Hi again," the Sietinen heir commented.

Shite! Ryan froze. There was no escape. "Nothing happened!" he exclaimed in a panic.

Wil cocked his head. "With what?"

Of course, he doesn't even know I was with his daughter all night. Ryan's mind raced, trying to figure out a way to backpedal. "I, uh…"

"Where were you coming from?" Wil asked.

"My lord, I can explain—"

Wil stared at him levelly. "Were you with Raena all this time? I'll know if you're lying."

"She asked me to stay," Ryan blurted out. "I must have fallen asleep. When I woke up—" He looked down at the floor. "I'll report the violation to my supervisor. I accept full responsibility."

The Tararian lord stood in silence for several moments. "As far as I'm concerned, there was no wrongdoing."

Ryan looked up slowly. "My lord...?"

"I know most of the highborn around here act in a certain way, but I grew up in the TSS. I think it's absurd that you can get in trouble for talking to someone. If my daughter wants to talk to you, it's not anyone's place to stand in the way of that."

He's not upset? It took Ryan several seconds to find his voice again. "I thought for sure you were going to have me banished."

"Banishment? Does anyone still do that?" Wil chuckled. "No, Ryan, far from it. In fact, I was going to ask you to join the TSS."

"The TSS?"

Wil nodded. "Are you aware you have latent abilities?"

"No. That's not possible..."

"It is and you do. You're a year or two past when we would normally have someone join, but you're still well within the window to draw out your potential. That is, if you accept."

Ryan swallowed. "I don't know what to say."

" 'Yes' would be a good reply."

Train in telekinesis? That was never a future I'd considered. "I'll need to think about it."

"For what it's worth, you'd be in the same cohort as Raena and Jason," Wil added.

That would be fun until Raena decided that she wasn't really interested in me and moves on to someone else. Ryan took a step back. "I can't make a decision right now."

"Of course," Wil yielded. "Take a couple days to mull it over."

"Thank you, my lord."

Wil smiled. "Please, the honorifics aren't necessary. First name is fine."

"I couldn't!"

"I'm sure you can find a way to adapt." The heir looked him over again. "You're quite an anomaly. How someone with your ability came to be in your position..."

"I don't remember my life before this," Ryan murmured.

"Well, regardless of if you want to join us in the TSS, I'd like to find out some more about your family. Do I have your permission to go through your file?"

"You don't need my permission to access it."

"It's common courtesy to ask," Wil replied.

Ryan nodded. "Sure. If you find anything interesting, let me know. It'd be nice to know where I was from."

"Deal. And please do consider the offer."

"Yes, my— I will."

"Good." Wil took a step in the direction he'd been heading before the near-collision. "Oh, and if your supervisor asks where you were all night, you can tell them I had a project for you."

Dumbfounded, Ryan resumed his dash back to the servants' quarters. *Join the TSS as an Agent? Have a chance to spend more time with Raena... This can't all be real.*

He took the familiar, plain interior corridor to the stairway that led into the basement beneath the mansion. He'd spent his youth getting to know every inch of the hill on which the Sietinen estate was constructed and the underground development that was a fully functioning city unto itself. Like the other staff for day-to-day administration, food preparation, and maintenance, he lived onsite in subterranean quarters. Though many of the estate's operations were automated or handled robotically, Tararian culture dictated a living person's touch for many activities, so people like him had a long history of employment. He often wondered, however, if that cultural norm of being served a meal by a person rather than an android was instituted as a means of job preservation on a broad scale rather than a genuine preference.

Unlike the marble floors and airy breezeways on the surface, the worker levels underground were cast in polished concrete with utilitarian amenities. Ryan raced down the stairs and glanced at the holographic reader board of the day's tasks as he entered the quartered housing for technical staff. Four maintenance requests had already come in and he should have claimed one of them. *Shite, they'll be checking in on me soon.*

He raced toward his quarters to take a quick shower and change. Unfortunately, he needed to pass by the common room to get there. Being 07:00, a number of people were gathered at the long bench tables for breakfast.

"Where were you last night?" Sophie called out from the nearest table.

She's the last person I wanted to see this morning. "I received a time-sensitive assignment late last night."

"Don't lie to me."

Ryan turned away and continued down the hall. "I'm not doing this here."

"You can't keep avoiding me!" Sophie jogged after him. "It can't keep going like this."

"There was never anything to get going in the first place."

Her glare bored into the back of his head. "So the last four months were nothing?"

"I told you I wasn't interested in anything formal. I was very upfront with that." He reached the door and palmed open the lock.

"I thought you were just saying that…"

Ryan stepped into his room. "I'm sorry if you feel otherwise, but this was always just a casual thing. I never considered you my girlfriend."

Sophie crossed her arms. "There's someone else, isn't there?"

There wasn't until last night. "I value your friendship, but clearly you're wanting something that's never going to happen between us."

"I thought you liked me."

Stars! I do not have the mental space for this drama right now. Then again, it'd been drama from the beginning. The entire arrangement had been a mistake he was too slow to admit. "I do like you and care about you. We're just at different places right now, and I think it's better we go our separate ways so you can find the deeper relationship you're looking for."

She stared at him with wide, pleading eyes. "But—"

"I'm sorry, Sophie." He started to close the door. "Take some time to calm down and we can maybe talk later. Now, I need to get ready."

"Ryan, please…"

"Sorry." Ryan closed and locked the door before she could

say anything else. Taylor had tried to warn him about her, but he hadn't listened. He hated feeling like he'd hurt her, but he'd been as clear as possible with his intentions and couldn't control her turning it into something inside her head that it wasn't in reality.

He rubbed his eyes and took several deep breaths to clear his head. Dealing with an obsessive ex-non-girlfriend was the lowest item on his priority list for the moment.

Ryan set about getting ready for the day as quickly as possible. Drama aside, life must go on. The future path, though, just might be headed toward an interesting detour.

— — —

Stars! When I set them up, I didn't think they'd spend the whole night together, Wil thought as he parted from Ryan and resumed his walk toward the breakfast patio.

The revelation did confirm that there was something genuine between them, however. Raena wasn't the sort to fool around with someone, so she must have seen potential for something significant. All the same, he could tell from Ryan's demeanor that nothing too serious had transpired overnight—at least not on a physical level. Wil had bigger things to worry about than two teenagers making out on a couch.

Still, maintaining a sufficient level of objectivity was easier said than done. On a conscious level, he was well aware that he'd been even younger than Raena when he first met Saera in the TSS. He also knew that experiencing a connection with someone was far from an enduring commitment and the could-be romance might go nowhere. All the same, he found a conflict brewing within himself as parental protectiveness faced off against a desire for his children to find happiness and fulfillment in their own lives.

If this guy is going to have a relationship with my daughter, the least I can do is figure out who he is. Based on the little Wil knew so far, Ryan was more than he appeared to be.

CHAPTER 15

THE PREVIOUS NIGHT seemed like a dream in the light of day. From the bizarre party to the new potential romance, Raena wasn't sure what to make of all the events. *This new life might be even more different than I imagined.*

She showered and dressed for the day, selecting a breezy skirt and tank top that seemed well-suited to the temperate climate. While she was braiding her hair, she received a text message from her mother directing her to a patio one floor down where the rest of the family was gathering for breakfast.

Raena finished styling her hair and then proceeded into the main residential corridor. No one else was around, but the hall was filled with sunlight streaming in through windows in the cut-outs leading to shared terrace spaces at various points along the walkway. Sounds of singing birds carried on the breeze through open windows, and she drank in the peace of the place as she strolled toward the staircase. With the new day, anything seemed possible.

Her family was already seated around a large, rectangular wooden table on a covered patio beneath one of the terraces on the upper level. Cris and Kate were on the far side of the table reading text projected from their handhelds resting on the tabletop, and her parents were sitting quietly across from them, absorbed in their own thoughts. Jason had apparently just arrived, settling into a chair next to Kate.

"Good morning," Cris greeted, minimizing the text on his handheld. "How did you sleep?"

"Pretty well," Raena replied, figuring it best to leave out the part about staying up half the night and spending the remaining time curled up on the couch with Ryan.

"You survived the party," Saera said with a smile. "It should all be easy going from here."

Now I have new complications to worry about. Raena took a seat next to her brother. "It wasn't that bad, thanks to all of you."

Kate minimized the text from her handheld, as well, shaking her head. "I still can't believe they're so intimidated by us even after all this time. One look and they run the other direction."

"In all fairness, your dagger-eyes can bring even the most battle-hardened Agent to their knees," Cris quipped.

Kate swatted him playfully. "You know what I mean. That line between those with abilities and those without is still as firm as ever."

"The irony being that almost everyone in that room was from an active genetic line," Wil commented. "In another generation or two they'll be the ones with the active abilities."

"Hopefully, a lot will have changed by then," Cris murmured.

In the silence that followed, Raena scoped out the breakfast spread. Two pitchers of juice were at the center of the table—one orange and the other red—surrounded by a bowl of fruit and several baskets of baked goods.

Raena stared at the pile of pastries on her mother's plate. "Mom! A little hungry?"

"They're *really* good," Saera said with a slight flush to her cheeks.

"Uh huh." Raena grabbed one for herself, finding it warm and soft in her fingertips. She set it on her plate and pulled off a small section of the flaky dough. The moment it touched her tongue, she flashed her mom a sheepish look. "All right, I get it."

Saera made a flourish of vindication with her hand and then resumed eating.

"So, Dad," Jason said, grabbing some breakfast for himself,

"a lot of people last night were talking about you like you're some sort of legend."

Wil inched back in his chair and looked down. "People say a lot of things."

Cris and Kate exchanged glances. "He's being modest," Cris said. "He's quite accomplished."

"I did what I needed to do," Wil muttered.

"Then it's true—about the independent jump drive?" Raena asked. "Whatever that is."

"It's an incredibly significant invention," her mother cut in. "Your father cracked a code that no one else had been able to."

"He was just about your age," Cris continued. "The official design was finished shortly before he graduated from the TSS."

"I can't imagine graduating at sixteen," Jason commented.

Wil nodded. "It feels like that was forever ago."

"What *is* the independent jump drive?" Raena asked.

"It's a navigation system," Saera explained. "Sort of like the equivalent of going from a dial-up modem to having access to satellite internet in the middle of nowhere."

"Well, it's a little more complex than that…" Wil said.

"How's it work?" Raena questioned.

"After you've had about two years of navigation theory classes, we'll get into that," her father replied with a smile. "And believe me, there's no way around it—navigation is the family business. You're going to learn more about it than you ever wanted to know."

"Right now, that sounds awesome," Raena replied with a grin.

Cris eased back in his chair. "Oh, just wait."

"I've always been partial to flying, myself," her father said.

"Oh, yeah, that's *way* better," Cris agreed.

Jason straightened in his chair. "And we can really start lessons when we get back to Headquarters?"

"Absolutely," Wil said. "Many students have had at least preliminary flight training before coming to the TSS."

"Wait," Raena said, "you wouldn't let us learn to drive a car but you're totally okay with us flying crazy-fast fighters in space?"

Wil smiled. "First of all, it was an irrelevant skill with the prevalence of self-driving cars. But the more compelling reason I resisted is because it's much easier to learn maneuvering in three dimensions first and then go back to the two-dimensional perception needs of driving a car."

"I can vouch for that," Saera added. "The speed and maneuvering are completely different. There are some bad habits to break from driver's ed. Then again, I was learning back before automated travel took over."

Raena grinned at her brother. "I can deal with flight lessons first."

"Definitely on board," he agreed.

"Okay, so navigation systems study and flight lessons..." Raena began, "and then I imagine we have all sorts of remedial information to go over regarding culture beyond Earth."

Her mother nodded. "Not to mention telekinesis training."

Raena perked up. "When do we get started with *that*?"

"Sooner the better, actually," Wil replied.

"My abilities came on rather suddenly, too," Cris stated. "When I joined the TSS, I entered into an apprenticeship to get caught up to a Junior Agent cohort."

"Will we do that, too?" Jason asked.

"Well, there were some extenuating circumstances," Cris clarified. "Extreme stress can trigger abilities beyond the expected level."

Raena tilted her head. "What happened?"

Her grandfather hesitated. "The Priesthood tried to kill me, and I fought back."

"What?" Jason exclaimed, eyes wide with alarm.

"That was the first time I ever 'stopped time', which is essentially creating a spatial disruption that lets you move faster than the rest of the physical world," Cris explained.

"Whoa! Will we get to learn that?" Raena asked.

Cris nodded. "You'll have the best possible teachers. Members of the Primus Elite group of officers your father trained—they have some of the highest CRs on record."

Wil glared at him from across the table. "They were a talented group to begin with."

"Even still, they exceeded their potential estimates by half a point," Cris shot back.

"A product of being around someone with your magnitude of ability," Kate added. "We can only imagine what you'll be able to achieve, Raena and Jason."

Jason looked over at their father. "You mentioned the high score before, but I'm still confused about what it really means."

As he folded his hands on the tabletop, Cris leaned forward. "The actual measures don't really matter. The only thing you need to understand for now is that abilities have a very strong genetic component, so we are quite anxious to see what you two can do."

Raena looked at her father. "Given your ties to the TSS and all this here on Tararia, I'm surprised you ever settled on Earth."

"Well, some things happened in the interim," he replied after a moment.

"He should really be the one commanding the TSS, not me," Cris said. "In fact—"

"That's enough," Wil interjected with bite in his tone.

What was that about? Raena glanced at her brother. "What don't you want us to know?"

Wil rose from the table. "Sorry, I need to look into some things." He stormed off.

Cris let out a slow breath and leaned back in his chair.

"Did I say something wrong?" Raena asked hesitantly.

"No," her mother assured her. "There are some old memories that have been raised over the last several days. It's nothing for you to worry about."

"They deserve to know," Cris stated.

A hum of energy registered in Raena's mind, and she perceived something silently pass between Saera and Cris. *Are they having a telepathic conversation?*

After a moment, Saera grabbed one of the pastries from her plate and took a large bite, seemingly on the losing side of whatever discussion had just transpired.

"What's going on?" Jason asked.

Didn't he just see that? Maybe Irina was right about me, Raena realized as it became clear that her brother wasn't yet attuned to the use of abilities in their presence.

"Your father's role in the TSS before is more than just standard service, but I'll give him the chance to tell you himself," Cris replied. "If he doesn't soon, though, I will, because I don't want you to get misinformation from others. It's one of those matters where there are some rather polarized opinions."

Raena and Jason exchanged glances.

"It's nothing to worry about," Saera went on. "Enjoy yourselves here."

This must have something to do with the war people have mentioned. If Dad was in command of the TSS, does that mean he was leading that fight? Raena spooned some fruit onto her plate and poured a glass of the red-colored juice, which reminded her a bit of a cranberry flavor.

Conversation was sparse for the rest of the meal, but with the promise of some time by the pool and a picnic lunch in the garden, whatever dark truth they were keeping from her was soon at the back of her mind.

—   —   —

No matter how hard he tried to move on and forget, Wil's past kept coming up to haunt him. *They don't know what the war did to me.*

Walking away from the breakfast table would only delay the inevitable, but it was the only thing Wil could do in that moment. Ever since Raena and Jason's abilities emerged, he knew that his role in the war would come up and he'd need to tell them about the Bakzen and everything he'd been through.

However, to hear over and over from others that he was a hero and had done great things stabbed at the dark stain on his conscience that he'd tried so hard to lock away. The walls around his guilt frayed with every mention of him being a savior and selfless leader. His vanquishing of the Bakzen may have been necessary, but the choices he'd made along the way made him far from a selfless hero. He didn't know how much longer he could maintain the front of innocence. Then again, admitting what he'd done might destroy everything in his life that now sustained him.

Either way, something had to give.

I need a distraction. Wil took a curved stairway from the ground level up to the guest wing. An investigation into Ryan's background might be just the project he needed to suppress thoughts of his own past.

With his mind made up, Wil located a private work room on his handheld and set a reservation. He followed the map to the office and unlocked it with his ID chip.

The space contained everything he'd need for his investigation—a desk with integrated holodisplay, encrypted work console for secure remote access to the TSS Mainframe, and a window of the garden to help pass the time while he waited for the results of the analysis.

He sat down in the swivel chair behind the desk and logged into the computer using his dynastic ID credentials, then augmented the rights with his TSS security clearance. Anything accessible without manual hacking would come up in the results, and if something was still sealed it could only mean that the Priesthood's highest order was directly involved, as he feared.

All right, Ryan, let's see who you are. Wil used the display to navigate through the personnel files until he located Ryan's. He configured a comparative analysis for Ryan's genetic records against profiles in the central archive to look for his parents.

Digging into a person's genetic legacy was a strange way to get to know someone. Part of Wil hated that he was reducing Ryan to his basic past like that and would use it to pass judgment, but there was no other way to determine his origins. *Why does it even matter? It shouldn't.*

Yet, it did. The Priesthood had driven them all to evaluate their genetic lines as a commodity more than a measure of family. Bloodlines determined a person's worth in society and could dictate their future path. It was counter to everything he'd been taught within the culture of the TSS—that a person's position was earned after starting from an equal footing. Some people had natural advantages of intelligence or other aptitude; there was no way around that. All the same, everyone could find some area where they could excel when given the chance.

When the Priesthood was involved, though, there was never

that opportunity for someone to find their own place. Destiny was determined generations ahead and some fates were unavoidable. Perhaps Ryan was just a naturally Gifted individual born into humble beginnings, but far more likely his future had been manipulated behind the scenes just like Wil's. That gave them an automatic sense of kinship, but Wil was determined to keep a detached perspective until he knew what the Priesthood might be after through this latest project.

Wil initiated the search and then spun around in the chair to gaze out the window along the back wall looking over the gardens and forested hills beyond. Long shadows still stretched over the landscape under the morning sun.

Despite the massive volume of data in the archive, the analysis shouldn't take long to complete. The search algorithm was set to only access plausible matches and run a matching sequence on those, greatly reducing the processing requirements.

Wil idly spun around in the chair while he waited. The initial scan of public records completed after three minutes, but there were no matches. *That's odd.* The search automatically dove deeper, accessing the sealed adoption records and other files in the individual worlds. Unfortunately, that information was far more disaggregated and the system would need to run a full analysis on each file rather than relying strictly on the metadata of the central public files.

This might take a while. Wil was about to leave the office and find somewhere else to hide out for the rest of the morning while the analysis concluded, but there was a buzz at the door.

He activated a video feed for the camera outside and saw his father standing in the hall.

"Come in," Wil said and released the lock via the desktop.

Cris swung open the door and immediately focused on the analysis running on the holodisplay. "What are you working on?"

"Trying to figure out who someone is."

"That sounds like a strategy to avoid confronting yourself," his father replied as he settled into a padded chair across from the desk.

"That was my intention." Wil swiveled to face out the window.

"Wil, the war is too big of a historic event for you to pretend like it didn't happen. Do you want them to read about you being Supreme Commander in a history book or tell them yourself?"

"Whatever they hear about the war won't be the truth. Everything I documented was buried under the Priesthood's propaganda."

"That's all the more reason they should hear it from you," Cris urged.

"But what could I tell them? The 'war hero' story is a lie and we both know it. I was forced to lead a genocide. There's no way for me to spin that in a way that is both truthful and doesn't make me look awful."

"You tell them that you were a military commander and you did your duty."

Wil spun the chair around to face his father. "And that doing so left me completely broken. What about that part?"

"It's been almost twenty years since then."

"Sometimes it feels like it was just last week." Wil glanced up at the genetic analysis still processing. "The Bakzen have been gone for a long time, but the war was never over."

"We're getting close. We might have our fourth vote."

"It'd be so much better if it were unanimous."

"Still, four is all we technically need," Cris said. "Besides, Raena seems to be a natural. She might be able to win over the rest."

"She does have a knack for getting her way," Wil agreed. "Is that who you think I should name?"

"Well, she's certainly demonstrated interest and aptitude, so that's a good sign. Do you think Jason is a better fit?"

"No. He takes after you, no offense."

Cris laughed. "None taken. I'd avoid anything having to do with politics and negotiations if I had any choice in the matter. It sounds like you have your decision."

"I suppose, but I want to hold off on an announcement until I've seen how they act once they're in the TSS."

"Sounds like a plan."

"In the meantime, there's this mystery to solve." Wil pointed to the projection of the analysis still processing above the desktop.

"Your mystery person, yes," Cris said. "Who is it?"

"His name is Ryan Pernelli—the maintenance tech I mentioned last night who appeared to have a resonance connection with Raena," Wil explained.

"Ah, yes."

"I wanted to make sure I didn't misread the situation when they bumped into each other, so I arranged for him to go work on her broken viewscreen."

Cris raised an eyebrow. "By which you mean you broke it?"

"Just a little light software recoding. But anyway, it sounds like he was over there all night."

"So, it's genuine."

"Yes. But is it natural or nanotech? That's what I'm trying to figure out now." Wil sighed. "And, apparently, his background isn't straightforward, because there was no genetic match in the public records. A Ward with a sealed file is pretty unusual."

Cris frowned. "That it is. Add in the strong telekinetic potential and that has the Priesthood written all over it."

"That's my concern. Is he friend or foe?"

"Hopefully, the analysis yields some answers soon," his father said. "While you're waiting, though, why don't you talk to your kids? If you won't, then I will."

"Do what you need to do," Wil replied.

"We'll be in the conference room next to where we had breakfast, if you want to come," his father said as he stood up. "You'll feel better after it's over."

"I'll think about it."

Cris strode out of the room and closed the door behind him. Wil massaged his eyes with his fingertips and leaned back in the desk chair. For every secret revealed, two new ones took its place. *I need to face my past eventually. We need a clear path forward.*

— — —

Cris found the twins still on the breakfast patio with Saera and Kate. They all seemed to be in good spirits despite the abrupt end to the conversation earlier.

"Is Dad okay?" Raena asked.

"He'll be fine," Cris replied. "It's time we talk about some things, though."

"Did Wil give you the go-ahead?" Saera asked privately.

"I told him I was going to and he didn't object."

Saera's frown indicated that she wasn't entirely pleased with his decision but she made no further comment.

"Let's go somewhere more private," Cris said, leading the twins and Saera to the nearby conference room he'd identified for the conversation.

The room was designed for visiting diplomats to have a secure place to make highly confidential offworld calls. Sound isolated and with retractable interior shutters, no one could see or hear what went on inside.

Cris activated the privacy mode for the room as he stepped inside, which caused the shutters to deploy. "Sorry for the theatrics," he commented, "but this is sensitive information. Please don't repeat what we discuss here, even to each other when you're alone. We can safely talk in broad terms once back at Headquarters, but around here it's hard to know who to trust."

Raena and Jason nodded their understanding.

Cris elected to stand rather than sit at the round six-person table in the center of the room. He clasped his hands behind his back and began to pace in front of the shuttered window. "Our family hasn't exactly had it easy," he began. "Holding influence and power often puts one at the center of plans, and we were no exception."

The twins and Saera took seats at the table facing him.

"Several hundred years ago, the Priesthood began genetic experimentations. They wanted to make a new, evolved race with stronger telekinetic abilities than had ever been harnessed before. This plan was twofold. The first component was to engineer a new line, called the Bakzen. The second was to introduce nanotech into the general population that would supposedly enhance everyone's abilities—"

The door chirped, indicating that someone was about to enter. A moment later, Wil stepped into the room.

"I decided that if you were going to talk about me it may as well not be behind my back," he said and took a seat at the table with his family. "Sorry to interrupt."

"Not at all," Cris said. "You can make sure I get this right. As I was saying, the nanotech was supposed to enhance everyone's abilities. And it did, temporarily. However, the side effect was a phenomenon we still experience today: the Twelve Generation Cycle. Seven generations with no abilities, followed by five with— the strongest expression being 10th Generation."

"So, that's why Corine doesn't have abilities, even though Michael and Elise are Agents," Raena said.

"Exactly," Saera confirmed.

"Meanwhile," Cris continued, "there was the other engineered race, the Bakzen. As people realized that their own abilities were fading, the Bakzen became villainized and ostracized. Eventually, they were driven from all the Taran worlds."

"The Priesthood tried to pretend like the whole thing never happened," Wil interjected, "and that the Generation Cycle had always been how things were. They control all the media and official data archives, so once they decide to propagate a certain message, it becomes complete and binding."

Cris nodded. "To that end, the Priesthood decided to make people forget abilities were once commonplace—it was the only way they could cover up their monumental mistake. They launched an anti-telekinesis campaign that resulted in most people hiding their abilities. Still, the Priesthood knew that the Bakzen were out there and could potentially pose a threat. To hedge their bets, the Priesthood secretly ordered the creation of the TSS—an organization to train people in weaponized telekinesis so they could fight the Bakzen if it ever came to it."

"But first, the Priesthood tried to eliminate the Bakzen completely," Wil added. "They sent a bomb to the planet where the Bakzen had taken up residence. Except, the Bakzen used their abilities to disable it. They told the Priesthood to leave them alone, but such a powerful organization wouldn't be bullied— especially not by its own creation. So, they declared war."

"*The* war," Saera clarified. "Any other conflict in the past two thousand years doesn't begin to compare with the duration and scope. Except, the Priesthood made sure to keep the war a secret."

"How could they keep it quiet?" Jason asked. "If it was so large-scale—"

"Because it didn't take place on this dimensional plane," Cris went on. "The Bakzen tore a hole between space and subspace— the Rift."

"And they stayed within the Rift, growing stronger and plotting their revenge against their Taran creators," Wil said. "When they finally made their first strike, the Priesthood immediately knew they needed a way to fight back. They began manipulating the bloodlines of those least affected by the nanotech that caused the Generation Cycle—a process of selectively pairing to create a new line with enhanced abilities just like their enemy, only one that evolved naturally rather than being created directly in a lab. The result of those efforts was known as the Cadicle, a term borrowed from theological texts." Wil couldn't meet their gazes. "That person is me."

Raena and Jason inhaled sharply. They looked at each other, processing.

"That's why your abilities are so much stronger?" Raena asked, breaking the silence.

"Yes," Wil confirmed. "And that's why the Priesthood manipulated our lives behind the scenes to make sure we ended up in the TSS. They made sure my parents would meet and that I'd be born into a life of service to the TSS. When I was fourteen, the Bakzen broke into Headquarters and captured me—with the help of a traitor. I made it back home, but that's when I learned about the secret war that had been going on for almost five hundred years without any of us knowing. There was a whole division of the TSS operating independently in the Rift. Finding out about the war and my future part in it changed the entire tone of my existence. My mandate was the complete destruction of the Bakzen."

Jason's jaw dropped open in horror. "And you found this out at fourteen?"

"Yeah." Wil stared down at the tabletop.

"I can't imagine hearing that... Not then or ever," Raena murmured. "How did you keep going?"

"Things were really rough for a while," Wil said. "I met your mom about a year later. She's the main reason I made it through." He fell silent again.

"The ensuing years were tough on all of us," Cris jumped in when it appeared Wil wasn't going to continue. "Our time in the war was on the horizon. After graduating to Agent, your dad spent the next three years working on the independent jump drive design—a piece of technology we needed to allow more precise maneuvering in the space battles spanning between the Rift and normal space. When that was done, it came time to train a group of officers to assist him with battle tactics. This team was the Primus Elites, some of whom I believe you've met."

"So, they're your war buddies," Raena commented.

"It's more than that," Saera tried to explain. "Agents that work together extensively develop a bond that's a sort of telepathic connection. Those of us that trained together for the war are tied together—like you and Jason as siblings."

"There were only five years to train," Cris continued. "The war was dragging on and needed to end. At that time, your dad was sworn in as Supreme Commander of the TSS."

"I had my mandate to fulfill," Wil murmured, still staring at the tabletop. "Eliminate all of the Bakzen."

"The rest of us didn't know at the time that the Bakzen were of Taran origin," Cris explained. "But Wil did. He spared the rest of us that knowledge so we could do our jobs."

Raena's face drained. "No wonder you didn't want to talk about it."

"We lost a lot of really good people." Cris swallowed. "One of them was your namesake, Jason. Jason Banks—the former High Commander of the TSS."

"He was family to us," Saera added.

"Wow." Jason slumped back in his chair.

Raena looked around the table at the drawn faces. "You won the war. Then what?"

"Your father didn't want the command any longer, so I stepped up from my position as Lead Agent to High Commander after Banks died," Cris replied. "At that point, I eloquently told the Priesthood to fok off and we've been operating independently ever since."

"Wow." Raena released a slow breath. "That's a lot to go through."

"The entire experience left me pretty broken," Wil said. "It took me a long time to come back from it."

"Yeah, I can imagine," Raena murmured.

"There you have it," Cris said, forcing a smile. "That is all the madness you were born into. Hopefully, now you understand why we feel so strongly that the Priesthood needs to go."

"No kidding," Jason said. Raena nodded her agreement.

"Now, I highly advise some lounge time by the pool for the rest of the day. This was a way heavier conversation than anyone should endure while on vacation."

"I'm pretty sure this was more of a business trip than a vacation," Saera corrected. "At least, that's what my expense report will state."

"You do realize that we're still the ones paying the bills around the TSS these days?" Cris joked back.

Saera grinned. "It's not my name on the account." She rose from the table. "Okay, pool time!"

"Go on ahead," Wil said to the twins. "Saera and Dad, hang back for a minute."

—   —   —

As Wil had listened to his father and wife give their account of the war, he realized that so many crucial details were being left out. *They don't know… They really don't know what decisions I had to make in those months.*

He had to come clean. They had been through too much together for him to continue harboring his dark truth alone. He could never explain it to Raena and Jason—they hadn't been through a war so they'd never understand. But his father and wife—they were by his side. They had asked him so many times what had happened and why he'd withdrawn. *If they want today to be about truths, then I need to tell them.*

Wil waved his children out of the room.

"Okay, we'll see you out there," Raena said as she headed out of the door. "And, thanks for filling us in."

Cris smiled at them. "Of course. We'll see you out there soon."

As soon as the door was closed again, Cris turned his attention to his son. "What's up?"

"A long time ago, you asked me what had happened—what so suddenly changed in the middle of the war," Wil said.

Saera came to attention. "Yeah."

Wil took a slow breath. "I'm sure you had your theories."

"Well, you were forced to take out all of the Bakzen, knowing who they really were. That would mess up anyone," Cris replied.

"That was a part of it. A big part," Wil acknowledged, "but it wasn't what put me over the edge." He fell silent and stared at the floor, still not wanting to admit what he'd done aloud.

"What, then?" Cris pressed.

"I— I knew about the attack on Cambion before it happened." The words caught in Wil's throat.

Cris paled. He needed no reminder about to which planet Wil was referring. "How?" The cold of his tone caught Wil off guard.

"Tek told me."

Saera and Cris looked at each other with horror.

Wil knew what they were suddenly thinking, that he had been consorting with the enemy all along. "It was my only communication with the Bakzen before the final minutes of the war. He messaged me because he had Saera's shuttle in a weapons lock."

"Oh my god," Saera brought a hand to her mouth. "So, something really *did* happen that day."

Wil shook his head slowly. "Tek gave me a choice between you and the planet. He gave me two minutes to decide. I ran through both scenarios every way I could think of them... and I couldn't lose you, Saera. That would have been the end of the war right there. But Tek also made foking sure that every time I looked at you I would also see the burning remains of Cambion."

"Shite." Cris collapsed back in his chair. "I…"

"I realize it was a treasonous act," Wil said with surprising calm. "I should have turned myself in a long time ago."

Cris and Saera sat in silence for what felt like an eternity to Wil.

Just yell at me and hate me and get it over with. He folded his hands on the tabletop, prepared for any reaction.

"That explains a lot," Cris said at last.

"At the time, it had to be done. Sacrificing those lives meant winning the whole war," Wil went on. "Afterward, I felt like I wasn't worthy of living because of the atrocities I committed. The guilt festered and ate away at me until I couldn't take it anymore. That's why I left for those three months—I needed to see if I could still reconnect with myself. And I did, just enough. I put up walls around the dark truth and buried it. But these last few days hearing everyone talk about the past and seeing the Aesir again… I remembered and it was too much to lock away again."

Cris took a shaky breath. "I don't know what to say."

Saera continued to stare into space.

"Say *something*," Wil pleaded. "You should hate me for what I did."

"No." Cris shook his head. "You were put in an impossible position. From the very beginning, you were set up to destroy the Bakzen. It's unfair to judge you for collateral damage."

Wil stared at him in shock. "Collateral damage? It was four billion people!"

"It's a scale I still can't comprehend even after all these years," Cris replied. "But I came to terms with that loss a long time ago. As High Commander, I had to review a lot of reports after the war, and though Cambion's loss was tragic, if the TSS fleet had been sent in to try to counter the attack we never would have had the forces left we needed to storm the Bakzen homeworld. The decisive military actions you took saved more lives in the long run by ending the war so quickly."

How can he be so understanding? I let all those people die! "What I did was selfish."

"It was a calculated decision, just like all the others you had to make. If it hadn't been that world, the Bakzen would have taken another. You need to let it go, Wil."

He couldn't—not while Saera was still sitting in silence with her inner thoughts blocked to him. He tried to reach out to her but she kept up her mental guards. "I'm sorry," he said aloud.

"That was a tough time for all of us," she said eventually.

"We all did what we had to do," Cris said under his breath. Then louder, "We can't forget how we got in that position in the first place. There's another entity at the center of the conflict, and that's the Priesthood. They were behind everything—the creation of the Bakzen and the entire clean-up effort where we were the center of their plan. Giving in to guilt wasn't a productive path then and it's not the way ahead now. The Priesthood needs to be brought down. Now, finally, we're almost in a position to do just that."

"But what I did—" Wil protested.

"What you did allowed all of us to be sitting here today," Cris stated, resolute. "Those lives are on the Priesthood's hands."

As his father looked at him with the same loving admiration that he had for Wil's whole life, the guilt that had plagued him for so long finally began to dissipate.

Saera met his gaze, and he was relieved to see that there was understanding in her eyes. "We have the upper hand now. The Priesthood made us to vanquish Taran enemies, and that's exactly what we'll do."

CHAPTER 16

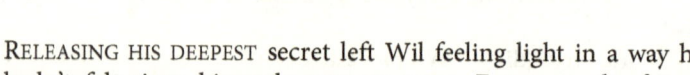

RELEASING HIS DEEPEST secret left Wil feeling light in a way he hadn't felt since his early teenage years. For once, the future possibilities were those of hope.

Saera remained reticent as they exited the conference room, but Wil could tell that she just needed some time to reprocess a highly emotional time from their past within the new context. There wasn't any of the hatred he'd feared she might feel toward him for having bartered her life in that way, but perhaps enough time had passed that such a visceral reaction was no longer possible.

For him, though, admitting his actions freed him of a weight that had been holding him back. He'd felt the anchor on him when he'd faced off against the Aesir, but he no longer perceived those restrictions. He'd been bred as a creature of war and he'd bring the war to the Priesthood's doorstep.

As much as he wished he could just storm their island and be done with it, he recognized that the Priesthood's tendrils ran far too deep to run headlong into anything. Further, the genetic analysis running in the conference room upstairs might unveil yet another layer to the Priesthood's plans that had gone unnoticed until the night before.

With promises to join them later, Wil sent his father and wife out to the pool with the twins while he returned to the conference room to check on the results of the analysis.

When he entered the room, the holographic representation of the scan had ceased and 'Match Found' was displayed in white script. The search had gone all the way into the most secured files, only afforded access by Wil's equivalent of High Commander credentials.

He stared at the results, mouth agape. *How is this possible?* Somehow, Ryan's lineage was far more intriguing than Wil could ever have imagined. What to do with the information was another matter.

He telepathically reached out to his father's consciousness. *"Dad, the pool will have to wait. Meet me in the western wing. You need to see this."*

— — —

I'm totally foked. Ryan wrung his hands as he took the final stretch of a servant passage toward the administrative wing of the Sietinen estate. There was no way he'd still be employed by the end of the impending conversation. He couldn't think of an alternative outcome from being called into a meeting with two dynastic heirs. The message from Wil was cryptic enough to leave Ryan open to speculation and all his thoughts were dire. *He must have changed his mind about me spending time with Raena. I can forget about that offer to join the TSS. I'll probably be shipped off to a prison planet!*

He took a deep breath as he swung open the door at the end of the corridor, careful to check the internal monitor for any passersby after his last collision with Raena. *I guess I'll never see her again.* The thought jabbed at his heart more than he anticipated.

The hidden passage opened directly across the hall from the destination office in the western wing. Through the open door, Ryan could see Wil and Cris seated at a small conference table in the center of the room. They spotted him after a moment and beckoned him inside.

"My lords." Ryan bobbed his head as he entered the room,

figuring he should at least keep up appearances.

An electric tingle passed through the air and the door swung shut behind Ryan.

He jumped with surprise. *Telekinesis?*

Cris smiled. "I stopped following the rules a long time ago."

Ryan took half a step backward, confused. *That isn't the demeanor of someone who's about to rip me to shreds for spending the night with his granddaughter.*

"You're not in trouble," Wil stated, seeming to almost read his mind.

He probably did, actually, Ryan realized. He swallowed hard. "How may I be of service, my lords?"

"No more honorifics," Wil replied. "Ryan… please, join us at the table."

Hesitantly, Ryan stepped forward and took the chair closest to the door. The two Sietinens exchanged glances as he sat down.

Wil cleared his throat. "Ryan, what do you know of your birth mother?"

"As I said before, my l— As I said before, she turned me over as a Ward when I was six years old. I don't really know anything about her. She didn't work, as far as I can recall, and spent time playing with me. I don't know why she gave me up."

"And your father?" Cris asked.

Ryan shook his head. "Never knew him."

Wil nodded. "We did."

Ryan's heart leaped. "What?"

"When I looked into your official file, it was pretty clearly a forgery—knowing what to look for," Wil explained. "So, I decided to run a manual genetic evaluation to see if I could figure out who you actually are. The results were… Well, they change things."

"Who was my father?" Ryan asked, his gaze flitting between the two men.

"He was the former High Commander of the TSS," Cris said. "My mentor, Jason Banks. At least, that's the name I knew him by. Apparently, like me, that was an assumed identity, too. He was actually the younger brother of the Head of the Bankris Dynasty, in the Second Region."

Ryan's mouth went dry. "I'm... I'm from a dynasty?" he stammered at last.

"Yes," Wil confirmed. "But that's only part of it."

My father was High Commander of the TSS? He couldn't begin to comprehend the implications of that revelation. "What else?"

"Have you ever heard of the Dainetris Dynasty?" Cris asked.

"We're not supposed to talk about the Fallen Dynasty," Ryan hastily replied.

"This room is secure, don't worry," Cris assured him. "So, you know it by reputation?"

Ryan inched back in his chair. "Only that it was once a seventh High Dynasty, but it fell many generations ago."

Cris nodded. "Yes, it was. And do you know what the 'fall' of a dynasty is?"

"Loss of power and influence?" Ryan ventured.

"Yes," replied Wil, "but there's more to it than that. It's the forcible removal from power, really. But Taran law is written in such a way that an entire family can't just be disowned. The Corporations are private—the most anyone could do is encourage people not to buy from them anymore. However, the corporations operated by the High Dynasties are so integral to society that cutting one off is impossible."

"Then how did the Dynasty fall?" asked Ryan.

Wil smiled. "That's the real question, isn't it? Truth is, we have no idea. All records of the event have been wiped from the official historical logs. As far as we can tell, the only way to really unseat one of the High Dynasties is by eliminating their chance of inheritance. No heir, no means to perpetuate the power."

"Then it's a matter of distributing assets. What's now the ship manufacturing division of SiNavTech was actually absorbed from Dainetris after its fall," Cris continued. "Several other components of the Dainetris' corporation, Dainetris Galactic Enterprises—or DGE—were divided up among the other High Dynasties. That's the protocol when there's no heir."

"Okay..." Ryan said slowly. "Why does any of that matter?"

"Well, what do you think would happen if there actually was an heir?" Wil asked, looking him over.

Ryan shrugged. "Generations later? It'd be hard to prove."

"Hypothetically, if it was proven, what would happen to the original assets?" pressed Cris.

"I don't know," Ryan responded after a moment. "If the assets had been absorbed into the other Dynasties for generations, it would be difficult to tell the market value of those components and break it out."

"Yes, it would be extremely difficult," Cris agreed. "Either they'd have to turn over the operational units or make a best guess determination at the current market value and arrive at a cash sales settlement. It's only one of those two options, since based on Taran law, the original asset distribution would have been in violation of inheritance rules."

Ryan eyed the two Sietinens across the table. "Does this have something to do with my father's inheritance?"

"Not exactly." Wil leaned forward and folded his hands on the tabletop. "Ryan, against all odds, it appears that you're a lost heir to the Dainetris Dynasty."

Time seemed to stand still in the room. Ryan's mind was blank—his entire sense of self temporarily shattered. *That's not possible!* He shook his head. "There must be some mistake."

"No mistake," Cris said, producing a handheld from his inner pocket. He brought up a genetic analysis on the screen, curiously not using the holographic projection.

Ryan looked over the results. He knew next to nothing about genetics, but the report seemed to indicate a match with absolute certainty. "I don't understand."

"We're still trying to piece it together," Wil admitted. "When Raena ran into you, I immediately identified that you had abilities. I figured you were probably handed over as a Ward when your parents realized you'd be Gifted, but this—I didn't see this coming."

"I'm just a servant…" Ryan murmured.

"Not anymore," Cris said, looking him in the eye. "I won't pretend like I have a plan because I don't have one—yet. We'll work through this development, though. You're inexplicably the son of one of my best friends. He was like a father to me—way more than my own here. You can be assured I'll look after you from now on like you're my own."

Wil nodded. "Given this news, I hope you'll accept the offer to come to the TSS. It's the safest place you can be while we sort this out."

Ryan's mouth still felt dry. "Yes, I'll come."

"Good." Wil glanced at his father before returning his attention to Ryan. "It goes without saying that this needs to be kept very need-to-know at this point. I know it will be difficult, but you can't tell any of your friends here. Right now, only the three of us know. We'll tell our wives and the twins, but that's it."

"I understand." Ryan expected to wake up any moment and find that it was all just a joke. *I can't really be a dynastic heir... can I?*

"I think the next steps are to talk with your mother," Wil continued. "She might know more than she let on with you."

"I haven't seen her since she gave me up."

"We'll find her," Cris said. "But even when we do, she can't know about this, either. Not until we can vet her."

Ryan nodded. "She abandoned me. I have no allegiance to her."

"This isn't about picking sides," Cris countered. "At least not among family. The Priesthood is another matter."

"Let's take it one step at a time," Wil cut in. "I think we've overwhelmed him enough."

Ryan swallowed hard. "I don't even want to know."

"Yeah, we'll get to that later," Wil said with a reassuring smile. "Take some time to process this. We'll get you moved up into guest quarters for the rest of the time until we go back to TSS Headquarters. Tell your friends whatever seems best—that you're preparing to join the TSS and are no longer employed. Just nothing about Dainetris."

"All right." Ryan still felt shaky.

In a daze, he wandered back down to the worker levels beneath the manor, possibly for the last time. *Is this really happening?* As he looked around at the familiar faces in the halls and common room, he suddenly felt like an outsider in a place that had been his home for almost his whole life.

He reached his door and palmed it open. The tiny space also

seemed strange from his new vantage. He had so many questions about how he'd ended up there he didn't know where to begin.

Ryan left the door ajar as he began packing some of his favorite clothes and his minimal personal items. If any of his friends happened to walk by, he wanted the chance to let them know he was going so they didn't hear it through the gossip chain. *What do I tell them?* he pondered. *They probably won't believe me no matter what I say. I can hardly believe any of it myself.*

There were few passersby in the hall at the mid-afternoon hour, so he was almost done packing by the time anyone more connected than a casual acquaintance wandered by. The first was Tony, another service tech with specialization in interior climate control systems.

"Hey," Tony said, poking his head through the open doorway. "Uh, are you packing?"

The voice caught Ryan by surprise, pulling him from his thoughts. "Yeah, I'm heading upstairs."

Tony leaned against the doorframe. "Promotion?"

"Not exactly." Ryan secured the clasps on his bag. "I'm joining the TSS."

His friend laughed. "Are you serious?'

"I was just invited to train as an Agent."

"They're inviting anyone to join now? I thought you had to have abilities for that."

"Apparently I do," Ryan replied.

Tony crossed his arms. "Oh. Um… Congratulations?"

"Yeah, I think it will be good," Ryan said. "It hasn't really sunk in yet."

"And in the meantime you get to hang around upstairs? Lucky you."

Ryan shrugged. "Cris and Wil are actually pretty friendly and easygoing."

His friend's eyes widened. "Now you're on a first name basis with them? Stars, that was fast!"

"I was just differentiating—" Ryan tried to explain.

"What trouble are you getting into now, Tony?" Sophie said from out in the hallway, beyond Ryan's view.

Of course she'd pick now to come by. Ryan slung his bag over his shoulder, poising for a quick exit.

"Not me this time," Tony replied to her. "Apparently, our friend here is joining the TSS."

Running footsteps sounded in the hall and the door to Ryan's room flew open the rest of the way.

"You're doing *what*?" Sophie demanded.

"I'm going to train as an Agent." Ryan decided to stay behind the bed as a buffer between himself and Sophie's wrath.

"You can't!" she exclaimed.

Ryan looked for a path between his friends, but he was trapped. "I got an offer this morning. It's a chance to start a new life—maybe the only chance I'll ever get."

"I think you're crazy to get involved with the TSS," Tony said, "but I hear where you're coming from. I'd probably go, too."

"But what about all of us here…?" Sophie stammered.

"It's not like I'm dying. We can stay in touch," Ryan replied. *Not that I'll be able to tell them what's really going on.*

Sophie spotted the bag on Ryan's shoulder. "When are you leaving?"

"I'm heading upstairs until they go back to Headquarters. It'll be a few more days, I think."

She scoffed. "Just like that, you go from being one of us to one of them?"

"Let's be honest, Sophie," Tony said as he stepped back out into the hall. "Ryan always considered himself above us. Just look at how he treated you."

"No, I—" Ryan protested.

"Enjoy your new life." Tony stomped down the hall.

Sophie hung back for a moment longer. "It won't be the same here without you."

"I'll miss all of you," Ryan told her. "And I'm sorry things didn't work out with us the way you hoped."

"Yeah, well, I'm used to that." Sophie retreated into the hall. "Goodbye, Ryan."

He stood in silence taking in his room one last time. For years, the three meter by three meter space had represented his whole world. To have his existence redefined as a dynastic heir and TSS Agent changed his sense of identity at the deepest level.

With nothing left for him down below, he strolled slowly through the halls up to the guest wing of the mansion. As he passed by the other servants, he gave them a parting nod and smile that they'd only understand after they heard the news through Tony or Sophie.

Unfortunately, by then the message would have twisted into a story of Ryan ditching his worthless underlings the first chance he got. That's how it always went when someone received an opportunity beyond the servitude they were born into or assigned at a young age as a Ward. For those that remained trapped, it was easier to pretend like someone had always been an outsider rather than wonder why they had been chosen over another. Ryan had done the same thing himself a dozen times in the past. Being on the receiving side this time hurt, but he understood.

As he stepped out from the servant halls into the guest wing, the reality of the changes in his life finally started to set in. *I'm a guest here now—I'm not at work. Eventually I'll be the 'sir' and 'my lord'.* He froze in the middle of the hall, overwhelmed by the magnitude of that upcoming transformation.

"Ryan?" a voice called him from his trance.

He turned to see Raena down the hall, wearing a mesh cover-up over a bikini. Her hair was wet and sunglasses set atop her head.

"Back already?" she asked.

"Your dad hasn't talked to you?"

She shook her head. "About what? I've been at the pool."

He searched for words. "Stars! Where to start." Then, he remembered Wil and Cris' warning about not sharing his lineage out in the open. "There's too much to go into right now or here. But I will be joining you at the TSS."

Raena's face lit up. "That's great!"

"And I'll be training as an Agent."

Her excitement turned to surprise. "You have abilities, too?"

"I had no idea," he admitted. "I guess your parents picked up on it right away."

"Is that what we felt, then, when we first met?"

"We both know it was more than just that."

She nodded. "All right. Well, I guess we do get to see where this can go."

Ryan resisted a sudden urge to kiss her right there in the middle of the hall. "I supposedly have a room up here now, until we leave later this week."

Raena smiled. "Good, then I'll see you soon. I need to go change now, though." She pointed toward her room.

"Yeah, see you."

He shook his head with disbelief as she disappeared into her room. Someone who the night before had been completely unattainable was now an ideal match under his new name. He kept waiting for someone to jump out and tell him it'd all been an elaborate prank at his expense, but an announcement never came. *I need to figure out who I am.*

CHAPTER 17

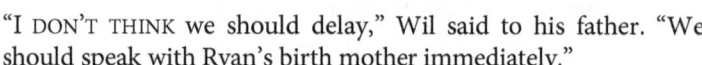

"I DON'T THINK we should delay," Wil said to his father. "We should speak with Ryan's birth mother immediately."

Cris examined the profile for the woman, Marie Pernelli. "How did Banks find her?"

"Maybe she knows. Or she might have information," Wil urged. *A secret Dainetris heir… I never would have guessed.*

"All right," Cris agreed. "Get Ryan. I'll arrange transport."

Wil proceeded to the guest wing. He pressed the buzzer on Ryan's door.

The teenager answered, still wearing his servant clothes. "Hi."

"We're taking a trip into town," Wil stated. "To speak with your mother."

Ryan's face flushed. "I have nothing to say to her."

"It's important that you set aside bitterness about the past so we can get some answers. There's no one else in a better position to answer questions about your lineage than her."

"Can't you go without me?" Ryan asked.

"We could, but I think it'd be valuable for you to come. For a number of reasons."

"All right." Ryan's reluctance was audible.

"But first," Wil said, looking over Ryan's gray servant uniform, "why don't you change into something more fitting for your new position. Do you have any street clothes?"

"Oh, right." Ryan looked down at himself. "I'd meant to change. Just a minute." He ran to the bedroom.

Wil waited in the hall, his mind wandering to what they might find out from Marie. *Did Banks have an arrangement with her, or was it an affair?*

Ryan emerged from his bedroom dressed in black pants and a blue form-fitted, long-sleeve shirt that could pass for any social standing depending on the context.

"Perfect, let's go," Wil said and led the way to the front entrance of the mansion.

Cris was waiting for them with a surface transport car, its doors spread open to either side to allow easy access to the middle passenger cabin.

"Thank you for joining us on short notice," Cris said. "I know confronting past issues with one's parents can be difficult."

"I barely remember my mother," Ryan replied. "I doubt she'll even recognize me."

"We'll see." Wil gestured to the car and they climbed in.

Cris tapped the console at the center of the passenger area to enter their destination. The doors automatically closed and the car autonomously began driving into town, accelerating after it left the stretch of gardens closest to the estate. It wove down the hillside into town.

"I figured we'd fly," Ryan commented.

"It's faster, yes," Cris said, "but much more conspicuous. There's no need to draw attention to our visit."

They rode the rest of the way in silence as the terrain changed from forest to swank, single-family homes on the hills surrounding the city, and eventually to the urban center. The tinted windows on the car allowed them to gaze out without fear of recognition from the people on the streets.

The car fell in line with the other automated vehicles on the roadway, eventually arriving at a block of mid-rise quartered housing in a working-class sector on the outskirts of town. When it reached the back side of a roundabout at the terminus of a dead-end street, the car pulled off into a parking area and powered down. The doors parted.

"Her unit is just up here," Cris said, consulting his handheld.

The three of them took stairs up to the second floor. The entrances all had identical dark green doors inset in the whitewashed building façade, only differentiated by a unit number on the upper right of each door.

"This is it," Cris said, stopping in front of unit 2734. He scanned his handheld over the door, which brought up Marie's picture and name.

Wil pressed the buzzer.

"Identify yourself," a woman's voice said over the intercom.

"Marie, we're friends of Jason Banks," Wil stated. "We're here regarding your son."

"My…" The intercom clicked off and the door unlatched. It swung inward a crack. "Who are you?" Marie asked through the slit.

"We're with the TSS," Wil stated, opting to keep the Sietinen Dynasty out of matters for the time being. "And Ryan is with us." He beckoned the teenager over to stand in front of the opening.

Marie's breath caught when he stepped into view. Tears welled in her eyes, and she opened the door the rest of the way. "I never thought I'd see you again."

"Why did you give me up?" Ryan demanded.

She shook her head. "It wasn't my choice."

"Why don't we talk inside?" Cris suggested.

Marie stepped back from the door, allowing them to enter.

The compact residence was only designed for one or two inhabitants, so Wil and Cris had to step into the living area as soon as they were through the door. Ryan hung back in the kitchen next to the door with his mother as she continued to stare at him with wonder.

"Look at you, all grown…" she murmured, brushing her fingertips over the side of his face.

He pulled back from her touch. "Why did you give me up?"

Marie's hands fell to her sides. "The terms of my agreement with your father were very clear. He gave me all the money I'd need to care for you and I'd get the child I always wanted. What neither of us counted on was the Priesthood getting involved."

"That figures," Wil said under his breath.

"Start at the beginning," Cris requested.

"Well, I was working as a nanny, living at the time in a building similar to this one," Marie explained. "One day, Jason showed up looking for my mother. He said he was a childhood friend. She had died when I was young, so we got to talking and, apparently, both of us had wanted a child but had never had the means. We came to an agreement: two million credits, and he'd provide everything else I'd need. He spent a week with me before going back to the TSS."

"Did you have any contact after that?" Cris asked.

"No. When he left, he said he wouldn't be able to make contact until Ryan was grown. Once he was old enough, I was supposed to give him that holopainting." She pointed to the image of a red flower.

Wil walked over to the framed holopainting sitting on the end table next to the couch. Nothing stood out about the image. He picked it up and searched around its frame. In the back, he found a tiny memory chip.

"Probably instructions," Wil said, indicating the chip to his father.

"You know Ryan's father was Jason Banks," Cris said, "but the name on his birth certification doesn't match."

Marie nodded and sank onto the couch. "Yes, the official father stated on Ryan's birth certification is a forgery. Jason insisted. I wasn't in a position to argue—I still got my son."

"He wanted the baby to remain as hidden as possible?" Wil suggested.

"Given his position within the TSS, if the Priesthood was watching he couldn't have his involvement known," Cris agreed.

Wil sat down on the couch opposite Marie. "All right, so you had the resources you needed and got the child you always wanted. When did things change?"

"Well, everything was great at first. With the money from Jason, I was able to move into a nice two-bedroom apartment in a better neighborhood, and I quit my job so I could care for him full-time." She stared at her hands. "Then, when he was six, representatives from the Priesthood came. They said that Ryan was Gifted and he'd need to be closely monitored so he wouldn't hurt himself or others."

"Abilities don't emerge until the teenage years," Wil pointed out.

"I'd heard that, too," Marie replied, "but they insisted it was what was best for him. I didn't want to give him up, but I wanted him to have the best life. They said I'd be able to visit him every weekend. Before I'd had time to think it through, they took him away."

"Did they tell you where they took him?" questioned Cris.

Marie shook her head. "And the weekend visitations never came. I tried to get in touch, and they pretended like Ryan had never existed. I spent all the remaining money trying to find him. I even reached out to Jason at the TSS for help, even though he'd told me not to, but I wasn't able to get in touch."

Cris eased into the chair across from Marie. "I'm sorry to tell you, but Jason died many years ago in the line of duty. Based on Ryan's birthdate, it was only a few months after he met you."

Marie's face drained. "He died?"

"He was a good man," Wil said. "He gave his life protecting us."

"That's why he never got back to me…" she trailed off.

"We never knew he had a child," Cris explained. "We would have helped you, had we known."

She wiped a tear from her eye. "I had a child with forged parental credentials—there was nothing anyone could have done."

"I ended up a Ward with the Sietinen Dynasty," Ryan said. "I haven't ever talked with the Priesthood, as far as I know."

Marie suddenly looked at Cris and Wil with fresh eyes. "Stars! You're…" She dropped her head. "My lords, there was something familiar about you, but—"

"We're here now as TSS Agents and friends of Jason," Cris told her.

Wil nodded. "We'll take good care of your son."

"I'm joining the TSS with them," Ryan said.

"Just like your father." Marie gazed at him lovingly. "I'm so glad you found me so now I know you're safe."

"I'm afraid this has to be a one-time visit for now," Wil said. *We need to keep a low profile. As it is, the Priesthood may already know we're here.*

"While you're training, of course," Marie acknowledged.

Maybe we can bring her into the fold later, but not until we're ready to make our move. Wil grabbed the holopainting of the red flower so he could extract the memory chip—not larger than the head of a pin. He yanked it out telekinetically and placed it in the slot on the side of his handheld. "We'll give you a few minutes to yourselves."

"I'll be right out," Ryan said.

—   —   —

Standing alone in his mother's presence, Ryan had no idea what to say.

"I still can't believe you're here after all this time," Marie murmured.

Ryan took a deep breath and let it out slowly. "I know you were just trying to do what was best for me."

"Can you ever forgive me for letting you go?"

"I don't even know what to say to that," Ryan said, leaning against the entryway wall. "I barely remember you. Growing up as a Ward was the only life I knew."

His mother reached out and took his left hand. "That's not what I wanted for you."

"Things don't always go the way we hope."

"No, they don't."

"Not everything unexpected is bad, though." *Raena and the TSS... This is a new start.*

Marie nodded. "You seem happy."

"I've had ups and downs, but I'm hopeful now."

"Then I guess everything worked out okay."

There are still so many unknowns. "Look... Mom," the title felt strange to say, "I'd like to get to know you, but the next few years are going to be... strange."

Marie tilted her head. "What do you mean?"

"I can't get into it. I think I'm going to be okay, though."

She released his hand and crossed her arms. "The Sietinens have always been kind. If you're in their favor, then I'm sure you'll be just fine."

"You should lay low, okay?" Ryan cautioned her.

"Me? I've always kept to myself."

"Good. Just… be careful." He paused. "I don't want to lose you now."

Marie smiled, stepping forward to embrace him. "I'm not going anywhere."

He savored her warm embrace as it brought back buried memories from his youth. He'd loved her more than anything else, and she him.

She released him and looked into his eyes. "I want you to have something."

"What?"

Marie walked over to the end table by the couch and picked up the holopainting of the flower. "My mother gave this to me, and now I'd like to give it to you." She came back over to him, hand outstretched with the painting.

He took it from her. "Thank you."

She embraced him again. "I've never stopped loving you."

Ryan's chest constricted. "I'll come back and see you when I can."

"I'll be waiting."

—   —   —

Cris and Wil paced on the front breezeway while they waited for Ryan.

Meeting the mother of Banks' son had affected Cris more deeply than he anticipated. For the entire time he'd been friends with Banks, he'd never known him to have many personal attachments. To realize that Banks had been on the cusp of having a family—something that had brought Cris such fulfillment in his own life—made his sudden death that much more poignant.

"I feel guilty keeping Ryan apart from his mother like this," Wil said telepathically, pulling Cris from his thoughts.

"Me too, but it'll be safer for both of them this way."

"Do you think the Priesthood is watching us here?" Wil

pondered.

Cris shrugged. *"Maybe. Probably. But if they were going to hurt Marie or Ryan, they would have done it already."*

"What do you think they're after?"

"A High Dynasty bloodline is valuable—especially when the people don't even know their own worth. But maybe Banks figured out something we don't know yet. We'll look at the recording as soon as we're back in a secure room."

Wil nodded his agreement.

After several minutes, Ryan exited from the apartment, looking like he might break down in tears at any moment. He carried the holopainting of the red flower.

Wil placed a reassuring hand on his shoulder. "You'll be able to see her again later, if you want to."

Ryan nodded. "I think I'd like that."

"Good." Wil headed toward the exit. "Now, let's go find out what your dad had to say."

Cris sat in quiet contemplation on the car ride home. Whatever information Banks had been hiding would likely change their understanding of the Priesthood's motives. That had the potential to help them in their mission to bring down the organization, but there was also the chance it would uncover an even darker truth—something Cris wasn't sure he was ready to know.

Despite his apprehension, Cris practically leaped out of the car as soon as they pulled up at the Sietinen estate. "Conference room," he said to Wil.

"You can join us," Wil offered Ryan.

"I don't think I can take any more revelations at the moment," Ryan replied. "If it's okay, I just need some time alone."

"Of course," Wil acknowledged. "We'll pass on whatever we learn later, if there's anything relevant."

Cris rushed inside to the conference room where they had met earlier in the day. The exterior shutters were still closed.

Wil sealed the door then placed his handheld on the conference table to access the memory chip. Only a single data packet appeared to be on the chip.

"What breadcrumb did he leave…?" Cris mused and tapped on the holographic representation of the file.

Words illuminated in midair: >>Find Cristoph Sietinen.<<

Cris glanced at Wil and then back at the message. "Subtle."

"Is there more?" Wil asked.

Cris dug into the file. "Looks like there's an encryption here. A combination of TSS login credentials and Dynastic ID." He entered in his information and the screen morphed into a display of genetic profiles.

"Stars!" Wil breathed. "This is it. This is the key to breaking the Generation Cycle. That's what he meant."

"What?"

"Raena," Wil clarified. "Rather, Banks left me a message, encouraging me to have a daughter. He knew about Ryan and the Sietinen-Dainetris match."

"And you think this combination will do it—break the Cycle?"

Wil let out a slow breath. "They're only 11th Generation so we won't know for sure, but based on this and what the Aesir told me, I think there's a chance."

Banks, you really did spend too much time with the Priesthood if you were devious enough to mastermind this. Cris returned his attention to the files and noticed that there was another file separate from the genetic profiles. He opened it. "These are instructions. I think it's referencing those encrypted files on the Mainframe that I was never able to crack."

"It must be the information about Ryan," Wil suggested.

"Must be." Sure enough, the key to the encryption was Ryan's genetic code—a combination no one would be able to guess.

Wil smiled faintly. "He knew we'd know what to do."

Cris' mouth felt dry. "I checked the timestamps on the sealed files on the Mainframe. He locked them within minutes of his death. This message here was for Ryan to find, but the rest was a last-second act of desperation. He entrusted us with his legacy."

"We'll make him proud."

— — —

Feeling sleepy after a day in the sun and with an hour to kill before dinner, Raena wandered into the common room adjacent to the guest wing. Across the room, she spotted Ryan standing by the window.

"I didn't expect you back already," she called out to him.

"There wasn't a lot to discuss there," he replied, not turning from the window. "Your father and grandfather got a key to some files, but I had little to say to my mother."

"I'm sorry to hear that," Raena murmured. She walked up next to him at the window. "I thought maybe you'd have a chance to talk to her about why she gave you up."

"We did," Ryan replied. "It just wasn't a very satisfactory explanation."

"What did she say?"

"The Priesthood told her I was 'Gifted' and needed to be monitored for my own good."

"It seems that the Priesthood is good at forcing people's hands."

Ryan turned to her, revealing reddened eyes. "But she let them take me!"

"My maternal grandmother was, apparently, faced with a similar choice."

Ryan returned his attention to the lake in the distance. "My life doesn't feel like my own."

"I'm feeling pretty lost myself. Just a week ago I was on Earth without any knowledge of the Taran civilization."

"It's really surprising to me that your parents would keep your identities from you."

"They had their reasons."

"But what?" Ryan pressed.

"They said they wanted us to see what life was like for a normal person—no abilities, no social standing, no authority. Just a commonplace existence."

"Is living on Earth really a good analogy for the average Taran citizen?"

Raena shrugged. "Based on what I've seen so far, doubtfully. However, I've also come to realize that my parents are very well-known. I don't think they could have gone to any Taran world without being recognized. Earth was probably the only place where they could assume an identity and give my brother and me any chance at the normal childhood they wanted us to have."

Ryan scowled. "I think normalcy is overrated."

"Says the secret heir," Raena shot back with a smirk. "My mom pulled me aside and filled me in while you were away."

"Okay, fair enough. But I was raised without any knowledge of that ancestry."

"As was I," Raena pointed out. "We do have that in common."

He was silent for several moments. "I can't help but wonder how it would be—two people from our backgrounds in positions of absolute power."

"I don't feel remotely ready to be any kind of leader."

"You have a presence," he replied. "I've seen how others look at you. You're a natural."

"Yeah, right," she laughed.

"That combined with your humility—maybe that's what your parents were trying to cultivate. I think that's the kind of leader Tarans needs now."

Raena stared down at the gardens below. "I dunno. Maybe."

Ryan inched closer to her. "Just remember, you're not the only one trying to figure out your place in all this craziness. We can help each other out."

"Thank you." She took his hand. "I'm glad we're in this together."

"Yeah, I guess we are."

"Hey," Raena said, "do you have dinner plans yet?"

"Huh, I guess I hadn't thought about that part. I moved to a room up here, but I guess I won't be eating down in the servants' mess hall anymore..."

"Come with us," Raena suggested.

"Really? That wouldn't be strange?"

"Sure, why not? It'll just be my parents and grandparents tonight."

Ryan was silent as he considered the offer. "I'd be honored to join you."

Raena smiled. "Good."

They waited in the common room for fifty minutes, exchanging small-talk and getting to know each other better. Raena was glad for the chance to hear more about Ryan's experience on Tararia as a child, which gave her insight into the culture that she wouldn't see otherwise. Hearing about the stark contrast between workers and the ruling elite, she once again realized what her parents had done by raising her and her brother on Earth where such distinctions were blurred. She found herself wondering if she'd even have given Ryan a chance had she grown up on Tararia—instead seeing him only as a servant rather than having an open mind and heart.

Ten minutes before the scheduled dinnertime, Wil and Saera walked past the common room on their way from their quarters. They spotted Ryan and Raena.

"I imagine Raena already invited you to dinner?" Wil asked Ryan.

"She did, if you don't mind," he replied.

"We wouldn't have it any other way," Saera said. "We're on our way down now."

Raena gave Ryan a reassuring nod and they followed her parents to a dining room on the lower level overlooking the garden.

Cris and Kate were already seated at the table when the group arrived.

"It looks like we have an extra joining us," Kate commented.

"So we do." Cris waved his hand and the two chairs on one side along the long end of the table spread apart to allow room for a third, and the extra glided across the floor into place.

Raena stared at him, mouth agape.

"Oh, right... We're not supposed to use telekinesis around here. Don't tell anyone." He flashed a devious grin and beckoned for them to join him and his wife at the table.

As Raena sat down at the ornate wooden table on the alien world in a house that looked like it was out of a fantasy book, she realized that she was surrounded by loved ones. Even on that foreign world, that made her feel right at home.

CHAPTER 18

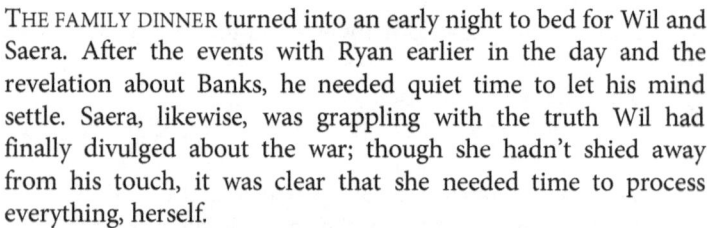

THE FAMILY DINNER turned into an early night to bed for Wil and Saera. After the events with Ryan earlier in the day and the revelation about Banks, he needed quiet time to let his mind settle. Saera, likewise, was grappling with the truth Wil had finally divulged about the war; though she hadn't shied away from his touch, it was clear that she needed time to process everything, herself.

Wil drifted off to sleep for three hours, but then he was roused from his slumber.

Something isn't right. He bolted upright in bed.

"Is everything okay?" Saera asked, propping up on her elbows next to him.

"No. Don't you feel it?"

She lay still for a moment. "You're right. There's someone here."

They jumped out of bed, quickly dressing. Wil only slipped on a pair of pants before running into the living room. He grabbed a show sword from above the fireplace.

"That's useless compared to telekinesis," Saera commented from the bedroom doorway as she pulled her shirt on.

"But it makes for great intimidation factor," Wil replied.

He rushed toward the door, sword still in hand.

"What's your plan?" his wife asked.

"We need to get everyone secure until we identify the intruder."

Wil telekinetically swung open the main door to the hallway and peered out into the dim light. No one was there yet—whoever was coming for them hadn't entered the wing.

"Get Jason, Raena, and Ryan and bring them to my grandparents' quarters. That will be the most secure place for now," he instructed.

Sounds of a door opening caused Wil to tense. He readied a telekinetic shield but relaxed when he saw his parents coming out from their bedroom.

His father evaluated him. "You felt it, too."

"There's definitely someone unknown with abilities nearby," Wil confirmed.

"Aesir?" Cris asked.

Wil shook his head. "It doesn't feel like them. I'm not sure what to think yet."

Saera and Kate ran to the twins' doors and pressed the buzzers, then Kate went down the hall to Ryan's.

Wil kept watch while they waited for the teenagers to groggily answer their doors.

"What's going on?" Raena asked, suppressing a yawn.

"We think there's an intruder," Wil replied. "Stay together and go to Reinen and Alana. We'll come get you there."

"Be careful," Saera told him and ushered the teenagers to follow Kate toward the main residential wing.

"The presence is coming from this way," Wil said to his father as he oriented toward the hall leading to the main entrance. "Their path should be safe deeper into the manor."

"Agreed. Let's go."

They set out at a jog toward the energy signature. The cool night air chilled Wil's bare chest and back, but he was too focused on pinpointing the intruder to notice.

"It must be the Priesthood," Cris suggested. *"We must have tipped them off when we went to see Marie."*

"If they're after Ryan, why wouldn't they just break in through the balcony?"

"The alarms blanket the upper levels. The only way in or out

without triggering the system is through select servant passageways," his father replied.

"Ah, yes. Of course you'd know that."

Wil stopped short when he detected the presence once again—much stronger than before. The intruder was close.

Cris nodded and pointed toward a darkened corridor. *"In there."*

"Pin him," Wil instructed. Simultaneously, he sent out a burst of energy to illuminate the hallway.

A figure dressed entirely in black and wearing a full face mask was being telekinetically pinned against the wall by his father, arms and legs spread.

"He's strong," Cris commented, not close to straining from what Wil could tell, but holding the individual immobile was taking sufficient mental resources.

"I'll take him," Wil said. He pinned the black-clad figure even harder against the wall, causing an old portrait painting to crash to the floor in its gold frame. He telekinetically yanked off the intruder's mask, revealing the face of a young man with glowing red-brown eyes.

"Who are you?" Wil questioned aloud while he also sent telepathic spears into the intruder's mind.

Though gifted with strong abilities compared to most, the intruder was powerless to resist Wil's commands. "The Priesthood sent me."

Of course. "Why?" Wil demanded.

Sweat beaded on the intruder's brow. "Your daughter, Raena. She is the one they want."

Wil tightened the telekinetic restraints. "What about her?"

"The bloodline. Her abilities. She is the key," the man stammered.

"What were you sent here to do?"

"Take her." The man gasped for air as the vise tightened around his chest. He shuddered, the telepathic spikes sliced deeper into his mind the more he resisted telling the truth. "Kill anyone else who resisted. But not the boy. Not Ryan. He— they need him, too."

Wil evaluated the man's ruined mind. His resistance had

destroyed him. He panted in Wil's suspended grasp.

I can't let him report anything back to the Priesthood. Without hesitation, Wil drove one final, deadly spear into the man's mind and released his telekinetic hold over him. The lifeless body crumpled to the floor.

"Wil!" Cris cried out. "Why did you...?"

"It was necessary." He was surprised to find he didn't feel any remorse. "They'd just send others. We need to send a message right back." *The Priesthood made me a killer—I'd managed to forget that for a while, but we're still at war.*

"I'm sorry you had to become this," Cris murmured.

"Better me than everyone else." Wil tossed the sword on the ground next to the body. "I'm surprised they only sent one person."

"He may have just been a scout. We're not safe here."

"No. We should all stay together for the rest of the night and then go back to Headquarters in the morning," Wil agreed.

"Why not just leave now?"

"We need the Priesthood to have time to realize their plan failed. We'll leave in broad daylight so there's no mistake that we're gone. It'll be safer for your parents that way."

Cris nodded. "Okay, let's go hole up for the night. My parents will be thrilled."

Wil kept a wary watch on their surroundings as they walked through the empty halls toward the main master suite in the mansion. *Was this planned all along, or did the Priesthood act because of our visit with Marie today? Do they want Raena and Ryan paired to break the Generation Cycle, or do they have some other plan?*

His father seemed to be absorbed in his own thoughts. Then, seemingly out of nowhere he asked, "Have you ever run a comparative genetic analysis between Raena and Jason?"

"No. Why would I have?"

"No, I guess not. But why would the Priesthood be interested in Raena and not Jason? In theory, they should have the same genetic markers."

Wil considered the proposition. "I suppose it's possible that there's a marker carried on the X that isn't on the Y."

Cris shook his head. "Think about it. The Priesthood was manipulating the dynastic bloodlines for generations. Certain families are known for having boys and others for girls. What if that family tradition originated through a mandate from the Priesthood so certain traits from each would be passed down?"

"And whatever 'key' the Priesthood is after rests with a Dainetris man and a Sietinen woman," Wil completed the thought for him silently.

"Exactly. They had to have known Banks visited Marie—no matter how well he covered his tracks. They probably would have found another suitable partner for her if it hadn't been him. Then, make the child a Ward where he'd be easy to track."

"Shite!" Wil breathed under his breath. *"Were they counting on us intervening? Was the plan all along for us to facilitate Raena and Ryan getting together?"*

"Have them in one place at the same time for them to come in and grab."

"But sending one person…" Wil shook his head. *"They know what I can do. No individual would stand a chance."*

Cris' face drained. *"Unless…"*

This was all a setup to get me to step away. Wil broke into a full-out sprint.

Shouts sounded from down the hall as they approached the residential wing. White smoke drifted through the hall, obscuring his vision. He felt his way through the whiteout telekinetically, searching for Saera.

He found her on the ground, stunned and just beginning to regain consciousness. He dropped to his knees next to her, helping her up. "What happened?"

Saera massaged her temples. "There was a flash. I—"

Wil shook his head. Few things could floor an Agent, but there was no way around the effects of a stun gun when caught by surprise. *This was all a setup. I should have known!*

Anger boiled within him, even before he sought confirmation for his suspicions. *Raena, Ryan…*

He rose to his feet as the smoke cleared. Jason and Kate were three meters away, both on their knees as their heads cleared. As he feared, the two other teenagers were nowhere in sight.

"Raena!" Saera screamed when she saw that her daughter was missing. She gripped Wil. "We have to find them!"

"We will," he assured her while running to his son. "Jason, are you okay?"

"I think so…" Jason rose to his feet.

Wil held out his hand to Kate and she took it to help herself up, legs still wobbly.

"How did they get in?" Cris questioned to no one in particular.

"I think there was a hidden TSD arch," Kate replied, finding her balance on her own. "I felt it just as I was losing consciousness."

Of course! What better way to enter when you can't walk in through the front door? Wil sent a telekinetic probe toward the walls, searching for a lingering energy signature from an arch. "They shouldn't even have that technology."

"It's on file with the TSS," Cris pointed out as he performed his own search.

A fair point, but Wil considered it an adulteration of the technology to use it for such underhanded means. Years of rage toward the Priesthood churned just beneath the surface— whispering for Wil to take action and seek revenge for old wrongs and this new assault on his family. He struggled to keep it in check.

"An arch could link to anywhere," he said, trying to stay focused.

"In theory, but there's only one place I can think of that they'd go," Cris replied.

"Their island." Wil found the signature he was looking for. "Here!"

The four Agents converged on the space he'd identified. At first glance, the wall appeared like any other of the carved relief murals around the halls, this one depicting a mountain scene over a lake. The carving was framed with a vine pattern. When Wil inspected the mural, he realized that the center segment had been replaced—and what appeared to be the vines was actually camouflaged framework of the arch.

What about the event horizon? This would be pulled through.

Wil tugged on the mural and it gave way, swinging outward to expose a shallow recess in the wall—just enough for someone to pass through.

"I'm going after them," Wil announced, only realizing after he'd spoken how impulsive that sounded as he stood shirtless and without even shoes.

"I want to go, too, but we need to be rational about this," Cris cautioned.

"What's there to rationalize? The Priesthood just kidnapped my daughter and the Dain... someone else of importance," he said for Jason's benefit. "Who knows *what* they have planned for them! I'm not about to sit around and find out."

Cris nodded. "I agree, but the intruder did say that they wouldn't be harmed."

"That same person also didn't know about the real attack, so I don't think we can regard that intel with any degree of certainty," Wil shot back. "Standing around here talking won't rescue them any faster." He began reaching out telekinetically toward the arch.

His father blocked him. "I can't allow you to walk into a trap."

Wil glared at him. "They can't stop me. I'll blow up their whole foking island!"

"While you could, yes, we have no way of knowing what's on the other side of that arch. You're no more immune to a stun gun than anyone if they catch you off-guard."

"I can be ready—" Wil insisted.

"And what about Raena and Ryan? They could easily get caught in the crossfire of a telekinetic battle." Cris shook his head. "No, it's too risky."

Saera stood with her arms crossed, glaring at the wall. "I'd run in there myself right after you, but Cris is right. It might be more dangerous for them if we follow right away. This operation was highly planned—if they intended to hurt them, they would have been dead in the hallway. We have at least a little time."

"So, what, we just ask the Priesthood to give them back?" Wil asked flippantly.

"Well, asking them what's going on is a logical place to

start," Kate said. "I know we're not on the friendliest terms, but this was a blatant assault on a High Dynasty."

"She's right," Cris agreed. "They can't expect that to stay quiet without opening a dialogue with us."

Wil stared at his father with disbelief. "You didn't just sit back and make a few vid calls when the Bakzen captured me! You expect me to—"

"What in the stars is going on?" Reinen bellowed from down the hall. He strode down the hall with Alana, both wearing dark blue silken robes.

"The Priesthood just declared all-out war," Wil stated levelly.

"What?" Reinen questioned, looking to Cris for confirmation.

"Operatives from the Priesthood broke in and captured Raena," Cris said. "Somehow they got a TSD arch in here."

Reinen eyed the hinged section of the wall. "This hallway was renovated two years ago, if I recall. But this…"

"So, they were planning this for at least two foking years." Wil ran his fingers through his hair. *It probably would be suicide to go through the arch after them. If Raena is the key, the rest of us are just obstacles in their way. None of us are safe.*

Then, Wil remembered that there had been someone else planning a move against the Priesthood since before he was born. "The files from Banks."

Cris came to attention. "There might be something we can use."

Reinen started to question them again, but Wil was already running toward the nearest secure conference room. *Please have the answers we need, Banks… And tell me my daughter is going to be okay.*

CHAPTER 19

WIL RACED TO the office he had been using for research. While not an ideal setup, the secure datalinks he'd established for the genetic analysis earlier would give them the connection they needed to access Banks' encrypted files without traveling back to Headquarters.

What was he hiding from us? Wil dashed into the room and activated the desktop.

"Stars! I feel like this is somehow my fault," Cris said as he followed him into the office.

Wil logged onto the system and reinitiated a connection with the TSS Mainframe. "It's the Priesthood's doing. We're all just players in their game."

"But what are they after?"

"Achieving their vision of the future," Wil replied. "And I think we're about to find out what that is."

The datalink established and Wil immediately set up an interface to unlock the file with the genetic code key. A series of locked files, indicated by red icons, appeared on the holographic display. The cipher began unlocking the files immediately, each icon turning from red to blue.

Wil glanced at his father. "This must be important if he went to such lengths."

"He was never one to take anything lightly."

When all of the icons were blue, Wil scanned over the list of newly revealed file names. One titled 'Summary' jumped out at him. *Looks like as good a place as any to start.* He swiped over the holographic representation to open the file.

Text illuminated on the projected screen. Though far from a comprehensive report, the summary was true to its name and highlighted the key points: the Priesthood had been keeping women with telekinetic abilities out of the TSS and had likely captured some of them for some unknown purpose.

Wil's stomach turned over as he read Banks' notes. There was no knowing how many more had disappeared since Banks' initial discovery two decades before. "What are we supposed to do with this information?"

"Stop the Priesthood, obviously," Cris replied.

"How do we retaliate when we don't even know what they're doing?"

"We'll figure something out. We always do."

Wil shook his head. "If I'd known what was in here, I could have tried to crack it manually years ago."

"I trusted Banks' instructions to wait until the time was right, same as you. And what could we have done before now?"

"I don't know, but I certainly wouldn't have brought Raena here had I realized that the Priesthood would go to these extremes!"

"And since Ryan wasn't in contact with his mother, we never would have found him," Cris pointed out.

No action exists in a vacuum. Taking a calming breath, Wil examined the files again. "We know the Priesthood has been watching the Dainetris bloodline and they took steps to curate the continuation of Sietinen through my match with Saera. Since they haven't taken any male prisoners—that we know of—until now, I'd wager that whatever would come from Raena and Ryan's pairing is near their endgame."

"They might be after the same solution to the Generation Cycle as the Aesir," Cris suggested.

"There's too much public benefit in that," Wil said, shaking his head. "No, whatever the Priesthood is trying to do it's for their own gain."

His father crossed his arms. "And knowing that, we can't let them proceed unchecked."

"No, we can't." Wil paused in thought. "Well, this research all points to the Priesthood's island. It's a fair bet that they won't move Raena and Ryan from there."

"That place is a fortress. I don't see a way to get in without it turning into a bloodbath."

"The Priesthood declared war the moment they broke in here and took my daughter," Wil stated. "A fight is exactly what they're going to get."

— — —

Light shone through Raena's eyelids. She snapped to, her eyes flying open to inspect her surroundings.

At first glance, she appeared to be in a medical exam room—bed in the center, on which she was laying, a light overhead, viewscreen on the wall behind her displaying vitals, and cabinetry along the side walls.

How did I get here? she wondered as she looked around the space. Then, the details of the attack came back to her. She had been running with her family and Ryan toward her grandparents' quarters, and a nearly invisible beam had rippled through the air from up ahead. Her mom and grandmother had immediately fallen to the ground. Someone wearing a mask dressed in all black had stepped out in front of her and... The rest was blank.

What happened to Ryan and Jason? And who would—

A door slid open in front of her, which had previously seemed like another smooth section of white wall. Two masked figures dressed in light gray robes stepped inside, followed by another in a black robe with a hood that obscured the individual's face.

Raena flinched as they approached her and she realized that her wrists and ankles were bound.

"Ah, you're awake," the black-robed figure said in a male voice.

"Where am I?' Raena demanded.

"You're safe in your new home," the man replied. "Don't struggle."

"This isn't my home!" she spat back. "Who are you?"

"You are now in the care of the Priesthood of the Cadicle," stated the man.

Raena's pulse spiked as she thought through everything she'd heard about the Priesthood in her short time away from Earth. They were a powerful political entity, but the notion of kidnapping someone—let alone a dynastic heir—seemed extreme. However, maybe her parents and grandparents hadn't told her everything.

She swallowed. "My parents will come for me."

"There's nothing they can do for you."

Raena fought against her restraints. "Let me go!"

"Be calm," the man in black said. "Don't harm yourself."

He grabbed a vial from the cabinet on the right and loaded it into a cylinder. He placed the device against her neck and she felt a slight prick followed by a cool tingle. While he stood next to her, she caught a glimpse of luminescent red eyes beneath the hood.

A sense of calm overcame Raena, quieting her mind as it numbed her hands and feet.

"Do you know Ryan Pernelli's origins?" the black-robed man asked.

Despite her instinct to resist, Raena was compelled to tell him everything she knew. "He's the lost heir to Dainetris. His father was the former TSS High Commander, Jason Banks—my brother's namesake."

"And who else knows this?" questioned the man.

"Just my parents and grandparents."

"Are you sure?"

"That's all I know," Raena replied. *You shouldn't be telling him this,* a voice in the back of her head tried to protest.

"What is your relationship with Ryan?" the man continued.

"I don't know," Raena said truthfully. "We cared about each other immediately, but it's still new."

"Have you had sexual relations with each other?"

The bluntness of the question shocked her even in her dazed

state. "No. We just kissed."

"Have you had any other sexual partners?"

Whoa, this isn't right, the voice in her head told her. This time, it was stronger. "No," she replied aloud. *I need to fight this.*

"Have you experienced any abilities?" the man asked.

I can't tell him. "No, my abilities haven't Awoken," she lied.

The man shook his head. "Be truthful, Raena. You must."

No! This is all I have. "A false alarm," she insisted. "They took us from Earth, but it was just a migraine. I don't have any abilities yet."

"Our tests say otherwise."

"The tests are wrong." *They can't prove it yet. My abilities might be the only thing that could get me out of here, if I could catch them by surprise.*

The man frowned under his hood. "I sense you are trying to deceive me."

"You're the one lying to me. I'm not safe here at all."

"Maybe we need to up the dose..." the black-robed man stepped toward the cabinet again.

"Your eminence, we won't be able to test her if she's under the influence anymore," said the gray-robed man on the left.

The leader stopped. "Yes, you're right. Testing them will be the easiest way to draw a definitive conclusion."

Them? "Who else do you have here?" Raena questioned.

"That's not your concern now."

"My brother? Ryan?" she pressed.

"Right now, you should be more concerned with yourself," the man said. "You have one chance to make this a comfortable experience." He stormed out of the room with the two others in tow.

Raena's heart raced. *What are they going to do to me? I have to escape!*

— — —

Ryan tested the restraints wrapped around his wrists. *I might be able to break it if I—*

A panel in the wall ahead of him slid open. Three figures stepped inside—one in a black robe and two robed in light gray. He immediately recognized them as associates of the Priesthood.

"Ryan Pernelli. Or, should I say Ryan Dainetris?" the figure in black asked.

Ryan glared at him. "The Priesthood has no right to manipulate people's lives like this!"

"On the contrary," the man replied, "so little would ever be accomplished without us. It's our duty to advance the Taran civilization."

"Not like this," Ryan shot back. "You can't just capture people in the middle of the night and expect them to cooperate."

"We don't need your cooperation. Whoever said we needed you conscious?"

Ryan hesitated. *Stars! Can they just drug us and do anything they please?*

The hint of a smile was visible beneath the shadow of the man's robe. "Now you're beginning to see your place."

"I'd rather die than help you."

"Oh, come now! That's not in the spirit of progress."

"You're sick."

The robed figure shook his head. "You're just as belligerent as her."

'Her'? Fok, no...! Do they have Raena? He swallowed his anger, knowing that lashing out at his captors wouldn't get him anywhere at the present. "What do you want with me?"

"You have quite the genetic legacy, you know," the Priest replied. "You can give us so much."

"And what's that?"

"Immortality." The Priest turned around and headed for the door. "Prepare him for the test."

"What are you—" Ryan convulsed as an electric shock passed through him, setting his nerves on fire. The world faded around him.

— — —

Wil expected his wife to be a little more enthusiastic about the plan he presented to her, but it did sound pretty simplistic when he said it aloud.

"You're just going to barge in?" Saera questioned from the couch in their guest quarters.

He continued pacing. "Go in with a team of the Elites, there's no way they could possibly have countermeasures. It's the best chance of getting them out quickly and unharmed."

Saera raised an eyebrow. "Couldn't possibly have countermeasures? This is the organization that made you and the Bakzen. I think they know a thing or two about telekinesis."

"I need to try, Saera. I won't let them use her."

"Neither will I, but we need to be smart about this. You're our best asset—getting yourself captured would be a major setback. For all we know, this is a trap to lure you in."

"That's possible, but—"

"You're approaching this like a father and not a strategist. I know because I'd rather be sobbing on the floor right now, but that would do nothing to help our daughter."

Wil sat down on the couch next to his wife. "So, what do we do?"

"You contact the High Priest and start making demands."

"That won't work."

"Of course not," Saera replied. "But if he's smart he'll at least take your call. And you can—"

"—pinpoint his location on the island, of course."

She smiled. "Now you're thinking."

"That gets us one person, though."

"But a very important person. I don't think we could realistically get to the lower levels of the island where any prisoners would be held, but his office might be somewhere more accessible. If you could apprehend him, we'd have leverage for a trade," Saera clarified.

"They've been working on these two genetic lines for generations—probably a thousand years. They're not going to trade those two people for one, regardless of how high up he is in the organization."

"But it will serve as a distraction and buy time."

Wil nodded. "And that might be enough."

"We'll get her back, Wil. Your family has a good record of beating the odds when it comes to this sort of thing."

"We do... But how are you not freaking out right now?" he asked her.

"Because I believe in her and us. Meltdowns and tantrums don't solve problems. We need to buckle down and act smart."

"You're right."

She took his hand. "I know you can do it because you've done it before." She paused. "We haven't talked about your big reveal."

His heart skipped a beat. "You mean about Cambion?"

She nodded. "I want to clear the air so we can focus on finding Raena."

"Saera, I—"

"You don't have to explain," she said. "I would have done the same thing for you."

"That doesn't excuse my actions."

"You did what was necessary in the moment to make sure you'd have a chance to address the real enemy."

"Yes, but..." ...*my internal motivations were far more selfish.*

"Wil," she swiveled to face him, "dwelling on your past actions now doesn't change anything. That was a tough time for all of us—you need to move past it. For good."

The Priesthood's corruption needs to be ended. That's what's important now. When his parents began laying the groundwork for a coup decades before, the actual methods of such an overthrow were only a vague idea. However, as the time for action neared, it was crucial that they not only had a clear tactical approach, but could also mitigate the Priesthood's countermeasures several steps in advance. The potential partnership of Raena and Ryan would provide the very leverage they needed—and the Priesthood probably knew it.

"All right, so we'll open a dialogue with the Priesthood. How do we know truth from fabrication?" Wil asked. "No one knows if the Priesthood possesses military power outside the TSS or how far-reaching their control stretches beyond the main organization. For all we know, one of the other High Dynasties is operating fully under the Priesthood's orders."

"Right now, none of that matters. This isn't about removing the Priesthood from power just yet—it's about gathering information."

Wil rose from the couch so he could resume pacing across the living room while he thought through the innumerable details that were still major unknowns. He massaged his eyes, trying to ease a growing headache. "We need to know what they're trying to achieve…"

Saera stood up and began to pace next to him. "Well, all of their original plans seem to revolve around physically augmenting current Tarans."

Wil nodded. "Really, we have no reason to believe those plans have changed. They tried one route and failed with the Bakzen. Then there was me—us."

"Do you think they started another genetic line?"

"Not out in the open," Wil mused. "But all of those disappearances… that was for something deliberate. It's too close to the other experimentations that we know about for us to ignore the potential implications."

Saera's face drained. "I was afraid of that."

"But the question is, what are they trying to accomplish? A new vessel for enhanced abilities… there has to be more to it than that."

"Maybe, or maybe not," Saera replied. "Thinking about all the selfish acts they've performed over the years—those that we know about, anyway—I wouldn't be surprised if all their plans were just extreme means of self-preservation. They've already shown that they'll stop at nothing to perpetuate their own existence. Regardless of how it may have started as a quest to better Tarans as a whole, now it's about the Priesthood making things better for themselves."

"My conclusion, as well."

Saera frowned. "But *what* would make things the best possible outcome for the Priesthood?"

"Absolute power," Wil suggested.

Saera frowned. "That's a bit nebulous."

"Whatever they're after, it must be a means to ensure their continued position of power. Something that would give them unquestioned authority over all others."

His wife stopped. "God-like powers."

Wil realized where she was going. "Abilities on a scale most have never witnessed. Like what I can do, but within their control."

"No wonder they wanted Raena," Saera said, slumping against the couch at the center of the room.

"I think we need to have that chat with the Priesthood."

CHAPTER 20

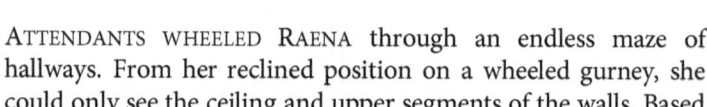

A{\scriptsize TTENDANTS} W{\scriptsize HEELED} R{\scriptsize AENA} through an endless maze of hallways. From her reclined position on a wheeled gurney, she could only see the ceiling and upper segments of the walls. Based on the lack of windows, her best guess was that they were underground—most likely beneath the Priesthood's island.

She still felt dazed from whatever drug they'd given her earlier, though it didn't seem to be as potent as the Priesthood thought. *My abilities are more advanced than they expect. How can I use that to break free?*

Of course, she'd never actually used her abilities and had no training on where to begin, but if her grandfather had been able to fight back against the Priesthood when his life was on the line, then maybe she could, too. She'd need to be perfect with her timing. With any luck, an opportunity would present itself.

Eventually, her gurney passed through a door with an electronic lock.

Something felt different in the new corridor—like there was a hum to the air. As she focused her senses, she realized that it was the same feeling as when she was surrounded by a group of Agents. *There are people with abilities nearby.*

Then, she saw them. Rooms with transparent walls lined either side of the hall, and inside each was a single woman. They varied from early-twenties to forties, but every one of them had the same blank expression of defeat and acceptance. Some of the women wandered in aimless circles around their cell and others lay back on the single bed in the small space. When Raena looked closer, she realized that most of the women had distinctly swollen bellies showing through their loose-fitting shirts.

Oh my god... They're all pregnant! Raena realized. Her heart pounded in her ears as the pieces began to fall into place. The Priesthood wasn't just interested in her genetic code, but the forced continuation of the line.

She fought the impulse to struggle against her restraints. If she was going to escape, she needed to pick the right moment—wasting strength now wouldn't get her free.

The attendants wheeled her into a room at the end of the hall, past at least three dozen women in their cells.

The destination was a rectangular room with two freestanding stations set up in the center of the space. Each station was equipped with a holographic display with placeholders for vital readouts. Above each station, a spotlight illuminated the floor.

Standing behind the equipment, three figures robed in black were accompanied by seven others wearing light gray robes. They stood in silence with their hands clasped in front, their faces hidden in shadow in the dim light beyond the bright spotlights.

Raena was wheeled under the spotlight on the left, facing toward the entry door with the ten robed figures out of sight behind her. She blinked in the bright white light shining down into her eyes.

As her eyes adjusted, she saw another gurney rolling into the room. After a moment, she realized that it held Ryan. He appeared to be unconscious. *So, I'm not alone... but what are they going to do to us?*

When Ryan's gurney was in place under the other spotlight, footsteps sounded at the back of the room, approaching Raena.

She turned her head to her right to see one of the black-robed figures pacing around the stations. He wasn't the same man who'd interrogated her before, as far as she could tell, but his face was obscured under his deep hood.

"Why are we here?" Raena asked him. "And who are you?"

"I am a High Priest, and you will be the mother of a new generation," he replied.

Yeah... no. Raena glared at him. "How about Option B—you let us go and forget about this little breeding program of yours?"

The man chuckled—an unnatural sound for his raspy voice. "Breeding? You misunderstand. We are the caretakers of the Taran genetic legacy. But what the Archive cannot provide, we seek through other means."

"Are you talking about the Genetic Archive?"

"Of course."

They never collected a sample from me for the Archive, and probably never got one from Ryan, either. "If that's what you're after, then take it and let us go."

"There's more to life than just two genetic donors coming together," the High Priest replied. "We need *you.*"

Raena's mouth dried. "What for?"

"We've tried artificial gestation, but the abilities of the offspring were never as powerful as those carried by a mother with Gifts."

Raena's stomach turned over. "You want me to have a baby for you."

"Oh, not just any child," the High Priest replied. "In only two more generations, we will have the template for a perfect vessel to give us eternal life."

A template? Raena's brow knit, trying to figure out what he meant. As she studied his face, she began to see a resemblance between him and one of the acolytes dressed in light gray that she had seen earlier. "You're clones, aren't you?"

"Ah, very good," the High Priest nodded. "You see, one person can only gain so much knowledge in a lifetime. To truly become an actualized self, we must perpetually study and grow."

"Are you talking about transferring consciousness to another body?" she asked. "Isn't that illegal?"

The High Priest's lips twisted into a sinister smile. "We couldn't allow such imperfection to perpetuate. For just anyone to live forever would destroy our civilization. We needed to be selective about who maintains the knowledge and power. Those deemed worthy are drawn into the Priesthood and made whole.

All others will die, and eventually we can reshape this civilization to fit our image—once we have the right vessel for our continuation."

Raena took a shaky breath. "If you're already cloning yourselves, then what do you need with me?" She glanced at Ryan, still unconscious on his gurney. "With us?"

"Our original attempts were flawed," the High Priest stated. "We knew we needed a new vessel. Your union holds the key—a new genetic line that will enable our continuation without degradation. The Bakzen were incomplete, and for generations their broken design is all that we've had. But with your progeny, we will finally have a purely Taran line with clean enough genetic code for endless replication. With such perfection will come true enlightenment."

"What makes a culture great is individual differences," Raena shot back.

"There can only be one expression of perfection. Any deviation is corruption."

Raena shook her head. "There's no such thing as 'perfection'! It's all subjective."

"Not to those who've had a thousand years to define their vision. The many forms I've taken have taught me what is needed and what is superfluous. Soon only the ideal will remain."

"And what will happen to everyone else?"

The High Priest's glowing red eyes focused on Raena. "They will live to serve their gods."

Yep, the Priesthood needs to go. She needed an escape plan, and fast.

"It's time to see what will come of this pairing," the High Priest continued. "Test their resonance."

Four of the people dressed in light gray stepped forward from their positions along the back wall, two flanking each gurney. The one to Raena's left swung out a support platform from the side of the gurney, which extended her left arm toward Ryan. The attendant on Ryan's right did likewise. Their fingertips were mere inches apart but too far to reach. She wished she could make physical contact with him and seek comfort, but she was powerless while he continued to lay unconscious on the gurney.

"What are you testing?" Raena asked.

"Your resonance connection. The nanotech you both carry will tell us everything we need to know about your genetic compatibility and potential of your pairing," the High Priest replied.

Suddenly, the light above their gurneys pulsed in rapid succession. Raena's blood momentarily felt like it was boiling. She cried out in pain but it was over in an instant. Next to her, Ryan's face contorted like he was also in pain, but his expression softened as soon as the pulsing stopped.

When the lights returned to normal, a holographic overlay appeared around Raena's and Ryan's bodies. Threads connected points between them, but Raena had no idea how to interpret the lines.

The High Priest studied the connections. "That's curious."

"Those gaps…" one of the acolytes began.

"There shouldn't be any." The High Priest frowned. "Run a complete analysis. We need to be sure."

The acolyte bowed his head and initiated a genetic analysis, which was depicted via the holographic projection in the open space above the two gurneys.

The attention of her captors around the room began to drift while the analysis ran in the background. It could be the opening she needed.

When is Ryan going to wake up? We need to communicate if we're going to get out of this. With talking out of the question, she hoped the little preview she'd been given of telepathy would be enough to help them coordinate. Drawing on the connection she felt with Ryan, she reached out to him, feeling his presence across the room. That connection would need to be enough to guide her.

She took a deep breath and tried to clear her mind of fear and uncertainty. She focused on Ryan's unconscious form.

"Wake up!" she implored him telepathically.

He twitched on his gurney but his eyes remained closed.

"Ryan, you have to wake up!" she shouted in his mind. *"We're in danger."*

This time, his eyes fluttered open. He tried to jump from the gurney when he caught sight of his surroundings but the restraints held him in place.

"*Stay calm. Focus,*" she told him. "*Are you okay?*"

No response.

She tried again, this time calling out to the invisible bond that connected them. "*I know you can hear me.*"

After a moment, he nodded.

Relief flooded through her. *That's a start!* She refocused her attention, thankful that the Priests were too distracted with their work to notice the telepathic exchange. "*Hold a thought in your mind. I'll try to pick it up.*"

There were only her own thoughts in the background at first, and then a message came forward. "*They're never going to let us go.*"

"*We have to break out,*" she replied.

"*How?*"

"*I need to catch them by surprise—try a telekinetic attack.*"

Ryan shook his head. "*We're hundreds of feet underground. There's no way out.*"

"*We have to try.*"

"*It's impossible, Raena. We need to hold on until someone comes for us.*"

"*There's one way,*" she told him. "*We need to stop time.*"

"*What are you talking about?*"

"*Controlled telekinetic spatial dislocation. My grandfather was able to do it without training. I might be able to do it, too.*"

He didn't respond at first. Then, "*That's a big gamble.*"

"*What other choice do we have?*"

"*We wait for—*"

"*For what?*" she cut in. "*For help that may never come? For them to 'breed' us, or whatever sick aim they're trying to accomplish. No. We're getting out of here.*"

Ryan smiled slightly, despite the grim circumstances. "*You know, I really like you, Raena.*"

Her heart warmed. "*Good, because I'm pretty fond of you, too. But you better start thinking in terms of 'must' rather than 'can't' or we'll never get the chance to see what's between us.*"

Before he could reply, the analysis displayed on the

holograph above them completed.

The High Priest frowned at the results. "This is not what we predicted," he said in Old Taran.

Raena came to attention. *They don't know I can understand them!*

Another one of the black-robed figures stepped forward, also speaking in Old Taran, "I told you that you should have taken him, as well."

"None of the models showed this scenario."

"That's why we must prepare for all contingencies."

The first High Priest nodded. "An oversight we will rectify. We will set them at ease and then make our move in transit."

Who are they talking about? Raena wondered. Whatever was going on, it sounded like there'd be a delay from whatever the Priesthood had planned before. *If we don't get out now, we might not get another chance.*

The High Priest returned his attention to the two captives, speaking in New Taran, "We will know the best path soon enough. You'll eventually come to understand that this is the only way." He departed through the door.

"When he comes back, that will be our chance," Raena said to Ryan.

"I have no idea how to 'stop time'," he objected again.

"Let instinct take over, like your life depends on it—because it does."

— — —

Wil gathered his family in the guest suite he was sharing with Saera. Morning light illuminated the gardens outside. Six hours had passed since Raena and Ryan's capture. They needed to take action.

Jason seemed particularly perplexed as he sat down between his mother and grandmother on the couch. Cris stood next to Wil, facing them.

"I know we're all tired and worried," Wil began. "Given the forces at play in this situation, I think it's best that we keep what will happen next confidential. The more we can keep the Sietinen Dynasty out of it, the better."

Cris nodded. "We've had a feud going with the Priesthood for years, but this is the first direct action they've made against us. At this point, we can't assume any of us are safe."

"Why take them and not me?" Jason asked.

"We don't know for sure," Wil replied, "but we suspect it has something to do with genetic coding. Certain traits are carried by men and women. Whatever they're after, they must be done with the Sietinen men."

"Regardless, we're not going to let them get away with whatever they're planning," Kate stated. She placed an arm around Jason's shoulders and looked up at Wil. "Do you know what you're going to say?"

"More or less," he replied.

"Wait, what's going on?" Jason asked.

"We're going to try asking the Priesthood nicely to back off," Wil told him. "If they don't, the TSS will initiate a coup."

Jason's eyes widened. "I thought the entire point was a political solution—to vote the Priesthood out of power?"

"Yes, but that was before they took your sister," said Wil. "I'll bring them down myself, if I have to."

"But first, we put them on notice. Their response will dictate what we do," Cris stated. "However, if we do have to turn to force, we'll need to get out of here immediately."

Wil nodded. "The four of you would go back to Headquarters while I go in with a team. I'm not sure what kind of retaliation they could launch, but that's the most secure place to ride it out."

"I—" Jason started to protest.

"We don't have the luxury of second-guessing or biding our time," Saera interrupted. "Go pack and be ready to leave if we need to." She stood and brought Jason to his feet with her. "Kate will stay with you."

He frowned but nodded his consent.

"I'll wait in the common room," his grandmother said as they headed for the door.

When they had exited into the hallway, Wil took a deep

breath. "All right, let's do this."

"Stars!" Cris fumed. "I still can't believe we're going to talk to them like this can be resolved without us smashing their faces in—"

"Dad… Just let me do the talking," Wil said.

Saera nodded. "We'll follow your lead."

Wil brought up the communications control interface on the viewscreen and initiated a manual contact protocol. Accessing the Priesthood's inner network was impossible, but he had figured out how to direct a message to a specific user based on their permissions profile. He couldn't be certain, but High Priest Quadris appeared to be one of the highest authority figures within the organization. "Here we go…" He initiated a video call to the account.

The viewscreen remained black with a swirling VComm logo in the center while the transmission awaited a response. A minute passed with no answer.

"Are they ignoring us?" Cris asked eventually.

"Maybe," Wil frowned. "Or this backdoor doesn't work anymore."

Then, the onscreen logo dissolved. The image resolved into a figure robed in black sitting at a desk with a smooth white stone wall behind him. The man's face was shrouded in shadow.

"I'm surprised," the High Priest stated. "I thought you'd come knock down our door."

Wil glared at the robed figure. "I didn't want to dignify your actions with a call, but here we are."

"You're wise to recognize you're powerless in this situation."

"That's not the term I'd use. I just want to resolve this in a civilized fashion." *If that's even possible dealing with such a monstrous organization.*

"Your daughter belongs to us now," the High Priest stated. "That matter is not negotiable."

"What have you done to her?" Wil demanded.

"She's safe. We left you your son—don't make us regret that kindness."

Kindness? These people are foking psychopaths. "I appreciate your consideration. However, I'm afraid I can't let matters go so easily."

The High Priest scowled beneath his hood. "You have fulfilled your purpose. Let us do what must be done."

"Which is?" Wil prompted. "At some point you assumed we'd be at odds, and since then you've tried to get us out of the way while still manipulating our lives. Didn't it occur to you that maybe we could work together?"

"You would never see things our way."

"Try us."

The High Priest scoffed. "Go, resume your lives with the TSS and keep plotting away. You'll never unseat us."

I guess they know what we've been up to. No wonder they swooped in to grab Ryan so quickly. "You should know by now that we don't give up easily. This is your one chance to resolve this matter peacefully."

"There's nothing to resolve," the High Priest replied. "We have taken what is rightfully ours."

"That's what we are to you—property?" Cris blurted out. "No wonder you always talk down to us."

A frown was visible through the shadow of the High Priest's hood. "We made you, just as we made the Taran civilization what it is today."

"You may have manipulated our genetic code, but we're sentient people," Wil replied. "You don't own us, and you certainly don't have the right to hold anyone prisoner."

"We have no prisoners," the High Priest stated. "Enjoy your freedom."

The transmission ended. The viewscreen displayed details about the call, including the exact coordinates of the receiving equipment.

"That was worthless," Wil declared. *Though at least now we know the location of Quadris' office.*

"Smug bastards," Cris muttered.

"That's it. We have no choice," said Saera. "You need to go in."

"Take Jason back to Headquarters," Wil told his wife and father. "I had some of the Primus Elites board a transport over here as a precaution. I was hoping it wouldn't come to this, but we'll do what we have to."

Saera hugged him. "Be careful."

"I'll try."

Cris gave Wil a quick hug, too, before running into the hall to retrieve Kate.

"Show no mercy," Saera stated, her tone cold.

"This time, I won't hold back."

— — —

Raena's heart pounded in her ears while she waited for the door to open. She had no idea if she'd be able to pull off the crazy maneuver she'd need to escape, but there was no way she would allow herself to be a part of the Priesthood's perverse experimentation.

Behind her, one of the other High Priests was conversing with an acolyte in Old Taran. "It appears that the line needs to be crossed back," the acolyte said.

"I feared that might be the case," said the Priest. "The margin of chance is great enough that such a cross-back is the only way to guarantee success."

"For certainty, it may require an additional pairing."

"We'll make that determination when the time comes." The Priest sighed. "Two more generations… I really thought we were ready."

"Soon, my eminence."

Raena swallowed hard. *I have no idea what they mean, but I don't like the sound of it.* She glanced over at Ryan and saw that he looked completely lost. *"They miscalculated something,"* she told him. *"This is our chance to get away."*

"You can understand them?" he asked.

"We got the imprinting for Old Taran when we got New Taran. Didn't think it'd come into play like this, though…"

A chirp sounded at the entry door. The lock clicked open.

This is it. We need to move. Raena cleared her mind. *"Now!"* she shouted telepathically to Ryan.

Instinct took over. Without conscious intention, Raena

yanked her arms upward and the tethers binding her broke away. She tore off her ankle restraints with a wave of her hand.

Ryan was still trapped on his gurney.

Raena jumped to her feet as the two High Priests and seven acolytes leaped into action. "No!" she shouted as they ran for her. She threw up her arms and the nine men flew backward against the wall.

Ryan stared at her, his jaw slack. "How did...?"

"You better find it in yourself if we're going to get out of here," she replied, dashing over to him. She tried to break his bonds like she'd done with her own, but nothing happened.

"Get me out of here!" Ryan pleaded.

"I'm trying—"

A shout sounded at the entry door.

Raena's skin tingled as the hum of energy filled the air. *Attack!*

She ducked just in time to avoid an energy orb hurtling toward her. It struck the monitor next to Ryan's bed, raining sparks over them.

Ryan raised his hands to shield his eyes—breaking the straps that bound his wrists.

The sparks ceased and he stared with wonder at his freed hands.

"Don't think. Act!" Raena told him. She ran headlong for the High Priest re-entering the room.

Another energy orb shot toward her from the High Priest in her path and an even stronger charge filled the air behind her.

I need to be behind the Priest, she thought to herself. *Ryan and I need to be in the hallway.*

Ryan came up alongside her as she barreled toward the Priest.

Her eyes met Ryan's in silent understanding. She had to get them out, no matter what. *"We need—"*

The world froze around her. The High Priest barred her path, an energy orb half-formed between his hands. She turned her head and saw the two other High Priests and the acolytes preparing attacks behind them. They only had a second to escape.

Next to her, Ryan swiveled around to take in the room—the only perceivable movement. He looked back at her, completely mystified. *"What..?"* he questioned in her mind.

"We did it!" she replied, intoxicated by the glow of energy surging through her. *"Now run."*

They dashed toward the open door while the world around them appeared to stay frozen. Raena nimbly side-stepped the High Priest and Ryan went around the other side. The door was beginning to close, but there was just enough of a gap for them to fit through.

The straight hallway through the women's cells was clear. Raena sprinted down the hall in the frozen world, the imperative to get away at the forefront of her mind. *We can't help them now. We'll come back for them.*

Her heart ached as she saw a young woman not much older than herself standing near the front of her cell with a hand on her stomach, just beginning to show the pregnancy that had been forced upon her. Raena wished she could set them all free, but there was no time.

She pressed on, silently willing Ryan to follow.

They reached the end of the hall. Another door barred their path.

"How do we get through?" Ryan asked.

"We just do." Raena placed her hands on the smooth surface and nodded for Ryan to do likewise.

The door groaned.

"Break!" Raena shouted telepathically.

The door gave way with a shrill, grinding shriek. The metal peeled back from the frame, providing an opening for them to slip through.

The women in the cells jumped up with wonder. With renewed panic, Raena realized that the spatial distortion had collapsed—they were once again moving in real-time.

Ryan grabbed her hand. "Run!"

They took off through the opening and sprinted down the hall.

Footsteps sounded ahead of them and shouts rang out from behind. There was only one way ahead and one path behind.

Forward was the only option.

"We did it once. We can do it again," Raena said.

"I'm with you." Ryan squeezed her hand and ran forward.

A tingle once again passed over Raena's skin. The sounds of footsteps and shouts lowered in pitch and then ceased entirely. As she ran forward with Ryan, they rounded a bend and saw a team of eight guards suspended mid-stride.

They ducked around the guards and wove their way through the halls. Passing around the next bend, the hall branched into two. Raena scanned over the walls and noticed a sign written in Old Taran that indicated an elevator.

We'd have to ride up in real-time. They'd be waiting for us to exit, if they didn't stop it in the middle of the shaft. They needed another way out. *"No elevator,"* she said to Ryan.

He nodded, seemingly to also intuitively understand the issue with that route. *"Air vent!"* he suggested.

They scanned the walls and ceiling for any sign of ventilation.

"There!" Ryan exclaimed, pointing to a grate at the base of the wall ten meters up ahead.

Raena waved her hand to rip the grate from the wall. As soon as it was clear, the sounds of footsteps and shouts resumed. Her head ached and a wave of nausea almost brought her to her knees.

Ryan wrapped his arm around her back and half carried her to the opening. He helped her into the cramped tube—barely more than half a meter wide and tall.

Stay focused, she urged herself onward as she began to squirm through. Ryan wriggled in after her.

They scrambled through the vent for twenty meters before encountering another grate. It was only secured at the top, and Raena was able to swing it upward to pass through.

The tube on the other side was tall enough to stand in.

"This must be the main shaft," Ryan said. "That means we're almost out."

Raena licked her finger and held out her hand, trying to get a sense of the wind direction. It seemed to be blowing toward her left. "This way!" She ran through the dark to the right, keeping her hands outstretched in front of her to avoid running into any obstacles face-first.

The guards would be right behind them. They had no time to waste.

After a full minute of running in complete darkness, faint light began to show in the distance.

Raena's fingertips brushed against a wall in front of her, and she realized that the tube was curving to the left. When they completed a gradual ninety-degree turn, they caught sight of direct sunlight shining through a metal grate.

A salty breeze gusted through the tube, carrying the crashing sound of waves.

Raena stopped short of the grate, grabbing Ryan's arm. With her other hand, she sent out a blast of telekinetic energy, rending the grate from the fasteners.

They were at least fifteen meters above the ocean. Water churned below, waves breaking on jagged cliffs.

"We're cornered!" Ryan exclaimed.

She glanced over the edge at the rock, but it was sheer, unscalable stone. "I'm not going back."

"Wait, is that…?" Ryan pointed out at a distant speck hovering above the water.

Raena strained to make out the form. It was a shuttle.

"Rescue or reinforcements?" Ryan asked.

"I'm not sure." Raena tried to identify the details of the craft, wasting crucial seconds.

Shouts sounded behind them, getting closer.

"We need to move!" Ryan urged.

Everything went quiet and still around her as voice spoke in her mind. *"Raena, if you can hear me, we're coming for you."* It was her father.

Raena took Ryan's hand. "That's our rescue."

She jumped.

CHAPTER 21

RYAN WAS PULLED from the ledge after Raena. The ocean rushed up at him, with white-capped waves slamming against rocks that were far too close to their path.

Raena released his hand four meters above the water and pinned her arms against her body with straight legs. Ryan did the same and took a deep breath.

The impact with the water almost pushed all the air from his lungs. He was blind.

He forced his eyes open despite the sting from the salt water, looking for any light to help orient toward the surface. The turbulent waters pushed him backward toward the rocks. He struggled against the current, only to find himself deeper under water.

For ten terrifying seconds, he couldn't find the surface. He swam up and up, his lungs burning for air.

Finally, he broke free. With a gasping breath, he swam away from the cliffs, hoping to find calmer water.

"Raena!" he called out, unable to see her bobbing in the water.

"I'm okay!" she shouted back from behind him.

Ryan looked over his shoulder to locate her and temporarily was forced underwater by a wave. When he resurfaced, she was two meters away and heading for him.

"You're insane!" he told her.

"It was that or let them catch us." She began swimming out to sea.

Hopefully, the rescue shuttle sees us. Ryan swam after her as best he could, but he wasn't used to the open waters. He and the other Sietinen Wards had swum in Lake Tiadon when he was a child, though that was years ago and the calm waters didn't pose a challenge.

The ocean battered him and he had to constantly swim to avoid losing ground. Raena kept a solid pace up ahead. He wasn't about to let her get out of sight.

A rumble sounded in the distance overhead. Ryan looked up and saw that the shuttle had dropped in elevation.

Raena slowed her strokes and waved a hand up in the air.

The shuttle positioned over them and the side door opened. Someone poked their head out—it was Wil, as far as Ryan could tell through the splashing water and glaring sunlight.

A tingling sensation washed over Ryan's skin. He could no longer feel the waves. Suddenly, he began rising upward. The air seemed to congeal around him as he continued to rise, heading straight for the shuttle door. Raena rose alongside him.

They passed through the open shuttle door and were released gently on the floor.

Ryan dropped to his knees and coughed out some water that had gotten into his lungs. When he looked up, he saw Wil, Cris, and six other men around Wil's age dressed in black surrounding him. Every one of them had glowing eyes. *Are these Agents?*

Raena smiled with relief when she saw them. "Thanks."

Wil embraced her. He held her in silence while the shuttle turned around and accelerated away from the island. The door closed and sealed.

Raena pulled out from the hug. "We have to go back. They have other prisoners."

"Not now," Wil replied. "We need to get you somewhere safe first. I wasn't expecting you to make it out on your own."

"I still can't believe we did…" Ryan murmured.

"How?" Cris questioned.

Raena slumped into a seat along the side of the shuttle. One of the men handed her a blanket and she began wiping off her face.

Ryan noticed another Agent had extended a blanket toward him and he took it. The soft, warm fabric was a relief after the chilly water.

"This is going to sound nuts," Raena said at last, "but you know back home when they'd have stories of someone who performed a feat of incredible strength—like picking up a car that fell on their kid, or whatever?" She looked at her grandfather. "Well, I remembered what you said about when the Priesthood came after you as a teenager, and how you got away. So, I told myself that I need to 'stop time' or I was going to die. And I just… did it."

The eyes of all the Agents in the shuttle widened with surprise.

"Really?" Wil kneeled in front of her. "That's how you got out?"

"Not just that," Ryan added, "but she busted out some doors, too."

"We both did. No thinking, just acting," Raena said.

Her father put his arm around her. "You never cease to amaze me."

She hugged him again. "Thanks for coming for us."

Wil held her at arm's length and gazed into her eyes. "I will always come for you. No matter what or where."

She smiled weakly.

Wil examined Ryan. "And what about you? Did she extend the spatial distortion around you, as well?"

Raena shook her head. "No, that was him. He kept up with me."

"Really?" Cris looked at Ryan incredulously.

It certainly didn't seem like I was doing it, if I did. Ryan took a shaky breath and pulled the blanket tighter around himself. "Like she said, we did what we had to do."

"I mean, I couldn't have done it all on my own. That'd be way too much, right?" Raena said. "It had to have been a team effort."

"That's incredible," Cris said after a pause. "Yes, I was able to pull off some advanced maneuvers in a life or death situation, but to perform coordinated maneuvers like that at will with no training… It's unprecedented."

"She is my daughter," Wil pointed out. "Regardless of the odds, they did it."

Ryan swallowed. *Or maybe I was just along for the ride.*

"This isn't over," Raena said, her voice growing stronger. "The Priesthood is up to something."

Wil sat down on the seat next to her. "What did you learn?"

"They're all clones—transferring consciousness from one body to the next," Raena said.

Wil shook his head. "I foking knew it. Of course they'd ban the practice and then keep doing it themselves."

"No surprise there," Cris agreed. "No wonder they never show their faces. I thought I saw hints of the Bakzen in there."

"What else?" Wil prompted his daughter.

"Well," Raena continued, "it sounds like they're trying to make a new vessel for eternal life. They said the Bakzen design was flawed but that through our pairing they could achieve their perfect vision."

Cris nodded. "That sounds very similar to what we pieced together."

"But there was something they didn't anticipate," she went on. "They were talking about needing to cross back the lines, or something. It was all in Old Taran—they didn't know I was listening. I lost track and don't remember the rest."

"Don't worry," Wil assured her, rubbing her back. "This is way more than we had before."

"Oh!" Raena sat up. "They also said that gestating a baby in a lab makes it weaker. When the mother has abilities, they're expressed better in the child."

"And you said you saw these women?" Cris questioned.

Raena nodded. "Most of them looked to be pregnant—second trimester, mostly, but it varied."

"Shite," Wil breathed. "I was afraid that's what they were up to."

Cris shook his head. "Surrogates for their perpetuation."

Ryan slumped down in a seat across from them. "I don't

know about Raena, but I was out for quite a while. They may have... taken what they wanted." He felt nauseated thinking about the violation.

"Doubtful," Cris replied. "They wouldn't have been testing you in the lab if that were the case."

"Exactly," Wil said. "And now we know that they're missing a piece they need to complete their plan. That means we still have time to take them out. Any idea what the missing piece might be?"

Raena's brow furrowed as she replayed the memory. "I think it was something about 'should have taken him, too.' "

Wil and Cris looked at each other.

"Jason?" Cris said.

"Fok, I wouldn't put it past them," Wil muttered.

Raena's face twisted with disgust. "You're not suggesting..."

"It's not worth speculating about the twisted musings of psychopaths," Wil assured her. "Now, let's just get you on the *Vanquish* and have Medical look you over. If everything checks out, we'll try to put this behind us until we can make our move."

"But what about the prisoners?" Raena protested.

"Where are they in the facility?" Wil asked.

Ryan shrugged. "Somewhere underground behind where we jumped out the ventilation shaft."

"Short of blasting a hole in the side of the island, our entry points are very limited, I'm guessing?" Wil asked.

"Well, yeah, but—" Raena began.

"Getting in is one thing, but getting dozens or hundreds of captives—most of whom probably haven't been outside in a decade?" Wil shook his head. "It's too many unknowns. We need to know that they'll be safe once they're released. There are no assurances right now."

Raena crossed her arms, pulling the blanket tighter around herself. "I hate knowing what's going on in there and not being able to do anything."

Wil rubbed her shoulder. "Welcome to true leadership. You know more than you want to and can't always do what you feel is right. But the best leaders never give up. We'll act when the time is right."

— — —

Cris stared out the viewport as he sat in silent contemplation for the rest of the shuttle ride up into space. The information Raena had brought back about the Priesthood's inner workings confirmed his darkest suspicions, but at least now they knew their adversary's motivations.

Eternal life through the perfect physical vessel. He shook his head. *Too bad it's not a consciousness worth saving.*

The shuttle headed to where the *Vanquish* was waiting for them just beyond standard orbit of Tararia. He didn't trust the Priesthood not to lock down the Tararian spaceports and make their departure impossible, so a remote rendezvous seemed like the safest option rather than joining up with the *Vanquish* at the dock where he'd left. He'd also ordered TSS battleships to be standing guard back at Headquarters' spaceport when they returned; he didn't want to take any chances when it came to getting Raena and Jason back to comparative safety inside the moon.

Kate and Saera had insisted they wait with Jason on the *Vanquish* rather than go back to Headquarters. Cris couldn't blame them—the idea of leaving behind some of the family in unspeakable danger would have kept him standing guard, as well.

The shuttle made the final approach to the *Vanquish*, swinging around to the port side entrance to the main hangar. It decelerated moments before it passed through the shimmering force field covering the entry to the hangar. After a short taxi it came to rest at the end of a row of TX-70s.

"Let's get out of here," Wil said.

"Couldn't agree more," Cris replied. He reached out telepathically to his pilot, Alec, up in the *Vanquish*'s Command Center. *"Take us home via the independent jump drive. We don't want them trying to intercept our route on the beacon network."*

"Aye," Alec acknowledged.

A moment later, Cris felt the familiar sensation of a subspace jump initiating. The vibration rattled the ship for five seconds and then everything was still. He heaved a sigh of relief. "No more kidnappings allowed," he declared.

Wil smiled and released the seal on the shuttle door. "It seems like we need at least one good abduction or runaway every generation. The good news is, now this one is out of the way."

Cris hopped out of the shuttle. "Some traditions should be broken."

No sooner had Cris' feet touched down on the deck plates than he sensed Kate running toward him from the entry door, accompanied by Saera.

His wife threw her arms around him. "How are you back so soon?"

"That's a little complicated…"

While he tried to think of what to say, Raena and Ryan stepped out from the shuttle, still wrapped in blankets. Their hair and clothes had yet to dry in the cool air. Wil climbed out after them, followed by the Primus Elites who'd volunteered for the rescue mission.

Saera rushed over and embraced her daughter. "I'm so sorry we let this happen."

"It's not your fault, Mom. I'm fine," Raena said.

"You're soaked," Saera commented as she pulled out of the hug. "What happened?"

"We sort of jumped off a cliff into the ocean…"

"What?" Saera turned to Wil. "Did you—?"

"No, they rescued themselves," he replied. "We just picked them up out of the water."

"It would seem exceptional abilities run in the family," Cris added. "We can do a proper debrief later. For now, get them to Medical for a preliminary examination."

"Already on it." Wil directed Raena and Ryan toward the door. Saera followed them, a gentle hand still on her daughter's shoulder.

"How'd they get out, exactly?" Kate asked.

Cris glanced at the group of Primus Elites and gestured Kate toward the door. "Let's head up to the Command Center." When they were clear of the shuttle, he continued, "Apparently they spontaneously taught themselves how to 'stop time'."

Kate's jaw dropped. "In a coordinated maneuver together?"

"From what they said, it sounds like it."

"That's exceptionally more difficult than doing it alone. With the variability, to sync things up—"

"I know." Cris massaged his eyes. "So, either Raena did it on her own without realizing it, or they really do have a unique connection."

"Either way…"

Cris chuckled. "I don't even think they realize how incredible a feat it was. Raena just said she knew she had to do it, so she did."

"It's really not so different, even when we've been trained. When it comes down to it, controlling our abilities is just a matter of freeing our minds enough to not hold back."

"Visualization," Cris agreed. "Once you know how to picture what you want to do, instinct takes over."

"But if she can do that on a whim…" Kate trailed off.

"I wonder if she's as strong as Wil."

"There's no telling what she could do."

Cris nodded slowly. "But I do know this: she is good and pure of spirit. However she ends up using her abilities, and however strong she becomes, she'll use it for good."

Kate linked her arm around his. "I believe that, too."

They walked in silence for the rest of the way up to the Command Center. Two meters from the door, Cris sensed Wil reaching out to him.

"Medical says they're clear," Wil said. *"No signs of extraction or other experimentation."*

"Thanks for letting me know. Get some rest—we'll be home soon."

Cris relayed the information to Kate.

She let out a long breath. "I always found it easier to know they were manipulating and using us as adults. But they're so young… It's almost like Wil all over again."

"That's why this needs to end."

Cris entered the Command Center and waved at Alec and Kari before heading into his private office on the right side of the room. There was one more person he needed to fill in about

Raena and Ryan's safe retrieval."

"CACI, initiate an encrypted call to my father on his private line," he instructed.

The TSS logo illuminated on the viewscreen while the call connected. After two seconds, Reinen's face appeared onscreen.

"We have them," Cris said.

"Thank the stars!" Reinen breathed. "Were they harmed?"

"Not as far as we can tell. They're exhausted but it's been quite an ordeal."

His father scowled. "I can't believe this level of betrayal."

"This is nothing new," Cris replied. "The Priesthood has been betraying all of us for generations."

"I should have listened to you."

"For what it's worth, very few other people took me seriously, either."

Reinen shook his head. "There was a time when I never questioned. Looking back on my life, I wonder how much I never saw because my mind wasn't open."

"What we do on the path ahead is what really matters," Cris told him.

"All the same, an old man can't help reflecting on his life." Reinen looked Cris in the eye. "Seeing you surrounded by family... it's made me realize how I could have done things differently."

"We're very different."

"We are. Still, I didn't consider the other side. I should have listened to you and tried to see things from your perspective."

Cris shrugged. "I doubt we would have ever seen eye to eye."

"Perhaps not, but I owed it to you to try, and I didn't."

"There's a chance for all of us to set things right now. We need to pave the way for a new generation."

His father nodded. "Yes. I believe it is time for us to look to the future and trust that it is in good hands."

Cris took a slow breath. "I know that you never felt I had the family's best interests in mind, but I have. So much of what I've done is to prepare for that future we all want."

Reinen smiled. "I see that now, Cris. I only wish I'd had your wisdom when I set about making my own plans. You've been both a father and a leader. I never got either one of those quite right."

"You did what you thought was best. That's all any of us can do."

"Indeed." Reinen swallowed. "All the same, your instincts are better than mine. The Sietinen Dynasty is about to enter a new era, and you're the right one to lead us there. A new Sietinen legacy is unfolding before us."

"I'll do my best to make you proud."

"You already have, Cris."

Such moments of appreciation were all too rare over their years together, but in that moment, none of their past rivalry or bitterness mattered. It was only a son with his father, accepting each other as individuals and uniting under the common thread of wanting to make things better for their loved ones than things had been for them. In the end, nothing else mattered.

—   —   —

"You did *what?*" Jason exclaimed, staring at Raena with disbelief.

"I know how it sounds." She shifted on the bed in her temporary quarters. Across from her, Jason was seated in a desk chair and Ryan was perched on the foot of her bed. Jason had pulled them aside to get the inside story the moment they were free from Medical.

"It still doesn't feel like I did anything," Ryan murmured.

"Well, get used to it," Raena said. "You're in the Telekinetic Club now. You broke your restraints and then you stopped time with me." *He must have. There's no way I could have done all that alone.*

Jason shook his head. "I miss out on all the excitement. After that initial headache at the same time as your Awakening, I haven't been able to do anything yet."

"Trust me, it was *not* the kind of excitement you'd want," Raena groaned. "I'm still so creeped out by the whole thing. What they wanted to do to us…"

"And to think everyone trusts the Priesthood." Ryan scowled.

"The truth will get out," Raena told him.

"But what do we do now?" her brother asked.

"We train and we get stronger." Raena glanced at Ryan. "Now we know what they're up to, and we're going to stop them."

CHAPTER 22

ARRIVING AT HEADQUARTERS felt oddly like a return home to Raena, despite having spent so little time there. Perhaps it was the proximity to Earth that lent a comfortable feeling to the place, or maybe it was just the company. Either way, she was relieved to have the ordeal with the Priesthood behind her—at least for the time being.

As she rode the elevator down into the main facility with Ryan, Jason, her parents, and grandparents, it occurred to her that her circumstances had changed considerably since they'd left to visit Tararia.

"What are we going to do until classes start?" she asked, adjusting her travel bag on her shoulder.

"You're going to spend most of your time in a practice chamber," Wil replied. "I'm still not entirely sure what to do with you."

"We might have to do what Banks did with me," Cris said.

"You mean the temporary apprenticeship?" Raena asked.

"Exactly—have some intensive training to skip you ahead to Junior Agent," her grandfather replied. "Your abilities are uncharacteristically advanced."

I was looking forward to the chance to train with Ryan. She frowned. "What about the Primus Elite cohort?"

"Like I said, we'll need to explore our options," Wil said.

"And you'll need to figure out what you want to study."

"Don't you assign classes?" Jason asked.

"Historically, yes. We're trying something different this year," Wil replied.

"There used to be set training tracks," Cris explained. "Command, Navigation, Tactical and Scientific support, Diplomacy, and Medical. Students would be assigned one of those tracks at the end of their first year based on aptitude. Those tracks were largely born out of wartime needs, though. We want to open it up for more purely academic pursuits—to attract students with abilities that might otherwise go to a traditional university."

"Why?" questioned Raena. "Isn't the TSS here primarily to train people in telekinesis?"

"If that were the case, there never would have been a Militia division," Cris pointed out. "No, the TSS is more than just a training organization—we offer a unique skill set through our position outside of everyday activity. Our value is in offering an outside perspective, and we now want to deliver that message to the masses."

Raena nodded. "To expose the Priesthood."

"And provide a voice for those who have gone unheard," her father added. "We want anyone who joins us to be able to pick an avenue that best fits them as they join us in that larger mission."

Do I even have a place in the TSS? With the political unrest, it seems like maybe my place is on Tararia. "I'll do whatever you need," she said.

Cris smiled. "For right now, that's taking some time to unwind and getting your bearings."

"Sounds good to me," Jason commented.

"Yeah, same," Ryan agreed. "The last two days have been a little… intense."

The elevator arrived at the residential floor of Level 2.

Wil was the first to step out when the doors slid open. "You can stay in the Junior Agent quarters for now," he said. "Don't get too settled in, though. You'll most likely move to the Primus Elite quarters at the end of the week."

"Will that be coed?" Jason asked.

Cris frowned. "That's still a point of contention."

"I think it's fine," Raena offered.

"Yeah, you would," Jason muttered under his breath.

Raena and Ryan flushed.

"The point," Wil interjected, "is to have one cohesive Primus Elite group. It was all men last time, but those circumstances were different. I'd like to give everyone the benefit of the doubt to behave appropriately."

"It's ultimately your decision," Cris yielded. "But you didn't have a roommate like Scott."

"I'd say that's exception more than rule," Wil countered.

"What about Scott?" Saera asked.

"Never mind," Cris and Kate said in unison.

"We'll sort it out. Go relax," Wil said to the teenagers.

"Okay," Raena acknowledged. "I guess we'll see you at dinner?"

"Yes, we'll message you." Saera squeezed her arm.

"Later." Raena headed across the lobby with Ryan and Jason. She released a long breath.

"Yeah, right there with you," Ryan said.

Jason glanced between them. "I still feel out of the loop."

"Lucky. I wish I could forget what I saw," Raena replied.

Ryan eyed some Junior Agents walking down the hall. "I don't think we should talk about anything out in the open."

"Yeah, good call," Raena agreed.

They walked in silence for the rest of the way to their temporary quarters. Jason palmed open the door.

Raena gestured for Ryan to go in first.

His eyes widened when he saw the space. "Wow, this is nice."

"I think they try to make it homey," Raena said. "Even coming from another planet, I felt comfortable here almost right away."

"I can't say the same about my last room," Ryan murmured.

"Well, let's get you set up here." She stepped over to the front room on the left, next to hers in the back.

Jason rolled his eyes and headed for his room in the back right to drop off his travel bag.

"Did I say something wrong?" Ryan asked.

"No. Ignore him." She tried to suppress the exasperation over her brother's sudden judgment of her. *So, he gets to go out with an endless string of girls and when I finally find a guy I like he gets an attitude? Whatever.*

Raena walked into Ryan's room with him and the light came on automatically. The room was just as Raena's had been when she first arrived, with a tablet and handheld charging on the desktop, and double bed. She had a sudden urge to curl up with him and try to forget the last two days.

Ryan must have been thinking along similar lines because he slid the door shut behind them. "We haven't had a moment to ourselves since we got away."

Raena hugged herself. "Did it all really happen?"

"It's all a blur for me, too." He placed his hands on her shoulders. "You were amazing in there."

"It wasn't all me."

"I'm not so sure." Ryan brushed the side of her face with his fingertips.

She swallowed and looked down. "The things they said in there about us…"

"Whatever's between us is what we make it."

Raena uncrossed her arms and placed her hands on his hips. "I'm glad you were with me."

Ryan smiled. "Me too. I'm pretty sure I'd still be strapped into that chair without you."

"I did kind of tear the place apart, didn't I?"

"In a pretty spectacular fashion, I might add."

Raena slid her right hand to the back of his neck and leaned up. A tingle passed through her as their lips met.

He embraced her and they lay back on the bed, casting aside the stress and uncertainty from the last two days as they focused only on each other.

For several minutes, Raena was lost in Ryan's presence, but she was pulled back to reality by a buzz from the handheld in her pocket.

She pulled back from Ryan. "Sorry." When she checked the notification, she saw it was a message from her father, asking to meet in the elevator lobby.

"My dad wants to meet with me," she said.

"Do you think it's about our escape?" Ryan asked.

"Probably." Her chest knotted. "I don't know what else to tell him."

"I'm sure it's nothing."

"Yeah." Raena got up off the bed and Ryan slid down to sit on the end facing her. "I'll be back soon," she told him.

He leaned forward and gave her a light kiss. "See you soon."

—   —   —

Going against protocol wasn't Wil's preferred strategy, but some matters were too important to let go.

The Priests have telekinetic abilities—probably strong ones. For Raena to have escaped... He had to know for sure just how strong she was already.

Wil paced in the lobby on the residential floor of Level 2, waiting for his daughter to arrive. No incoming Trainee would ever see the testing sphere before classes began, let alone go through the final stage of the Course Rank test. Something told him, though, that Raena was unlike any other—not even her brother.

Raena emerged from the adjacent Junior Agent wing. She waved when she spotted him and jogged over. "Hey. What's up?"

"I know you've been through a lot over the last couple of days and I said I'd let you rest, but I was hoping you'd humor me with a little exercise."

She hesitated for a second. "Sure."

Wil called the elevator. When it arrived, he set the destination for Level 11.

Raena restyled her ponytail while the car descended and she seemed to be keeping watch on the pulsing white light next to the door.

"Almost there," Wil told her.

She nodded.

The elevator came to a rest and opened into the plain

hallway on Level 11. Wil stepped out and directed his daughter toward the isolation chamber used for Course Rank testing.

When they arrived at the entrance, Wil palmed open the door to the main chamber. "Wait in the center of the room. I'll be up in the observation area."

"All right," Raena said and entered.

Wil jogged up to the monitoring room overlooking the chamber. He hadn't attended any tests since the Primus Elites had been tested at H2; the last time he'd been in the room was Saera's Course Rank test shortly before they were married. It was hard to believe that was more than two decades prior.

He activated the intercom while the control interface for the testing equipment initialized. "We'll get started in just a minute. This should be quick."

"What is this place?" Raena asked, examining the chamber.

"We test Agents here," he replied. "I wanted to evaluate your abilities."

His daughter nodded. "I'm curious, too. I'm not sure I could do those things again now that I'm not in danger."

"We'll see."

The system interface was ready. Wil activated the pedestal to raise the testing sphere from its storage space under the floor.

Raena stepped back when the hatch opened by her feet. "What's that?"

"It will measure telekinetic input," Wil explained as the sphere rose into position. "Place your hands on the sphere and try to feed energy into it. Don't strain yourself—just see what you can do."

"Sure." Raena gripped either side of the golden sphere.

The energy readout on Wil's screen flickered as her fingertips brushed against the sphere, then stabilized as her palms curved around it. She closed her eyes.

Four seconds passed without even a shudder on the meter. Then, the readout spiked, sending the intensity line on an upward trajectory: 3… 5… 7…

Wil stared with disbelief. *That's already more than a Trion Agent…*

The numbers continued to rise, though more slowly than the

initial spike. Raena's face remained calm and serene as she passed 8, and then 9.

Stars! How is this possible? Wil found he was holding his breath as he watched the screen, glancing between the readout and his daughter below. The intensity ticked upward: 9.2… 9.5… 9.7… 9.8…

"Stop!" Wil commanded into the intercom.

Raena opened her eyes and released the sphere. "Whoa, that was weird."

"What did you feel?" Wil asked, his heart racing.

"It was like I was floating in subspace."

"Did you sense any sort of barrier up ahead, or something holding you back?"

She shook her head. "No. I only stopped because you told me to."

Shite! Even my dad only scored 9.7. If she can do this now… Wil took a deep breath. "Thank you for humoring me. It looks like you're just fine."

She smiled up at him. "Good. So, was that it?"

"Yes. I'll be right down."

Wil cleared the test results from the console, logging a single exported report into an encrypted folder. He had to be careful—few could be trusted with knowledge about that kind of power.

—   —   —

Raena trudged back to her quarters, still feeling wired from the test. She palmed open the door and found Ryan sitting on the couch facing the door and Jason on a chair across from him. They were each playing on their tablets.

Ryan's face lit up when he saw her. "What did your dad want?"

"He ran me through a test down on the practice level. Sounds like everything checked out fine, though."

"Good."

Raena sat down on the couch next to Ryan, leaning against him slightly.

Across from them, Jason finally looked up from his tablet and scowled.

"Is there a problem?" she asked her brother.

"What's going on with you two?" he asked.

Raena glanced at Ryan. "We're just hanging out here."

Jason crossed his arms and leaned back, eyeing them.

She glared back. "It's been kind of a crazy week. Can you lay off on the interrogation?"

"I asked one question. That's not an interrogation."

"You're looking at us funny."

"What are you, five? I'm just sitting here."

Raena groaned and stood up. "Come on, Ryan."

He looked confused but rose, as well. "See you later, Jason."

Jason just scoffed and shook his head as Raena led Ryan into her bedroom.

She closed the door. "Sorry."

"What was that about?" Ryan asked.

Raena sat down cross-legged on her bed. "He's always been a little protective of me, I guess. Where we grew up, there were some people that just wanted to get in someone's pants and then would move on to their next conquest."

"Yeah, I know all about that." Ryan sat down next to her. "Does he really think that's what's going on here?"

"No. I think he's worried it's more than that. We've always been close, and casual dating didn't get in the way. But if I'm in an actual relationship…"

"He won't be able to talk to his friend in the same way anymore," Ryan completed for her.

"Exactly." She sighed and lay back on the bed. "Why didn't anyone warn us that growing up was so complicated?"

Ryan reclined next to her. "Seriously. It was tough enough without throwing in all the dynastic heir stuff."

"So, let's ignore all that," Raena suggested. "No one's actually imposing any mandates or forcing us to do anything."

"It doesn't feel that way."

"I know…" She rolled to her side to face him, propping her arm under her head. "But we like each other, right?"

He nodded.

"So, let's forget about everything going on outside and get to know each other like normal people—just like we've started to do."

Ryan rolled over to face her. "I'd like that."

She inched closer to him. "Besides, we really are just two Trainees here in the TSS. Nothing in our outside lives is supposed to matter."

"Good point."

"Who we are, and what we went through on Tararia, let's just keep that between us."

Ryan grasped her free hand in his. "There's no one else I could possibly talk to about it."

"Me either."

She shifted around to bring her head to his chest. There was still so much to process, but she felt better knowing that someone else knew what she was going through. Regardless of what lay in store for them, they were now bound by that shared experience. Maybe, with time, it could be even more.

—   —   —

Cris reviewed the test data on his desktop while Wil sat in the visitor chair across from him, awaiting his assessment.

"This is… surprising," Cris said at last. Any commentary would be an understatement. Raena was already on pace to match benchmarks Wil achieved as an advanced Junior Agent. Though she was the same age he'd been at the time, she had none of the formal training.

"She might actually be stronger than me," Wil stated, vocalizing what no one had wanted to say aloud since her remarkable escape from the Priesthood.

"I didn't think that was possible."

"The Aesir knew she was special. At the time, I thought letting them test her would have been a death sentence, but now I'm not so sure."

Cris collapsed the testing logs and placed them back in a secure file. "If she were anyone else, I'd hesitate to have her with the other Trainees."

Wil leaned forward. "The thing is, I don't even think she realizes what she can do."

"And you don't want to tell her?"

"I know what it's like to be handed a fate."

So we let her find her own way—what we never had the chance to do. "Okay."

"We keep this between us," Wil said. "Not even Saera or Mom."

Cris despised keeping anything from Kate, but in this matter, he had to agree. They had one chance to let Raena grow into a true leader for Tararia, and dangling that power in front of her would only distract from the bigger goals at hand.

"We'll guide her as best we can," Cris said.

Wil hung his head. "I wish I'd never had to find out what I can do."

"Whatever power Raena masters, it won't be for destruction."

"I hope you're right."

CHAPTER 23

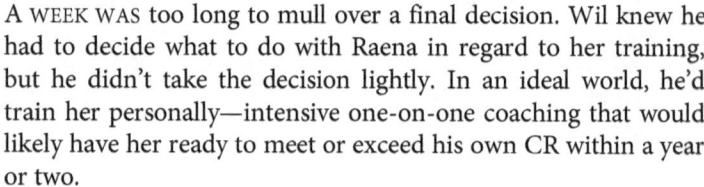

A WEEK WAS too long to mull over a final decision. Wil knew he had to decide what to do with Raena in regard to her training, but he didn't take the decision lightly. In an ideal world, he'd train her personally—intensive one-on-one coaching that would likely have her ready to meet or exceed his own CR within a year or two.

However, there was more to consider than just her prospects as an Agent. More pressing was the need for someone to handle the delicate political dealings that would ensue in the coming years on Tararia. While Jason was an exceptional heir prospect by most standards, Raena's temperament was far more suited to a life of politicking. Compounded by her budding relationship with Ryan, there was no denying that she was the better choice for that life.

It's not mutually exclusive, but would she really step into a life of politics if she knew her power? She might be more inclined to join the Aesir.

The open offer he'd been extended appealed to him in the darker moments—an escape from the often mundane existence of administrative duties and politics. He wondered what it would be like to be among others so advanced in their knowledge and understanding of the fabric that made up their reality.

Yet, there were too many loved ones in his home to seriously consider joining them. Saera, his children, his friends... The ties were too numerous and the danger they still faced was far too great for him to turn his back on them.

He paced his office as he mulled over the options: tell Raena her true potential, let her discover it on her own, or intentionally keep her from tapping into that potential.

The latter was the safest, but it would also be the easiest to backfire. If he was to guide her, he needed to be viewed as a trusted advisor. Betraying that trust would ultimately drive her away.

Telling her about her true potential could equally backfire. She was too curious by nature to not want to push the limits of her abilities, especially since the advances came so effortlessly.

That left the option of allowing her to discover her strength at her own pace. Her realization could come at any moment, but as long as it was a natural progression, she was less likely to harm herself or others by reaching too far, too fast. She would almost certainly remember the time he tested her and ask what he had learned, but he could figure out what to say when that time came.

He ran his fingers through his hair as he came to terms with the decision. *She'll advance so much faster than the others, but maybe they'll benefit from her presence in the way that Saera and the Primus Elites did from me.*

His mind made up, Wil left his office and strode the short distance down the hall to the High Commander's office. He knocked on the door and Cris bid him entry.

"Hey, what's up?" his father asked.

Wil closed the door. "Raena should stay and train like we planned. Either accelerating her or holding her back could cause her to drift from us. We need to keep her close."

Cris nodded. "That's the direction I was leaning, too. Agreed."

"That brings us to the matter of the Primus Elite cohort," Wil said. "I've gone over the potential candidates and have made a selection. Ten men and ten women."

"To share Initiate quarters?"

"Yes. And given Raena's abilities, I'd wager that the constant proximity will benefit all of them."

"Okay," Cris agreed. "Upload the list and we'll pull them when they arrive. We should get a few early arrivals tomorrow and the rest by the end of the week."

"I guess I'll get the twins and Ryan moved over, then."

"Good idea." He paused. "Are they still getting along?"

"Ryan and Raena are great. I think they're taking things slow and getting to know each other properly, which I appreciate. I haven't been able to get a good read on how Jason is taking everything."

His father folded his hands on the desktop. "It has to be strange for him seeing Raena branching out on her own. Their lives were once so intertwined."

"I hope they'll reconnect once they start training together. I'd also like to see a good relationship between Ryan and Jason— we need a secure alliance between Tararia and the TSS."

Cris tilted his head. "Is your intent to groom Jason for High Commander?"

"It's occurred to me. We'll see how things play out."

"Indeed. I'm not about to give up the job yet."

"I'm well aware that you'll avoid getting into Taran politics at any cost."

Cris smiled. "Guilty."

Wil chuckled. "All right. I'll go talk to them about the move. I'll get you the other seventeen names this afternoon."

With a parting nod, Wil headed down to Level 2 to speak with his children. The halls were still relatively empty as the older trainees took advantage of their down time between terms to catch up on video games and mindless entertainment from across the Taran worlds.

Wil arrived at the door to their quarters and hit the buzzer. Five seconds passed before the lock clicked open.

Jason answered the door. "Hey."

"May I come in?" Wil asked.

"Yeah, of course." He stepped aside. "Dad's here!"

The door in the back left slid open and Raena emerged with Ryan.

Wil glanced between them and Jason, gaining a new appreciation for the awkwardness of the arrangement. Still, he couldn't fault Raena and Ryan for hanging out in her room when he had stolen a spaceship to get some alone time with their mom.

"Everyone have a seat," Wil said, deciding to shrug off whatever may be going on behind closed doors.

The three teenagers sat down on the couch facing the door and he took the one adjacent to them.

"Like I said, these quarters were temporary," he began. "The other Trainees will start arriving soon, so I think it's time you move into the suite you'll share with the other Primus Elites in your cohort."

Raena let out an exaggerated sigh. "I'll have to share a room, won't I?"

"With four other lovely young ladies." Wil grinned. "I'm sure you'll love it."

She scoffed and tossed her head back on the couch.

"How many total?" Jason asked.

"Four rooms, five a piece," Wil replied. "Since coed quarters are new for the TSS, I think we should at least keep the rooms divided. Jason and Ryan, you can decide if you want to room together or not."

"When do we head over?" Ryan asked.

"I can take you now, if you like," Wil said. "You can move over your things later."

"I'm game," Raena replied.

"All right, let's go."

Wil led them through the halls and across the lobby to the Initiates wing. He'd managed to secure the same suite his previous Primus Elite trainees had occupied. Since many of those men would play an integral part in training the new generation, it only seemed fitting.

He palmed open the door and ushered them inside.

The copper-colored walls no longer held the memorabilia that had decorated the room for years, but Wil had no doubt that the new group would find their own way to make a personal mark on the space. The furniture had been updated in the recent TSS remodel, but the new couches were still gathered around the main viewscreen like always and a round conference table with a central holographic projector still dominated the back of the room.

"Girls on one side, boys on the other?" Raena asked after making a brief assessment of the space.

"Works for me," Jason said.

Wil noted that Ryan and Jason headed for separate rooms, with Ryan across from Raena at the back of the common room and Jason in the front left.

That actually worked out to his benefit, per his preferred method of having Captains share their room with a squad. The three of them were natural fits for the leadership positions, though he needed to make sure the other students responded to them before making a final determination.

Raena was the first to emerge from her chosen bedroom. "This is going to be an adjustment."

"You have been pretty spoiled your whole life. Remember, you were all geared up to go to college and live in a dorm."

"That would be one roommate, not four," she countered. "At least it's pretty spacious."

"You'll get used to it," Wil assured her.

Jason and Ryan walked out from their rooms.

"What's the best bed?" Jason asked.

"I always preferred either one of the back corners across from the door," Wil replied. "That way you don't get anyone walking by."

"All right, claimed," Jason said.

"It's always nice knowing the right people so you get first pick," Wil jested. "This will be home for quite some time so get to know it and treat it well."

Ryan looked around the room. "We'll do our best."

Wil admired them in the familiar space. *A whole new generation... It's hard to believe.* "With that, welcome to the TSS."

— — —

Ryan settled onto his bed in his new quarters. The room seemed entirely too large and empty with just him in it, but he figured he should enjoy the privacy while he could. In a matter of days, he'd have four new roommates and be on the path to becoming a TSS Agent.

I still can't believe how much has changed. I never would have dreamed this kind of future was possible. Joining the TSS was a radical enough change, but the future prospects of reviving a fallen High Dynasty was still too much for him to process.

Coming to terms with that eventuality was further hampered by Raena's distance from her own heritage. When spending time together, he often forgot how different their lives had been. She acted like any other teenager most of the time, giving no hint of her ancestry. For that matter, Wil and Cris seemed to keep their Sietinen lineage at arm's length when it came to day-to-day interactions. While Ryan appreciated their openness and casual attitude, it didn't provide a useful model for how a dynastic heir was supposed to behave. Or, maybe they were the perfect role models and all of his preconceptions were wrong. Only time would tell.

He turned on his tablet and began scrolling through the myriad of course offerings for his first term in the TSS. The flexibility to choose his own course of study was appealing in theory but he was overwhelmed by the options.

Do I study what interests me or what will give me the skills I'll need to run a High Dynasty? For either route, he had no idea where to begin.

Ryan's thoughts were interrupted by a light knock on the door. "Come in," he said, figuring it was Raena.

To his surprise, Jason entered. "Hey. Have a minute?"

"Sure, of course." Ryan set his tablet off to the side and sat up cross-legged on the bed. "What's up?"

"I don't feel like we got off on the right foot," Jason said. "We're going to be spending a lot of time together, so we should probably be able to carry on a conversation."

"Agreed. I'm sorry if my presence has caused any hard feelings."

"Nah, it wasn't you." Jason sat down on the adjacent bed in the middle of the room. "At any rate, I realized that I never thanked you."

"For what?"

"For getting my sister out of there safely."

Ryan shook his head. "Really, she's the one who rescued me."

Jason chuckled. "Yeah, she likes to do that."

"I will do what I can to look out for her, even though she does a plenty good job taking care of herself."

"I can see that. You really care for her."

"I do," Ryan admitted. "I know all of this has happened fast."

"It has. I was pretty shocked when my parents adopted you practically overnight."

Ryan hesitated. "They didn't tell you, did they?"

"What?"

"About who I am."

Jason's brow furrowed.

"I guess with all the Priesthood craziness it didn't come up directly."

"Yeah, I was sort of sidelined as soon as you were captured. I think my parents didn't want me to worry, or something. I did wonder why they took you, too."

Ryan nodded. "Well, apparently, I'm the lost heir to the Dainetris Dynasty."

"The what?"

Of course, he wouldn't know all the history. "It was a seventh High Dynasty."

Jason frowned. "That doesn't make any sense."

"How do you think I feel? I grew up as a servant, for planets' sake!"

"I'm guessing there's a long and convoluted explanation that would make little sense to me."

"Yeah, to say the least." Ryan laughed. "It's been a foked up week. I don't even know where to begin."

"Dude, you're telling me. As of a week ago, I thought Earth was the only populated planet."

"All right, you have me beat there."

Jason smiled. "Life can be weird sometimes. But seriously, secret High Dynasty heir?"

"So I'm told. But I'm not supposed to tell anyone."

"I'll keep it to myself." Jason crossed his arms. "Wait, if

you're an heir that means you and Raena…"

"Yeah, everything took on a very different meaning as soon as they made that connection."

"Damn. Have they been forcing you together?"

"No. I mean, they laid out the political case pretty clearly for us. They want us to be together, which is crazy to me because in my head I'm still a servant and all of you are people I'm not supposed to talk to because you're in a whole other echelon of existence. But Raena and I like each other. I knew there was something between us the moment we met."

Jason nodded. "I could tell. She's always been very… selective about the people she's let into her life. When she took to you so suddenly, it was obvious she cared."

"I care about her, too. And going through what we did, I think that's made us even closer."

"Yeah, that happens." Jason stared down at the floor.

"All the same, we've agreed to take things slow. There've been so many changes for both of us, we want to make sure what we've felt isn't just a product of shared experience."

Jason rose from the bed. "Good for you. But yeah, that's where the bro talk will end. I don't really want to think about you sleeping with my sister, you know?"

Ryan nodded. "Sorry."

"Nah, it's all good. Compartmentalization is an amazing thing. I hooked up with a couple of our mutual friends on Earth—she and I have an understanding."

"Okay, good. Because I would like us to be friends. I think we're in this together for the long haul, one way or another."

Jason smiled. "Yeah, we're good. As long as you're in Raena's favor, I'll have your back."

"Thanks."

"Now, we're supposed to figure out our class schedules or something?"

Ryan groaned. "I have no idea what to study. I kind of wish they'd let us go back to the old way of them assigning us classes rather than having us pick."

"Yeah, a lot is new this year, I think." Jason sighed. "I guess I'll take a little of everything and see what sounds fun."

"Too bad there isn't a class for 'how to secretly be a High Dynasty heir and learn everything you need to know about being an effective leader without telling anyone who you are'."

"I would one-hundred percent take that class with you."

Ryan laughed. "I'll suggest it for the 'independent study' block."

"Perfect. Well, I'm going to go stare at a list of classes and pretend like I know what Applied Computational Astrobiology actually entails."

"Good luck with that." Ryan grinned.

"I'm gonna need it. I'll see you at dinner."

"See you then."

Ryan reclined on his bed and returned to perusing the course offerings. A class on effective negotiation tactics for political engagements caught his eye. *I think I'm going to need that.* He enrolled. *This is going to be quite the year.*

— — —

Cris completed his refresh review of the incoming Agent Trainee files. He'd gone over all the applicants in the previous months as they were accepted into the training program, but to go through the list in one sitting reminded him of just how much things had changed since he joined the TSS.

The latest cohort would be nearly four hundred Trainees. That was more than double what it had been a decade prior. *If this keeps up, we're going to need a bigger facility.*

Despite the new logistical challenges of accommodating the newcomers, he was excited for the future. *This is a proud time to be High Commander.*

As soon as he closed the personnel list, a priority call illuminated on the screen. Its origin was the head administrative office for Sietinen but the contact code was Marina's.

Cris answered the call. "Hi, Marina. How are you?"

Her face was drawn. "Not great." She wiped an eye with her hand.

His heart dropped. "What is it?"

"Cris..." Marina searched for the words. "Your parents Left."

The air was knocked from Cris' lungs as if he'd been struck in the chest. *If they Left, then...* "Are you sure?"

She nodded. "They provided a full accounting and everything that's required for the transition. We'll need you to come here right away."

"I..." Cris leaned against his desk. *How can they be gone?*

"I'm sorry, Cris," Marina said. "I lost my parents several years back. I know how difficult it is."

"Did they Leave, too?"

"My mom did, after my father died."

Cris shook his head. "The whole practice—"

"I agree. It makes it that much harder for us survivors, to know they're still out there somewhere."

"I can't imagine walking away like that." Cris wrung his hands, his chest aching. "I wasn't ready for this."

"You're a natural leader, Cris. You'll be fine."

I don't have a choice. When I escaped my life on Tararia, I knew I'd have to go back eventually. "Give me a day to sort everything out with the TSS."

"Of course, but there are some immediate matters..."

He nodded. "Let me tell everyone what's going on. Kate can help you while I wrap here."

"All right. I'll be in touch with her shortly," Marina agreed. "And Cris, they left a note for you. I'll forward it."

Cris nodded and ended the call. He collapsed into his chair, shaking his head.

It was hard to believe his parents would participate in an antiquated practice such as Leaving, but then again only those with adequate means participated in the tradition in modern times. After deciding that life had been lived to the fullest, those that decide to Leave would make their final arrangements and then set out on their own to die in peace. Those last days or hours could mean different things to different people—a chance to check off one final wish list item or just to go out while still in possession of one's faculties. The commonality was to die on one's own terms, wherever a shuttle could take them.

For Cris' parents to have Left, they must have felt a sense of closure. He couldn't blame them for wanting to have a say in the end of their own lives, but part of him resented them for dumping the responsibility of the Dynasty on him without any clear warning. Though he'd been skirting his responsibilities for decades, he'd always envisioned there being some sort of formal handover. To have everything fall to him so suddenly was too much to process.

As he sat quietly in the midst of his thoughts, his desktop flashed with an incoming email from Marina. An attachment to the message was titled 'To Cris'.

His throat tight, he opened the attachment. It read:

Cris,

We know our departure will come as a surprise to you, but we are confident the Dynasty is in good hands. With everything that will come in the ensuing years, it has become clear that our time has come to an end. We depart now as leaders from an old era so a new can begin.

It's unclear where our final days will take us, but we look forward to a few moments free of responsibility. As we contemplated this decision, we often thought of you when you chose to depart Tararia to find yourself. Though our adventure comes at the end of life rather than the beginning, we hope to find the same sense of fulfillment you found.

Know that though we are gone from your daily life, our thoughts will always be with you and our family, even after we have finally passed. We hope you succeed in your mission. It's time for a change, and we know you're the one who can make that a reality.

Take care of yourself. The future is what you make it.

Love,
Dad and Mom

The note left him speechless. Rarely had he ever called them

Dad and Mom, yet he now wished he could give them a farewell hug and do just that.

He took several minutes to process his parents' final words to him, then shook himself free of the fog. There was too much to do. He sent a telepathic message to Kate and Wil requesting they come to his office.

They arrived at the same time.

"What's going on?" Wil asked, closing the door behind him and his mother.

"Have a seat," Cris said.

"What's wrong?" Kate asked. He knew she must feel his hurt through their bond.

"My parents Left."

Kate inhaled sharply and Wil slumped back in his chair.

"Are you okay, Dad?" his son asked.

"It doesn't feel real yet." Cris swallowed the lump in his throat. "I've been summoned to Tararia."

Wil nodded. "Right…"

"I need to step down as High Commander," Cris continued. "Normally, command would pass to Lead Agent. But officially, I've been an interim High Commander while you were on personal leave."

"Yeah, I guess so," Wil replied.

"Do you want to take over now, or…?"

His son sat in silent contemplation for several seconds. "I'd thought about it before hypothetically, and I was certain I'd turn it down. But after what happened with Raena and Ryan, I know now more than ever what direction I feel the TSS should go. If Saera agrees, I'll step in. I'm ready."

"Then she should join us," Cris replied.

Cris sensed Wil reach out to her. She was in her office just down the hall and it only took twenty seconds for her to arrive.

Saera's face drained the moment she stepped into the room. Wil must have filled her in telepathically because she immediately rushed to Cris and gave him a hug. "I'm so sorry."

"They lived full lives. There's nothing to be sad about," Cris told her.

"I know what this means for you, though," she said.

Cris shrugged. "I had a good run. There are worse fates than a life as a politician… I think."

She gave him a weak smile. "Let me guess, we're here to figure out who takes over the TSS?"

Cris nodded.

"I'm willing to step up as High Commander," Wil said, "but I don't want to supersede you if that's a title you want."

Saera scoffed. "Are you kidding? High Commander is a bunch of administrative tedium. Lead Agent lets me have my own starship and go out on missions. No offense…"

Wil eyed her. "All right. Administrative tedium it is."

"It's not *that* bad," Cris said. "Either way, I guess that settles it."

"We should let everyone know about the transition," Saera said, turning to business.

"Yes," Cris agreed. "Call an assembly for tomorrow. In the meantime, I need to review some contracts with you to make sure no details are lost when I step away. And Kate, I told Marina she can coordinate with you in the interim for transitioning the Dynasty and SiNavTech."

"Of course. I'll help in any way I can," she told him. *"I'm here for you, my love."*

"Thank you." Cris took a deep breath. "This is it. We have control of Sietinen now."

Wil cracked a smile. "Let's go make history."

CHAPTER 24

I swore I'd never take a leadership role in the TSS again, but this is something I need to do. Wil stared out at the expectant faces gathered in the large lecture hall on Level 5. They knew something big was coming but he doubted anyone would have guessed this news.

When the final Agents had found their seats, Cris stepped to the podium at the center of the stage. "Thank you for joining us on short notice," he said into the camera at the front of the podium. "I make this announcement today with a heavy heart. I must resign as High Commander of the TSS."

Gasps sounded around the room.

"As many of you know," Cris continued, "I was born as the heir to the Sietinen Dynasty. That's not a position anyone can take lightly, and though I recognized early on that I wanted to make a life for myself outside of that birthright, I knew one day I would need to fulfill my obligations to my family. I've had more than fifty years of doing pretty much whatever I wanted and probably getting into more trouble than is advisable, but I have no regrets.

"That time has come to a close now, though. I've been called upon to return to Tararia and so I must." He took a slow breath. "While I wish my position within the TSS and my station as Head of Sietinen weren't mutually exclusive, in this case they must be.

No one person can offer the time and attention that's needed for both roles. The TSS, in particular, is in the midst of a delicate transition, and it needs a leader to dedicate their full attention to making these changes a success.

"For that reason, there is no one more suited for the task than my son, Wil. He has already served you as Supreme Commander of the TSS during the Bakzen War so he understands the weight of the responsibility. But more than that, he, too, regards the TSS as his family. When I left Tararia, I never dreamed I'd find a place to belong in the way that I have felt within this organization. I am proud to call all of you my comrades and my kin, whether by blood relations or not.

"That is the future I see for the TSS—a place where Gifted and everyone else can come together as one. No longer can we be those with abilities and those without. That is not how our people began and that's not how we'll be in the future. These have been dark times, but those times will soon pass.

"As difficult as it is for me to think of leaving the TSS, I am excited for the possibilities that will come from this momentous transition. To step into the position of Dynastic Head as someone with open telekinetic abilities is unprecedented, to say the least. This is truly the beginning of a new age that will bring the TSS from the shadows into the spotlight. With the changes we already have planned and the new opportunities this transition in power will allow, I have no doubt that we are about to begin the finest era of the TSS."

The announcement would call into question why Cris was stepping up as Head of Sietinen now after all these years. Most would be able to read between the spoken lines, and that would be enough for now. During the silence that followed as the audience processed Cris' words, Wil joined his father at the podium.

"I know I haven't been very present within the TSS of late, but I want to pledge to you now that I will be the most attentive and true leader I can be for you," Wil began.

Cris gave a nod and smile of approval before stepping back to the side of the stage.

Wil looked out over the audience. "I've spent my entire life here. For the first two-thirds of my life, this was an organization ravaged by war. We were trained in the ways of battle and that violence was the only way forward. I don't know about you, but I hated having to use my abilities in that way.

"As we look forward to the path of this next generation who were never personally touched by that war, I hope the TSS can become something new. With the defeat of the Bakzen, the most immediate danger to us and the rest of the Taran people evaporated. For years, I've wished that the TSS could be a place where Gifted people could come train without the requirements of military service or the expectation of battle. Our abilities can be used for so much more than combat.

"Instead, I want this to be a place where committed, smart individuals—with or without abilities—can come together to learn how to be ambassadors for all Tarans. We can be mediators for those who need an outside voice to resolve a conflict, or we can provide protection when a community is in danger. These will be missions of peace, not war. No one will need to raise their hand or mind in battle unless they elect to participate. Academic or political studies that were once ancillary to the TSS curriculum will now be central to our training—a preeminent institution where someone can learn about their full self and how best to use their innate talents to benefit the greater good."

The faces of those in the audience expressed a sense of joy—or even relief—as Wil's words sunk in. The years of transition since the war had been a time without focus or direction. It was no fault of Cris' but just a product of the times. The renovations and changes that had been in the works behind the scenes for years could now finally be brought to light.

I'm sorry he won't be here to witness all of it in person, but I'll make sure he has the chance to share in this success. Wil beckoned Cris and Saera up to the center of the stage with him. "Even though there will be a formal transition of leadership, I look forward to maintaining an open dialogue with the governing authorities across the Taran worlds. We will spread the word that the TSS is a safe place for all to come.

"To help oversee these operations, my wife, Saera, will remain in her position as Lead Agent. She has been instrumental in designing our new training curriculum and advising on new testing protocols to better match our future vision for TSS graduates.

"But despite the time and thought we've put into designing these changes, I know we won't get all of it quite right the first time around. Please know that we value your feedback, and don't hesitate to reach out to us if you have concerns or questions. Thank you for going on this journey with us."

Applause sounded in the audience as Wil stepped back from the podium, but his focus had already turned to what came next. It was one thing for him to have moved down to Earth for the last sixteen years, where he was only a short shuttle ride or trip through the TSD arch away, but to have his parents moving to Tararia... They had never truly been apart as a family in his entire life.

Though he had been largely independent since he was a teenager, Wil had always found it comforting to have his parents nearby. Their departure to Tararia meant that Wil could no longer shy away from responsibility, as he had been inclined to do since stepping down from his leadership role after the war. He needed to be accountable and true to the words he had just spoken to the TSS. A new future was ahead, and he was at the forefront of shaping that new reality.

Wil exited the auditorium with his wife and father, still trying to process what it would be like to have everyone looking to him for guidance again. He paused outside the door in the hallway. "Should you have sworn me in, or some sort of formal ceremonial gesture?"

Cris smiled. "We did that long ago. Technically you never formally resigned—I just kind of took over for you."

"Yeah, I guess I didn't," Wil realized. "Well, I'll try to do you proud."

"You always do, Wil," his father said, embracing him.

He pulled out from the hug. "Where's Mom? I thought she'd be here for this."

"She's been busy handling the administrative aspects of the transition with the Dynasty," Cris replied rubbing his temple. "I've been so preoccupied trying to tie up loose ends here with the TSS—"

"Dad, it's okay," Wil assured him.

"We've got it," Saera added. "Between Michael and me, we can piece together the outstanding items. Take care of yourself."

Cris nodded slowly. "I just can't believe they're gone…"

"Neither can I." Wil placed a hand on his father's shoulder. "But we're still here, and we have a lot still ahead of us."

"I know we do." Cris gave Wil another brief hug. "Stars! I can't believe I'm leaving this place."

"It's been home for a long time," Wil agreed.

"But now you're finally back, and the twins… We were just about to all be together." He shook his head.

"Hey, don't talk like that," Saera said in an upbeat tone. "We'll come to visit. It won't be like it was before."

"I know." Cris released a slow breath. "I wish I could stay to talk more and say a proper goodbye, but things are a mess right now on Tararia and we need to get there as soon as possible."

"Of course, I understand." Wil directed his father toward the elevator, recognizing he was floundering in the awkward situation. He hated seeing someone he'd always admired for his poise under pressure now in such a stressed state, especially since it so easily could have been avoided. *It wasn't fair for my grandparents to Leave so suddenly like this. They could have given us some notice.*

"We'll take care of everything here, don't worry," Saera said as she fell into step on the other side of Cris. "I'll be in touch if we have any questions."

"I know you can handle it," Cris replied. "It's me that isn't ready to go."

Wil smiled. "There'll always be a place for you here."

"I wish I'd listened when he told me to come to Tararia," Cris murmured. "They've been asking me to come for so many years, I dismissed it like always. But this was different. I should have been there."

"You'll be there now when it matters most," Wil said.

"Well, I guess I should finish packing." Cris shook his head. "I can't shake the feeling that this is a dream and I'm going to wake up at any moment."

Wil nodded. "I know what you mean. Me being in command of the TSS again... I didn't think that'd ever happen."

"Hey now, you two," Saera interjected. "That's enough reality-questioning for one day. We'll get through this just fine. We still have each other."

Wil took her hand as they walked toward the elevator. "You're right. And we always will."

— — —

As Cris rode the central elevator up to the spaceport with Kate and a travel bag in hand, his heart was heavy with thoughts of all the changes ahead. He was leaving his home and family for the one place he'd tried to avoid for the entirety of his adult life. Though he now held the power to shape that loathed environment into something more palatable, it was still far from where he wanted to be.

"We'll make it our own," Kate commented, not needing to read his mind to know what he was thinking after forty-eight years together.

"I'll miss this all the same."

"Me too."

When they reached the surface of the moon, they strolled down the corridor slowly, pausing at the railing where they'd gazed out at the stars on their first date. Cris took his wife's hand while they took in the view one last time as Agents.

"I'll miss this the most," Kate said. "Stargazing through a planet's atmosphere just isn't the same."

"Especially with the light pollution from Sieten. I guess we'll have to get used to staring *up* at a moon."

Kate smiled. "Or two."

"And being at the center of civilization as we know it. No longer the outsiders looking in..."

"The revolution we've been planning is finally coming."

"I really did get you talking crazy like me." Cris grinned at her.

"No, you just enlightened me."

The sound of voices in the elevator lobby carried down the hall. Cris looked over to see Wil and Saera approaching with the twins.

"You didn't think you could leave without saying goodbye, did you?" Wil called out.

"You said it yourself, this isn't goodbye... Just a 'see you later'," Cris replied.

Wil shrugged. "Well, all the same—"

Before he could finish, all the elevators in the lobby opened almost simultaneously and three dozen Agents and senior Militia officers poured out, led by Scott, Marsie, Alec, Kari, and all their other friends who'd been a central part of their lives for the past five decades.

Cris' throat tightened as he looked over the familiar faces. "You didn't need to see us off like this."

Scott smiled and walked up to him. "But we wanted to. We'll miss you, man."

Cris smiled back. "Don't you mean 'my lord'?"

"Whatever," his friend quipped. "You High Dynasty types are still people just like the rest of us. I guess you aren't that hard to talk to, after all."

Cris stepped forward to embrace him. "Take care of yourself."

"You too. I'd tell you not to cause too much trouble on Tararia, but I know better."

"Oh, we're going to cause *all* the trouble."

Scott clapped him on the shoulder. "Go get 'em. We'll be waiting."

— — —

Wil ran his hand over the edge of the desk in the High Commander's office, noting the details in the grain of the wood. He'd known the desk for his whole life but had never really studied it. Now it was his, as well as the responsibilities it represented. *High Commander of the TSS. That's going to take some getting used to.*

Though technically a demotion from the Supreme Commander title he'd held during the war, this new role held more weight in his mind. It wasn't just a title bestowed upon him during extenuating circumstances but rather a position many had worked toward for their entire career. He would soon be tasked with steering the TSS in a new direction and forging an identity for the organization that would see them through the political trials ahead and into the future.

Also unlike the war, the lives and careers of those he now directed were his family and close friends—not the faceless statistics he'd had the luxury of commanding during the war. His attachment to individuals within the organization gave him a different perspective, and he was committed to honoring their best interest.

Everything that's about to come is for them. I can't think of myself—not like I did before. This time, though, rather than having Saera driven from him she would be right by his side. Partners in life and in their leadership roles within the TSS, she'd be there to keep him on course and make sure they didn't lose sight of their goals.

As he sat down in the padded chair behind the desk, he reached out to her telepathically and beckoned her to him. She arrived two minutes later, slowly swinging the door open.

"This is weird…" she commented as she stepped inside. "Are we really the ones in charge here now?" She closed the door behind her.

"I know, right? I keep feeling like I should have some oversight."

"Yeah, now that I think about it, you're *really* bad with administrative duties. The entire time I've known you, I'm pretty sure you've only filed four reports on time."

"And I maybe read a quarter of the reports submitted to me." He laughed. "Yeah, the TSS is pretty screwed."

"Or this is a chance for us to rethink how things are run—not just in terms of the divisions and training program, but mundane operations, too," Saera suggested.

He gazed at her. "You're so incredibly brilliant."

"Stating the obvious is all it takes to be called 'brilliant' these days? I've been going about this all wrong." She grinned.

"Come here." Wil waved her over to him and she leaned against the desk right next to his chair. "I never would have taken this position if you weren't Lead Agent, you know."

"We are always at our best when we get to work as a team." She stroked the side of his face.

He cupped her hand in his. "Yes, we are."

She looked into his eyes. "Are you okay, Wil? You've barely said two words about your grandparents. I know you weren't close, but…"

"It's strange," he admitted, "knowing they aren't there and having my parents taking over that role. Everyone close to me has always been here in Headquarters, for the most part. Being divided will take some adjustment."

His wife nodded. "I feel bad for them. We promised time with the twins after they came of age but they never got the chance."

"Raena, though, should spend some serious time on Tararia."

"It does make the most sense to name her as your heir, doesn't it?"

"She has the temperament, aptitude, and now a promising partnership. I don't think Jason would have the patience to put up with the politicking, at least not for years."

"I agree, Raena has a knack for diplomacy. She could learn a lot from Cris working alongside him."

Wil nodded. "We could probably have her ready for graduation in four years, then send her to Tararia for her internship."

"I like it."

He wrapped his arms around Saera's waist and she scooched in front of him. "We need to keep each other balanced," he told her. "Husband and wife in the two most senior positions might get tricky."

She smiled. "I'm pretty sure we established that Michael will jump in when we start acting stupid."

"That's true. We'll just have to make it clear that he should."

"I think they're planning to enroll Corine in Militia next

year," Saera added.

"Good. We'll need everyone we can get."

"And in the meantime, we'll have each other." Saera leaned down to kiss him.

Their lips parted. "Stars!" Wil exclaimed. "How suspicious are people going to be every time the High Commander and Lead Agent have a private meeting?"

"You're probably over-thinking it. But since you brought it up, we may as well give them something to be suspicious about."

"Is that so?" Wil rose to stand in front of her and leaned in for a kiss.

Saera halted. "I wonder how many others have in here…"

Wil pulled back. *Like my parents…* He grimaced and quickly blocked the notion from his mind.

"Sorry! Nope, forget it. I did not just say or think anything."

"Already sealed in the vault." He lay Saera back on the desk. "CACI, suspend all telecommunications. And lock the door."

CHAPTER 25

W᷊IL GAZED AROUND the conference table at the twenty most senior Agents in the TSS. With the formal setting, seated at the head of the table with Saera to his right and Michael to his left, it was the first moment he felt the true weight of his new position as High Commander.

"I know we're already going through a lot of transitions around here, but with this change in leadership, I'd like to make a few more," Wil stated.

"Before you go any further," Irina cut in, "I'd like to tender my resignation."

The announcement caught Wil completely off-guard. "Pardon?"

"It's not you, Wil," she clarified. "This is something I've been mulling over for a while now. With all the other changes going on, I think this is the right time for me to step away. I wanted to make the announcement publicly so you couldn't talk me into staying."

"Are you sure we can't persuade you?" Scott asked.

"Retirement is far too appealing," she replied. "I'll stay for another month to assist with the transition."

Wil nodded. "You'll be missed." *She's been here my whole life. It won't be the same without her.* "Any other imminent retirement plans?" he questioned the group.

"Was that an open offer?" Ian asked.

"You're not getting off that easily, Ian. I have plans for you," Wil smirked.

Ian slumped back in his chair. "Yeah, that figures."

No one else spoke up. "All right. So, regarding assignments," Wil continued, "I'd like to try something new with the instructors and division heads. The historical arrangement of making assignments based on Agent class was useful from a command perspective, but I'm not sure that's the most beneficial setup for students. I'd like to experiment over the next couple of years with having high CR Agents spend more time with the students that have lower estimated potential to see if we can get any lift effect."

"There is anecdotal data from the original Primus Elite cohort to support that theory," Irina said.

"Exactly. To that end, Ian, I'd like you to take over as the Division Lead for Sacon, and Ethan, for you to take over Trion," Wil announced.

Agent Elra, the current lead for Sacon bowed his head. "I welcome the experimentation."

The Trion lead, Agent Cordan, also inclined his head. "As do I. My aspiration has always been to help our students realize their greatest potential. All I ask is that I remain an instructor."

"Of course!" Wil hastily added. "We need all the instructors we can get, especially experienced ones held in good esteem by students. Please, don't take any of these changes in a negative light. My only aim is to see if the regular presence of CR 9 Agents can elevate someone with 7 potential to, say 7.2."

"If it's as simple as that, we can all feel foolish for not trying it sooner," Elra stated.

Wil shrugged. "The old priorities were not what they are now. My intent is to find the best way forward."

"You have my support," Cordan said.

There were murmurs of agreement from around the table.

"In addition to new instructor assignments," Wil continued, "Michael will step in as the lead trainer for the new Primus Elite cohort. I'd intended to lead it, myself, but my new position won't afford the required time. However, I'd like all of us to take an active role in the training of every student. The more of our knowledge we can pass on, the more well-rounded our graduates will be."

Wil dove into the minutia for the remaining assignments and was relieved to find that the other Agents all seemed supportive of the changes. With such an exceptional team supporting him, High Commander might be his easiest assignment yet.

As soon as the meeting adjourned, Michael pulled him off to the side of the hall.

"I just received word that the last of the Primus Elite Trainees has arrived," his friend said. "Could I convince you to give an impromptu welcome speech to start things off right?"

"Now?"

Michael grinned. "Isn't a sudden and unexpected announcement the way of things in the Elites?"

Wil laughed. "You have a point."

Michael led Wil to a classroom on Level 2 that was serving as a staging area for the new arrivals. When they entered, Wil immediately saw Raena, Jason, and Ryan in the front row of the tiered seating along with the seventeen other new Trainees.

A couple of the students inhaled sharply when they spotted Wil.

My reputation still precedes me. He smiled up at the twenty young men and women. "Your formal induction into the TSS isn't until tomorrow, but I wanted to be among the first to greet you. I am High Commander Wil Sietinen. Though my primary role is running this organization, I hope to also take an active role in your training.

"I'll be perfectly upfront with you," Wil continued, "because that's how it's always been with the Primus Elite group. You have been identified as the best and brightest, so I will hold you to a higher standard.

"TSS central command is now an old club of friends. That makes it like pretty much any other organization out there, and that means you either need to play nice with the club or you'll find yourself in an uncomfortable place on the outside. You're in luck, though, because the Primus Elite group is my pet project— and my own children are a part of it. You'll get favoritism—no sense denying it—but in return I expect your unwavering loyalty and following of directions."

A young man Wil recognized as Hank Guilin, the heir to one of the Lower Dynasties in the Second Region, raised his hand.

"Yes, Hank?"

"Why be so open about your bias?" the youth asked, his dark green eyes narrowed. "That doesn't seem like a great way to gain followers."

"So, it's better for me to be dishonest with you? No, this only works if we're transparent with each other," Wil replied. "This group will hone the skills I know to be critical for effective leaders. I want you to challenge yourselves and each other to establish a firm ethical and moral foundation that will guide you for your careers. You will be the model of future student generations to come and will help transition the TSS into its new role."

"And what's that role?" a young woman named Samantha asked.

Wil smiled. "A new compass for the Taran civilization."

Hank's eyes shifted to the faces around the room. "That's the role the Priesthood plays…"

"That's what they're supposed to do, anyway," Wil told him. "Should they falter, another entity needs to be ready to step in to prevent complete chaos."

In the front row, Raena smirked and flashed a knowing look to Ryan and her brother.

"To guide you through your studies," Wil went on, "your primary trainer will be Michael Andres. He's one of my best friends and was also my second-in-command for many of my most critical moments as a leader. If anyone can teach you how to become respectable authority figures, it's him."

Wil gazed around the room. "But I'll be there, too. As will many of the other senior officers. One person cannot turn out a group of well-rounded students; it takes input from many people. I would be nowhere near the person I am today without the guidance of multiple perspectives. Together, we will try to prepare you for anything because we honestly have no idea exactly what we'll face."

Michael stepped up and clapped Wil on the shoulder. "Wil taught me everything I know, and I am honored to be able to pass that knowledge on to you."

"And to begin that journey," Wil continued, "you need to set aside whoever you were on the outside. You represent all Taran citizens and will respect everyone for their unique position in our society. That is our guiding tenet. We come from different places but together we can make a bright, new future. Get to know and trust each other—these are relationships that will last a lifetime. Today, you begin training to be Agents of the TSS."

—   —   —

After the short introduction meeting with her father and Michael, Raena returned to the Primus Elite quarters with the other new Trainees. In contrast to having only three people in the space for the last several days, she could already tell it was going to get crowded really fast.

Behind her, a group of three girls had already started to form a clique. They were whispering amongst themselves just below intelligible volume a meter back, much to Raena's irritation. She could feel their eyes on her.

Someone tapped on Raena's shoulder. She spun around to see that it was one of the girls.

"Sorry," the girl said, "but are you the High Commander's daughter?"

"Yes," Raena replied.

"So, you're a Sietinen?" one of the other girls breathed.

Raena shrugged. "It's really not that big of a deal. Don't treat me any differently."

A young man walking next to Raena, who'd been identified by her father as Hank during the introduction, perked up when he heard the conversation. "Was he serious about us leaving behind who we were on the outside?"

Raena gave him a sidelong glance. "Yeah. That's sort of a key thing with the TSS."

Hank scoffed. "You can't walk away from an upbringing like

that—especially when genetics talk. Some of us are just naturally more refined."

"We're all in this group because of our aptitude and potential," Jason pointed out from the other side of Raena. "We've been screened and are worthy, regardless of where we came from."

"Easy for you to say as a Sietinen—and son of the High Commander. But some of the others here," Hank's gaze flitted to one of the girls who'd mentioned being from a mining colony, "will never be up to our standard."

"What standard is that? You mean a dynastic bloodline?" Jason shook his head. "If you want to look at things in those strict terms, then you and I are as far apart as you are from the 'commoners' you seem so intent on putting down. Or maybe we can just think of people as people and forget about class distinctions."

Hank shook his head. "Yeah, whatever you say." He pushed past them and went to the front of the group.

He better change his attitude or he won't last long around here. Raena looked back at the girls behind her and their eyes were wide. The one in the middle whispered something to the others.

"If you have some commentary, you can say it to my face," Raena stated.

The girls flushed.

"Sorry," the middle one said. "It's just that we've never met anyone highborn before."

Raena smiled. "I grew up on Earth. I wouldn't know how to act highborn and fancy if my life depended on it."

The girls relaxed.

"Well good," said the one on the left, "because I grew up on a salvage ship where they swear like their foking lives depend on it, so I'd rather not have to watch what I say."

"It's all good, no worries," Raena said through a grin. "Call me Raena."

"I'm Tiff," the girl on the left replied.

"Susan," said the middle girl.

"Nora," said the girl on the right.

"Nice to meet all of you," Raena told them. "Watch out for my brother, Jason," she gave him a shove, "and that's Ryan," she pointed to where he was walking two people over in an attempt to downplay their relationship for the time being.

"Hey," the girls greeted in unison.

The group arrived at the Primus Elite quarters and filed inside. A pile of luggage occupied the center of the common room, and the Trainees dove in to locate their possessions. Raena immediately dashed to her bed to defend her claim. The three girls she'd met in the hall wandered in after her carrying their bags.

"Are these beds taken?" Nora asked.

"Help yourself." Raena flopped back on her bed.

Nora claimed the middle bed next to Raena, Tiff on the far bed of the back wall, and Susan took the bed on the left side of the door across from Raena.

After a minute, a slightly older young woman with red hair and ice blue eyes appeared in the doorway. "I guess I get last pick." She ventured a smile.

"You lucked out, 'cause you get the cool room," Raena said.

"I'm Adaline." She grinned and placed her bag on the remaining bed.

Everyone introduced themselves.

Tiff looked around the room with wonder. "Shite, I'm really in the foking TSS."

"Not just the TSS, but the Primus Elites," Raena added.

Nora grinned. "Oh, yeah. This is going to be good."

—   —   —

It took Ryan all of thirty seconds to decide he preferred having a room to himself, but at least his roommates seemed good natured enough. To his relief, the uptight dynastic heir who'd spoken up in the hallway had elected to room with Jason after muttering something about the dynasties sticking together.

A brawny blond with dark brown eyes who'd introduced himself as Ned plopped down on the bed next to Ryan. "So, when do classes start?"

"In three days, I think," Ryan replied. "Or as soon as the course schedule can be set based on interests."

"You were here when we arrived," Sten said from across the room. "When did you get in?"

"A few days ago." *I don't need them digging too deeply into my life.*

"Where you from?" Ned asked.

Ryan hesitated. He'd been instructed to be transparent with the history of the persona he'd been, but he wished he could shed that anchor that had been holding him back his whole life. "I grew up as a Ward on Tararia," he said at last.

"Oh man, sorry," Jared said from the bed across from him.

"It wasn't all bad." Ryan shrugged.

"With which family?" questioned Sten.

"Sietinen," Ryan admitted. "I came back here with them."

"Hanging with the right crowd. Nice!" Liam exclaimed from two beds over.

"Yeah, well, I don't expect the special favors to go beyond getting me into the TSS," Ryan stated, already hating that he needed to lie to the very people whose trust he was supposed to earn.

"That heiress is super fine," Jared commented.

"Oh, yeah, I'd totally move in on that," Sten agreed.

Ryan didn't bother to overtly shut them down because he knew Raena would have no trouble doing so herself. "We should probably not talk about our fellow trainees in such objectified terms."

"Dude, unless you don't swing that way, you can't disagree," Jared countered. "Objectively speaking."

"No argument. But be careful—her brother will end you if you look at her wrong," Ryan warned. *Or I will.*

Sten tossed up his hands. "Fok! None of us stand a chance, anyway."

Ned stroked his chin. "Didn't Wil marry someone from Earth?"

"Yeah! The absent heir, that's right," Jared said.

Ryan got up from his bed. "Romantic prospects or not, we

should probably meet the others."

"Good call," Sten agreed. He and the others followed Ryan out into the common room.

Within two minutes, the other Primus Elite Trainees had migrated into the central space. As a matter of efficiency, they decided to gather around the table at the back of the room and make introductions one-by-one, including name, age, and a brief statement about where they were from.

When Ryan finished his introduction, other Trainees nodded and smiled in greeting like they had with the previous students, but Hank shook his head with a thinly masked expression of disgust. *What's his problem?*

Raena must have noticed, as well, because she glared in Hank's direction.

"Don't worry about it," Ryan told her.

Her gaze flitted to him and she gave a slight nod.

As soon as they'd made it all the way around the table with the introductions, Jason held up his hand. "Hey, I just got a message from Scott that we're supposed to meet up in the mess hall. Early lunch before physical assessments this afternoon."

"Good, I'm starving!" Ned exclaimed.

The group headed for the door.

Seeing the other Trainees eyeing Raena as they walked through the hall, Ryan wished he could go up and take her hand. There was no way they'd be able to keep their relationship secret for as long as Wil and Saera had reportedly done, but trying to explain a High Dynasty heiress dating a Ward on Day One was probably not the best way to start out. Over the coming weeks and months, a relationship could naturally emerge in public, mirroring their private feelings as they continued to grow.

For the time being, he kept a respectable distance while he offered meager insights into TSS operations for the newcomers based on his few days in Headquarters.

On their final approach to the mess hall, though, Raena turned around from her conversation with her new roommates and said louder, "…and that's how Ryan ended up joining us here."

Shite! What did she just say about me? He complied with her gesture to come join in their conversation.

As he jogged up to Raena and her new friends, Ryan caught Ned's and Sten's shocked expressions.

"Uh oh. What have you been saying about me?" Ryan asked with a lighthearted smile.

"Only good things," Raena replied with a wry grin. "You have a knack for electronics repair."

"Is that so? Could have used you on the salvage ship!" Tiff said.

"He's been good moral support, too." Raena nudged him with her shoulder.

"Well, now you can have some more appropriate company," Hank interjected from behind them.

Ryan rolled his eyes and turned around to face the other Trainee. "Oh, do elaborate."

"I saw the way you look at her. Do you really think you have a chance?"

Fine, he wants a fight? Let's do this. "I think Raena can befriend whomever she wants."

Hank chuckled. "Oh, the Ward thinks just because he's in the TSS now he can forget his place!"

Ryan glared at the other teen. "Actually, that's *exactly* what it means to be in the TSS."

"No, people like you will always serve people like me. Leaving your home doesn't change who you are."

Raena opened her mouth, but Ryan brushed her hand and she stepped back.

"You have no idea who I am." Ryan rounded on him.

"You're a Ward," Hank spat. "Not even your own parents wanted you. Why should the TSS take you on?"

"And what, you think you're special just because you belittle others?"

"I have the right name and connections. You have nothing."

Ryan glared at him. "You really consider yourself to be a better person than me when you can talk to another individual like that? You're pathetic."

"At least I'm someone. Do you honestly think you'd be able to get with someone like her?" Hank nodded toward Raena.

"Our relationship is none of your business," Ryan shot back.

Hank scoffed. "Stars, you do! Unbelievable."

"And you think I'd rather be with a grade-A asshole like you?" Raena finally interjected.

"Have a little self-respect and stick with your own kind," Hank told her.

Jason stepped in front of Raena. "You want to deal with someone on your level, then take it from me. You're out of line."

"Me? I'm just telling it like it is. We need to stop polluting our bloodlines. Your family has already done a good enough job at that."

In one motion, Jason slammed Hank up against the wall. "If that was a crack about my mom, you just made a very grave mistake."

"Jason, let it go," Ryan said, but only half-heartedly. Secretly, he was hoping to see the smug sneer wiped off Hank's face by a fist.

"At least I'm not tainted by those defective human genetics—"

Jason's fist connected with Hank's face in a more spectacular punch than Ryan could have imagined, knocking Hank's head back against the wall and causing him to lose his balance. He stumbled to the side, clutching his face.

"You broke my foking nose!"

"Maybe you should have considered that possibility before picking a fight with me."

"I'll ge—" Hank froze mid-stride.

"What's going on?" Wil demanded from down the hall, running over to them.

Hank was released from the telekinetic hold and took an awkward step forward. "He attacked me!"

"After he insulted Ryan for being a Ward and then proceeded to trash-talk anyone from Earth," Jason clarified.

Wil tilted his head. "Really?"

Hank telekinetically flew against the opposite wall, paralyzed under Wil's gaze.

"People like you are precisely why we insist no one's life outside the TSS be factored into decisions. We define people by their own merits, not holding anyone back by whatever status they were born into. All of them deserve to be here. It's *you*—with your narrow-minded ways and bigoted attitude—that's not worthy of being in the TSS."

Hank tried to squirm but his arms and legs were pinned. "You're crazy! You'd choose them over someone like me with all my connections? No wonder Sietinen is faltering."

"I'd rather live with a convalescent peasant than someone who doesn't know a good heart when he sees one. I don't know what they taught you while you were growing up—or if you got your special brand of stupid all on your own—but you'll never be a TSS officer and you can sure as fok bet that Sietinen will never be doing any further business with the Guilin Dynasty. Congratulations." Wil released the hold and Hank dropped to his knees on the ground.

"You can't do that!" Hank protested, shakily finding his feet.

"You're right—I can't control with whom the Sietinen Dynasty does business as I don't sit on the board, but I happen to be pretty close with the Chairman, so I can put in a recommendation. When it comes to the TSS, however, I have complete and final authority to terminate the training contracts of any student. Consider yourself expelled. You have ten minutes to be on the elevator up to the surface or you can expect an armed Militia guard to forcibly remove you." Wil looked around at the other students in the hallway. "Is there anyone else who'd like to say something about their fellow Trainees?"

"That was so badass," Tiff whispered.

Wil cracked a smile. "That's an acceptable reaction. Now, why don't you see Hank on his way?"

Two Junior Agents stepped over to Hank.

"Whatever." He stormed down the hall back toward the Primus Elite quarters.

"So... uh," Jared began, "are we going to get a replacement?"

"Yes, there were a number of prospective candidates," Wil replied. "You can expect someone new to arrive this afternoon. Carry on." He strode into the Mess Hall like nothing had happened.

Ryan smiled to himself. *Yeah, I think I'll be able to get used to life around here.*

— — —

Cris leaned forward in the head seat at the SiNavTech board table. The men and women around the table were the brightest minds in business but he couldn't help feeling like they had no experience. *They've spent their whole lives in conference rooms. Do they even know what life is like for most Tarans?*

Kate, seated to his right, would at least offer another voice representing an outside perspective. *"We'll show them the new way,"* she said in his mind.

Cris looked around the table at the board members' faces. *They're not going to like this.* "The first order of business regards the TSS. I'm issuing an executive order to allow the TSS free and unrestricted use of the SiNavTech network."

Ronald scoffed. "Give up our third-largest contract? You can't be serious."

"The TSS is a public service organization. They should never have been paying usage fees."

"You may be a Sietinen, but that doesn't mean we can't replace you on the board if you don't act in the best interest of the company," Ronald replied.

Cris folded his hands on the tabletop. "That's absolutely right. So, let me tell you why I'm an asset. It's because I don't give a fok about pleasing the shareholders and making the company books look good."

Everyone's eyes widened around the table.

"That's not helping your argument," Ronald stated.

"Let me finish. I don't care about those things because people count on us to get them safely to their destination. SiNavTech focusing only on the bottom line is what caused the TSS to reduce patrols, and as soon as that happened, piracy rose to the highest levels in two generations. By allowing the TSS free travel, we gain built-in security at all the ports, which encourages recreational travel.

"I've been out there, but you rarely see beyond the walls of a conference room. I know what life is like in the Outer Colonies. They need us to stay connected to the rest of the worlds—to get deliveries of their essentials. We shouldn't be charging people for something they *need*. Instead, we should be focusing on those with disposable income, because that's where there's growth potential. Don't charge higher usage fees, but rather invest in the overall travel experience for higher-end travelers, promote ad placement opportunities to offset reduced fees through sponsorships. As a result, our investment sponsors better connect with the right people to grow their own businesses and we, in turn, gain reliable revenue from the deepest accounts—the other corporations."

Marina raised an eyebrow and leaned back slightly in her chair. "We'd never looked at it that way before."

"I intend to make a lot of changes around here," Cris said. "I want to make this company a model for all others in our position—trusted, reliable, enduring. We offer an essential, core service. That means we have a responsibility to uphold. Not to shareholders, but to society."

"Anyone who isn't interested in exploring that new perspective is welcome to step away with full compensation," Kate added. "But we have plans and some of it might sound a little unconventional at first."

The board sat in silence for a full minute.

"I, for one, think it's time we reexamine our practices," Marina said, breaking the silence.

Elard, one of the elder advisors seated at the far side of the table, folded his hands on the desktop. "Let's hear what you have in mind."

CHAPTER 26

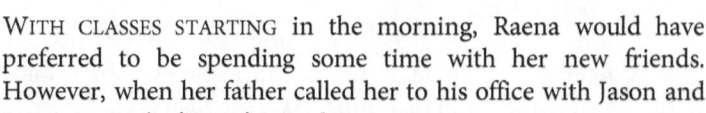

With classes starting in the morning, Raena would have preferred to be spending some time with her new friends. However, when her father called her to his office with Jason and Ryan, saying 'no' wasn't exactly an option.

She sat down on the couch facing the viewscreen between her brother and Ryan.

Wil stood before them, hands clasped behind his back. "Ryan, you're getting into the details of our family's business probably more than you'd like, but I thought it appropriate to include you given the overlap with your impending political situation." He paused for a moment, looking them over, then proceeded to pace while he spoke. "Dynastic inheritance rules dictate that one heir must be named. Now that I'm a direct heir rather than one generation removed, I no longer have the luxury of delaying that decision. I've watched both of you, Jason and Raena, over the last two weeks to see what interests you and where your strengths lie. Through those observations, I feel that Raena is most suited for the political responsibilities on Tararia."

Jason leaned back on the couch. "Phew! I was worried for a second you were going to pick me."

Raena gave him a playful punch. "I think that's pretty obvious, Dad."

"Do you accept the nomination?" Wil asked her.

She glanced at Ryan. "I do." *Of course, there's more to it than just my personality...*

"I know you already understand the larger political context, so I won't bother to spell it out. But I will say this: if we, as the Sietinen Dynasty, come forward in several years with a lost heir to Dainetris and the means to form a binding alliance between the two dynasties, we will achieve all the political leverage we need to instigate a major upset." He sighed. "At the same time, I spent the first twenty-five years of my life being manipulated for others' ends. I don't want to do the same thing to you, so it's up to you how to proceed. Consider it your first decision as heiress, Raena."

She shrank back into the couch. *Decide if I want a lifelong commitment to a guy I met two weeks ago? There's liking someone, and then there's that.*

"You don't need to make a decision now," Wil continued. "Think about it. Talk about it. Let us know when you have some notion of which way you're leaning so we can plan accordingly."

"Dainetris was never part of your plan before," Raena pointed out.

"No, it wasn't. But it's a game-changer. As long as any Dainetris heir is alive, there's a seventh vote that should be counted that hasn't been in play. We no longer need to sway the existing Dynasties—with Dainetris, we have a majority. But further, unveiling what happened to Dainetris and the Priesthood's involvement might give us the leverage we'd need to make the vote unanimous, which would change the situation even more. Until now, a unanimous decision was out of the question, so we hadn't even considered trying."

"What's the difference between unanimous and not, in terms of how things would play out?" Ryan asked.

"With a unanimous vote, we could go in and strip the Priesthood of its power immediately. Their ties are strong, but we'd have the numbers to make it swift and permanent. If there's opposition, though, it could take months or years to break the Priesthood's influence, with operatives seeking refuge with sympathizers. Of course, that will happen with either scenario, but with the unanimous option, not having the backing of any

High Dynasty will make it that much more difficult for the Priesthood to accomplish anything once their main administrative head is figuratively severed."

"So, it's a single show-down rather than a drawn-out war?" Ryan summarized.

"Essentially."

That doesn't seem like any decision at all from a political standpoint, regardless of how we feel about each other. "All right, we'll talk it over."

Jason grinned. "I got off easy."

Wil smiled back. "Oh, just wait."

They adjourned the meeting and headed back toward their shared quarters. Four doors down from theirs, Raena hung back. *"There's no privacy in there. Should we talk?"*

"Yeah, good idea," Ryan replied aloud.

Jason glanced between them, shrugged, and continued on his way.

"Let's grab a study room," Raena suggested. She located the first open room and they stepped inside, closing the door to the windowless space.

"What my dad said..." she began.

"I know. You don't have to say anything." He collapsed into one of the four chairs around the miniature conference table and rested his elbows on the tabletop. "It's all a ruse, isn't it—giving us a choice?"

Raena sat down across from him. "Considering that I would have been paired up with a total stranger, had my great-grandparents had any real say in the matter, the situation could be much worse. We at least like each other."

"It's easy to like someone when you first meet—who knows what we'll think of each other five months or a year from now?"

"This isn't about our personal feelings, though," Raena replied. "To some degree, the political necessity goes beyond whatever else is between us."

"True, and I can't argue that it makes sense for us to be together, given what your dad said."

"And what we saw for ourselves with the Priesthood..." Raena shuddered.

"If our partnership can help bring them down faster, that's not something we can ignore." Ryan looked her in the eye. "That said, you already mean much more to me than just some convenient political arrangement."

She smiled back. "You do to me, too."

"Still, agreeing to anything at this early stage…"

"We can still get to know each other at our own pace," Raena said. "It's not like we'd be getting married tomorrow."

"Not tomorrow, but that's what they're talking about. This isn't just parading around as two friends."

"I know that."

"And it's not just marriage—but ultimately merging the two lines. As in, having an heir of our own. Probably two, actually—one for each of the dynasties," Ryan pointed out.

"I'm not just a broodmare."

"I didn't mean it like that." Ryan released a low breath. "I'm taking this seriously, that's all. I don't want you to rush into something you'll regret."

"Does that mean you've already made up your mind?"

Ryan reached across the table and took her hand. "Raena, if I had to be stuck with someone for the rest of my life, I can't imagine a better partner than you."

She tossed her head. "You hardly know me!"

"And you hardly know me, but like it or not, we were both born into a life with a certain track, even though the course has only recently become clear. We're talking about the future of a galactic civilization here—whether two people like each other enough to get married seems like a pretty trivial issue when the alternative is civil war."

"Yeah, when you put it like that…" *Are we really going to do this?*

Ryan studied her face. "Besides, I get the impression you've already made up your mind, too."

Raena swallowed. "We may have just met and it'll still take more time to get to know each other properly, but I think it speaks volumes that we're not repulsed by the idea about where this can lead."

"Agreed."

She smoothed her hair with her free hand. "It's going to take a while for everything to sink in."

"No joke. I barely know who I am anymore."

"Me either. But I do know that I'm happy when I'm with you."

Ryan nodded. "Me too." He paused and flashed a coy smile. "You know, I'd still want to try to make things work with you, even if the fate of the universe wasn't at stake."

Raena smirked at the melodramatic characterization of their circumstances. "I would, too." She took his other hand in hers. "No matter what, we'll be stronger together than apart. All of us in this cause need to be united going forward."

Ryan smiled, warm and genuine. "I'm in."

She smiled back. "Good. Let's see where this takes us."

— — —

Sometimes being a leader meant making the tough decisions. In this particular matter, Wil knew the morally right choice wasn't the correct tactical move.

"It makes me sick, thinking about them being trapped down there," Saera said.

They'd just finished reviewing Raena and Ryan's accounts from their time with the Priesthood. Seeing the details of their experiences in writing made Wil appreciate the gravity of the situation even more.

"I don't like it, either," Wil replied, "but we can't just run in there."

"Why not? We have the forces to take the island."

"The physical means, yes, but what about the political fallout? We're so close to being able to do this the right way. We need a long-term solution that will stick."

Saera shook her head. "So, we just stand back and leave them there?"

"I don't know what to say. Until a few days ago, we didn't even know there was anyone trapped that needed help."

"But now we do."

"We can't jeopardize a plan that's taken two generations to put in place for a few hundred people." His heart dropped. *Billions have already died in the name of this war. How do we decide the worth of each life?*

Saera crossed her arms and turned away.

"We'll get them out as soon as we can."

"If they make it that long."

Wil looked her in the eye. "Justice will be served for all the lives the Priesthood has manipulated. This will be the last generation under their reign."

— — —

Quadris stormed into the Council Room. "Well, what have you come up with?" he demanded of the other High Priests.

"Have patience. It will take time to identify another opportunity," Tarlaen replied from his seat around the oval table at the center of the airy room. "We squandered our best chance."

"We don't have time!" Quadris bellowed. "Every transfer the degradation is worse. The next…"

"We should have taken them as children on Earth," Baeron muttered from the other side of the table.

"And we should have had security contingencies in place for advanced abilities. Hindsight doesn't change that we weren't prepared for the contingency of spatial dislocation abilities of that magnitude," Quadris shot back. "Now all of our plans are in jeopardy."

"They're with the TSS now. What can we do?" Baeron asked.

Quadris sat down at the table in the seat closest to the door. "We have no choice. It's time we reach out to our long-lost brethren."

Tarlaen's eyes widened. "The Aesir?"

"They're Priesthood as much as us, regardless of their new name." Quadris passed his gaze around the table. "They understand the importance of our work, even if we don't agree on the methods. It's time we complete what we started."

— — —

The first morning of official training had finally arrived. As Raena entered the mess hall with the Primus Elites in her cohort, she felt the eyes of the other trainees sizing her up. *We're the ones everyone is going to be watching. And me especially—High Dynasty heiress and elite Agent all in one.*

It was a lot to take on, but she was up for the challenge. When it came down to it, she didn't have a choice. The Aesir would be back for her in five short years and she needed to be ready—but not just her; she had to make sure Jason was ready, as well. They'd always had each other's backs and that was more important now than ever.

The Primus Elites all grabbed their breakfast and brought their trays to one of the long tables in the center of the room.

Raena sat down next to Ryan. "You know, this is really starting to feel like home."

"Oddly, it is," he agreed.

"Good thing, because we're going to be here for a while," Jared chimed in.

Ned grinned. "Like, a lifetime."

"That's a little overdramatic." Raena rolled her eyes.

"Hey, just telling it like it is," Ned stated. "The life of an Agent, you know…"

I have a lot more ahead of me than just that… Raena smiled. "I welcome the challenge."

"It's only been a few days, but I already can't believe I was once anywhere else," Ryan commented.

"Yeah, it's weird," Jason agreed. "The right people seem to end up here."

"They're not afraid to trim the dead weight, that's for sure," Jared said, taking a sip of orange juice.

"Lucky for you, Rory!" Ned nodded to the new arrival that had replaced Hank.

"Yay for being first runner up…" Rory said sarcastically.

"For what it's worth, that spot should have been yours from

the beginning," Jason said.

"We're happy to have you," Raena added.

Ryan nodded. "Everyone here just 'gets it'. I guess I never felt like I was on the same team with others before."

"Well, we are on the same team—literally," Tiff said.

"You know what I mean." Ryan flushed slightly. "I didn't realize how much I had been missing until I was around all of you."

"An intuitive connection," Jason said.

Ryan nodded. "Yeah. We're all working toward becoming our full selves."

"And to do that, we need to help each other," Ryan said. "What better way to bring everyone together?"

"Everyone expects us to be the best, so we better act like it," Jason told them.

Raena looked around the table, her gaze finally resting on Ryan. "Somehow, I think we'll do just fine."

CONTINUE THE STORY...

Volume 7: Scions of Change

As Raena's and Jason's training with the TSS nears completion, the return of the Aesir is imminent. Whether the Aesir are adversaries or allies will be put to the test as the final pieces of the Sietinens' plan to bring down the Priesthood fall into place.

Facing an unstable political landscape and with the future of telekinetic abilities among the Taran people on the line, Wil and his family must wage one final war to correct past injustices and usher Tarans into a new era of peace.

Scions of Change brings together the final pieces for the High Dynasties to attempt an overthrow of the Priesthood and restore equity in the Taran worlds.

OTHER CADICLE UNIVERSE BOOKS

CADICLE SERIES
Volume 1: Architects of Destiny (in *Shadows of Empire*)
Volume 2: Veil of Reality (in *Shadows of Empire*)
Volume 3: Bonds of Resolve (in *Shadows of Empire*)
Volume 4: Web of Truth
Volume 5: Crossroads of Fate
Volume 6: Path of Justice
Volume 7: Scions of Change

MINDSPACE
Book 1: Infiltration
Book 2: Conspiracy
Book 3: Offensive
Book 4: Endgame

VERITY CHRONICLES *with T.S. Valmond*
Book 1: Exile
Book 2: Divided Loyalties
Book 3: On the Run

SHADOWED SPACE *with Lucinda Pebre*
Book 1: Shadow Behind the Stars
Book 2: Shadow Rising
Book 3: Shadow Beyond the Reach

IN DARKNESS DWELLS *with James Fox*

TARAN EMPIRE SAGA
Book 1: Empire Reborn
Book 2: Empire Uprising
Book 3: Empire Defied
Book 4: Empire United

ACKNOWLEDGEMENTS

I really owe this book to my readers. When I began on this journey, I never expected to be publishing Volume 6 less than two years after I released the first book. The messages of support from readers have been such a motivator for me.

As always, I must thank my amazing group of beta readers and advanced reviewers for helping to elevate this book from the initial draft. Eric, Kurt, Julie, Liz, Dewald, and Katy were instrumental in identifying areas for improvement and helping me realize my vision. I must also thank Charlie and Nick for their great eyes, as well as my mom for her tireless support. My husband, Nick, is my greatest cheerleader and kept me focused even when I was tired and just wanted to watch Netflix.

I would also like to thank the extremely talented author M. D. Cooper for being so generous with his time and supporting me as an author. I have made many author friends in recent months and feel incredibly lucky to be surrounded by such cool colleagues. They have made being a sci-fi indie author the best job in the world!

GLOSSARY

Aesir - A mysterious group of people known to be of Taran descent that live on the outskirts of explored space, engaging in metaphysical pursuits.

Agent - A class of officer within the TSS reserved for those with telekinetic and telepathic gifts. There are three levels of Agent based on level of ability: Primus, Sacon and Trion.

Ateron – An element that oscillates between normal space and subspace, facilitating high levels of telekinetic energy transfer.

Baellas - A corporation run by the Baellas Dynasty, producing housewares, clothing, furniture, and other textiles for use across the Taran civilization. Additional specialty lines managed by other smaller corporations are licensed to Baellas for distribution.

Bakzen - A militaristic race living beyond the outer colonies. All Bakzen are clones, with individuals differentiated by war scars. Officers are highly intelligent and possess extensive telekinetic abilities. Drones are conditioned to follow orders but still possess moderate telekinetic capabilities.

Cadicle - The definition of individual perfection in the Priesthood's founding ideology, with emergence of the Cadicle heralding the start to the next stage of evolution for the Taran race.

Course Rank (CR) - The official measurement of an Agent's ability level, taken at the end of their training immediately before graduation from Junior Agent to Agent. The Course Rank Test is a multi-phase examination, including direct focusing of telekinetic energy into a testing sphere. The magnitude of energy focused during the exercise is the primary factor dictating the Agent's CR.

Dainetris Dynasty - Formerly a seventh High Dynasty, the Dainetris Dynasty was responsible for ship manufacturing before its fall from power.

Earth - A planet occupied by Humans, a divergent race of Tarans.

Considered a "lost colony," Earth is not recognized as part of the Taran government.

H2 - The nickname for the TSS headquarters in the rift. The facility was created to serve as a base of operations for the Bakzen War.

High Commander - The officer responsible for the administration of the TSS. Always an Agent from the Primus class.

High Dynasties - Six families on Tararia that control the corporations critical to the functioning of Taran society. The "Big Six" each have a designated Region on Tararia, which is the seat of their power. The Dynasties in aggregate form an oligarchical government for the Taran colonies. In descending order of recognized influence, the Dynasties are: Sietinen, Vaenetri, Makaris, Monsari, Talsari, and Baellas.

Independent Jump Drive - A jump drive that does not rely on the SiNavTech beacon network for navigation, instead using a mathematical formula to calculate jump positions through normal space and the Rift.

Initiate - The second stage of the TSS training program for Agents. A trainee will typically remain at the Initiate stage for two or three years.

Jotun - The codename assigned to the division of the TSS dedicated to the war in the rift, based in H2.

Jump Drive - The engine system for travel through subspace. Conventional jump drives require an interface with the SiNavTech navigation system and subspace navigation beacons.

Junior Agent - The third stage of the TSS training program for Agents. A trainee will typically remain at the Junior Agent stage for three to five years.

Lead Agent - The highest ranking Agent and second in command to the High Commander. The Lead Agent is responsible for overseeing the Agent training program and frequently serves as a liaison for TSS business with Taran colonies.

Leaving (Left) - An act of stepping away from one's life while still in possession of physical and mental capacities. Individuals that exercise this final rite feel that their life is complete and wish to die peacefully in private or with their spouse. Most commonly, an individual will Leave in the night and document instructions for carrying out their final wishes.

Lower Dynasties - There are 247 recognized Lower Dynasties in Taran society. Many of these families have a presence on Tararia, but some are residents of the other inner colonies.

Makaris Corp - A corporation run by the Makaris High Dynasty responsible for the distribution of food, water filters, and other necessary supplies to Taran colonies without diverse natural resources.

Monsari Power Solutions (MPS) - A corporation run by the Monsari Dynasty, responsible for power generation systems for the Taran worlds, including geothermal generators, portable generators, and reactors to power spacecraft.

Rift - A habitable pocket between normal space and subspace.

Sacon - The middle tier of TSS Agents. Typically, Sacon Agents will score a CR between 6 and 7.9.

Simultaneous Observation - The act of separating one's consciousness from the physical self in order to observe multiple spatial planes (i.e., normal space, subspace, and the rift) at the same time.

SiNavTech - A corporation run by the Sietinen High Dynasty, which controls and maintains the subspace navigation network used by Taran civilians and the TSS.

Spatial Dislocation - The act of physically transitioning from normal space to the brink of subspace, either by means of a jump drive or telekinetic abilities.

Starstone – An extremely rare gem. Only ten such gem veins are known anywhere in the galaxy, and each of the six High Dynasties has claim to one. Only enough material for one set of wedding rings is produced by each vein every generation. Starstones emit a luminescent resonance when positioned near other stones cut from the same vein.

TalEx - A corporation run by the Talsari Dynasty, managing mining operations and ore processing across Taran territories.

Tarans - The general term for all individuals with genetic relation to Tararian ancestry. Several divergent races are recognized by their planet or system.

Tararia - The home planet for the Taran race and seat of the central government.

Tararian Selective Service (TSS) - A military organization with two divisions: (1) Agent Class, and (2) Militia Class. Agents possess telekinetic and telepathic abilities; the TSS is the only place where individuals with such gifts can gain official training. The Militia class offers a formal training program for those without telekinetic abilities, providing tactical and administrative support to Agents. The Headquarters is located inside the moon of the planet Earth. Additional Militia training facilities are located throughout the Taran colonies.

Trainee - The generic term for a student of the TSS, and also the term for first year Agent students (when capitalized Trainee). Students are not fully "initiated" into the TSS until their second year.

Trion - The lowest tier of TSS Agents. Typically, Trion Agents will score a CR below 5.9.

Priesthood of the Cadicle - A formerly theological institution responsible for oversight of all governmental affairs and the flow of information throughout the Taran colonies. The Priesthood has jurisdiction over even the High Dynasties and provides a tiebreaking vote on new initiatives proposed by the High Dynasty oligarchy.

Primus - The highest of three Agent classes within the TSS, reserved for those with the strongest telekinetic abilities. Typically,

Primus Agents will score a CR above 8.

Primus Elite - A new classification of Agent above Primus signifying an exceptional level of ability.

VComm – A telecommunications corporation owned and operated by the Vaenetri Dynasty.

ABOUT THE AUTHOR

Award-winning author A.K. (Amy) DuBoff has always loved science fiction in all its forms—books, movies, shows, and games. If it involves outer space, even better! She is a Nebula Award finalist and *USA Today* bestselling author most known for her Cadicle Universe, but she's also written a variety of space fantasy and comedic sci-fi. Now a full-time author, Amy can frequently be found traveling the world. When she's not writing, she enjoys wine tasting, binge-watching TV series, and playing epic strategy board games.

www.amyduboff.com

www.ingramcontent.com/pod-product-compliance
Lightning Source LLC
Chambersburg PA
CBHW051956240626
47153CB00005B/1775